Praise for
THE PROPHET'S WIFE

"Seventy years after the publication of *As a Driven Leaf*,
readers will marvel at Milton Steinberg's unfinished symphony,
The Prophet's Wife. Rabbi Steinberg brings the reader into a
world of deep conflicts in life and religious outlook. As he did
for the rabbis seven decades ago, Steinberg now illuminates
the world of that most querulous of prophets, Hosea, and his
wanton wife Gomer."

~ **Rabbi Burton L. Visotzky**
author of *A Delightful Compendium of Consolation*

"Steinberg conveys the life of Hosea in such vivid and compelling
fashion that I couldn't stop reading. . . . An extraordinarily
sympathetic and psychologically astute characterization of both
Hosea and Gomer."

~ **Dr. Adriane Leveen**
Hebrew Union College – Jewish Institute of Religion

"*The Prophet's Wife* provides a window into both the world of
Biblical literature and the soul of one of the most penetrating
theological minds of twentieth century Jewry. Milton Steinberg's
novel will serve as a trusted companion and guide for spiritual
seekers in generations to come."

~ **Rabbi Elliot J. Cosgrove**
editor of *Jewish Theology in Our Time: A New Generation
Explores the Foundations and Future of Jewish Belief*

Praise for
AS A DRIVEN LEAF

"Imposing. . . remarkably effective."
  ~ *New York Times*

"Perhaps so completely frustrated a life has never before
  been presented in fiction. Sheer beauty!"
  ~ *Christian Herald*

"A windswept novel of a turbulent age strangely like our own."
  ~ *Chicago Daily News*

THE
PROPHET'S
WIFE

THE PROPHET'S WIFE

MILTON STEINBERG

With a Foreword by Ari L. Goldman

Commentaries by Rabbi Harold S. Kushner and Norma Rosen

Behrman House, Inc.
www.behrmanhouse.com
www.prophetswife.com

Published by Behrman House, Inc.
Springfield, New Jersey
www.behrmanhouse.com

ISBN 978-0-87441-140-9
Printed in China

Cover design by Marc Cohen
Interior design by Howard Levy/Red Rooster Group
Edited by Beth Lieberman

Library of Congress Cataloging-in-Publication Data

Steinberg, Milton, 1903-1950.
  The prophet's wife / Milton Steinberg ; with a foreword by Ari L. Goldman ;
commentaries by Harold S. Kushner and Norma Rosen.
     p. cm.
  ISBN 978-0-87441-140-9
  1. Hosea (Biblical prophet)—Fiction. 2. Bible. O.T.--History of Biblical events—
Fiction. I. Kushner, Harold S. II. Rosen, Norma. III. Title.
  PS3537.T32343P76 2010
  813'.52—dc22
                                                      2009043304

CONTENTS

A NOTE FROM THE PUBLISHER

"YOU KNOW, THERE'S ANOTHER STEINBERG NOVEL."

Thus began this ambitious project, with a simple offhand remark. Another Steinberg novel? I was intrigued. Milton Steinberg's other work of fiction, the widely read and admired *As a Driven Leaf,* has had unusually enduring appeal. In it Steinberg explores, with widely recognized compassion, talent, and style, the struggle between religious life and secular pursuits, a struggle that is as present today as it was in the rabbinic period he describes. Generations of Jews report the novel as their first significant encounter with adult Judaism.

What an unexpected opportunity: to provide these readers with a second Steinberg literary experience, and to introduce Milton Steinberg to a whole new generation of readers!

The story of the publication of *The Prophet's Wife* is well told by Ari Goldman in his Foreword—Milton Steinberg's intellectual odyssey up to his writing of the novel, how it fits like a matching bookend with *As a Driven Leaf,* and the challenges of publishing an almost-finished novel sixty years after the author's sudden and untimely death.

And so we have at long last published this unique novel. And rather than having it finished by someone else, we have gone another way, assembling a stellar array of contributors to provide context for the reader and a framework for giving meaning to this last work of Milton Steinberg.

My thanks overflow to these colleagues whose careful attention and inspiring vision took Rabbi Steinberg's final book and gave it a breath of life. Professor Ari Goldman of Columbia University, former religion correspondent of the *New York Times* and author of *The Search for God at Harvard,* has shepherded the project for many years. He has been its passionate advocate, exploring with us options for finishing it, helping polish the manuscript, and providing insightful editorial guidance. Rabbi Harold Kushner, author of *When Bad Things Happen to Good People,* has provided startling illumination into Steinberg's view of human nature, drawing parallels between Gomer's relationship with Hosea and the Jewish people's relationship with God. And Norma Rosen, author of the novel *Touching Evil,* has given us an audacious, almost breathtaking, interpretation of the novel and of its leading character, Gomer, as a model of feminism a full half-century before its time.

Special acknowledgment and thanks go to Beth Lieberman, project editor for both the novel and its accompanying commentaries. Beth had an almost impossible task—providing narrative and stylistic continuity, while working with a manuscript of whose author she could make no inquiries and for which there were no notes. She did so with a fierce intensity of commitment and a desire to get it just right, spending time on even small points almost certain to go unnoticed by others. It is a pleasure to work with someone of such dedication and integrity.

A heartfelt thank-you also goes to Carolyn Hessel, director of the Jewish Book Council, who is a discerning critic and has been a longtime supporter of this project.

I am deeply grateful to Professor Jonathan Sarna of Brandeis University, who was working on a book with Behrman House when he made the offhand remark I referred to at the beginning of this note. Dr. Sarna has been a steady source of valuable advice for almost all of my twenty years at the Firm; I look forward to many more years of the same.

And finally, profound thanks to Dr. David Steinberg, president of Long Island University, and Dr. Jonathan Steinberg, professor of history at the University of Pennsylvania, the sons of Rabbi Milton Steinberg and his literary heirs, for their encouragement of this project, and for their courage, as part of this process, in allowing all of us into the life and the mind of their father. He was a cherished part of, and remains a permanent inspiration for, our extended Jewish community.

David E. Behrman
Springfield, New Jersey

FOREWORD
by Ari L. Goldman

WHEN RABBI MILTON STEINBERG DIED SUDDENLY and tragically in 1950 at the age of forty-six, there was a keen awareness that the Jewish community had lost one of its great literary, intellectual, and spiritual voices. Steinberg was a preacher of uncommon eloquence and depth, a literary craftsman of prodigious output, and a scholar at home with both rabbinic and classic literature.

Even today, more than a century after his birth, Steinberg is known for his historical novel *As a Driven Leaf*, a book that grapples—in a way few had before or since in fiction—with Judaism's core values and beliefs. First published in 1939, *As a Driven Leaf* remains in print and is praised as a literary masterpiece in nearly every major survey of Jewish books.

What is not widely known about Steinberg, however, is that he was feverishly at work on another historical novel at the time of his death. In his study, on his desk, he left a 401-page typewritten manuscript titled *The Prophet's Wife*. The book you have in your hands is the first ever release of this remarkable tale to the public.

As the reader will see, *The Prophet's Wife*, based on the book of Hosea, vividly and creatively brings to life the prophet and his world. But it is an unfinished work. Not all the characters are fully drawn and not all the plot lines neatly concluded. Regardless of these facts, and even perhaps because of them, I am convinced that the novel will prove to be an unforgettable reading experience for the public and a major contribution to modern Jewish thought. *The Prophet's Wife* will fascinate scholars of Steinberg, as well as fans of his earlier work and those who are hearing about him here for the first time.

Why it took so long—sixty years—to release *The Prophet's Wife* is an epic story in itself, but one that can be best understood if put in the context of Milton Steinberg's life and legacy. So let us begin with a brief review of his life.

Milton Steinberg was born in Rochester, New York, in 1903. His father was a Lithuanian-born refugee who had received a traditional Jewish education at the great yeshiva in Volozhin. Although Samuel Steinberg was, for a time, a committed labor-socialist, he considered the pursuit of knowledge to be life's highest calling. Young Milton attended synagogue as well as cheder. Steinberg's American-born mother, Fannie, was determined that her children succeed. She moved the family to New York City when Milton was fifteen so that his sister, Florence, could further her singing career. Milton soaked up the intellectual and Jewish life of New York. He attended DeWitt Clinton High School, where he was valedictorian of his class, and later went to City College, where he graduated first in his class and with prizes in history, philosophy, Greek, and Latin.

He contemplated the academic life but chose the rabbinate instead because he wanted to bring Jewish ideas to a wider audience. It was during his rabbinic training at the Jewish Theological Seminary that Steinberg met Rabbi Mordecai Kaplan, the founder of Reconstructionist Judaism. The two would become significant influences on each other over the years.

Steinberg was only nineteen years old when he fell passionately in love with an even younger Edith Alpert. The two married and moved to Indianapolis so that he could take a position as a congregational rabbi there. They stayed for just a few years. Edith very much wanted to return to New York City. When Milton was given the opportunity to serve as rabbi of the Park Avenue Synagogue, they moved back. Their sons, David and Jonathan, were born soon after.

During Steinberg's tenure at the Park Avenue Synagogue, the congregation increased from approximately 120 families to 700. His preaching and his writing, first in national magazines and later in books, made him a highly sought-after lecturer who crisscrossed the country giving talks on contemporary Jewish life and thought. He wrote seven nonfiction books, including *Basic Judaism* and *The Making of the Modern Jew,* but the book that became his most enduring work, *As a Driven Leaf,* was a work of fiction.

As a Driven Leaf animated philosophical questions through a compelling literary character. The story describes how Elisha ben Abuyah, a brilliant scholar of the early rabbinic period, has a crisis of faith and turns his back on God and the Jewish people.

Elisha's crisis of faith, as recounted in the Talmud, is a searing one. Elisha knows his Scripture well. There are two places in the Bible in which God promises Israel long life. Long life is promised to one who honors his parents. And long life is promised to one who observes another Jewish law: the requirement to send a mother bird away before taking her eggs. According to the Talmud, Elisha witnesses a scene along the lines of the following:

A father and son are out walking. The father instructs the boy to climb up to a tower and bring him eggs from a bird's nest. The boy obeys his father and climbs to the tower, only to find a mother bird sitting on the eggs. In accordance with the biblical law, the boy sends the bird away. But the promise of long life is not fulfilled. As the boy reaches for the eggs, he loses his footing, falls to the ground, and dies.

Seeing this tragic scene, Elisha denies the existence of God. He is excommunicated as an apostate by the very sages who were once his colleagues and friends.

In *As a Driven Leaf,* Steinberg takes this thin reed of a tale and places it in the context of the Greco-Roman world with which the early rabbis struggled. Steinberg puts flesh on Elisha, his teachers, his friends, and his ideas by taking the reader on a great philosophical adventure through the ancient world.

The Prophet's Wife is similarly based on the vague outline of a story. The prophet in question is Hosea, who lived in the eighth century BCE, toward the end of the First Temple Period. In his prophecies Hosea rails against the Israelites who have strayed from righteous living, were worshiping foreign gods, and might have been engaging as well in ill-conceived political alliances. Hosea's tale is startling. After introducing the prophet and his time, the book of Hosea begins with these words: "The Lord said unto Hosea: Go, take unto thee a wife of harlotry and the children of harlotry; for the land doth commit great harlotry, departing from the Lord."

Can this be true? Take a harlot as a wife? Hosea obeys by marrying Gomer, only to find himself betrayed time and again. Hosea complains to God, but God orders him to take Gomer back. She will be faithful.

No one takes the story literally. The book of Hosea is seen as a metaphor for God's love for Israel. No matter how much Israel sins, God's heart will always be open to her and take her back.

No one takes the story literally, that is, except Milton Steinberg. The empathy with which he has portrayed Gomer, one of the most enigmatic women in the Bible, and the humanity he gives to both her and Hosea is extraordinary. In the pages of *The Prophet's Wife,* Steinberg imagines someone so much in love that he is blind to his beloved's faults and even infidelities. Steinberg conjures up a flesh-and-blood Hosea and follows him through the hardships and disappointments of his young adulthood. Hosea, in Steinberg's rendering, is a boy who, early in life, is mercilessly teased by his brothers and then loses his mother. His emotionally detached father is distracted by other concerns. Hosea learns the value of silence and becomes a scribe in the king's court, a position that allows him to be exposed to the great controversies of the day.

The Prophet's Wife demonstrates that the "gift of prophecy" is not something bestowed but earned through the travails of life, not least of which for Hosea is a passionate but troubled marriage to the wayward woman Gomer.

How come *The Prophet's Wife* wasn't published when it was discovered sitting on the rabbi's desk in 1950? The official reason was that it was a fragment and not something that could hold up as a literary work. Steinberg seems to have left no notes, no outline, no plan for the book. After Edith's death in 1969, the couple's sons and literary heirs donated the manuscript, along with all of Steinberg's papers, to the American Jewish Historical Society. It remained in the archives until now.

Without Milton Steinberg to finish the story and explain it, perhaps it was for the best. But I think there is another reason *The Prophet's Wife* wasn't published. It was too hot to handle.

It was well known that Steinberg had a complicated relationship with his adored Edith. On the one hand, she was the midwife to many of his literary works, collaborating with him and editing his manuscripts for publication. At the same time, she was a force in her own right who felt intensely ambivalent about being a rabbi's wife. The two continued to love each other deeply throughout their tempestuous marriage. The story of Hosea and Gomer cut too close to the bone.

I think Steinberg was also working out some issues about the relationship between God and Israel in his novel. The turn of the mid-century was a troubling time in Jewish history. The full horrors of the Shoah were just coming to light, even as the modern State of Israel was emerging. These were subjects that occupied a great deal of Steinberg's intellectual life in his final days and were themes that no doubt found their way into *The Prophet's Wife*.

The novel is set in another tumultuous time, the eve of the Northern Kingdom's destruction. Steinberg creatively brings together two prophets, Hosea and Amos, who, as far as we know, were contemporaries but never really met. While they both warn that Israel's sins will result in the nation's downfall and its people's exile, Hosea is the far more optimistic prophet. He reassures the people that God will ultimately bring them back under divine protection. In 1950 there may have been little reason for such optimism. Whether Hosea's vision or Amos's vision would prevail vis-a-vis the modern State of Israel, then in its infancy, was an open question. Perhaps this, too, was too volatile a story to try to understand at the time.

It wasn't until 1999 that David Behrman, the head of Behrman House, began to think about publishing it. This was in part occasioned by the company's success a few years earlier of a reissue of *As a Driven Leaf* in paperback with a new foreword by the great Chaim Potok. Behrman shared the manuscript of *The Prophet's Wife* with numerous authors and asked them for advice. He remembers asking Potok if he would be willing to finish what Steinberg had started. "How can I finish another man's work?" Potok answered.

I had no such scruples when Behrman asked me to get on board with this project in 2001. I instantly fell in love with *The*

Prophet's Wife and spent many years, including a semester at Oxford, trying to craft a proper ending. Without success. Potok, I learned, was right.

Steinberg's magnificent tale remains open-ended, as he left it. There is one thing, however, that the reader needs to know. The last page of the story, in which Hosea's companion Binyamin praises God for letting him see "the angel of death on his way," was written by Steinberg on the night before his death.

What a curious place to leave off, because, with the release of *The Prophet's Wife*, Milton Steinberg is vividly brought back to life for a whole new generation. Readers will once again be able to partake of Steinberg's brilliance, to debate and discuss his life and his contribution. We begin that discussion later in this volume with two extraordinary readers, each with a particular genius for bringing the story into our understanding—Rabbi Harold Kushner and the novelist Norma Rosen.

It is with pride that I introduce to you *The Prophet's Wife*. I remember the first time I read *As a Driven Leaf*, more than thirty years ago. I finished the book, was hungry for more, and asked, "Did Milton Steinberg write any other fiction?" Turns out that he did. How lucky we are to finally have it in our hands.

Whosoever is wise will understand these words,
Whoso is prudent will know them.
For the ways of the Lord are right,
And the just will walk in them;
But the transgressors will stumble therein.

– HOSEA 14:10

PROLOGUE
Eighth century BCE, Israel

HE CONSIDERED THE THING HE MUST SAY, chose the words with which to say it, tried them on his tongue, and fashioned them tentatively on his lips. Revulsion welled up in him, raised the gorge in his throat, and without assent or awareness on his part set his feet in motion.

But as he fled, the kindling within him burst into flame. He could not leave. When he reached the street which led beyond the palace he slowed, and stopped. Then he swept back in the other direction, toward the arched entrance to the assembly hall of the princes. To and fro he went, from one side of the great market square to the other.

Time and again he returned to his original place, that block of battered marble, the pedestal of a long-vanished statue of Omri, king of Israel. It had been erected by Omri when he had built a city in this place, and had toppled and shattered on that wild day when his house had fallen. So plain a thing it was now, a platform supporting nothing, no higher than a man's shoulder. Yet it stood in the center of the Great Square of Samaria, with the city itself and the land of Ephraim and of all Israel surrounding it. The pedestal had come to serve as a rostrum for all who would address the king in his palace fronting the square on one side, or the princes and elders in their assembly hall on the other, or the people of Samaria and Israel who, whether free or bond, noble or serf, rich or poor, passed this way and loitered here at all hours of the day and night.

Long since he had lost track of how often he had escaped, only to return. A sense of unreality had descended upon him, the hypnotic notion that he might go on so forever. In the end, the spell was broken from somewhere outside himself.

He was standing before the pedestal, just on the point of tearing himself away from it once more, when there came to his ears the noise of song. The words were too blurred by distance and the tumult of the marketplace to be distinguishable. But there was no mistaking the coarse, lewd melody in which they were chanted, nor the voices that lifted them—the shrill not-mannish, not-womanish voices of the castrated priests of Baal. He did not need to inquire as to the occasion. It was high noon. This was the litany of the noonday sacrifice to the bull-god of Samaria, bestower of fertility on man and beast. That golden image of a bullock rampant so as to expose its monstrous male organ stood enthroned in the king's private chapel, there on the far side of the palace.

"Whoredom!" he muttered fiercely. "The whoredom of a people..."

His indecision had fled, leaving only rage and great pity.

He put his hands on the sun-baked stone and felt the tingle of its heat in his palm. Hoisting himself onto its surface, he stood upright, and raised an arm.

"Ho, men of Israel!" he cried out.

Of those passing by, most looked up at him, hesitated

momentarily, and then went about their business. But there were others who, whether for want of better employment or out of curiosity, paused and clustered about him, a shifting clot in the restless stream of traffic.

He stood before and above them, this man of middling height and years, his frame slight but wiry, his hair and tapering beard of finest texture, brown in hue except where it was frosted with gray. His eyes were as black as a winter's night and, as such nights sometimes are when the moon is extinct and the stars obscured, aglow with a light not to be accounted for. His face was fine-featured, youthful in its impression and yet deeply lined, the visage of one who has endured much while still young.

He waited quietly, the shadow thrown by the noonday sun a dark circle ringing his feet.

At that very instant, far, far to the east, where the day was already turning, a dark-skinned hermit in a forest sang an ancient hymn in honor of Varuna and Mitra. He thought meantime that those two and the other gods could not be distinct or many, since they and all else were one.

At this selfsame moment, in the opposite direction, in the remotest west, where morning was still fresh and moist with dew, a farmer made his way across a marshy plain that began at a river's edge and spread itself among seven hills. He was startled to see a wolf skulking in the dense underbrush.

In Nineveh, nearer at hand to the northeast, Tiglath-pileser III, newly crowned king of the Assyrians, was just then resting his hands on a leathern map spread over his knees.

"First here," he said to his counselors. His broad thumb ground the spot where Babylon stood. "Afterwards, that way." His hand swept toward Egypt and the lands that lay between.

And in Egypt itself, in the great court of the Temple of Amun-Re, in the capitol city of Mo, Shabako the Ethiopian watched the white-robed priests enact their strange rites. His head ached from the weight of the high double crown of the pharaohs. Under his bejeweled and embroidered robes, his body sweltered. The arid scent of incense parched his nostrils. All the time his keen little eyes never left off darting this way and that in spurts of suspicion. They loved him, these milky-hued native priests and nobles, he told himself, about as much as he loved them. The spittle of contempt collected in his mouth.

Elsewhere, on a mainland promontory beyond the islands of the Aegean, at the base of a steep hill sacred to the high-helmeted goddess, a peasant strained to hear a voice. A rhapsodist in one of the priestly houses on the summit above him told a well-loved tale of warfare in days gone by. But the chant came from afar and the wind was noisy in the leaves and grass. And so he raised his pruning hook once more, his heart heavy with discontent over his lot and with yearning for brighter and more heroic days which once had been.

Closer at hand, in the City of David directly to the south, king Uzziah kneaded, wearily and without hope, still another ointment into the leprous flesh of his forearm. He wondered as he did so why the God who had forgiven so much to his ancestor David should be so unrelenting toward him.

Nearest of all, no more than a few hundred paces away from the great market square, tough old Jeroboam, king of Israel, sat down to his midday repast. He held himself at arm's length from the table, on account of the monstrous growth which caused his own belly to bulge outward as though he were with child. With a keen glance he appraised his son, Zechariah, heir to his glorious crown. He noted Zechariah's lusterless eyes and unassertive chin, marveling that he should have sired such a weakling.

• • •

HE WHO STOOD on the marble block waited.

As men assembled to hear him he looked down into each face, seeing it in the unsparing brightness of the noonday sun. Nowhere, not on a single one, could he find either the faintest trace of old insights and pity, or the slightest signs of understanding or compassion.

So stark and merciless is necessity. And immediate, for those gathered about him stirred restlessly while he hesitated.

He breathed deeply and gave forth his voice.

"The word of the Lord thou shalt know," he said, "that came unto me, Hosea son of Beeri."

CHAPTER I

THE HOUSE OF BEERI, LIKE THE MAN HIMSELF, was solid and respectable without being in any way conspicuous or great. Neither the largest dwelling in Samaria nor yet the smallest, it was located on the slope of the mountain, halfway between the palaces near the great market square on the plain below and the mansions of the merchants, money changers, and upstart nobles on the crest above.

Its moderation was deliberate. Though Beeri was a rich man, the owner also of a sizable and profitable estate in the valley of Jezreel, he could well have afforded a larger and more fashionably situated home—let alone an ample supply of the brocaded wall hangings and couch spreads which had come into vogue in recent years—but he did not hold with luxury or extravagance in any form. The house had been constructed of fired brick rather than hewn stone or cedar wood inlaid with ivory. Simplicity was to him a matter of principle. Indeed, in his eyes, everything was a matter of principle. Beeri lived by rules.

There were the rules for tilling the soil and breeding animals, the meticulous observance of which served to ward off drought, the plague, and the loss of the young of herds and flocks. There were the terse and salty precepts of men of old as to right-doing with God and man. There were the ordinances of Moses and the teachings of the prophets.

Beeri was one of those who honored the Lord. Never once in all his life had he done obeisance or made sacrifice to a Baal. Never once had he gone into a sacred grove to lie down with a temple prostitute, not even in the days of his youth when his blood ran hot at every reference to what went on under the sheltering tree of an Asherah, not even in that terrible time when, for two years in succession, his sheep and cattle had lost more calves than they had brought forth alive, and his servants and friends alike had counseled him to appease the Baalim of fertility.

As strictly as he withheld service from the false gods and the other abominations, so conscientiously did he render it to the Lord God of Israel. He offered at their prescribed time the required sacrifices on the high place of his estate in Jezreel. Thrice each year, circumstances permitting, he undertook pilgrimages, traveling not only to Beth El but on occasion as far as the oaks of Mamre, in distant Hebron. He paid his tithes faithfully and gladly. From Dan to Beersheva there were others of his wealth and rank, but there was not another as scrupulous as he about what was due to the Lord. Such had been the way of his fathers, such therefore was his way also.

Honoring the Lord, Beeri honored the prophets, those who spoke in His name, declaring His will to Israel, His statutes and ordinances to Jacob. And there was no family tradition which he recounted more often or with greater pride than the story of how Elhanan, his paternal grandfather, had risked his life and imperiled his entire household to give asylum to Elijah the Tishbite. For nigh a full month Elhanan concealed Elijah in the homestead in Jezreel when, having slain the prophets of Baal at Mount Carmel, the prophet fled the wrath of Queen Jezebel, their protectress and patron.

By heritage from his fathers, Beeri was an adherent of the prophets. But not without reservation.

The household had been assembled about the altar of unhewn stone on the high place of the family estate in Jezreel—Beeri, Ophra, and their seven children, of whom Gadiel, the eldest, was at the time a lad of ten and Sarai, the youngest, a babe in her mother's arms. Talmon, the overseer of the estate, had been there also, along with the priest, the Hebrew bondsmen and maidservants, the three hirelings, the Canaanite slaves, and the families of all, each person dressed in white robes in honor of the holiday. It was the Festival of First Fruits, which was the fiftieth day after the Passover. The morning sun was high in the heavens. The household waited for it to pass its zenith so that the garlanded baskets of first fruits, now resting before the altar, might be accompanied by the afternoon meal offering and sacrifice.

The day was white with sunshine. A soft breeze stirred, surprisingly cool and pleasant for early summer. From below and before the hillock on which the celebrants stood, the land rose slowly, at first in open fields and then more steeply in terraces toward the forested shoulders of Carmel to one side and Mount Megiddo to the other. Megiddo itself was to their left, the new city rebuilt and fortified in the days of King Solomon, gleaming white in the near distance. The brooding, haunted mound of the ruins of the old city, ancient beyond man's memory, loomed beyond. Behind them Jezreel fell away in a gentle slope to the valley floor, a tapestry of squares in dun and green of all shades, dotted with the whites, grays, and maroons of homesteads, amongst which their own stood nearest at hand.

Though the season and the setting were festive, the mood of the celebrants was not. The winter just gone had been hard. The rains, interlaced with hail, had come late and with violence. As a result, the fields and the orchards had been compromised. The fruits in Beeri's baskets, the best of the yielding of his orchards, were badly misshapen. And though no one had presumed to partake of them before the offering had been made to the Lord, they would prove, one could see readily, either tart or tasteless.

Beeri's household was too solid to be shaken by a single unfortunate season. In a strongbox in a cellar under the house, silver in bars and coins was hidden. Other monies were on deposit with the most trustworthy of the money changers in Samaria. And in the event of a long, continued period of misfortune, whether through famine or drought, there were slaves to be sold, and slate, hangings, and jewelry also. Like everyone else, Beeri had had to eat this year into the wealth he had amassed. But if certain calculations revolving in his mind came to pass, he had reason to believe that the general calamity might yet prove advantageous.

Except for a few favored households like his own, the outlook was bleak everywhere. There was talk of hunger, of the mortgaging of lands, of free men selling themselves as bondsmen and their daughters as maidservants, even as slaves. If the sacred day was less than joyous at Beeri's high place, it was heavy-hearted indeed under its smiling face through most of Jezreel, in all the kingdom of Israel, and, if reports were to be believed, in Judah as well.

Yet a festive day it was and a day of duties also that waited to be discharged.

And so they stood, Beeri and all his household, with the priest, awaiting the proper and auspicious moment, meantime occupying themselves or idling, each according to his duties and inclinations.

The priest sharpened his ritual knife on a whetting stone, calculating the portion of the shoulders, cheeks, and maws which were to be his in the sacrificial feast.

Children, elated by the awareness of a holiday yet restrained both by the fresh whiteness of their robes which they feared to soil and by the fear of reproof for unseemly conduct before the Lord's altar, played furtively, one shoving or taunting another, then taking refuge hastily behind the skirts of an adult.

Ophra, as was her wont, stood somewhat to one side, withdrawn, her eyes watching anxiously for some duty which she had neglected.

And Beeri, his back to the others, stood facing the valley, rehearsing the prayer he was to speak over the baskets of first fruits before they were brought up to the altar.

"A wandering Aramean," he whispered to himself, "was my father, and he went down to Egypt, and sojourned there, few in number; and he became there a nation, great, mighty, and populous. And the Egyptians dealt with us harshly, and afflicted us, and laid upon us hard bondage. And we cried unto the Lord, the God of our fathers, and the Lord heard our voice, and saw our affliction, and our toil, and our repression. And the Lord brought us forth out of Egypt with a mighty hand, and with an outstretched arm, and with signs, and with wonders. And he hath brought us into this land, and hath given us this land, a land flowing with milk and honey. And now, behold, I have brought the first of the fruits of the land, which thou O Lord hast given me...."

He broke off abruptly at the sight of a newcomer striding vigorously up the well-trodden path from the homestead to the high place.

"Who is it that comes?" Beeri asked, squinting into the sunlight.

The others turned about to face as he did.

"It is Hodiah," someone in the company answered.

"Aye, Hodiah the prophet," another confirmed.

"Hodiah?" Beeri clasped his hands in prideful joy.

Was not Hodiah a great prophet of the Lord? Had he not ministered to the mighty Elisha? Was he not even now foremost among the sons of the prophets, that guild of men of the Lord who dwelt in Tirzah, an ancient city close to Samaria? Possessed by a conviction of Samaria's impurity, Hodiah was among those who revived the ancient city, living in tents and going about barefoot and clad in skins. Hodiah's name was often on Beeri's lips as an instance of a true prophet, deserving of honor.

No soothsayer or diviner he, Beeri believed. And no mercenary, either, to whom the Lord's word is a purse from which bread is to be purchased. Here was a sober, simple person such as one might take to be a householder. In all Israel there is in these times not another to rival him in wisdom and strength, in zeal for the Lord or in jealousy against the Baalim and evil rites. Beeri felt that if all prophets were like Hodiah, one might indeed pray with Moses: 'Would that all the people of the Lord were prophets.'

"Verily, honor is done this day to all our house," said Beeri. "Come, Gadiel, let us hasten to bid him welcome." Seizing his firstborn by the hand, he went down the path, the child stumbling along at his side and slightly behind him.

When the two men met halfway on the slope, they did not pause only so long as would suffice for an exchange of greeting and the speaking and acceptance of an invitation. To the surprise of those who stood on the hilltop and watched, able to see but not hear, they entered instead into a dialogue which, to judge from their manner and gestures, rapidly turned into an altercation.

There they stood, at high noon on a day sacred to the Lord, the long, gaunt, gray-robed Hodiah and the slight, stalwart figure of one of his most zealous adherents, shaking their heads and waving their arms toward each other, the prophet deliberately and with determination, Beeri now with indignation and bewilderment. Gadiel fidgeted at their feet, his head tilted back, looking first at one and then at the other of the men who quarreled above him. All of which while the astounded spectators at a distance stared at the pantomime below them, taking their eyes from it only long enough to address wordless questions to one another and to shrug silently by way of answer.

In the end, Beeri's shoulders sagged. But if he yielded the point of the controversy, it must have been with reluctance. For as the two men and the boy started to remount the hillock together, Beeri's slow and uncertain gait became a stride, increasingly dominated by a stiffness that grew more perceptible as he drew nearer. He began to address Hodiah in short spurts of speech until, by the time they reached the crest, he stopped, no longer able to contain himself, and in the full hearing of his entire household cried out to the prophet:

"And what think you? That because I do not, none other will? Shall those who revere the Lord be disadvantaged against the worshipers of the Baalim?"

Hodiah, who had paused along with Beeri, now looked down into his face so that countenance was set against countenance, one deep-lined, hollow-cheeked, and thick-bearded, the other agitated and flushed, its tapering wisp of a whisker quivering forward like an accusing finger.

"May it not turn out so," the prophet answered gravely. "Perhaps if you do not, no one else will. Certain this is," he went on, his eyes kindling, "that the Lord's will must be done regardless of advantage or disadvantage, and whether the event can be foreseen or not.

"Most certain of all is it that a man shall not bring the Lord's sacrifices," one hand gestured impatiently toward the altar, "and then do the deeds of the Baalim," the other hand pointed to the valley.

"So be it, my lord," Beeri appeased hastily, "I shall obey."

"For which," Hodiah countered, "the Lord will bless you—

and him also concerning whom we speak, so that you shall both live in peace on this godly land which was given to your fathers and to you, and to the generations that shall come after you."

They turned to the deferred rituals of prayer, song, and sacrifice for which the hour had for some time been at hand.

Beeri, however, was still not at peace. Though the deeds over which he presided were of thanksgiving and the words he pronounced of joyfulness, he bristled throughout with anger and rebellion so visible and, on one occasion, so close to an outburst, that only the intervention of Hodiah prevented it.

At the moment when the animal for the feast had been slaughtered, and the priest was beginning to cut it apart, Hodiah spoke to Beeri:

"Know you not, O Beeri, what the prophet Samuel did say to Saul the king:

> *Hath the Lord delight in burnt-offerings*
> *and sacrifices,*
> *As in harkening to the voice of the Lord?*
> *Behold to obey is better than sacrifices,*
> *And to hearken than the fat of rams.*
> *For rebellion is as the sin of witchcraft,*
> *And stubbornness is as idolatry and Terafim.*

Thereafter the sacrifice was conducted and the feast held, if not with gaiety, then at the least without further untoward incident.

Only after the rituals had been completed and the celebrants had dispersed, Hodiah on his way, and Beeri and Ophra to their private chambers, did the household have an opportunity to seek an interpretation for the strange events before their eyes. Then Talmon, the overseer, and the others who were not required elsewhere—which was nearly all of them, since no one labored on the festival day—gathered in a body in the rear courtyard of the homestead. They waited until Gadiel should chance to pass and descended on him, demanding excitedly that he relate what had occurred between his father and the prophet.

"I tell you," he said in the midst of a circle of eager faces bending over him, "this was indeed a festival, to see our father who is so free with counsel and instruction being himself counseled and instructed. Nay, 'twas fairer than that. For when he chides us it is mallows which he gives us to eat. When Hodiah reproved him, it was gall and wormwood which he received."

Shameful was the disrespect for his father in Gadiel's speech, and at any other time he would have been reprimanded, assuredly by Talmon, perhaps, too, by any of the three hirelings, and even by the older among the Hebrew bondsmen and maidservants. But now their questions seemed too pressing.

"The occasion, lad," Talmon urged. "What was the occasion?"

Another said, "Over what was their quarrel?"

Now Gadiel had at the beginning been too engrossed in his amused recollections to think of ought else. But now he became aware of the fierceness of the curiosity of his interrogators. Never one to miss an opportunity to taunt others, he seized on his advantage, refusing to speak until Talmon and the others all but burst with exasperation.

Next, Gadiel turned the situation to his profit, exacting as the price for speech a variety of promises, fortified by oaths, as to special liberties and extra delicacies to be given him. Only when he was certain that he had achieved everything which could be extorted, did he disclose his secret.

"It seems," he said, "that Charun, our neighbor, has grown poor this year, and has neither food for his household nor seed for another planting, and that he came to our father for assistance. But our father instead proposed to purchase Charun's land. And

Charun went off, troubled and perplexed, and did tell all this, this very morning, to Hodiah. That is why the prophet did turn aside to see us—an honor, our father called it." And Gadiel chuckled at the thought.

"So," Talmon reflected, "it was for that reason that our master inquired so often how it was with the house of Charun."

"But what more was there?" another pressed.

"Tell us the rest," said the others.

"The rest is this," offered Gadiel. "When our father first addressed Hodiah to bid him welcome, Hodiah would not say 'Peace' in return, but straightway told our father that it did not beseem one who did not design peace to his neighbor to bespeak the word, nor was it fitting that one who revered the Lord should cast a stone after a falling brother. And our father replied that reverence for the Lord was to one side and the purchase of fields to another. Hodiah said that it was not so, that therefore the Lord did apportion the land by lot to our ancestors so that each family might have its own patrimony, and that it was the work of those who whored after the Baalim to move the ancient boundaries. And then our father said that he was grieved that a prophet of the Lord should speak so of him. But Hodiah answered that his was the greater grief and that he, being a prophet of the Lord, would not join our feast unless our father gave promise not to purchase Charun's land but to lend to him as befitted a brother. Then they spoke angrily one to another and, I believe, they would have come to blows, but Hodiah exceeded our father in anger and in the end he threatened to denounce our house as once Nathan denounced King David, and to curse it as Elijah aforetime cursed Ahab in the matter of Naboth's vineyard. At which our father grew affrighted and did give way. But not willingly," said Gadiel.

How unwillingly became clear to the household later. For though Beeri did as the prophet had instructed, his face was set and gray. Though he was forever saying that the wise man speaks softly always and is ever master of his spirit, he was for many days harsh of voice and quick to anger. What is more, though heretofore he had had the prophets ever in his mouth, he did not now make mention of them at all the long week.

In the end, however, the teachings of his father, the instruction of his youth, and the ways of a lifetime prevailed. Beeri began again to speak as often and as ardently of the Lord and His commandments as of old, to be as zealous as of yore against the Baalim and the evil ways of their worshipers, and even to make favorable discourse concerning the prophets—though whenever he had occasion to refer to true prophets and that wherein they were true, his words would falter and he would end up lamely with vague, disjointed phrases. He could neither fully embrace nor fully banish the prophets from his heart.

CHAPTER II

EVEN AS A LAD, BEERI LIVED BY THE PRINCIPLES and precepts sent down by the sages long ago. He had been but a half-grown boy when Elhanan, his father, and Bilhah, his mother, perished together in the plague which had been in the days of Jehu, king of Israel. Ever since then, Beeri had been his own master. Though he was the sole son to his parents and none remained to tell him otherwise, he comported himself gravely, with the wisdom of someone older. He guarded the purity of his ways. He watched over his three sisters conscientiously and, when the time had come, sought out befitting husbands for them. Nor did he take a penny of their marriage prices for his own use.

Only after his brotherly duties had been faithfully discharged, and the season of marriage for himself was at hand, did he consider whom he should take to wife. Beeri did not look for high birth, wealth, or beauty, but for good blood, chastity, and fear of the Lord. All these he found at last in Ophra, daughter of Jehonadav, a girl modest and pleasant to look on, as he was well aware. He had seen her time and again from afar, and she was well spoken of by all who knew her.

Jehonadav was a poor man, the tiller of a scant and stony patch in the upland above the valley. But he was of good pedigree, being the hereditary chieftain of one of the hundreds of the tribe of Ephraim, and, most important of all, a man zealous for the Lord who knew full well how a daughter should be raised.

Having set his mind and heart on the maiden but possessing no kinsman or friend to act as intermediary on his behalf, Beeri served as his own emissary.

So one morning it came to pass that the robust, toil-hardened man, wise in the ways of the world, and his visitor sat together on the terrace outside the upper chamber of the house. Beeri felt manifestly awkward and ill at ease, and was therefore even graver in manner and more solemn and verbose in speech than was his wont. First they talked to each other of indifferent matters, as though neither knew what was on the other's mind. Then, by what he deemed skillful maneuver, Beeri spoke of husbands and wives and their duties to each other. It was at this juncture that he presented to his future father-in-law that catalog of expectations which he had thought through and rehearsed so carefully. Of his wife, he made clear, he would require that she serve the Lord alone, keeping herself clean of all evil contamination, whether from the Baalim and Ashtarot or the Terafim. He assumed further, he persevered, that she would not eat the bread of idleness nor be among those light women who are forever gossiping at the fountain, nor behave in any fashion beneath her station. Finally, he stipulated, she would of course raise the children whom the Lord would grant to her and to her husband to piety and righteousness as he, her husband, would direct, being dutifully obedient on this score as on all else, as could be expected of a chaste and well-bred woman.

Half blinded by the glare of the noonday heat, which penetrated even into the shadows in which they sat, Jehonadav looked at the suitor who had come for his daughter's hand. He nodded gravely as each stipulation was entered on the record, thinking meanwhile with considerable amusement how the fellow strutted and played the man of affairs, and how he spoke many words where one would serve. But, being an experienced judge of men as Jehonadav was, he knew of the solid virtues behind the young man's composure. The dower price was larger than he had ever dared to hope. As for Beeri's conditions, these appeared thoroughly reasonable, such as he might himself have detailed, though to be sure with greater brevity. Last of all, his daughter, though abashed before her suitor, did not find him at all distasteful. A betrothal was arranged without difficulty, and the marriage consummated not too long afterward.

On his part, Beeri treated Ophra always with a formal but dispassionate courtesy which was, however, thoughtful rather than spontaneous, more a tribute to his principles than to her demands. As is the master's hand, so is the servant's. Beeri's retainers displayed careful politeness toward the mistress of the house, without, however, paying her excessive heed or consulting her opinion. Ophra, timid all her life and now in awe of her husband and the grandeur of the house, accepted this. Over the years she became ever frailer and more faded, as Beeri grew more portly, dignified, and self-assured.

Their marriage was fruitful. Seven children had been born to them, and Beeri had reared them all according to his likes. Unfortunately, they had not turned out as he had hoped.

Not that his four daughters had ever occasioned him the slightest distress. They were comely girls and, since he had no need to haggle over marriage prices, he had not the slightest difficulty in marrying them off to suitable husbands, to whom they in turn would make dutiful wives.

But it is not with daughters that a man builds his house. And Beeri's three sons—Gadiel, Iddo, and Hosea—afforded him little of the joy for which he had hoped and to which, as a man conscious of his virtue, he felt entitled.

Gadiel, the oldest, was self-willed, it seemed, from birth, early aware of his favored position in the household as its firstborn and heir, and quick to take advantage of it. He grew accustomed to having his own desires met without regard to reason or right, and without thought of anyone else. He issued the most outrageous demands and developed ingenuity in procuring their fulfillment. He learned to wheedle and plead so as to melt the most obdurate heart, to play the innocent skillfully, to slip at will into screaming fits of hysteria, and to engage in campaigns of malicious slander against anyone who ventured to stand in the way of his whims. So he became accustomed first to domination and the seeking of revenge, and then to enjoying them for their own sake, without purpose, or occasion. His indifference to the welfare and comfort of others turned into deliberate cruelty which he practiced for the keen delight it afforded him at the expense of anyone and everyone who could not resist, most particularly the lowlier servants and his younger brothers and sisters. He became adept at pinching and hair pulling, at tormenting and teasing, at ferreting out secrets, and at publishing them at the most effective moment. It was a madness not unlike a strong drink, this desire to lord over and terrorize others, to see them cringe and cower. But when the wine of young manhood began to flow in his veins, he was intoxicated indeed. No maidservant was secure against molestation at his hand, no manservant against his capricious tyranny. Eventually the entire household—except for its master, mistress, and overseer—lived in terror before him, avoiding his presence whenever possible and concealing with the utmost care all private matters and secret dreams from his prying sight.

Of all this Beeri became aware too late. To begin with, hope and high expectations blurred his vision. For a long time Gadiel wore a mask of pretense in his father's sight. Besides, did not Beeri give to his firstborn son instruction in the sacred traditions of Israel? And was not such instruction the truest and the surest way to lead a child to righteous manhood?

As was required of him by that tradition, Beeri instructed his son each day at a prescribed hour in the lore which had come down generation to generation from remotest times. He told to Gadiel the tales of the first fathers of the Hebrew tribe, of the enslavement in Egypt, of Moses and the miraculous deliverance from the house of bondage, and of the almost equally miraculous conquest by Israel of its land. He recited the words of Moses and led the lad in the repetition of them, so that they might be engraved upon the heart of the son as they were on that of the father. He schooled Gadiel in the fear of the Lord, the invisible and imageless God of Israel who dwelt in heaven. Beeri trained his son in the rites of sacrifice, prayer, and pilgrimage and in ungrudging generosity as to tithes and other perquisites due to priests. And he admonished Gadiel sternly and often against adopting heathen practices; against the idols of the Baalim and the Ashtarot, their groves, holy pillars, temples, altars, priests, and sacred prostitutes; and against the bringing of sacrifices, whether of beasts or of humans, to such abominations. All this was looked after with ardor and great patience on Beeri's part.

Gadiel listened, and, though the lessons of his father were a suffocating bore to him, he gave every appearance of attentiveness. Indeed, among the many skills which he acquired in boyhood, this was not the least: to listen without hearing. But he did not learn, nor did he take the instruction to heart. And when Beeri chided him, the wily boy pleaded that he strove to learn but to no avail. Beeri concluded that his older son was not destined to be a scholar, and told himself a child could not be punished for an incapacity to learn.

In contrast to Beeri's instruction, Talmon's stories never failed to excite Gadiel and his brothers, Iddo and Hosea. In all the household, in all Jezreel, the boys were certain, no one had such tales to tell or was so skilled in telling them as their beloved steward. Talmon would perch on a stool, his great shaggy head bent forward and tilted somewhat to the left side by a scar, token of an old wound on his neck. His massive hands were clasped, except when he opened them to illustrate the position of the persons or things of which he was speaking. This is the way he sat by the hour in the courtyard or common room at dusk on workdays or at any time of Sabbaths and New Moons, spinning out for the children and servants the sights he had seen in his lifetime and the adventures which had befallen him.

He related how in the middle years of Jehu, king of Israel, the Assyrians had come into Gilead and ravaged the land. This was the saddest of all Talmon's stories, for it had been then, when he was only eleven years old, that his parents and brothers had been killed, and his sisters led away to be sold into slavery, never to be seen or heard from again. He had saved his own life by hiding in a dry cistern in the family's courtyard. There were other tales also of his wanderings as an orphan boy, of how he had hungered and all but starved, of those who had befriended him and those who had oppressed him, of the farmer who had devised to claim him as a slave and of his escape from his hand, and endlessly of the Assyrians.

"Ho," he would say, "you children do not know your good fortune to live now when Jeroboam has humbled the Assyrians. It was different in my day, I tell you. Then they were always on us, coming into the country as they pleased, murdering, pillaging, and enslaving with none to hinder them. The roads were untravelled then, you may believe me, the open villages deserted, the walled cities breached. There were more people hiding in the forests of Carmel than dared to remain in their homes in Jezreel. So had the Assyrians ravaged the land. But the Lord was good to us; he gave us a king who is a man of war, and with him going before us we set the world aright."

When Talmon was sixteen years old he became a soldier, being for all his youth as strong as a full-grown man. Nor was he of those soldiers who are farmers and herdsmen picking up their spears or bows or swords when the enemy draws near and laying them aside as soon as he has been repulsed. He was a soldier of the king, one of those men of valor who do naught else, eating the king's bread and serving only him. This had been in the ninth year of Jehoabog the son of Jehu, from which time on there had been no going forth to war in Israel in which he had not gone also.

These were the most exciting stories of all, the tales of how he had become a captain of a hundred and how the hosts of Israel had driven the Assyrians back, first out of the inheritances of Asher, Naphtali, Zebalon, Menasseh, and Dan, then out of Gilead and Bashan, until the land was free of them and, in the second year of Jeroboam, Israel's armies were camped at the very walls of Damascus.

The older children remembered Talmon's coming to Beeri's house, but Hosea, who had been only two years old and just weaned at the time, knew of it only by hearsay. Talmon loved to tell this story—it was one of his most important—but only did so when his wife was present. It was such a story as made one angry beyond bearing in its former part but very glad in its latter end, so one listened to the first willingly for the sake of the second which was to follow.

"We were fighting at Bikuth then, which is hard by Damascus," Talmon invariably began, "and two misfortunes overtook me. First we delivered from the hands of the Assyrians some Israelite women they had held for slaves, among them some fair to look on, or wise, or of wealthy family. But I was never unfortunate and when we cast lots I acquired—whom do you suppose?"

The children knew of course whom he intended and by a well-established practice always called out together.

"Shualith, your wife."

"Aye, Shualith, my wife, who was neither comely nor wise nor young and, by the altar of Beth El, certainly not sweet of palate or sparing of tongue. But sell her I could not; who would buy her? For a handmaid what need has a soldier? Or for a wife either for that matter? But she wanted it so and I knew not then that a little creature could be so fearsome. And so it came to pass that I took to wife one whose name means vixen and as is her name so is she. Is it not so, old woman?' he would ask Shualith.

Shualith had indeed been named appositely. She was tiny, coming no higher when she stood than her husband seated. Her features were small and pointed, her eyes beady bright, and her speech short like the fox's bark and as painful as his bite.

"And you," she would snap at him, "does not your name signify badger? Is there a stupider beast or a stupider man? Who save for me would have wed you? Were you not close to fifty years old and well nigh broken down? And were you not nursing that sword cut in your neck, the scar of which is still to be seen, and half dead because of it? Your misfortune, do you call me? Who pressed out that wound and bound it up and mollified it with oil and stood you up again on your feet? And in that matter of your inheritance, when you went to claim it and the judge cheated you out of it—perverting your cause in judgment though you bore a wound incurred in fighting to defend him—and you would have drawn your sword, which he, looking for an occasion against you, desired, so that then he might be justified in setting the guard upon you—who restrained your arm and so saved your soul?

"And when you came to Samaria to press your suit and, because you lacked friends for influence and money for bribes, there was none in the king's house who would even listen to you, and you in your discouragement wished to sell yourself as a bondsman, who urged you to wait?

"And when we wandered on and the Lord in his mercy brought us here just at a time when the former steward had died and Beeri our master required one to oversee this house, and he asked of you whether you knew aught of tilling the soil and tending beasts and you said nay and had begun to turn away, who then said that the steward does not work himself but directs others, and that one who has led a hundred men of war in battle can learn to lead twenty bondsmen and slaves in the fields?"

Speaking so, Shualith would come closer and closer to Talmon, who watched her with a smile of admiration as she advanced toward him a few paces at a time, until she spoke and gesticulated directly into his face and seemed for all the world as though she were on the point of assailing him. But to that she never came, though the children hugged themselves with the expectation that she might. Having come so close to him that she could proceed no further, having poured forth all the protests and accusations she could think of, she would stand, her sharp nose the shortest distance from his, quivering with speechless indignation. Then she would turn her head to one side of him to spit contempt, next in another, and, still spitting, take herself off. At which the children and servants would laugh, but none so loudly or delightedly as Talmon himself.

But otherwise no one either in Beeri's household or in all Jezreel laughed at Talmon. Even at the beginning when he had claimed to be no farmer he was not altogether ignorant—who in Israel was?—of husbandry or tillage. And what he did not know to begin with he learned soon enough, until in all the valley few were more expert than he. Nor for all his love of tale-telling did he engage in it except after his tasks were finished or in sacred hours when the doing of work is forbidden. At other times he labored long, steadily, indefatigably. From the servants he never asked more than he was prepared to do himself, nor would he take less than that of which they were capable. Accustomed to command, he issued his orders with quiet firmness and no one ventured to do less or differently than he had indicated. And all this without the least trace of the shrieking and cursing, the raising of fists and the laying on of staves by which alone other overseers ruled their households.

Toward all the children he was long-suffering and gentle, with a delicacy of touch and utterance, surprising in one so large and strong, and so schooled in violence. To the boys he imparted more than his tales; he trained them also in his skills.

"A man is no man," he would remark, "whose fingers are not trained to weapons of war.

"There is peace in the land now, while Jeroboam is yet on the throne, may he remain there forever. But who knows what will be when Zechariah, the prince, of whom the reports are not good, sits in his room. Perhaps then it will be as when I was a boy. If so, he who cannot defend his own life and possessions will have neither."

He used to say to each of them, "What your father can teach you, I cannot. What I can teach you, he cannot. Between us, each of you will be what he is, a man of learning, and also what I am, a man of war."

But it did not turn out as he prophesied, for in the end each was one or the other but not both.

Gadiel ended up proficient with some weapons but untutored in others. To the many-edged sword, for example, the mace and the heavy spear, for beating and thrusting, all of which require force rather than skill, he took naturally, easily. But the bow, sling, light sword, and javelin that is thrown he never mastered. Ungainly to begin with, he also lacked the patience for practice, preferring, as he put it, to beat his opponent, rather than trick him into submission.

Iddo on the other hand excelled in all weapons, from the heaviest to the lightest, for in him nimbleness, strength, and intelligence were united.

Hosea proved Talmon's despair. He lacked neither the required agility nor, for that matter, strength. To be sure, even then, in the boyhood years before the dawn of first manhood sprouted on him, he was tall for his age and very slender, with an elongated, seemingly undeveloped body and thin, unmuscular arms and legs. But his appearance was deceptive. There was toughness in his frame, and his limbs could be as tenacious as threefold ropes. He managed then to bend even a fairly stiff bow and hurl a man's javelin.

His difficulty with weapons was a matter of spirit rather than flesh. Hosea's imagination was so vivid that when he thrust with the sword or shot an arrow, he saw the piercing of his opponent's flesh and the spurting of his blood. Not only did he picture all this, he also thought about it. As a result, he was the more reluctant about these exercises at arms, as the steward and his brothers were the more enthusiastic.

But if Talmon was disappointed in his youngest pupil in one regard, he was pleased by him in another. Nothing more delighted the old soldier than to sing the hymns of the army, both those which were from of old and those newly composed. Yet whenever he opened his mouth in song, all who heard burst into laughter. His voice was strong but toneless, like the lowing of a cow, and the expression of his face displayed the greatest of feeling. The combination was more than the most respectful and sober-minded could endure. It vexed him to no end.

Hosea sang prettily. In a child's voice, to be sure, which was scarcely suited to songs of battle, but clear and true, and quite sweet. What is more, as he sang, he saw it all through his own eyes; he felt in his veins the joy or grief, the fierceness or triumph, the pain or fear of death of him in whose name the song was rendered.

Thus Hosea was all exaltation as he intoned the praise of the prophetess arisen in days gone by from his own tribe of Ephraim to judge Israel and lead its people in battle:

> *Until that thou didst arise, Deborah,*
> *Until thou didst arise, a mother in Israel....*

So also pride swelled in him whenever he repeated Moses's description of the sons of Joseph, among whom Beeri's house was numbered:

Blessed of the Lord be his land;
For the precious things of heaven, for the dew,
And for the deep that croucheth beneath,
And for the precious things of the fruits of the sun,
And for the precious things of the yield of the moons,
And for the tops of the ancient mountains,
And for the precious things of the everlasting hills....
The firstborn of His bullocks, majesty is his;
And his horns are the horns of the wild ox;
With them he shall gore peoples to the ends of the earth;
Such are the myriads of Ephraim,
Such the thousands of Menasseh.

Never, though, was he more moved nor did he stir others more deeply than when he sang songs of sadness. Such songs as David's lament for Saul his king and Jonathan his friend:

...the lovely and pleasant in their lives,
Even in their death they were not parted....

Then into the melody already plaintive and into the poem already heavy with melancholy there crept all the pity of which, young as he was, he was already capable. With it he echoed the pain which thus early he had come to know—yearning for his mother, loneliness that his brothers left him so long and often, grief that his father loved him least of all his sons.

For Hosea was not beautiful in himself; contrasted with his full-bodied, ruddy-complexioned brothers, he was plain indeed. His thin face was pale, high-foreheaded, bony. His mouth was large. His hair was a nondescript brown, springing straight upward to fall helter-skelter. Whereas Gadiel and Iddo favored their mother and her kin, all of whom were extraordinarily colorful and comely, he was entirely his father's son.

When he sang, all who knew him considered him afresh and with vague surprise, so changed did he appear from their notion of his appearance. At such moments, his eyes were kindled, and one became aware that they were very large indeed, and warm and luminous. One saw, too, now that his face had come alive, how intensely alive it could be, how intent on and at one with his theme. But equally with these, it was his utterance—eloquent, understanding, and sympathetic beyond his years—which was affecting. Later, when the animation had faded from his countenance and the glow from his eyes, when his speech had again turned timid, even—in moments of stress—hesitant, he was again merely a shy little boy undistinguished in himself and outshone by his brothers. But not when he sang.

He did not sing for long, at least not in the presence of the members of the household, because of an untoward incident which befell him. It happened at a time when, after long refusing it, Beeri seemed on the point of allowing Hosea to learn to play the lute, that there might be music with his song.

One day, it must have been in Hosea's eighth or ninth year, Gadiel took him aside and requested of him that he learn a particular song which he desired to teach to him.

Now it was not Gadiel's wont to interest himself either in Hosea or his songs, and the younger boy, surprised, looked suspiciously at his brother. He wondered whether Iddo, the author of all jests and adventures, might not have a hand in this one also. But the desire to please his older brothers and the hope, never encouraged but never surrendered, of yet winning their favor were stronger than his caution. The song was a song of love, many of the words beyond his comprehension. When he learned it and sang it for

Gadiel, his older brother listened, and seemed transported with pleasure and amusement.

One Sabbath day when Hosea was singing before the entire household, he sang this song also. From the first lines he knew that something was amiss. The silence in which he was listened to was taut and deeper than usual. He was watched with queer looks and unfamiliar expressions. His father stared at him incredulously. Under all this strangeness, the boy faltered, but his father waved to him to continue, as, a moment later, he prevented Talmon from interrupting him. And so he completed the ditty.

Then it was as though the heavens had fallen. First he was questioned as to the meaning of the song, and then from whence he had acquired it. Determined not to implicate his brothers, Hosea would not answer. At first, he was asked specifically whether it had been Gadiel or Iddo or this one of the servants. Later, his brothers protested their innocence. Their father threatened dire penalties and in the end pronounced judgment.

"Then so be it. Keep your secret. But so long as you do you shall not have the lute for which you have petitioned nor shall you continue to amuse this household. When you have spoken, you shall sing again."

After which he was whipped, though not too severely, and confined to the children's room from this Sabbath to the next. But there he was comforted, for in the first days at least his brothers came to visit him, bearing him tribute for manliness, promising undying friendship, swearing to include him as an equal in all their future adventures. Which vows were forgotten even before the week was out. As for Beeri's denying Hosea a lute, this chastisement was grievous for a time but not too long a time. For, some few weeks after the incident, Hosea became aware that two fine black hairs were sprouting in each of his armpits, and not long thereafter when he was speaking to one of the servants his voice shrilled unexpectedly so that he jumped at its sound. The days of his singing, he knew then, were over for a time—as the event proved, forever. For his voice, when it steadied, though musical in speech, was no better than pleasant when alone in the fields or in the company of others when over festive sacrifices on the altar he attempted song.

Nevertheless, Hosea gained a heritage from his singing. Ever after he sang inside himself, where only he heard, and his voice was sweet and true as he desired it. At first his singing was only of the war chants which Talmon had taught him. Later as he grew older he acquired also the songs of love which the youths and maidens chanted in the vineyards in the springtime. He learned further the songs of sacrifices and festivals, of things that had been in days gone by such as when Balak, king of Moab, had brought Balaam from Pethor to curse Israel and he instead blessed. No priest chanted over an altar in his presence, no potter hummed over his wheel, no mother crooned over her crib but he attended, repeated until he possessed what he had heard. From the peasants, shepherds, and herdsmen in particular he acquired many songs, for he lived among them, and they of all men were the quickest to take pipe in hand or raise their voices. Hearing them sing of earth and sky, of forest and field, and of the seasons and their signs, seeing with their eyes, hearing with their ears, smelling the scents their nostrils noted, he learned after them to mark the green blush of sprouting corn, to observe the first ripe fruit on the fig tree, to predict from the texture of the morning dew, whether it was thick and wooly or thin and wispy, what guise the day would take; to distinguish the west wind for that it was tangy with the fragrance of the cypresses of Lebanon, and the north, chilled by the snows of Hermon, and the east, at once hot and dry from the desert and yet lushly scented from the jungle of the Jordan. But for those times, spectacles, sounds and smells for which there were no established songs, especially for his own heart astir with elusive causeless, nameless joys, sorrows, and disquiets, for these he prepared his own music, inventing such melodies and words as were congruous with his thought and mood.

Thus Hosea came to live in two worlds. The first was public and spoken, but frugally spoken, in speech severely utilitarian and naked of adornment. The other lay within him, secret and in song. This world was multicolored, unhindered, where nothing came into being but found expression, an expression which never faltered and was ever true to the reality it bespoke.

Then, because he saw the two lives in himself, he detected them in others. But this was not a theme for song. It became the cause of an endless unslakable curiosity and, on occasion, flashes of insight and spurts of pity. For how can one look into another's heart and not feel as it feels for itself, sometimes even more so?

• • •

GADIEL, WHO HAD BEEN FAIR ENOUGH to look on as a boy, grew into a handsome man: big-boned, ruddy-cheeked, bright-eyed. He grew also into a glutton and drunkard, heedless of his father's counsel, sullen under correction, rebellious against his authority. The same stolid incomprehension which he affected toward Beeri's formal teaching served as tactic toward his moralizing as well. Bored to suffocation by the long-winded homilies to which he was subjected whenever his father chose to indulge in one of his general discourses, and smarting with resentment under reproof for some specific misdeed, Gadiel turned large dumb eyes and a blank face toward the lecturer, even as he appeared intent on understanding.

Gadiel learned that there was nothing graver to fear from his father's preachings than the discomfort of listening to them and of pretending assent. Beeri could always be counted on for sermonizing and, when the provocation was sufficient, even for threats. But he lacked altogether the heart to lift his hand against his firstborn, let alone his staff. He was also too fond a father and too proud of his household's good name ever to haul a child of his before the elders for graver punishment.

Once he had arrived at this conviction, Gadiel knew neither bridle nor yoke. What was right in his eyes, whatever his heart desired, he did. For his companions he chose the base and idle fellows of the countryside, the sons of Belial, who spent their days in taverns gaming, drinking, and feasting, and their nights in even less reputable pursuits. Nor did he deign any longer to pretend respect for his father's corrections, nor to conceal his deeds. Instead, he was free to show his impatience with Beeri's reproof.

What will a father not endure? To what anguish and humiliation will he not submit himself for the sake of his flesh and blood? And especially on behalf of his firstborn? Agonizingly aware of the contempt to which Gadiel was subjecting him, humiliated before his entire household by the defiance of his will, Beeri was still incapable of resorting to appropriate discipline. He ate the bread of affliction, gagged on it, but swallowed it in the end, feeling its indigestible weight heavy against his heart. He bowed his head and turned away, incredulous that a child of his, a descendant of such honorable forebears, should go so far astray. In quiet hours, whenever he was free from other occupations, his mind was drawn to a searching of his days for those offenses which might have merited so grave a visitation on himself at the Lord's hand. Or he pondered where he had gone astray with the child, regretting that in years gone by he had not on one occasion or another said or done this or that. But though he reflected, examined, and searched, there was no light in the matter. And in the end, he resigned himself to his hard destiny, consoling himself that before him lay one of the dispensations of the Lord, and not the first to be beyond man's comprehension.

So matters ran on many a long and troubled year and might have gone on forever had not Gadiel, in his arrogance, filled the measure to overflowing and committed such an offense in the eyes of God and man as not even Beeri could pass over in silence. One year, at the time of the festival of the pressing of the grapes, when all the world was drunk with the taste and smell of new wine, when the idolaters, to whom this was more a festival than to those who served the Lord, celebrated with an abandon second only to that of the resurrection of the lost god Tammuz, Gadiel and a group of companions, being drunken beyond all restraints, danced together into the sacred grove of the Baalim on the slope of Mount Megiddo. This alone was a graver offense toward his father than Gadiel had ever yet ventured.

Having so affronted the Lord God of Israel, Gadiel proceeded to do offense to man as well. Assembled in the sacred grove, recumbent, each on a pallet spread under one of its trees, were the virgin daughters of the Baal-worshiping families of the countryside. These young women each waited for some man to come to the grove and to lie with her, so that she might make sacrifice of her virginity—and also of her harlot's fee, whereafter she would be free to wed whatsoever man her father elected and she desired. Of the virgins assembled there, those who were fair did not tarry long, particularly in a season such as this when men were inflamed by wine and therefore especially mindful of their duty to the she-goddess of fertility. But others, those who were not comely to look upon, remained, some of them, for many a month until their continuance in the grove of the Baalim became a jest to all who knew them and their kinsfolk.

One such was a woman, no longer young, named Jezebel, the daughter of one Achimelech, a Canaanite master of a farmstead across Jezreel from Beeri's. Achimelech was a devotee of the Baal and Baalith of Tyre. But the god and goddess that Achimelech revered were not content with his fealty, or else, as Beeri insisted, had no power in the land of Israel, which belonged to the Lord God of Israel alone. Whatever the cause, they gave to Achimelech as his firstborn a girl-child and misshapen to boot, with a hump upon her back, one withered hand, and features which, though not ugly, were not fair enough to cause men to forget her twistedness. So she sat in the grove, not one month nor two but nigh onto a year, and no man did come near her to lie with her and to set her free. Now Achimelech might have freed her by paying some man the fee which was due to the goddess, and also a token for himself to keep in return for freeing her from her virginity. But the man was not only a Canaanite and an idolater, but somewhat miserly also. He was reluctant to spend his silver on what should be without cost or price. And then, having been taunted by all who met him, he had taken a great oath by the gods he revered and by the Terafim of his house that his daughter should sit in the sacred grove forever if need be before he would release her with purchase money.

It was to this Jezebel that Gadiel turned when he and his friends came into the sacred grove. He drew her near him with cunning and guile, and feigned to hesitate over whether to choose her from the many young women roundabout. And she, broken by shame and moved by hope, did seek to make herself beautiful in his eyes. And when he seemed to hesitate still further she did plead and urge that he lie with her. Long skilled in the art of taunting and tormenting, Gadiel did prolong the sport to his own amusement and to the laughter of base fellows who were with him. He even compelled the girl to allow him to touch the hump which was on her back and the withered hand, as though examining them before making up his mind. And then, when wearied of the game and the last laughter had been extorted from it, in his drunkenness he spit in her face and led his companions off to women fairer to look upon.

The story of what happened spread throughout the valley. Some there laughed to hear it; others grew hot with indignation. Achimelech kept his own counsel, and when he was asked whether he would not avenge his daughter's disgrace, he responded by saying that he was a Canaanite living in the midst of Israel and glad enough to go unmolested. He pointed out that Gadiel was the firstborn of a by-no-means lowly house and the grandson of a chieftain of one of the hundreds of Ephraim. Besides, was it not he who had exposed Jezebel to humiliation, having left her to sojourn so long beside the Asherah? What then, he inquired, was left to him except to be a reasonable man and swallow his anger?

Beeri was sitting in the early morning sunlight at the inner gate of his courtyard when a remote kinsman, a base fellow, himself fresh from the grove, came to bring the evil report concerning Gadiel, gloating as he spoke. Beeri turned pale and trembled as he listened but asked no questions and attempted no denial, saying naught until the entire tale was told. Then he rose uncertainly to his feet, his eyes blank.

"A serpent, not a son, have I nurtured in my bosom," he whispered to himself, turning away to enter his private chamber. He barred the door behind him.

It was the noon hour by the time Gadiel came home, his garments crumpled and filthy, the reek of stale wine enveloping him like a cloud. As soon as he entered the courtyard, there were those waiting to inform him that the news of his exploits had returned home ahead of him. He shrugged his indifference, but it was feigned. This time, he feared, he had overstepped all bounds.

His well-warranted fears grew with each hour, as it became apparent that Beeri would not come forth from his chambers all that day. And when, on the next day, his father still denied himself to the household, Gadiel took deep alarm. Never before had Beeri withdrawn so long.

Not until the third day did Beeri send word from his apartment that all his household should assemble in the courtyard at the end of the second watch, which was the mid-afternoon. In this, for the first time, Gadiel saw a hopeful sign, for it had never been his father's way to shame anyone, let alone his firstborn son, by chiding him in the presence of others. When the appointed hour had arrived, Beeri came forth to seat himself in a chair which had been set up for him in the courtyard. Gadiel was reassured still further, since his father's face, composed and unimpassioned, was not the countenance of a man whose anger was still in him. And when Beeri began to speak, slowly, sententiously, with the obliqueness of approach that marked all his longer utterances, Gadiel felt his last apprehensions ebb away in the confidence that this was once again the old story of chastisement with words.

"There is," Beeri said deliberately, "some evil seed in every planting. Who has ever sown wheat or barley and not found, no matter how favorable the sprouting, some sheaves blasted or mildewed, or some ears empty and spotted? A few years ago, when we planted a vineyard on the middle terrace, you will remember how carefully we chose the cutting so that every one came only from a proven good vine. And they flourished as we hoped. Yet is there not to this day among them one vine, in the very center of the yard, which though of good stock as all the others, gives only small, sour grapes such as grow on wild vines?

"As with grains and plants, so with animals and so also with men. The Lord God of Israel, who made heaven and earth and man, has woven some evil into all things, even the best. Blessed is the sower who is not compelled to look on when, as it must sometimes, that evil breaks forth."

He paused, looked at the semicircle of those standing before him, Ophra, Gadiel, and the other children in the center of the first row, the servants and slaves—male and female, Canaanite and Hebrew—to either side and behind. Then he fixed his eyes on Gadiel and continued, "Our family is a goodly planting in Israel. Since the days of the judges it has been a goodly planting, yielding men and women who revere the Lord and do His will, but you, my son, my firstborn whom I love, Gadiel, you are an evil seed in this planting, the vine which has reverted back to wildness and sourness and sets teeth on edge. And I am the unfortunate one in whose time the evil has broken forth.

"It is a shameful thing which you have done, a disgrace to you, to me, and to all our house. You have given insult to the daughter of a neighbor, wanton and cruel insult. You have been drunk. You have consorted with base fellows. You have uncovered the nakedness of a woman who is not wed to you. And you have despised the Lord your God, debasing yourself and all His house with idolatry. All these years have I labored and prayed that you would turn from your sinful ways. But now, after what was a third night ago, I hope no more. There remains for me only to do that which should have been done long since: to tear out the blasted sheaves before they infect the whole supply, to pluck away the wild grapes lest they sour the entire vintage and turn it to vinegar, to fulfill the commandment of Moses: 'Thou shalt uproot the evil from your midst.'"

All who listened to Beeri stared silently in fright. Little cries broke forth. Ophra struggled to maintain her breath and trembled visibly before forcing a hand to her lips. Gadiel, whose composure had disintegrated with the unfolding of his father's mind, groaned and shook under the blow of his concluding utterance. For a moment, it seemed that he would move to plead or protest. But pride, and his habitual contempt for his father's weakness, restrained him. And then, an instant later, the need for self-humiliation passed. Composure surged back into him. A faint smile of knowing relief played over his lips as Beeri went on to correct the impression left by his words.

"It is not my design to impeach you before the elders, though such would be your dessert," Beeri said wearily. "And though it were better were you to be stoned in the gates so that you might no longer vex your God, shame our house, disturb its peace, or involve it in blood vengeance, which, the Lord forfend, you may have done already—and in the end squander its substance as you will no doubt once my eyes are closed and I have been gathered to my fathers, the strength is not in me. Full well do I know that it were better so, but I cannot do this to my own flesh, the child of my loins whom I have loved.

"Therefore, this is my judgment. On the morrow you shall depart this place unto the fields which we possess, which are near to Laish in the boundaries of the tribe of Dan, and there you shall abide until the scandal you have raised is subsided, and my heart is turned soft toward you again."

Like clouds in the time of the wheat harvest, Gadiel exalted in himself, *all thunder and lightning but no storm. And I did fear....*

But aloud he spoke humbly and penitently.

"My father is justified. I shall do as he commands."

At which Beeri rose and stalked toward his chamber, stopping however at its door for one bit of final instruction.

"Do you go on," he ordered, "and not alone."

Gadiel rode forth the next morning, armed and with a stalwart bondsman at his side. Late that very day they were found, master and servant, lying slain in a thicket alongside the northward road, where it curled over the crest of the hill to leave the valley of Jezreel. Both had been murdered in like fashion, their throats having been cut. But Gadiel's body had been dishonored in addition in that it was mutilated in the groin.

It was eventide when the dire news reached Beeri's household. At the hearing of it, Ophra shrieked once horribly and fainted. Beeri balled his hands into two tight fists, bowed his head, and said nothing. But when his son's corpse was borne in, limp, blood-stained and lifeless, a wordless moan tore itself from his throat, and he wept like a lost, inconsolable child.

"I did not think," said one of the bondsmen who watched, "that he would weep so for a perverse and wayward son. After the fashion in which he spoke yesterday..."

"Fool," Talmon, the overseer silenced him, "if you have no eyes in your head to see the ways of men, have your ears never heard of David the king and his son Absalom?"

Blood had been spilled; the ground was unclean with it and cried for purification. Therefore, the elders assembled from all the towns round about the thicket in which the bodies of Gadiel and his manservant had been found. And, measuring to see to which town the place was closest, they discovered that it was nearest unto Dothan. Then the elders of Dothan did inquire diligently to discover who had done this wicked thing, to shed blood and defile the land. Of suspicions and conjectures there was an abundance, and the names of Achimelech and his sons were on the lips of all. But only by two witnesses could a grave matter such as this be established, and of witnesses there were none. Nor did Achimelech or any of his household show wounds or scratches such as were to be expected on them who had contended in mortal combat with others. Nor were the beasts which had carried the two who had been slain found in their hands. Furthermore, they did swear, and their servants did confirm them in their oath, that on the day of the murders they had not departed from their fields. And as for the mutilation of the body of Gadiel, which seemed to point to Achimelech and his family, they protested that, had they been guilty of the murder, they would not in idle bloodthirstiness have left tokens to direct attention to themselves. And indeed, it did appear reasonable that anyone who thirsted for Gadiel's blood—and there were others whom he had offended in time gone by—might divert attention from himself by just such a device.

In the end, then, it became clear that the murderer could not be found. But blood which had been shed could not disappear under its own power. Since it could not be washed out with the blood of the guilty, it was required to be washed away in the blood of a sacrifice.

So it came to pass that one day the elders of Dothan did lead forth from their city a heifer on which a yoke had never been placed. They took the heifer into a rough valley which had never been ploughed or sown and broke the animal's neck. Then the priests poured water over the hands of the elders above the body of the heifer. The elders washed their hands and, having done so, did speak and declare together in one voice, "Forgive, O Lord, thy people Israel, whom Thou hast redeemed, and suffer not innocent blood to remain in the midst of thy people Israel."

So the elders of Dothan did thus put away the reproach of blood from the midst of themselves and from the land in which they lived. Blood had been spilled for blood so that, in accord with the Law of Moses, no more would be shed.

Still, when the body of Gadiel had been laid away to rest, Iddo, now sixteen, visited Beeri in his chamber.

"I am the proper avenger of my brother's blood," the boy declared.

Beeri would not permit it. "Are we of the desert folk, to seek blood revenge each for himself? Are there no judges and elders in Israel? Is there no law?"

"Law?" the boy hooted in scorn. "See you not what the judges and elders achieve? They ask questions, are given lies in response, and accept them as the truth. Meantime the guilty one sleeps securely in his bed at night, for he knows that, even should the judges and elders come to suspect him, he will have time and more to travel at his leisure to a city of refuge where he may be safe forever. It shall never come to pass," the boy protested, "so give me leave and this night his soul shall wander through Sheol, along with my brother's."

"Whose soul?" Beeri questioned. "Who is the guilty one? Is it Achimelech, or one of his four sons? And if one of his sons, tell me his name. Declare it, you who know so much."

"What matters it which," Iddo cried, "so long as blood is shed for blood?"

"Innocent blood for guilty? This kind of justice is not acceptable before the Lord."

A violent, blasphemous utterance hovered fleetingly on Iddo's lips, but, enraged as he was, he forbore to speak it.

"Then shall I be put to shame before men," the boy resumed, "and be held as a coward among them?"

Beeri looked at the boy, saw that his cheeks burned and his eyes glowed with defiance, observed that he was strong and handsome in his youth, being even fairer to look upon than his older brother had been. Beeri's eyes flooded with tears and he said softly, brokenly, "And shall I and your mother and all our house be bereaved yet a second time?"

He denied to Iddo consent to serve as the avenger of Gadiel's blood and bound him furthermore with a solemn oath before the Lord. But, knowing the spiritedness of the boy, he did not put his confidence in these alone. Beeri arranged for his household to reside mostly in the royal city of Samaria, traveling to the homestead in Jezreel only for the plantings, the harvests, and the holy days, at which times the father did not permit his second son out of his sight.

There was another reason why Iddo did not run away to avenge his brother's death. Their mother was dying.

Only days after Gadiel's body had been carried home, Ophra took to her bed. Iddo at first thought nothing of it, but Hosea, barely ten years old, told him of the dire whispering he overheard between one maidservant and another. Fear seized them when, in a moment of lost loneliness, they were turned away from the door of her chamber.

Iddo did not try again, but Hosea tearfully persisted. At long last, he was led to her bedside in her darkened room. Ophra looked at him through fevered eyes and managed a smile. She put her hot, dry hands on his. Her kiss was like withered leaves on his forehead. Then she broke into high, thin weeping, and the maidservants joined her until the room was filled with wailing.

• • •

FOR HIS MOTHER'S SAKE, Hosea, his brother, and father journeyed to Beth El soon afterward. Hosea's recollections of the pilgrimage itself swam in mists, except here and there for fragments: the toy sword they had given him to wear so that like the others in the party he might go forth armed against the perils of the way; his discovery, among the animals for sacrifice which brought up the rear of the cavalcade, of a heifer, not yet broken to the yoke, which was his favorite; his anguish of fatigue and saddle soreness on the second interminable day.

As for Beth El and what took place, various isolated episodes remained with him.

One was the sight of his father standing before the Sacred Pillar of Jacob, his arms upraised toward the top of it just above his head, one hand holding a cruse of oil for anointment and his voice raised in supplication. He remembered, too, the many-stepped colonnade of the Temple of the Lord across the Broad Place from the Shrine of the Pillar, and how his father mounting it had expressed reluctance concerning his sacrifice, since the Lord was represented there in the form of a golden bullock.

Nor did he forget the sacrifice itself, the frightening aspect of the great image which seemed to leer at him through its sightless eyes and to grin also, the blood everywhere on the altar and in the bowls and on the arms of the priests to their elbows and over their robes, and the flies humming through the chanting. He felt nausea and horror both at once when they cut the throat of his pet heifer.

Finally, he retained a vivid memory of the meeting between his father at the head of the cavalcade now homeward bound and Talmon, sweaty and dust-covered like the horse he rode toward them. He heard the steward's news and the rasp of his father's cloak as he rent it, and he saw the seemingly muffled figures of his father and Iddo as they pressed on, each of them covered in mourning.

CHAPTER III

BEERI AND HIS ENTIRE HOUSEHOLD were in Jezreel to gather in the harvest and to celebrate the good days of thanksgiving. It was autumn, the season of the Festival of Booths, the second after Ophra's death.

All went, if not joyously, in peace. First, the long, hot days of backbreaking toil in orchard, vineyard, and meadow, each followed by a long cool night in the lean-tos which had been set up in the field, so that those who toiled might not be burdened with going home at dusk only to return to their labors in the morning. Then the threshing and winnowing on the floors, the pressing of olive and grape, the careful storing in the storehouses. Finally, when the harvest was over, the fields and orchards were stripped, and the barns and vats filled with produce, masters and servants alike continued eight days more in the shelters which had covered them during the harvest season. Now the booths, heretofore crude huts of board and boughs, were adorned with palm, willow, and myrtle, hung with ripe golden citrons and other autumnal fruits, adorned with embroidered hangings, strewn with rugs, and furnished

with the costliest of furniture. For the sojourning in them was no
longer for labor but for thanksgiving on behalf of the harvest, and,
some said also, because so the forefathers of Israel had lived in the
wilderness when they came forth out of the land of Egypt.

On each of the seven festive days, sacrifices were brought on
the high places of the homestead, and banquets were ordered at
which the meat of the offering was served together with the fruits,
greens, and new wines of the harvest. Songs of joyful thanksgiving
were chanted. Some got drunk, while others recited the words
of Moses and told tales of the patriarchs or judges or prophets
or kings who had been aforetime, or spoke of the forefathers of
the family. But the eighth day was a solemn assembly. Then all
households came together to the great high place in the center
of Jezreel, there to bring up, not each man a sacrifice for himself
and his kin, nor to seek his private gratitude, but altogether to
pay collective tribute to the Lord on behalf of the community
and Israel's house. Prayers were also made for rain. Therefore the
prayers of the eighth day were spoken with tears and supplication,
and tall urns of water were emptied onto the ground about the
altar as symbols of abundant rain, brimming cisterns and wells,
and drenched soil, while all looked on in silence and dread.

Once the Lord had been entreated and nothing remained
to do except to await the answer of His will, the people turned
altogether, as though assured of a favorable response, to feasting,
drinking, and singing beyond any of the preceding days. And the
young people, youths and maidens, danced—not those of one
household only, but of all; and not the well-born in one place, the
poor in another, and the bondsmen by themselves, but all in one
company.

Iddo and Hosea joined the procession during the late afternoon
festivities of the eighth day. Iddo, still very much a lad though in

his eighteenth year, was long and slender of limb and body, his temperament fiery and intense. His face, more than handsome, was beautiful in repose for its blending of strength and delicacy, and in speech and laughter for its nobility and the white flash of his teeth.

There was wildness in him too, not the brutishness of Gadiel but the impetuosity of high-spirited youth. It was such a wildness that caused old men to shake their heads indulgently and smile wistfully and moved young men to appoint him their leader in exploits and drinking bouts.

Beeri often wished him more sober in spirit. But then, as he would tell himself and others, there is no sobriety in a man until he has come to bear responsibility for a wife and children. And so, from Iddo's fifteenth year on, Beeri urged him to marry, promising to pay any dower price if only the maiden of his son's choice were chaste, of good blood, and not of those who put their trust in idols. But the boy was reluctant to marry for the very reason for which his father urged it: that it would restrict his freedom. Since, furthermore, his fancy had never been taken by any maiden beyond others, he responded to his father's promptings with delays and evasions. In this fashion time slipped by. Beeri had already begun seeking a suitable wife for his son, and told him so. But Iddo had other plans.

As a boy of twelve, Hosea showed no sign that he would turn out either massive in frame and ruddy in complexion like Gadiel or long-limbed and vivid like Iddo. He was spare and of moderate height, with sandy hair that fell haphazardly onto his shoulders. He looked pleasant but not handsome or distinguished in countenance. His thin face was pale, high-foreheaded, bony. His mouth was large. All in all, Hosea was neither ugly nor handsome, much like his father, and his father's father before him.

Neutral in appearance, he was neutral in temperament also, or seemed to be such, being quiet, shy, and reflective in manner. When he was gripped with enthusiasm, his eyes became very large and warm and luminous. But Hosea's most remarkable characteristic was his manner of speaking—eloquent, understanding, and sympathetic beyond his years.

Hosea could convey the most precise ideas and intensely moving emotions in any situation, should he so choose. But he rarely spoke up, time and time again allowing himself to be intimidated by his brother. Hosea admired, revered, and adored Iddo. Of him he was certain that there was no equal in all Israel. Were it not blasphemous to utter it, one might have said that he worshiped Iddo as though he were a heavenly being, one of the messengers of the Lord, shaped like a man and yet compounded by fire, who reveal themselves in the world as flesh and blood. And in truth it was such that the older son appeared in the eyes of the younger. Was he not comely in his towering height and carriage? Did he ever fear aught, or care for the morrow, or doubt his powers? When he walked, and especially when he danced, did he not seem to spurn the earth and almost fly?

Of the adulation of his younger brother, Iddo could not be unaware. But he gave it no serious thought. It amused him when he did think of it, which was rarely, and then only fleetingly. He was kind enough to the child, as to everyone else, with the offhanded casualness of a self-centered, pleasure-loving man. When Hosea addressed him, inquiring of him concerning this or that, or stammering out some confidence or other, he listened as a rule with such patience as was in him or as he could muster. But he had not the slightest notion of what the awestricken child had endured before he spoke and was undergoing in the process—the long hesitations and the mustering of the courage to speak at all;

the painstaking preparations of what would be said and how to say it; the sinkings and soarings of the heart with each indication, favorable or adverse, of how the words were being received; and then the sickness of soul to be outlived or the memories to be treasured through many days, as the event might be.

Insensitive and unconscious of all this, Iddo could be impatient with the boy when his mind was on his own concerns, some feat of strength or skill, some dance, or some maiden. Even worse, he was not above making good-natured fun of the child's vagaries, and not in his presence alone but before the entire household. Once, when Hosea had looked into the cistern which contained the overflow of the fountain and had seen the whole courtyard reflected in it, he had wondered whether there might not be, there or elsewhere, perhaps in the sky, other worlds where other children like him sat and looked into cisterns and marveled about him as he marveled about them. He had ventured to ask Iddo whether this might be so. Iddo's response had been to tease him all through the noonday repast and in the eyes of the entire family. Hosea was shamed by the mockery. His pale cheeks burned, tears were in his eyes, and a lump was in his throat so that he could not swallow his food. He vowed to himself in his heart never again to tell his secret thoughts to anyone in all the world, not even to Iddo.

This pledge he made often to himself and as often broke. When Hosea was gripped by an idea, he burned to share it. Normally the consequences when he told his brothers were either embarrassing or disastrous, but on rare occasions they turned out to be pleasant, even exciting, as in the matter concerning Gomer.

Iddo refused to allow Hosea, being only twelve years old, to join the youths at the dance. Hosea bridled at the edict, especially when he saw that a girl a year younger than he danced among the maidens. Nonetheless, he contented himself to watch from the sidelines.

The maiden was Gomer, the niece of Charun, whose fields had bordered their own until he had grown poor and been compelled to sell to some stranger. Had they not, Hosea and Gomer, played together when both had been younger? When he saw her among the maidens and watched her dance with aliveness and abandon, he observed for the first time that she was beautiful to look on, indeed more graceful and beautiful than any others there. Being the youngest, she danced not in the first rank but the second.

Halfway through, the dancers ceased to dance for a while and stood still, all singing and beating time, the maidens on tabrets, the young men clapping hands, and whichever youth or maiden dared to do so came forth and danced alone between the two companies until someone from the opposite party danced forth in answer. Then they danced together in the eyes of all.

Sometimes it befell that one ventured forward and found no favor and remained dancing alone until the onlookers began to mock. Sometimes another one whom many find delightful came forward and none was so bold as to respond.

So it was when Iddo advanced. Half the virgins desired to be partnered with him. But they each feared the jealousy of the other, and all alike lest they be not welcome to him or else that they be accounted forward. Thus he stood alone for a long moment while all waited to see what would occur.

Then, abruptly and in a rush, a girl danced into the open space between the ranks. She was slender and not tall, her body showing the first curves of womanhood, her hair a great loose tangle of curls that overflowed her shoulders almost to her waist; her face olive-skinned; her eyes dark; her mouth full, appealing, and vital.

"Who is she?" the onlookers inquired of one another.

"Why, it is the little orphan, Diblaim's daughter," came the astonished response.

"Mean you Charun's niece? The one called Gomer?"

"Aye, that one. And a bold one to take the prize from under the very eyes of the others."

"A bold one, say you?" one of the matrons interrupted. "A brazen one says I—to push herself ahead of those better and older than she."

"Tamar here," a man jibed, "speaks from the bitterness of her heart, being jealous for her daughter who has seen fifteen years and still sits in her father's house."

"Jealous," the woman spat in derision, "of that little vixen? They say of her that there is not her like for wildness and that Charun has vowed that if only he had the money he would pay any dower, even though she is but his niece and not his daughter, so does he fear that she will yet disgrace his house. And they say…"

"Let them say what they will," the man replied, his attention elsewhere, "but the child knows how to dance. See then how he and she move together." And he fell silent in admiration, as did all the onlookers.

Iddo, when he had seen Gomer come forth, had been displeased. She was half-crazed and unworthy in station to dance opposite him. He was about to turn on his heels to leave her to the shame she had invited.

But pity moved in him for her, for, despite the boldness of what she had done and the defiance with which she held her head high, she was frightened, as the quickened steadiness of her breath disclosed. And so, hovering somewhere between curiosity and compassion, he began to dance, and she in turn danced opposite and with him with a grace and sureness that, before the first measures were over, surprised him. Half-maliciously, for his resentment against her was not altogether vanished, he entered upon more difficult steps, those such as he thought would teach her the lesson she merited. But she did not falter and, responding to a challenge as explicit as if it had been spoken, danced with increased accuracy and confidence. Then, as the magic of movement bewitched him, he forgot her and everything else, the place and those who stood about watching, and abandoned himself to the rhythm of song and motion. And she, no less joyous in the dance than he, did not turn her eyes from him, not so long as they continued to dance, not even later when they had returned, he to the company of the young men and she to the maidens.

Tongues wagged afterward. There were those who said that Diblaim's daughter was without modesty, and others who said she was but a high-spirited girl who had done what the other maidens wished to do but did not dare, and still others who said only that not in many a year had there been such dancing in Jezreel.

As for Hosea, an aching excitement had welled up in him as he watched the dance, so intense and poignant that he could not speak of it, not when the dance had concluded and not all that day until its very end. When the festivities were over and the household of Beeri was trudging homeward in a struggling band along the dusty road, southward to where the hills begin, Hosea walked at Iddo's side, holding the skirts of his robe lightly so that no one might come between them.

"Ah, ah," he burst forth, his emotions exploding at last, "it was truly wonderful."

"What was wonderful?" Iddo inquired.

"The dancing! How you danced and the daughter of Diblaim with you."

"So," Iddo smiled down in amusement, "you did approve of our dancing."

"And not the dancing alone," Hosea pressed on.

"And what more, pray?"

The boy paused. He saw the two swaying whirling figures—this towering tall and strong, and that more than a head shorter—and those delicate yet firm stomping feet raising clouds of dust, and the heads crowned—one with shining straight hair, smooth and close and clinging through all the wild tossing, the other enveloped in a cloud of dark curls, now floating gently to rest, now whipping in the tempest. And, most beautiful of all, visible only fleetingly through the flying arms and for the sudden turning, the girl's face, her lips half open, her eyes glowing, her cheeks rose under tan with the breathlessness of excitement and effort. Thinking of all this, Hosea found words.

"It was beauty and beauty," he reflected.

"What was?" queried Iddo, whose mind had already strayed onto something else.

"You and that girl Gomer."

The eyes of the older brother glimmered mischief. "So," he said, "it was beauty and beauty. And which, think you, was the more beautiful?"

In all gravity Hosea thought for a moment on the question.

"It cannot be said," he decided. "You are beautiful in your fashion, as befits a man, and she in hers, as is proper to a woman."

"So," Iddo drawled, "my brother finds Diblaim's daughter beautiful."

"Oh yes," the boy breathed impetuously, "the most beautiful I have seen in all my days."

Then, aware all in a rush of what he was saying, he stopped abruptly, looked up into his brother's face, and, reading the amusement unmistakably written there, cried out, "You mock me."

At which Iddo roared with mirth.

"Hearken, house of Beeri," Iddo called to those walking before and behind. "Hear these tidings. Our younger brother has fallen in love. With that little brand from the fire with whom I danced this noon. For he says concerning her—"

"Iddo, stop," Hosea shouted. "Stop, I say."

But the joke was too tantalizing for Iddo to abandon it.

"He says concerning her—"

At this, his face aflame with embarrassment, Hosea threw himself upon his older brother, twining his arms about him as though by confining his person to restrain his speech. But Iddo held him off, neither disturbed nor prevented, concluding, "He says she is the most beautiful maiden he has seen in all his days."

The jest was after all but a jest, not unkindly in intent, and somewhat feeble. No one did more than smile or, for the next day or so, tease Hosea mildly. The boy, however, felt himself shamed and humiliated. He had given all when he revealed his heart. His brother had betrayed him.

Hosea loved Iddo too unreservedly to nurse a grudge against him. But at the same time, he planted firmly in his mind a lesson— the only dream safe from desecration is a dream one keeps to himself.

Shortly thereafter, and without warning, Iddo disappeared. It was at a time when an embassy from the seren of the Philistine city had just left the royal seat of Israel. Together with other youths, Iddo had picked up and followed after the Philistines who, having transacted their business with the king of Israel, had improved on the occasion by enlisting young Hebrews as mercenaries in the service of their overlords in their coastland cities.

Grievous enough for Beeri to bear, Iddo's departure from his father's home was made the more grievous when it was revealed as no suddenly impulsive act or youthful prank, but a calculated and deliberate flight. For now that he was gone, many of his sayings, obscure on utterance, became clear.

"Let not my father suppose," he had said to his bondservant, "that he shall bind me to his will with a wife of his choosing. I shall not be here to be wed."

And to Talmon the overseer he had once declared, "I am wearied to death of the weight of my father's yoke, and even wearier of his endless instruction."

Nonetheless, Beeri would have pursued after him and searched the cities of the Philistines one by one—Gath, Ashkelon, Gaza— had not a report come from Jezreel to deter him. Leaving his father's house, Iddo, accompanied by some of his fellows, had traveled up the valley where, in the dead of the night, they had beset the house of Achimelech, seizing him from the midst of his family while his unarmed sons stood helplessly by.

"Leave him where he left my brother," Iddo called on parting, "and in like condition."

And though Achimelech's servants mounted as soon as Iddo and his band were gone and rode breakneck to the thicket at the crest of the hill, they were too late. Achimelech's body was still warm, but he was dead and had been mutilated as had Gadiel.

Wherefore Beeri did not follow after his second son but stayed at home, telling himself that it is better to have a live son in the heathen cities of the coastland than one dead for blood vengeance in his father's house.

Beeri was now so broken by disappointment that he dared hope no more. Considering his third son, the sole one remaining to him, he made a solemn and embittered covenant with himself, that neither would he dare to indulge in ambition, nor expect joys, nor, beyond all else, expose himself, out of excess of love, to hurt. He would do his duty as a father, but no more.

Hosea was cut off now from his brother and his father. The habit of silence grew in him.

CHAPTER IV

CONSCIENTIOUS AS HE WAS, Beeri would not allow a male child of his to go untutored in the sacred lore of Israel. Dutifully then, each day at the end of the second watch, at which time the servants went forth to resume their labors after their noonday repast, he met with the boy in his private chamber—in earlier years in Jezreel and also later, when Gadiel was dead and Iddo had departed and the household had come to Samaria.

Beeri was of those who knew how not only to read but to write a little as well. Nevertheless, he did not hold with teaching from books, nor did he follow any prearranged order of presentation in his lessons. He had been instructed by his father, by word of mouth and memorization, and so he instructed his children. Whatever occurred to him at the moment as necessary or desirable for imparting he related, discussing the matter until the child understood it or repeating the saying over and over again until it had been fixed in his mind.

In this fashion, Hosea learned the teachings and ordinances of Moses and the sayings of other wise men of days gone by. His father schooled him in rituals: the details of the observances of Sabbaths, of New Moons and festivals, of tithes and offerings, of sacrifices after their different kinds. He told him the tales he himself had heard from his own father, the stories of how the Lord God had created heaven and earth; of the first man in His garden to the east; of Abraham, the first of the Hebrews; of Moses and Joshua; and of the judges, kings, and prophets who had been men of fame in the land aforetime. He trained him to distinguish between the clean and the unclean, between the foods one may eat and those that are forbidden. He explained to him the difference between the lawful fashion for a man and a woman to come near one to another, as when they are wedded to each other and not close kin, and unlawful relations, as when a man coerces a maidservant or lies with one married or betrothed to his fellow, which is a grave sin deserving of death, or with his own wife during the time of each month she is forbidden to him.

Nor was Beeri content merely to rehearse rules and sayings; he interpreted them also. Thus he explained why the firstborn of a man must be redeemed from a priest: to show the father's recognition that the child is from the Lord and has been born unto him. And why must the child be purchased for a price from a priest, rather than be sacrificed by passage through fire before Molech, which is the practice of the Canaanites and of the Edomites? For to murder a human being, even if it be one's own to do with as one may please, is a vile deed. And the God of Israel, unlike the gods of the nations, desires not that children be killed in His honor.

Sometimes they drifted from interpretation to speculation, and Beeri would meditate aloud over why Israel, which serves the Lord, should be a small nation—though not weak or poor during these times—whereas Aram and Ashur and Babylon and Egypt, though they flouted the Lord, were great and powerful. Or for what reason the kings of Israel and Judah were so inclined to fall away from the God of their people, vexing Him by going astray after alien gods. Or whether these alien gods were indeed gods, given that they were less than the Lord and rule in other lands, or only demons, or perhaps mere shadows and emptiness as some among the prophets contended.

Had Beeri paid closer heed to the boy, he would have noted the keenness of his intellect, his spontaneous interest in instruction, the quickness of his comprehension, the speed with which he fixed in his mind whatever he was bidden to memorize, and the tenacity with which he retained it. But Beeri's heart, if not his mind, was usually elsewhere. And when he did mark, as on occasion he could not help but do, Hosea's talents and responses, he was as likely as not to resent them, asking himself, half bewildered, half rebellious, why it should have been the Lord's will that of his three sons, this should be the one who was willing, diligent, and understanding? But then, aware that his question was not only impious toward God but unfair to an innocent child, he would choke it down, telling himself that it was better not to see, not to ask, and not to think.

Hosea was quite unaware of what went on in his father's mind. If he found Beeri to be aloof and unapproachable, he took it for granted that his father had been with him as he was with his brothers. He learned because he was naturally alert in mind, because he was curious, and because he was dutiful toward his father and deeply reverential of the sanctities of their household.

Then, suddenly, he was more than a good student, more than a dutiful, correctly devout son.

The change took place all at once, in a moment, on the morning after the day Beeri had given up hope of bringing Iddo home from the cities of the Philistines, after learning that his second son had shed the blood of Achimelech in revenge for Gadiel's slaying. On that morning, at the end of the first watch, Hosea stood uncertainly in the courtyard of the house in Samaria, just outside the doorway of his father's private chambers. It was the time of his daily lessons. Normally, he would have come to the door and called through the woven hanging to ask whether he might enter. But today he hesitated. He had seen with his own eyes the grief of his father the night before, and, more than a little stirred with concern and compassion, he desired to spare him. But Beeri, never one to neglect duty because of sorrow, came forth to seek the boy when Hosea did not come to him.

"Hosea," he chided, all but falling over the lad as he came out of his chamber, "why do you loiter here in the courtyard when you know you should be with me?"

"I knew not, my father," the boy began to explain, "whether you would desire to have me come for instruction this day."

"When I desire not, then I shall tell you so," Beeri snapped, irritable with hurt and sleeplessness. "Come in, lad, come in. How long will you stand like a stock of wood?"

Hosea followed his father into the private chamber, waited until the man had seated himself on the bed, which with a woven spread over it served also as a day couch, then proceeded unbidden, for it was their regular practice, to do what was required to make the room as comfortable as it might be. It was midwinter. The tessellated stone flooring was cold to the feet, even through sandals. A chill, moist breeze blew through the lone latticed window, ruffling the hanging over it. Hosea drew a reed mat which had been stacked in a roll against the wall and unfurled it before his father so that Beeri might rest his feet on it. He carried a waist-high tripod, on which a brazier rested, from the center of the room, where it stood to the side of the couch, and blew on it until the coals glowed and sparked and gave off a generous warmth. Then, his duties to his father done, he carried a stool almost to the man's knees, sat himself on it, wrapped his long cloak over his legs, folded his arms with his hands in his armpits for comfort, and sat upright, waiting expectantly.

Beeri, who had lost himself in his thoughts while Hosea had been busy, came to with a start, paused for a moment to recall what instruction he had last imparted to the boy and on what he had settled with him for this lesson, and then began:

"I said to you yesterday—nay it was the day before, since yesterday we heard evil tidings...." He trailed off into silence. Then, after a long, aching interval, he resumed.

"I did say to you that I would speak today concerning practices that are forbidden unto us who serve the Lord, the ways of the idolaters, those deeds which vex our God and did cause him to cast out the peoples of the land our fathers possessed.

"Of gross and palpable idolatries you already know, and there is no need to discourse concerning them—such abominations as graven images, which though men make them with their own hands they yet set up and worship as gods; or the foulness of sacred pillars, with their unclean men, and groves, with their unclean women; and their weeping for Tammuz so that the fields may become fruitful. Today I would speak of other practices which are yet idolatrous, though they do not have an idolatrous guise.

"Wherefore did Moses forbid unto us that we should trim the corners of our beards or shave our heads or put baldness between our eyes by removing our eyebrows, or write with ink upon our body? Because this too is idolatry. For so do the priests of Baal who, having unmanned themselves, go about hairless, as though they were neither male nor female, so as to be pleasing equally to the Baal and the Baalith.

"Or wherefore is it forbidden that an Israelite shall seethe a kid in his mother's milk? For this too is idolatry, though it appears far from it. The Canaanites who do these things and the Israelites who follow after them say that by making a rich broth and pouring it over the corners of the fields they thereby help the fields to be rich themselves. But the words which they recite are in the tongue of the Philistines. And there, among the cities of the Philistines, when they do these things it is in honor of their great god, the corn-god Dagon. Can it be other than idolatry in the land of Israel if it be idolatry among the cities of the Philistines?"

Beeri's mention of the cities of the Philistines was inadvertent. But once he had spoken of them, his mind moved restlessly to the thought of Iddo. All his days Beeri had kept his heart to himself and his emotions under control. But not today. He spoke the last words falteringly, then lapsed into silence, unable to continue.

Hosea looked on covertly and saw his father's eyes grow vacant with abstraction. He observed the tightening of the lines about his father's mouth, listened to the desolate silence into which he had lapsed. And suddenly he understood that this moment was to Beeri like that other moment when Gadiel's corpse had been borne into the courtyard of the homestead in Jezreel. Now not one heart ached but two, the father for the missing son and the remaining son for the father.

A yearning engulfed Hosea, a desire to comfort his father. He started from the stool, thinking to move to his father's side and warm him with a near presence, only to sink back in fear of a rebuff. His hand then reached forward to take Beeri's, but faltered and dropped as it occurred to Hosea that even this might be overly bold. The boy opened his mouth to speak but, not certain what to say or how to say it, and having long since been habituated to shielding his heart, he closed it again.

"Father," he began tentatively and not knowing what he intended to say, concerned only to break Beeri's anguished abstraction. "Father, will it weary you should I ask a question?"

"Eh?" Beeri grunted, coming to with a start. "What say you?"

"I have said that I would ask a question."

"Then ask," the man said, his mind and heart still elsewhere.

In a flash of inspiration, Hosea knew what to ask. He would speak of one of those matters of which Beeri loved to discourse.

"The gods of the nations, I do not understand about them."

"What do you not understand," Beeri inquired, his attention beginning to be arrested.

"What are they? I do not intend the images which I know are things that men fashion with their own hands and then foolishly worship. I mean high gods like El and Baal and Chemosh, which, though there be images of them, are yet said to be more than their images, as our God is, though He dwells in His shrines at Beth El and Dan and Jerusalem, yet is at every high place at which His name is invoked...."

"You must not speak so," Beeri interrupted, entrapped as Hosea had expected. "It is not lawful to speak of the Lord as though other gods could be compared to him."

"But," Hosea persisted, emboldened to rashness by the success of his ruse, "this is my very question. Why is it unlawful to speak of them in like fashion? Is not Ashur a god in Nineveh and for his people, the Assyrians, as the Lord is for us here in Israel?"

"They are not to be likened one to the others," Beeri repeated, his words touched with anger because he was not altogether clear in his own mind of the proper answer. "Ashur is a god in Assyria. But is he invisible like the Lord? Did he create earth and heaven? Is he mighty like Him? Nay, he is more like a..." Beeri went on in relief, seeing his way out, "Ashur is a demon, a spirit like the spirits and demons which are in places, fountains, or woods, save that his place of dwelling is an entire land."

"Then would it be lawful," Hosea inquired, "for us, if we came to his land, to call on his name or bring sacrifice to him?"

"Silly child," Beeri scolded, now completely absorbed in their conversation. "And do we call on the names of the demons and spirits who are in this land? Know you not the Lord is a jealous God before whom an Israelite may have no others?"

"Even should the Israelite travel to Assyria?"

"Even in Assyria."

"Then the Lord must be there too."

"Yes, and that is still another difference between Him and the others."

By now Hosea had himself been taken in by his own guile and had forgotten all else, except the matters of which they were speaking.

"Will it tire you, my father, if I ask yet another question?"

"It will tire me," Beeri said, a not unkindly smile on his lips, "but you will ask nevertheless, having always been a great one for questions."

"What I do not understand is this: if the Lord be mightier than Ashur, wherefore is it that the Assyrians are a powerful and rich nation, whereas we, though not poor, and not weak in these times when the house of Jehu rules on the throne here in Samaria, are yet nonetheless so much weaker than they?"

"A deep question, my son. A question over which our prophets and wise men have pondered much. Concerning it, they say two things. First, that the Lord is biding His time. There is a day to come, a day of the Lord, when His might will be made known in the eyes of all flesh, and great glory will come to Him and to all

Israel. But there are those who say that it is not for want of might on the part of the Lord and not because He is awaiting a more favorable time that Israel is weak, but for our own sins. For we have vexed Him by going astray after other gods and transgressing His statutes."

"But not more than other peoples," Hosea objected. "Do not the Assyrians in their worship of Ashur, or the Arameans who bow down to Baal, offend Him more grievously than do we, seeing that they do not acknowledge Him at all?"

"But they are not His people," Beeri hurled back, "therefore He looks to them for naught. We, however, know Him. We are His chosen covenanted nation, which has sworn to do His will. From us He expects more than from them. Therefore is He harder with us than with them, as a master may be sterner with a more advanced pupil or a father with his older son."

Hearing his own words, Beeri stopped short.

"Not always is it so," he added slowly, "sometimes a father should be stern and is not...."

The floodgates of memory burst wide open. Beeri fell altogether silent in an anguish of pity for his dead son, of yearning for his missing son, and of self-reproach for the things left undone. And his third son, looking on, understanding his hurt but powerless to assuage it, ached with a pity rarer than that of a father for his child: a child's compassion for his father.

And not at that moment only, but always. Hardly a day passed during which for some moment he did not yearn tenderly toward Beeri out of compassion for the man's lonely hurt. Therefore, the boy learned more readily and more thoroughly than even his considerable talents and interests might account for, and he took what he learned to heart, making Beeri's teachings his principles, loving what he commanded, rejecting what he despised. For the boy hoped to comfort his father, to make up to him for the wrong done him by his other sons. Therefore, between what he did deliberately in this spirit and what he did out of unconscious imitation born of love and admiration, Hosea became, as it were, the second Beeri, a Beeri in younger miniature. He took on the man's demeanor, the gravity of his deportment, his measured and didactic speech, his very gestures, until all who saw him were somewhat amused at the spectacle of a child comporting himself with the seriousness of a solemn and pompous adult.

So on the stone he rejected, Beeri inscribed his dream. For though he took little heed of the fact and derived slight joy from it when he did notice it, Hosea came to be made in his father's image, as surely as Adam was fashioned in the likeness of the Lord God who created him.

One day, the boy came to Beeri's private chamber, expecting no more than his usual period of instruction. But his father was preoccupied and did not speak to him for some time.

"My son," he said finally, "you are now fifteen years of age, and it is time for us to think of your future and how you will live, and from what you will live, when I am dead and gathered to my fathers."

"May my father live forever," Hosea offered.

Beeri nodded his head gravely in acknowledgment of the blessing.

"But the days allotted to man are numbered, and no one knows in the morning what may be at eventide. It is therefore only prudent that thought always be given for the morrow and its changes. Therefore, I have been asking myself what will be with you when I am gone and the houses, fields, cattle, and slaves of my possession are passed on, as is the way of the world, to my oldest male child, your brother Iddo. For though I have seen him not these three years, it is he who must lawfully inherit them.

"Silver and gold I can bequeath to you, and I shall. But how long can a man live on money, unless he lends it out on usury or traffics with it in merchandise—to which you, my son, I trust will never stoop? You are a child of an honorable house and honorable houses such as ours derive their livelihood from herds, flocks, and the soil. Therefore, I am concerned that you shall not be dependent on your brother, for I have seen the lot of younger sons in a household, and it is often bitter.

"Having considered these circumstances and weighed all the possibilities, I have decided that you would be most secure if you will enter the service of our king. Not in the first ranks, for no safety may be found there. Not alone, because those in a court are enemies one to another, forever seeking to supplant each his fellow. The house of Jehu has sat firmly since it overthrew Ahab and Omri's house, and were it more zealous for the Lord I should say let it sit forever. But who knows what enemies, whether within or without, plot against it even now? And when a royal house is overturned, it falls not alone.

"Not so, however, with those who serve the king in the middle ranks—the overseers of the royal money, the chroniclers, scribes, and secretaries. For so long as the king reigns, he has need of them. And if—may there be no omen in my words—insurrection or war should rise against him and he should fail to withstand it, as happened when the Arameans in my father's time did sit here in Samaria, the new rulers will require such services equally and even more. Of our nobles, of our chiefs of tribes and captains of the host, they had no need. But of our scribes and accountants they did make use, paying them according to the monies which had been dispensed to them before the city fell.

"To serve in the king's household is not, therefore, an evil thing. It is a dependable livelihood and modestly profitable. And you, my son, are suited to it, being quiet, studious, quick to learn, and long to remember. Therefore, I have spoken this day with one of my acquaintances, Noam the Naphtalite, who is the first of the king's secretariat, and a good man who reveres the Lord. I have arranged with him that once the Passover festival is gone and we have returned from Jezreel, he shall take you to apprentice. It will not be necessary that you live with him, for he resides in Samaria but a short distance from our house. Nay, you will continue to dwell in our midst as always, except that you shall attend him each day from the middle of the first watch to the middle of the third, whether in his own home or in the palace. And he will teach you to write not only our tongue but whatever other tongues kings employ to do business one with another...."

Beeri spoke of this matter at considerable length. Hosea listened attentively until he was done.

"I thank my father for his great kindness and forethought concerning me." He would have spoken so in any case, since Beeri's will sufficed for him. But in this matter, his heart was glad also. The prospect of learning the writer's craft pleased him, and he was especially happy that it would not be necessary for him to leave his father's house to that purpose.

• • •

WITH THE APPROACH OF EACH FESTIVAL, Beeri's household went into a fever of uncertainty. How would the master decide this time? Would he elect to disregard the risks of an attempt at blood vengeance by Achimelech's kin by traveling to Jezreel so that he might worship the Lord in the high place at which his fathers had worshiped before him? Or would his fears bind him to the safety of Samaria and the altars sacred to the Lord in that city, even though they were not his own? Or might he resolve to render the offerings of his lips at some ancient, storied shrine, as he had in his earlier years, when he was both more vigorous in body and less burdened by a large and prospering household?

Among these possibilities, Beeri's household hesitated during the sacred time of the first fruits, the harvest, and at the great New Moon in the autumn. But not at Passover, the one festival most properly celebrated in the family homestead. For whence should the paschal lamb be taken except from one's own flocks, and whence the grain for unleavened bread save from one's own granaries? Besides, did not the stems of new barley await their master that he might select a sheath, mark it, cut it with his own scythe, thresh and winnow it, so that an omer of it could be brought each day for forty-nine days in thanksgiving to the Lord?

In all years then, even those of Gadiel's death and Iddo's flight, the household traveled from Samaria down to the valley of Jezreel, a procession of six ox-drawn carts groaning under their bundles of goods, on top of which sat the women and young children. On either side of the procession were the bondsmen and sturdier maidservants who went afoot, as well as Beeri, Talmon, Hosea, and many of the more honored free laborers.

The journey was pleasurable or difficult, depending on family circumstances, the state of the weather, and the condition of the roads. The first spring after Iddo left, every heart brooded over the past and dreaded to look on familiar scenes from which two familiar faces and figures would be missing. As though out of fellow feeling, that winter had been unseasonably prolonged, so that the skies were grim, rain fell in solemn persistence, and a chill wind blew gustily. The roads were morasses in which the wagons mired time and again. The entire cavalcade seemed more a funeral than a festival procession.

But for the third Passover after Iddo's flight, when Hosea had passed his sixteenth birthday and was considered a man soon to be apprenticed to Noam the Naphtalite, every circumstance conspired for joyfulness, both on the road they traveled without obstacle and at the homestead at which they arrived in safety.

The sorrows of Beeri were by now old sorrows, somewhat mellowed. The spring was in him with a sweet potency that lifted the heart and brought song to the lips. The sky was so blue and breathtakingly high that it seemed not a heaven but in its exceeding loftiness a veritable heaven of heavens. The wind, blowing in long, even breaths was so strong in scent that all turned slightly giddy from the inhaling of it. And flowers were spread over the ground—crocuses, anemones, irises, and lilies—glowing and dancing in their many colors, looking like the jewels of some Canaanite trafficker, set against a cloth to show them off against the solid green of grass, solid green since there was no brown or barren spot anywhere.

At each dusk during that season, the world put away its daytime adornment of flowers, slowly and with reluctance, and put on, one by one, the spangles of hugely lavish, almost garish, displays of stars. The wind blew at twilight as strongly perfumed as before, save that it took on the coolness of a chilled wine and was moist as if with the vapor that condenses on a polished bowl. And night by night, the moon, which had been just newly born when the household came to Jezreel, grew prodigiously as the Passover approached and rose higher in the sky with each shining forth, until by the eve of the festival it was at the full, standing round and bright yellow overhead.

In its light, tables were spread in the courtyard of Beeri's homestead, as in every household in Israel and Judah in which men and women revered the Lord. A great fire was kindled for the roasting of the paschal lamb, which had been slaughtered at dusk, and a feast was made of its meat, together with unleavened bread and bitter herbs. Then, as they sat in the mingled light of the moon and the flames, still eating and drinking the wine, Beeri related to them the tale of Egyptian bondage and of the miraculous deliverance, after which they sang hymns of praise deep into the night.

On the next morning there began the annual "walking out" of the youths and virgins, of their going abroad in the fields and on the roads; addressing one another freely as was proper only two times a year, on the Passover and on the Festival of Booths; singing songs of love one to another and looking each to see who was fair and winsome.

Most of the young men went about in bands, as did the maidens also, compromising so between unconfessed eagerness and equally unconfessed timidity. Those whose hearts were already set on one person walked alone, as did those who were friendless, or so shy as to cringe at the company even of their own kind.

Such was Hosea. He knew no one whose company he might seek out freely and without embarrassment, his long absences from the valley having broken his acquaintance with other youths of like station. And such a flight of emotions had been awakened in him by the anticipation of walking forth—reluctance and ardor, desire, curiosity, and bashfulness—that he feared the presence of anyone by his side, lest he betray himself.

On the first morning, therefore, he went forth alone. Lacking boldness, he wandered side paths on the outskirts of the groves and fields rather than the main roads and other places where young people foregathered. He saw them from afar, heard their songs and laughter, and yearned, but did not dare, to approach them. Occasionally he encountered other youths as solitary as he, and once he encountered a maiden, a not uncomely maiden to whom he would have spoken. But she was hurrying toward the town and had brushed him by before he found words.

In his loneliness the day dragged for him, all the more painfully because he was aware of its passing and the slipping away of its promise. At its end he trudged home, heavy at heart.

Had he some pretext, he would not have gone forth at all the next morning. But a wine jug and a generous luncheon packed in a pouch had been set out for him at the doorway of his chamber. And he could not bring himself to face the mockery of the entire household which certainly would descend on him, and for a long time, were he to loiter at home. With studied nonchalance, therefore, he donned festive attire once more, raised the skirts of his mantle, pulling it up through the girdle so as to free his legs for walking, swung the pouch over his shoulder, and lifted the jug into the crook of his other arm. Calling casual farewells to all within hearing, he sauntered off. As he did so, a resolution which had been forming in him crystallized. He would not visit the places where youths and maidens congregated. Not again would he skulk about, looking and yearning from afar. Better to pass the day as best he might in solitude in some spot where no one would come upon him, amusing himself in whatever fashion he could until the dusk descended and it was safe to turn homeward. So at the least his pride would be spared and he would not be sickened at heart again with disappointment and self-reproach.

But though he struck off in the direction of the hills, he found himself drawn, despite himself, toward the town. He did not allow himself to venture inside, but neither did he go so far from it as to be beyond all hope of some happy chance encounter. He compromised by settling himself in an open space in a vineyard, as close to the midway point as he could determine between his home and the fields and paths where the other young people walked.

The hours did not go quickly. Having nothing else to do, he was compelled to invent matters, childish matters, with which to concern himself. He studied the vine leaves with painstaking and prolonged care, examining the network of veins, the mottled light and arc of the tissue. He watched a colony of ants at work. In the end, unable to think of an alternative, he took to staring up into the sky through half-closed lids, admiring the mysterious little luminous shapes that floated in and out of his vision. Hypnotized by the play of light and shadow, lulled by the whisper of the wind in the leaves, and somnolent with the mounting heat of day, he drifted into a half trance in which all thought and all awareness of time were blessedly swallowed up.

A shadow fell across his face, startling him into consciousness. He sat bolt upright, blinking up at a young woman's figure silhouetted against the sky.

He scrambled to his feet and set nervously to making himself presentable, brushing the dust from himself, pulling at the skirts of his mantle, all the time volunteering hastily invented and broken phrases for fear that the truth about his solitude be guessed. "I grew weary...all my friends..."

The girl's voice seemed strained, as from anger. "May I be your partner today?"

He wished, but could not bring himself, to say yes.

"Then you are not alone?" she continued after a moment, misconstruing his silence. "You have friends for whom you are waiting? I watched for a while and saw no one...forgive me...." She shrugged ruefully and turned to leave.

"Don't go," he interposed, hastening to stop her. "I am alone...."

"But your friends!"

He hesitated on the verge of lying again, but, being calmer now, he lacked the will.

"I have no friends," he confessed, "I did not tell the truth to you. I am alone."

She tossed her head defiantly. "As am I."

From his first startled glimpse of her, he had been aware that she was pretty. But now she suddenly appeared to him breathtakingly lovely.

Her hair was a swirl of very dark waves about her head, a cascade tumbling down her shoulders. The smooth olive of her skin was deep with sunburn and touched with the blush of her blood. Her eyes burned black under eyebrows that glared upward as though about to take flight. Her nose was not thin and her mouth was full, but there were hollows under her high cheekbones which lent delicacy and wistfulness to her face. She was tall for a girl, her eyes on a level with his. And there was in her an intensity which made her seem gloriously alive.

"You?" he wondered, "Why should you be alone?"

She struggled between shame and indignation.

"Because," she burst forth, "because the other girls will not walk with me, saying that I am a nobody. And the boys, when I go along with them, are over bold, mindful that with me they need fear neither a father nor brothers, since I am an orphan and alone. And because of this."

She swept the fingertips of both her hands down her sides, calling his attention to her robe, which he observed was threadbare, faded, and ragged at the fringes.

"And because of this," she went on in mounting passion, putting forth a bare, dust-stained foot. "It is not enough that I must appear in rags to be mocked at by all the world. I must also go without sandals so that I cannot even dance."

At this, he recognized her.

"Why, you are Gomer, Gomer the niece of Charun and the daughter of…"

"Diblaim," she supplied. "And you?"

"You do not know me?" he questioned, first touched by disappointment and then telling himself that he could not expect her to recognize him, as he had not recognized her. "We have met often before, but long ago. I am Hosea...."

She looked at him blankly.

"Hosea," he repeated, "Beeri's son."

"Of course," she cried, "Hosea, Iddo's brother. Where is Iddo? Is he still among the Philistines? Do you hear from him?"

"Not often, and then indirectly, as when some traveler comes from Ashkelon. That is where he is. He has become a captain of fifty of the palace guard of the city's seren."

For a long moment she said nothing, and while he waited, the misgiving beset Hosea that she would turn to leave.

"Will you eat with me? I have enough for two, for a whole company indeed," he stammered. "And it is not pleasant to be alone."

"Do I not know it," she replied solemnly.

"And you need not stay all day," he assured her, "though I would like it. You may go on whenever..."

She looked into his face. Whatever remained of sullenness in her face vanished in a swift, warm smile. "No, it will either be all day as I suggested when I first spoke to you or nothing. Which, I pray you, will you have?"

It was noon. His heart leaped with relief, with an onslaught of pleasure.

"To the very dusk," he said.

They turned at once to the pouch, undid its fastenings, and explored its contents—the cakes of unleavened bread, the meats wrapped in a cloth, the dried figs, dates, and nuts.

"This is a feast," she said. "One such as Solomon the king might have eaten."

They fell to zestfully, eating eagerly and steadily, and drinking from the jug as they ate, passing it back and forth whenever one or the other thirsted. The wine was, on Beeri's prudent instruction, well-diluted, but it was refreshing and had enough strength that, even if fleetingly, Hosea was partially liberated from his usual difficulty of speech. He talked with a spontaneity and articulateness which surprised and delighted Gomer, especially when he told her of Samaria, the multitudes who lived there, and the magnificence of its palaces and temples.

As he sobered from the wine, however, his speech faltered once more. She noticed that his courage began to fail him. He groped for things to say, lapsing into intervals of silence, from which he emerged into hesitant speech, only to slip back again with an ever heavier sense of anxiety and inadequacy.

Gomer was not without understanding. She suppressed any impatience she may have felt, and, whenever some period of quiet became intolerable or his inner anguish too painful, she tried to help him. As one supplies to a stammerer a word for which he struggles, she asked him leading questions.

But it was all slow and dull; she wished so very much that she were elsewhere that in the end her capacity for pretense was exhausted. She continued to sit, her face turned toward him as though she were all attention. But her fingers toyed with a twig, twisting and untwisting it interminably. Her eyes were either averted or, when she looked at him, vacant. Eventually, she stopped taking any part whatsoever in the conversation. Watching her furtively, anxiously, he came at last to the point at which he could no longer conceal from himself that she was bored. Despair overcame him. He gave up and fell as silent as she.

How long they sat wordless together he did not know, plunged as he was in a hopeless lethargy. But somehow, suddenly, he was aware of her again. And he was seeing her, all at once, not as someone who might leave him at any moment and whom he must strive to detain, nor as one with whom he must make conversation, no matter how difficult, but simply as one to be looked at and be marveled over for beauty. She was seated near him with her head somewhat bowed and her averted face visible only in profile. He had been lying on his side, his head propped up on an angled arm, his gaze fixed idly on the ground, his consciousness deep in the great, colorless tide of his loneliness. A moment later, nothing had changed except that his eyes had been raised.

He stared at her. His sight invaded and lost itself in the waves and curls of her hair. Recovering, it traced the clean line from her forehead to her chin; returned to her generous lips, where it paused for a trembling moment; wandered down her arms to her long, thin fingers, busy with the twig; retraced its way upward and forward as to round the swelling curve of her breast; then drew quickly away, returning to her face, where it found rest for a long interval on her lips, then on her long-lashed, lowered eyes.

A sweet tremulousness was born in him, a half-pleasurable, half-painful sensation in his chest.

She raised her eyes. He was too absorbed and lost to think of averting his own. Their glances locked.

"You are very beautiful," he murmured, speaking without forethought or self-consciousness.

She flushed at the compliment, a dark tide flowing upward in her face. Instantly he blushed too for the daring of his utterance, the openness of his self-disclosure.

• • •

THE NEXT DAY, SHE DID NOT COME. He loitered away the interminable hours, alternately seething with indignation against her, though she had not bound herself to spend this day with him when he had proposed it the afternoon before, and aching, first with hope and finally with dull despair.

But on the third day, she returned. There was in her something of surliness, as though she had come reluctantly. But he was too joyous to sense her mood, not that he would have understood its import if he had. It was enough for him that his anxiety had proved false. She had come, and a long day stretched before them. This time, he was not unprepared for her arrival. Through the two long nights since they had first met, he had planned carefully their next encounter, what he should talk about to her and how he should express it.

It did not go quite as smoothly as he had designed. His words were not as fluent as he had intended, nor was she so interested as he had hoped in the matters of which he spoke—his studies, for example, or the scribe's craft which he was to learn from Noam the Naphtalite. But it went much better than on the first occasion. There were matters which fascinated her. And at no time was there a recurrence of those long, awkward silences during which his heart perished for want of what to say and her thoughts wandered off where they would.

Thereafter they met each day, Hosea invariably arriving first, she coming tardily and always with a sullenness which did not disappear until the morning was far advanced, and which was liable to return whenever the conversation lagged. Occasionally she withdrew into herself and her private, unhappy concerns.

It was never so between them that they were altogether at ease. But there were periods in which both of them chatted spontaneously, gaily, and lightly of heart.

Meantime his admiration for her mounted steadily. He did not again bespeak his wonder of her. But each day she seemed more beautiful.

He became aware of details of her loveliness, the flash of her teeth when she smiled, the tapering slenderness of her fingers, the faintest dimple in her chin. He became conscious of her intriguing mannerisms, the way laughter welled up in her throat, the huskiness of her voice, the proud toss of her head, the volatile quickness of her mood.

All these he found pretty and appealing. But as he came to know her better, he discovered other traits which disturbed him. One was that she was not overly devout. It had been when they were ransacking the pouch for their first luncheon. As they examined their treasure, she cried out in playful regret, "What, no parched corn in honey? I had been hoping there would be some. It is my favorite dainty."

"Oh, no," he answered. "Have you forgotten that parched corn is suspect as leaven and may not be eaten on these days?"

"I had forgotten that. And I had forgotten too that in your household such customs are strictly observed."

"But is it not so also in your home, Charun's home?" He was more than a little shocked.

"No leavened *bread*. But for the rest, Charun, my uncle, is not overzealous for the details of the law. He will eat and give us to eat of parched corn, and even of beans and peas, holding that these are not the leaven of grain. And I must say that I agree with him. It is one thing to eat outright leaven such as bread; that, everyone agrees, is unlawful. Besides, it is not safe, for a man and his household may be cut off from the family of Israel if they are discovered doing so. But all these other little rules, they are so difficult. Besides, what purpose do they serve? Will it matter to the Lord?"

As with ritual, so he suspected with other matters. Never, when he referred to the Lord and the teachings of Moses, did she say anything in response. And whenever he mentioned the principles taught him by his father regarding dealings between man and man, she would merely look at him, a cryptic smile on her lips.

Also, she disturbed him from time to time with a bitterness of mood which welled up in her. She was capable of speaking harshly and angrily of people, of flaring into angers against them as though they had done her some personal wrong.

But these were to him but the momentary disturbances, the ruffles of a smoothly flowing delight in her.

And they were completely wiped out of his consciousness by the wondrous incident which befell on the last day of their walking out, on the seventh day of the festival.

The place of their meeting, isolated by vines and terrace walls, could not be seen from the road. But sounds carried from it, so that they always heard the noises made by passers-by—the clank of sodden hoofs on the stones, the babble of voices, the whistling of a lone boy playing his pipe, fragments of conversation.

On this last day of the festival, a band of youths and maidens, accompanied by musicians trooping up the hill, stopped at a level place in the roadway and began first to sing and then to dance.

The words and the melodies carried to Hosea and Gomer clearly, and even more clearly there came the rhythm, beaten on a drum and tabrets.

Gomer's eyes lit up.

"Come, Hosea, let us dance."

"But I cannot," he protested.

"Cannot? Iddo's brother not be able to dance?"

"Oh, I can," he admitted, "but I do not do it well."

She coaxed, but he was too unsure of himself to give in. At last, as much to free himself from her beseeching as for any other reason, he said to her, "Do you dance for both of us, dance for me."

"Would you truly desire to see me dance?"

As she asked the question, he knew all at once that there was nothing he desired more.

"Yes," he whispered, "I would."

Gomer rose from the ground on which they were sitting. Lifting her head so that her face was turned upward to the sky and her hair flowing free of her back, she raised her arms as if holding tabrets. She then began to turn and sway before him.

He looked up at her and saw not her face, at which he had always looked heretofore, but her body. As he noticed the slenderness of her ankles, the length of her legs, the curved aliveness of her thighs and waist, and the fullness of her bosom, fire flared in him. It was clear to him as a springtime day. He loved her.

CHAPTER V

IT WAS A HAUNTED HOSEA who journeyed to Samaria the next day with his family. He was haunted by the question of whether he should have spoken of his love to Gomer; haunted by regret that he had not come to love her earlier, so that he might have looked upon her with his new vision for longer than a few hours; haunted by anguish over the need to depart from Jezreel, by misgiving as to when he might return, knowing full well that in no case would it be before the Festival of First Fruits, an interminable six weeks hence at the least; haunted by unendurable fear that in his absence she might come to love another, or be pledged in marriage by someone who would arise to purchase her at Charun's hands. Haunted by all these things, he ceased altogether to be a boy, becoming all at once a man who loved.

Through the turmoil of all this ran the deepest and most persistent concern of all: should he, dare he, speak of this to his father?

Only by speech would he ease his heart. Yet with speech he might cast away all hope. Suppose his father should prove indifferent, saying that his son was too young and immature to think of marriage? Or suppose Beeri should refuse to consider his choice, declaring that being the father he would choose a wife for his son? Or, most terrible of all, suppose he should say that he did not approve of Gomer, either because she did not find favor with him, or because she would be without dower, or because her lineage was not high enough, or because—and this was most likely—Charun's household was lax in its duties toward the Lord?

On the road from Jezreel to Samaria and at their home the first days and nights after their return, he grew giddy and weary thinking about all the possibilities. Moments of desperation beset him. *Anything would be better,* he thought, *than this tormented uncertainty.* Yet he could not bring himself to talk to his father.

On the third day of their return, Hosea appeared before Beeri for instruction.

"My son," he began, "it is nigh six weeks to the time when we go again to Jezreel for the Festival of First Fruits. I have considered waiting until after that holiday for the matter I shall put before you. But I have already deferred it too long...."

Hosea's blood began to pound in his ears. Wild joy, wild relief had soared up within him. Then they *would* be in Jezreel in six weeks, weeks long and many to be sure, but not so long and so many as to be an eternity. He would see her again. And when he did, he would be as sure of his love as he needed to be. How fortunate! How fortunate!

Happiness bubbled in him like secret laughter. He gave himself over to it completely. Then a voice broke into his transport.

"Hosea, boy," his father was saying indignantly, "what is with you? Thrice I have spoken and you have not answered."

"Pardon, my father, but my mind did wander."

Beeri threw Hosea a stern look, hesitated, and went on.

"Today will be your last day of instruction under my watch," Beeri concluded. "On the morrow I will take you to the home of Noam the Naphtalite, who will instruct you in the scribal arts."

"On the morrow," Hosea echoed. He was happy.

• • •

WHEN THEY SET FORTH THE NEXT MORNING for Noam's house, Beeri hesitated at the first street corner.

"The most pleasant route to follow," he said, "is down our shoulder of the hill, almost to the royal palace, and then up the other. The streets, both ours and that on which Noam lives, are wide and clear. But the journey is long. Let us go through the cleft. It is shorter."

Beeri turned, Hosea with him, into a narrow side street descending into the ravine which ran between the two bulging hills of Samaria, to almost the heart of the city and the king's palace on the plain below.

Here, on the steeply-pitched sides of the cleft, lived the poor of the city—a teeming multitude, dwelling in caves cut into the rocky cliffs; or in huts of twigs and reeds daubed with clay; or in tents of black goatskin like those of the desert folk; or in windowless, one-story brick houses, their doors gaping black holes covered each, if at all, by some ragged hanging. This jumbled ramshackle mass was broken not by ordered streets and roadways but by narrow passages and alleys, unplanned; unpaved; foul with refuse, leaves, clay, and the mud droppings of disintegrated walls.

Through this uncleanness Beeri and Hosea made their way, keeping direction through the maze only by noting the pitch of the land and following it downward to, then upward from its bottom. At the lowest depth of the cleft there ran an open, slimy drainage ditch, the stench of which was so revolting that the man and the boy were compelled to hold their noses while they crossed and breathe through open mouths as little as possible.

Squalid as the place was, the people who lived there were even more so. Faces skeletal or bloated appeared momentarily at the doorways of houses and the openings of tents to stare at the travelers through savage eyes as they passed. An almost naked toothless hag lay sprawled, perhaps unconscious, perhaps dead, across the pavement in their way. Crippled, blind, maimed, twisted wretches whined after them for alms as they passed, as did the unspeakably filthy and naked urchins who played noisily in the streets, some of them so persistent that Beeri was compelled to raise his staff to them. On several occasions, painted women leered at them, suggesting proposals which Hosea did not understand but which set Beeri into more rapid movement. And once, when they were in the deepest and most tangled part of the maze, a hand reached forth to pluck unsuccessfully at the purse which hung from Beeri's girdle.

Father and son pressed on, eager to emerge as soon as might be from the noisome stench and the lurking peril into clean sunlight, fresh air, and safety. With relief they detected the first sign of the world they knew, the first token that they were making the upper reaches of the shoulder, when a clearly-defined street emerged out of the tangle of passageways. At that point they stopped to rest, breathing deeply for a few minutes to free their nostrils of the cloying, acrid stinks.

"How ugly," Hosea burst forth, speaking for the first time since they had entered the cleft.

"Indeed, it is ugly," said Beeri. "And it is all the more so because these are children of Israel, fellow descendants of our fathers."

"But why should it be? Why should people live so?"

Beeri shrugged his shoulders. "Who knows? Some say—and disposed I am to agree with them—that it is because they are lazy and wish it that they live so. After all, their fathers, too, received a patrimony of land, as did ours."

Hosea reflected on his father's answer. He did not believe it but said nothing.

Beeri himself seemed not altogether satisfied. "Maybe it is for sin that this has befallen us—perhaps their sin, perhaps the sin of all Israel," he added. "After all, is not the Lord just? And if evil be the portion of these persons, it must be because somehow they have merited it. Or if not they, then perhaps it is for the sins of the whole House of Israel that they are being punished. And enough sin there is in the House of Israel: idolatries, whoring, forsaking the God of our fathers for heathen gods. And perhaps, right are the prophets who say that it is against the Lord's will that we dwell in houses and that one of us is rich and another poor so that the land is made foul with such corruption as we have seen this day. Therefore they prophesied the time will come that the land will spit us out as it banished the people who lived here before us."

To Hosea these explanations seemed somewhat better, though not altogether convincing.

Beeri sighed and concluded, "It is a high and a deep matter. I know not the answer."

Lost in thought, the two of them resumed their course, trudging up the steeply pitched shoulder to the avenue that ran up its spine, where, in a house which proved to be much like their own, dwelt Noam the Naphtalite.

• • •

IT WAS NOAM HIMSELF who opened the outer door of his house at Beeri's knocking.

"Peace unto you both," he greeted his visitors.

"Peace," they responded.

Noam the Naphtalite was a little man, shorter even than Hosea, with a round face which sprouted hair everywhere and in all directions. His fat body was draped in an ungirdled, threadbare robe which had once been brown but which was so stained by ink, especially down the left side from the drippings of the ink horn which he wore about his waist, that it was now of no recognizable color. He was thoroughly shabby, unkempt, tousled, almost dirty. But he wore one magnificent ornament. Suspended by a fine gold chain from about his neck a large onyx dangled on his chest, a rare and beautiful onyx which bore the inscription, "Unto Noam the Naphtalite, scribe to the king."

While Hosea had been looking at Noam, a little taken aback with surprise, Noam had been looking at Hosea. His eyes alert through a tangle of brows, lashes, and wisps of beard which grew high and loose on his cheeks, he resembled some wakeful little animal looking out from its shelter.

"So," he spoke at last. "This is the sheep that has been brought to the shearing."

Humming tunelessly, he appraised Hosea openly, frankly, until the youth stirred with awkward embarrassment under the screening.

"Ah well," the scribe concluded, "we shall have to see. Come," he was speaking now to Beeri, "let me show you his fellows and his place of labor."

"No," Beeri objected. "It is he, not I, who has business in your household. I shall not intrude."

"You will not be intruding," said Noam. "Do come in."

"But you have work to do."

"I always have work to do and that regardless of how much I have already done. The plague can take it."

Beeri leaned over to Hosea. "It is only his manner of speaking," he said.

Noam stared at the man incredulously. "Ah, Beeri, I forgot for a moment that you are a serious fellow. And you," he looked speculatively at Hosea, "no doubt you are the serious son of a serious father. But we shall see, we shall see." He resumed his humming once more, not pressing his invitation on Beeri.

Thereupon Beeri repeated to Hosea the instruction he had given him on several previous occasions as to dutifulness to his master and proper behavior to other members of his household. He added a word of caution about traversing the cleft alone on his way home. "Unless you are accompanied by others," he instructed him, "do not go that way. Go through the avenue, even though it is longer."

He then thanked Noam for receiving his son as an apprentice, expressed a hope that the boy would measure up to the father's description and the master's expectation of him, requested that his good wishes be communicated to the other members of Noam's household, voiced the wish that there be peace in his family and in all Israel, and bade them both farewell.

Noam sighed deeply.

"Your father," he said to Hosea, "is a very courteous man. But come, to work."

He led Hosea through the smaller outer court into the larger inner enclosure and across it to a small arcade at its rear where three youths were at work. One pounded with a pestle into a stone mortar, another polished a leather sheet with pumice, a third wrote laboriously on a piece of potsherd, his iron pen grating in a shrill treble, his tongue caught at the corner of his mouth in the intensity of his concentration.

"Here they are," Noam chuckled, "my assassins of pens, tablets, and languages. Eh, Binyamin?" He nudged the lad who was engaged in writing.

"I am but my master's disciple," the boy replied with humility.

"You sly one!" Noam roared his approval, his hair and beard tossing, his belly shaking with laughter under his robe. "Rogue, son of Belial." He rumpled Binyamin's hair.

"And yonder," he gestured toward the two other lads, "are the twin sons of Bichri the priest, whose father is not content with the dues of the priesthood—tithes, offerings, redemption monies, portions of sacrifices, and the like—and hopes to enrich his house even further with the earnings of scribes. A delusion, a vain dream."

"Alas for the poverty of our master," one of the boys murmured with mock sympathy.

"No doubt," the other chimed in, "he serves our king for naught."

A game broke forth of remarks and retorts, the three boys thrusting, now one, now another, then all together at Noam while he chuckled, teased, prodded, parried, and gave impartial applause to every successful sally, whether theirs or his own.

Hosea looked on and listened in total bewilderment. He was not accustomed to frivolity, especially not on the part of a grown man of years and station akin to his father's. He found Noam's manner undignified and the attitude of his apprentices toward him incredible in its impudence. Nor could he altogether follow the jests in their lightning interchange. The prattle was a novel experience for him, one in which he was totally inexperienced and unskilled.

As abruptly as the explosion had erupted, so abruptly did it cease.

"Enough," Noam roared suddenly. "If this continues there will be even less work done in this household this day than is usual. Back to the millstones, slaves."

Still smiling but instantly obedient, the youths resumed their work.

"And now for you," Noam said, placing his hand on Hosea's shoulder. "An artisan should know his tools. First, then, I shall teach you how to prepare the things you will be required to use. Then you shall learn writing."

He set Hosea to a task that occupied him for the rest of the day: the stirring together of oil, acid, and soot for the making of ink. Aside from measuring out the proportions which Noam had indicated, there was nothing in his labors to occupy Hosea's mind. He thought first of Noam and his manner, its startling indifference to propriety. It was hard for him to believe that a man so unconcerned with his own dignity could be truly wise; there must be in him, he reasoned with himself, something of the fool. Having arrived at this conclusion, his mind drifted off, as it did so constantly of late, to reveries of Gomer.

• • •

HOSEA DID NOT PERSIST LONG in his adverse opinions of Noam, but he never did come to approve of him altogether or to be thoroughly at ease in his presence. The man was an incorrigible jester, full of jokes, witticisms, and laughter; free with pinches and nudges; forever humming gay tunes to himself as he worked; constantly interrupting his serious speech to tell of this or that pointless incident which he found amusing. Hosea did grow to know what to expect from him. But unaccustomed as he was to lightness of speech, he was slow to understand it and did not know how to comport himself with it. Sobriety was the ideal to Hosea. He responded to Noam's flippant remarks with that seriousness which was the rule in Beeri's house. But Noam was not altogether able to resist the temptation of having his sport with this solemn, overly dignified youth. The other apprentices followed his lead. As a result, the humorless Hosea became very much the butt of the humor of master and apprentices alike. But there was kindliness in Noam; he permitted neither himself nor the others ever to be cruel in their jest. In the end, then, Hosea was not too happy over the atmosphere of his master's house and his place in the esteem of those about him, but neither was he too discontented. He learned to endure what he had to endure; he protected himself on the outside by an assumed indifference, and he grew even more serious within himself, concentrating all his thought and energy on what was being taught to him.

On that score, he had no complaints. Noam was an extraordinarily fluent penman, reading and writing the Israelite, Judean, and Canaanite dialects of Hebrew with equal ease, but also the tongues of Edom, Moab, Ammon, the strange language and picture script of the Egyptians, and the speech and wedge-writing of the Babylonians, which are the languages and scripts that kings use in their dealings one with another. Capable as a scribe, he was equally talented as a teacher, being one of the three or four in all Israel to whom the king looked for the training of his scribes. The king chose from among his penmen the most gifted teachers in their craft, compensating his teachers from the royal treasury with remunerations over and above the tuition fee paid by the fathers of the pupils.

With Hosea, as with all his apprentices, Noam was thorough,

patient, clear, and earnest in his instruction. When Hosea had learned to mix ink in various colors, he then set to the making of pens and brushes, the preparation of clay and metal tablets, the polishing of leather sheets, the rolling and smoothing of Egyptian papyrus, and the baking and selection of potsherds, which were the commonest writing material of all. Then, and not until then, did Noam introduce the youth to reading and writing, and to forming the characters of the alphabets.

There was further knowledge which Hosea derived from Noam beyond that which pertained to a scribe's craft. Noam was among those who were forever fascinated by what had been. He was informed about ancient times and passionately absorbed in the study of them, beyond anyone whom Hosea had ever met. It was characteristic of him, for example, that he called himself a "Naphtalite," though long since most men of Israel had grown indifferent to distinctions of tribes, clans, and fathers' houses. Among his scrolls was one devoted to the genealogy of the tribe of Naphtali, which included the names of the fathers and the sons who had headed families all the way back to Naphtali himself, the son of Jacob.

Quick as he was to jest at the least provocation, there was one theme about which Noam was never flippant, and about which he would not tolerate lightness on the part of his apprentices: reverence for the Lord and for the Law of Moses. On this score Hosea found him like his father. He resembled Beeri in the passion with which he was devoted to the Lord God of Israel and His ordinances. But unlike Beeri, Noam possessed a great curiosity concerning the traditions that had come down from the past and their authenticity. He was always comparing copies of the Law of Moses by diverse hands, embodying diverse traditions that differed from one another, whether much or little. All the time that Hosea served in his household Noam was busy with comparing two scrolls, both of which purported to be the authentic embodiment of the Law of Moses—one very ancient which had come to him from the royal scribes in Jerusalem, and another more recent which had been executed at the sanctuary in Beth El. Some day, he hoped to write a composite account which would reconcile the differences and embody the materials of both.

Therefore, whenever Hosea grew restless over the monotony of the tasks assigned to him, or indignant over some especially bold prank at his expense, he had consolation beyond the thought that he was doing his father's will. He knew that if there was a sting to his master, there was honey in him also.

• • •

NOT UNTIL THEY WERE ON THE ROAD TO JEZREEL did Hosea give much thought to how he would contrive to see Gomer. This was the Festival of First Fruits, not the gathering when the entire populace of the valley came together on the eighth day for public sacrifice, nor the Passover when all the youths and maidens walked out together. There was nothing in the observance of this holiday to throw them together. The alternative, to go to Charun's house openly for the purpose of visiting her, was to declare himself in the eyes of all men, something he was neither prepared nor sufficiently courageous to do, and something which would have required his father's consent. There was no way then, except the way of chance, some good fortune, to bring them together. But even chance would require his assistance. Most certainly, he knew there was no hope at all if he stayed at home. He sought opportunities to be away from his father's estate.

However, with the family sacrifices he must attend, and feasts from which he could not absent himself without explanation, there remained only an hour or so in the mid-morning and a somewhat longer period in the mid-afternoon when he was free to do as he wanted.

During these intervals, he wandered the fields and orchards around Charun's house, not so close to it as to be in peril of being observed, but not so distant either as to fail to see Gomer, should she come forth. As he roamed, he burned both with eager anticipation of what might happen next, and with shame and self-reproach over the indignity of his conduct. Yet, for all his plotting, his yearning, and his humiliation, he did not see her at all.

The visit to Jezreel, so long and eagerly awaited, so tremblingly and hopefully embarked on, turned out a protracted anguish of disappointment, for during the course of it he did not catch so much as a glimpse of Gomer. Yet the visit was not all frustration and loss. On the very first day, he acquired through discreet inquiry the welcome and reassuring information that Gomer was not yet betrothed, and that no suitor was known to have asked for her. The extremes of his rapture and despair gave him the answers he sought about his heart's constancy.

CHAPTER VI

CLEARER IN PURPOSE, if not quieter in heart, Hosea returned to Samaria and his studies—which now became studies indeed.

"Enough of child's play," Noam informed him upon his reappearance in the master's workshop. "Leather scraping, potsherd glazing, ink mixing—these are to a scribe's craft as plowing and digging and clearing of stones to a farmer's. All but preliminaries to the planting. Now we plant. Today we begin to write. Come." He drew Hosea to a scribe's bench, seated him on a mat before it, and set before him pen, inkwell, potsherds, and baked clay tablets, on which various letters of the alphabet were inscribed in large bold characters. "Let us see what you can do with these," he said.

Hosea took pen in hand for the first time. He held it in his fingers after the fashion in which Noam instructed him and began to trace the specimen letters.

Through almost all that day and several that followed, Noam stood over Hosea's shoulder or sat behind him. When necessary, he leaned over to correct his apprentice's grip on the pen, shake his forearm to relax its strained intensity, or suggest an easier method for fashioning some of the more difficult characters.

It did not go too badly, even at the very start.

"You will be a scribe," Noam pronounced at the end of the first week of practice. "Not the fleetest, perhaps, but already you do passably enough, and I shall see to it that you do better."

And so did it turn out. With the weeks and the months, Hosea became a competent, though not more than competent, craftsman. Always more agile in mind than body, he never acquired the facility of natural scribes such as Noam, who could write with breakneck speed and also with superb clarity, evenness, and grace. In the end as in the beginning, whatever characters he fashioned were certain to be clear and well turned, but they were always fashioned with slow deliberation.

It was only with the beginning of instruction in spelling that Hosea showed the first evidences of his exceptional gift. For then, he who had heretofore lagged behind the other apprentices now outstripped them one and all. As natural as the wielding of the pen was to them, so natural was the compounding of the names of things to him. There was, it appeared, an instinctive wisdom that instructed him as to the letters from which words were to be compounded.

This same instinctive wisdom availed Hosea also when Noam set him and his fellows to the next course of instruction for scribes: the composition of phrases, sentences, and whole narratives. Here too, in unique and unprecedented measure, Hosea excelled. Though ever hesitant in utterance, he became a freed man when a pen was in his hand and a clean tablet or leathern sheet before him. Whatever the assignment to which Noam set his class, be it the relating in his own words of some ancient tale of Israel, the imagined inquiry from the master of an estate to his overseer, a letter such as the governor of a city or the head of a tribe might send to the king, or the answer which the king might return, Hosea wrote with an absorption, authority, and effectiveness above and beyond the others.

As a result, he took pleasure in the composition. He loved the challenge of the imagination in the moments when he set himself to it, and the excitement and release he felt in its execution, as well as the glow of fulfillment when it was finished. Occasionally, when he reread what he had invented, he also surged with a pride of accomplishment.

But the scribe's craft was not the entirety of what Hosea was learning during the months of his apprenticeship. Little as the young men of Noam's workshop had in common, they shared the desire to take the short course to their destination each day. And so those apprentices who lived on the other shoulder of the mountain of Samaria made it their practice to band together each morning and again each evening to walk through the cleft on their way to and from home.

It was not merely the shortness of the distance that sent them on this route. It held a morbid fascination for them. To travel by highways was to go in safe dullness. But to go this way was to court the experience of novel, strange, and even horrible sights, made all the more alluring and adventuresome for the slight edge of peril involved.

Thus it befell one morning that they crossed the ravine just as the king's guard was conscripting a levy of forced labor for new fortifications at the mountain at Samaria. Had the neighborhood been visited by the plague, like the cities of the plain of Gomorrah which the Lord overthrew in Abraham's time, it could not have appeared more desolate. Not a person was abroad, not a house gave the least sign of tenancy. All was still except for the steady tramping of the heavy boots of the soldiers, the intermittent crash of splintering doors, and the occasional wild outcry of some wretch rooted out of his hiding place, accompanied, if he had kinsfolk, by their shrill laments.

For the young men whose blood coursed hot, the cleft had one other attraction, the women who sat in the doorways soliciting passersby: ancient crones, wrinkled and often toothless; little girls chanting the invitations they had memorized, performing vile, provocative gestures in which they had been schooled; women of unmistakable breeding, almost—despite the rouge on their cheeks, the paint about their eyes, and the henna on their hands—of respectability, perhaps abandoned wives or widows left without dower.

Having been warned by their parents and teachers, sternly and impressively, against the wiles and snares of women such as these, none of the young men dared to have dealings with them. The sons of Bichri, however, bolder than the rest, ventured now and again to engage them in conversation. With one they teased; with another they exchanged fantastically indecent proposals; with a third they haggled, as though in utmost seriousness, over the harlot's price.

It was all a prank to them, but a prank not without its earnestness. After they had gone on snickering or shouting laughter, not infrequently pursued by curses, there was left in them a disquiet, and a sharpened hunger. For it was the flaming mystery of the flesh, that burning secret, into which they awaited initiation. If the woman was comely, then her spell might remain with them, tormenting them with some echoing of her voice, or some lingering image of her body.

All this Hosea felt along with the others. There was also one thing which perhaps they shared with him, though neither he nor they ever made mention of it. Through the curiosity and desire, the eagerness and the shame that attended it, he felt pain and protest. It grieved him to look on these women and the hardness, misery, and squalor of their lot.

Because of this, Hosea held a vast hurt, a hot indignation that things should be so. He took away with him a sense of defilement and degradation, and a sense that not only these wretches but he, and Israel, and Israel's God, had been humiliated and made unclean by their condition.

In this fashion, between studies and other pursuits, with alternations of speed and slowness, the year fulfilled itself. The Passover returned, and once again Beeri and his household went down to the homestead in Jezreel.

This time, however, the courage of a hope too long deferred had entered into Hosea's soul. He would not again undergo the emptiness, the futility, the humiliation of his last visit, when he had done no more than loiter about Charun's house, catching not so much as a glimpse of Gomer. And the anxiety he had always felt concerning her, the fear lest she be spoken for, had hardened into a dread that froze and burdened his inward parts whenever he considered that evil turn which any day might bring. On the first day of the feast, immediately after the sacrifice, he mustered the courage to ask of the steward that the wallet of food and refreshment for the walking forth be prepared for him during the coming night, to be ready by sunrise. The next morning, while none of Beeri's household was even awake yet, he was on his way.

The sky overhead retained everywhere the star-strewn azure of night, except to the east, which was hemmed in green, fading through yellow, to the brightening white of the not-yet-visible sun. A moist wind blew; dew was heavy on the grass and shrubs. Hosea went on his way, shivering now and again. Whether it was from the chill of earth and sky or the fever of excitement within himself, he could not discern.

It was in a proper hour that he entered Charun's courtyard. The sun was well up, and even on a festival morning a family might be expected to be about. However, he had not calculated on two circumstances. Accustomed to an ordered, firmly-administered homestead, he had not reckoned on the slipshod confusion which was the sole rule in Charun's household. Nor had he counted on the fact that the Passover, an occasion in Beeri's household for joy and solemnity together, for feasting and drinking but also for religious instruction, was in other, less earnest families little more than a rout of gluttony and imbibing.

To its last male, Charun's family and retinue slept the sodden sleep of wine. The floor of the courtyard was littered with refuse. Tables and benches stood helter-skelter about, spread with remnants of food, empty jars, and overturned cups. The two slaves of the household slept in a corner huddled together on a pallet, under a ragged cover. Not a person, as far as Hosea could see from the threshold, was awake.

He was on the point of stealing away to return at a later and more auspicious moment. But from somewhere in the shadows a dog barked an alarm. Another joined, and then a third, after which there was no getting away undetected.

One of the slaves sat up grumbling, cursing, blinking in the daylight. He caught sight of Hosea. "What do you want?" he asked gruffly.

"I'll come back later," Hosea replied hurriedly. "I have come to call on Gomer, but it's too early."

But the slave, befuddled with sleep and wine, caught only the girl's name.

"Gomer," he called toward the bedchambers in the rear of the court. "Gomer," he repeated raising his voice to a bellow.

"Gomer, do you hear me? Wake up."

"I hear, I hear," came her voice in answer, husky with sleep. "I'm coming. What is it?"

"There's a young man here for you."

"A young man," she echoed incredulously. "It can't be. I'm not dressed....The house..."

In her chamber there was the sound of rushing feet, the pulling of the curtain over the door.

"Oh, no," Gomer half gasped, half wailed. "Of all times..."

"I'll come back," Hosea volunteered, "I didn't think..."

"No," came the answer after a moment. "It won't be any different. Wait for me."

The curtain dropped.

The entire household seemed to wake. Children appeared in other doorways, a brood of them of various ages and sizes; a maidservant; a woman whom Hosea recognized as Charun's wife; and still another whom he remembered vaguely as Charun's concubine, all staring at him with open-eyed undisguised curiosity, before which Hosea, already discomfited, became more wretched by the moment.

Last to appear was Charun. Emerging from his bedchamber, he stood blinking into the daylight, his face puffy with sleep, his black wiry beard uncombed, his sparse hair standing every which way. Short, stout, and bloated, he was dressed in a stained, shabby day cloak, the wrinkles and creases of which suggested that it had just done service also as a nightshirt. He stared at Hosea through red-rimmed, bloodshot eyes, scratching absentmindedly at his bulging belly with such vigor that the cloth of his garment swished from side to side with the rhythm of his fingers.

"Do they not sleep in your household," he grumbled, "not even of a festival morning? And what household may it be whose son calls on my niece?"

"I am Beeri's son."

For a moment, Charun seemed not to have heard. His face remained surly, his fingers still scratching at his belly. His fingers slowed as a look of comprehension—then of total amazement—swept his face.

"So," he breathed, "you are a son of Beeri. The second one, the one who ran off to the Philistines? Nay, he was a different manner of man, and older too, if I remember—"

"No," Hosea corrected, "I am Hosea, the third of Beeri's sons."

"The one whom I have heard is learning to be a scribe?"

Hosea nodded.

There followed a pause, brief but not uneventful, while neither the man nor the lad said anything. During it the change in Charun's manner, which had begun a few moments earlier, completed itself. The astonishment which had replaced Charun's initial surliness now gave way to an exuberant cordiality, broad smiles, and a bluff heartiness of voice, through which his calculation and cunning showed legibly.

"And how fares your father?" Charun inquired.

Hosea, though he had himself never been one to speak with double heart and was therefore inexpert in looking for hidden intentions, could detect the low, crude cunning of the man and felt sickened by it.

"My father is well," he managed to reply.

"Praise therefore to Him who sits above the clouds." Charun raised his eyes and his hands piously.

"But come, my boy," he went on, his enthusiastic hospitality mounting apace, "we must not leave you standing like some unwelcome guest when you are welcome, most welcome indeed. You must sit down while you await our young lady."

He came forward, put an arm around Hosea's shoulder, and,

blowing wine- and sleep-soured breath into his face, escorted him to one of the benches. They had no sooner seated themselves than Charun leaped to his feet.

"A luncheon," he reminded himself. "You will require food for the day. Ho, Abishag, Naamah," he called loudly. "Let us have food and drink for the young people—wine, good wine, and fruits and cakes of the best unleavened bread. Spare nothing. Is aught too good for our niece and our neighbor's son?"

"I have luncheon," Hosea said.

The old man had to be convinced that Hosea was speaking the truth. And when the cross-examination on that score was ended, there followed the uproar of the countermanding of his original instructions.

By the time quiet was restored, Hosea was in an agony of embarrassment. The embarrassment was then made worse by the confidences concerning Gomer which the man began to whisper into his ear.

The girl, he told Hosea, was known for her beauty and virtue through all the countryside. And he, her uncle and guardian, had been offered great marriage prices for her, and not merely by common men, but by nobles and priests. But though all was not well with his household, as no doubt Hosea had heard, though he had fallen on evil days when the very elements had become the enemies of his prosperity, he was not one to sell a kinswoman, especially such a one as Gomer, a veritable jewel, into a loveless marriage, let alone into a concubine's lot.

So he went on. Hosea, pretending attention, tried not to hear. He was humiliated for Gomer—and suspected that there was little truth in her uncle's claims. But one thing he heard, for Charun related it with an assurance that carried conviction. Returning in his speech to his boasts concerning the number and desirability of Gomer's suitors, Charun described in considerable detail one of them, a certain Othniel, a trafficker in slaves and cattle, who came through the valley twice a year on business, and who of late had spoken for Gomer.

"But he wants her as a second wife," he explained, "which she says she will not be. Besides, if he is rich, he is ungenerous also. Over such a one as Gomer he haggles. But he will come around; I have no fears. I can see in his eyes how he desires her." With a wily smile on his lips and a glow of cunning in his eyes, he continued. "Now, if the Lord would only send to Gomer a man of a good and prosperous family, of her years, who is seeking his first wife, such a young man as yourself, why for such a man I would accept a marriage price less, aye, much less than this Othniel offers. Which is no more than right, seeing that because of the reverses which have befallen me, I have no dowry to bestow on her."

In another instant, certainly Charun would have been specifying sums. But, suddenly aware that Gomer was standing by, he broke off abruptly. Both of them looked up, Hosea with a spurt of anxiety lest she had been there long enough to have overheard. The high flush on her cheeks, the quickness of her breath that forced her lips open and caused her chest to rise and fall visibly could well be explained by the haste with which she had dressed. But when he saw how straight she was carrying herself and how high she was holding her head, even higher when he rose to greet her, he looked down into her eyes and saw there tears. To her embarrassment over the state of the household, he sensed, had been added the humiliation of being so eagerly offered for sale. And because he ached for her and desired beyond all else to comfort her in her hurt, he thought to tell her, in the fleeting instant before he spoke, that she was beautiful beyond his recollections of her, that nothing which had occurred that morning, that nothing which could possibly occur, could lessen her in his eyes. But Charun sat there listening, and others stood about within earshot, and the reticence of a lifetime welled up in him, and so he said only, "Peace, Gomer."

"And unto you, Hosea," she answered.

"It would make me proud and very happy if I might escort you on the walking-out of the young men and maidens this day."

And because he said this with utmost sincerity, in a voice gentle with solicitude and a courtesy beyond her expectations and experience, the defiant pride which had sustained her gave way.

"I shall be honored," she managed to say. Then her eyes overflowed, her speech choked up, she extended one hand behind her toward Hosea to communicate the appeal she could not utter, and she hurried through the gateway.

Some distance down the road, well out of sight of Charun's house, he overtook her. She was standing still, facing away from him, her arms taut at her sides, her hands clenched, her head and shoulders bowed. When he circled around her to stand before her, she turned with him.

"No, don't," she said in a choked whisper. "Just let me be for a moment, and I shall be over it."

And so he waited patiently while slowly her body untensed and stood at ease. Then, as with a sudden resolution, she turned to face him, a gay, warm smile on her lips and in her eyes, though her lashes were smudged with tears.

"There, that's over," she said brightly. "It's all forgotten. Now let us have a glorious day as befits a holy day," she said, looking at him with warm intentness, "as you deserve for being so loyal and sweet."

That day and the days after it were the gayest and happiest in all Hosea's life. Gomer was all lighthearted vivacity from the moment he met her each morning at the gateway of the courtyard of Charun's house to the time he left her there at sundown.

Whether she had planned it so or not, she seemed never at a loss for something pleasurable to do, for light mirthful things to say, for places for them to visit. Nor did the two of them stay by themselves, alone from other young people, as they had the previous holiday. This year she led Hosea without hesitation or self-consciousness into the places where the youths, men, and maidens gathered.

Still she had but one patched, threadbare, and graceless robe, perhaps the same one she had worn the year before, but she seemed totally unconcerned over the fact. But she did not complain, as she once had, of feeling excluded and looked down upon by the others. All the shadows seemed to have vanished from her heart. Joining boldly, naturally into the group games and sports, she, and Hosea with her, were accepted with equal naturalness. She seemed to have out-grown her old anxieties and discontents and posessed a new assurance. She was as beautiful, tempestuous, and capricious as he remembered her, but now added to that was a delight-ful blitheness and a lightness of heart. Beyond all else was her awareness of him, gentle and concerned, which he found remarkable, intoxicating, all the more so because it had been altogether missing the year before.

Thanks to all this, he put aside the misgiving that had plagued him heretofore, that the core of bitterness and hardness in her be incorrigible. His love for her was now free to be untroubled. And free to take on a new dimension and quality.

He discovered a pretty charm in her appearance and ways, the slender-fingered grace of her hands, the straight flight of her eyebrows, and in the fashion which she laughed—warmly, richly, spontaneously. To look at her, to watch her, which before had been spellbinding, flame-kindling, tormenting, now took on the new aspect of being simply and sunnily pleasurable.

On the last day of the walking forth, by consent they made their way to that glade in the vineyard which they had frequented the year before.

And because they had been companionable with each other for almost a full week, playing, laughing, and talking, the floodgates of speech burst open. They talked, not all the time or without long spells of silence, but for longer intervals and with greater ease, intensity, and release than ever before between them—and in Hosea's case, ever before in his life.

Contriving, delighting to speak, they told each other much about their circumstances. He described the regimen of his days as an apprentice to Noam, revealing more than did she, who, having only Charun's household to discuss, said as much as she could while retaining some pride. But both of them disclosed enough so that she became aware of his hopes and expectations, and he, though by indirection, of her desperation.

It was in the freedom engendered by their intimate speech that Hosea felt bold enough to ask the question which all week long had cried for utterance.

"Your uncle said—" he began.

"My step-uncle," she corrected at once.

"Yes, your step-uncle," he amended, and began again, "your step-uncle said when we talked together that there is a merchant, a trafficker in slaves and cattle, I believe, who seeks to take you to wife...."

The relaxed easiness with which she had been sitting disappeared. A resistant stiffness came into her posture, her face became set, lips closed tight, eyes staring off.

"I had not meant to offend you," he said.

"Nay, the offense is not yours." She smiled at him briefly, bleakly, with effort. "It is Charun, ready to sell me to anyone, it matters not how foul or ugly, if only his price is met. That is all that stands between Othniel and him; they are not yet agreed on the purchase money. My precious step-uncle hopes, by holding out, to sell me dearer, and that hideous old man, though he lusts after me so that it is a shameful thing to see his eyes when I am about, he hopes by holding out to buy me cheaper."

"Is it likely that they will come to an agreement?"

Gomer shrugged.

"If Othniel continues to desire me, they must in the end. Charun is hard-pressed for the money. But then, perhaps Othniel will not return this way again; he comes only each half year. Perhaps he will die, as I pray day and night."

"But if they should agree," Hosea persisted, cold dread clamping his heart.

"I do not know," she answered slowly. "Sometimes I think I would rather die or do murder than submit myself to that vile old man. He is fat, Hosea, and when I am near him he quivers and his lips get wet. It's disgusting to see. Even worse, he is forever trying to lay his hands on me. His fingers are thick and round, and there is thick black hair all over the backs of them. I have told Charun, at times like that, that if he sells me into that marriage, I will kill him or the old man or myself. But he only laughs. And then, I do not know..."

Everything was terror in and all about Hosea. He did not stop to think.

"You need not," he said firmly, "you shall not marry that man."

"But how," she cried, bewildered.

"Before it comes to that," he went on simply, "I will marry you. My father can pay as great a marriage price as...that is," he hesitated, "if he would be willing.... And if," he went on, aware suddenly and painfully of the arrogance of his assumption, "if you would wish it so... I had no right to assume..."

She looked at him as, face averted, he spoke, her eyes filling up and swimming with tears, a smile of anguished tenderness on her lips, such a smile as a mother bestows on her child when he has brought her his most precious toy as a gift. "So," she whispered, "to save me, you would marry me yourself."

He looked straight at her, startled.

"Oh, you…you do not understand. It's not that I feel sorry for you. I love you."

So it was said.

Gomer watched him and listened.

"As Moses says we should love the Lord, with all our heart and soul and might, so I love you."

She reached out for Hosea, grasped his forearm with both hands, and leaned forward until her head rested on it. Bent over almost double now, she began to weep, such a weeping as Hosea had never witnessed before. Not that she cried aloud; only faint, muffled sounds escaped her, but her body shook as with a convulsion and her sobs came without remission and her tears flowed in such abundance that his forearm was wet with them.

As he had never desired anything in all his lifetime, he wished to comfort her. With his free hand, he tentatively, timidly, patted the back of her head and stroked her long hair. But he did not know what to say to her, for he did not know over what she wept, whether with joy or sorrow, fear or release, or because she was touched by what he had said.

In truth she wept for all these things, and for things which in his innocence did not occur to him. She wept for her fears, for the impasses in which she was trapped, for the perils of an escape she might attempt. But she wept, too, for his simplicity and sweetness, at once so welcome and so demoralizing to her, braced as she was for harshness and cold. She wept over a generosity too generous to know itself as such. Most of all, she wept for herself and him together, her orphan's lost loneliness, his opening up a door of hope when all the world was shut against her.

For all these she wept, at first with an abandon so total that there was within her only a wild chaos of feeling. Then, as the convulsive shaking of her body subsided, as her sobs quieted and her tears flowed more slowly, she began to think—at first with only a glimmer of reason, then with increasing coolness and clarity—of what had befallen her and what she needed to decide and say concerning it. She strove desperately to be hard, cold, self-concerned; her life being in balance, she could afford no sentimentality. But it was beyond her. She had been too recently possessed of passion to be dispassionate, too grateful to him to be only calculating. It was then with as much cunning as she could muster, but cunning not untouched by affection, that she spoke at last.

"Your father," she murmured, her head still bowed, "what of him? Have you told him that you escort me? Would he allow...?"

With her question, he was flooded with the fear that he had for some time suppressed. So long as she had wept disconsolately, he had thought only for her and her sorrow. But as she had stilled, ceasing to command his compassion, he too had begun to think—and his thoughts with each passing moment had grown more chill and disturbing. There was in him the misgiving that he had committed himself irretrievably to a future he could not foresee. And before he was ready for such finalities, was he altogether sure of who or what she was? Was he, now that the hour of decision was at hand, altogether certain of the constancy of his feelings for her? Perhaps they would change today, tomorrow, in one year, ten years hence, and then they would be bound together, he and she, with no love in him to give in return, when it was love he had promised her, love which he did not doubt for an instant she deserved to the full. From some frigid place inside him a chill spread, until he was all cold. Now she had made reference to his deepest anxiety of all, and all at once an apprehension was on him so close to panic that, incapable of words or thought, he sat in glum, miserable silence.

Gomer lifted the hem of her skirt to wipe her tears away. Perceiving his distractedness, sensing its cause, she was instantly sorry—profoundly, warmly sorry—and would, if she had not restrained herself with an effort, have wailed only to comfort him. But pity being a luxury she could not afford, she suppressed it and repeated her question.

"Your father?" she prodded.

"No, he does not know."

"But if you should tell him, what would he be likely to say?"

"I do not know. I cannot say."

But through his words, she read his apprehension, almost a conviction. Quickly calculating the risks and hazards in either alternative, she said, "Then do not tell him, at least not now. He may forbid us to meet, and then there would be no hope at all."

He knew that he should demur, but the weight of his anxieties was too fierce for pretense.

"Very well. I shall wait."

Then they were both heavy-hearted with disappointment; she because, though it was the wiser course, which she herself had counseled, she had been hoping all along that he would counter it with some device, or at the least some confident utterance as to the outcome. In any case, she had not expected him to surrender so unprotestingly, unreservedly. And he—because in addition to her disappointment in him, which he sensed—was disappointed in himself for being deficient in constancy and courage. But most of all because, now that the anxieties over his father were no longer exigent, his anxieties over her were once more released: compassion for the unhappiness of her plight, fear for what might befall her, and dread lest he lose her, were all up on him again in full, in redoubled force.

"But what will be if that Othniel returns, and Charun and he arrive at a marriage price?" he asked. "Gomer, if that should come to pass, you must let me know at once. Somehow, I know not how, but somehow you must send me a message. Nay, I know. Talmon, the steward of our household, comes up to Samaria each month at New Moon to render an accounting to my father. To him you must say something. He shall not understand, but I shall. Say to him only that the slave buyer is returned. Or, better still, have one of the servants or children give him the message, not revealing its source. And I shall speak boldly to my father and shall come at once. Allow nothing to be settled. Wait for me; I shall come. I swear it by the Lord, God of Israel. Do you understand?"

"Yes, I understand."

"And you will remember the message: 'The slave buyer is returned'?"

"I shall remember it, I promise."

"You must give me oath."

"It is not necessary," she protested. "I have already agreed."

"I shall not be content with less."

"Very well then," she indulged him, but not without being stirred by his earnestness.

They rose. She lifted her hands, palms up, turned her face also to the heavens, and pronounced: "By the Lord, God of Israel, I swear it."

"Amen," he whispered after her, "and may the Lord hearken to your vow to fulfill it."

The wind of nightfall began to blow. They became aware suddenly how far the day was gone.

"I must take you home," he said. "It would not be fitting, even on the last day of the walking forth, for us to tarry after twilight."

She nodded her head, looking up at him. His slender length seemed all at once pitiably frail; his earnest, ardent face, his guileless eyes, overcame her. She struggled against the temptation which beset her; it was stronger than she.

"There is one thing I must tell you. I dislike to say it; I scarcely know how…"

She broke off speech, making one last effort to subdue this wild, senseless impulse which was betraying her, but his countenance was before her, all tenderness and expectation, and the words poured forth of themselves.

"I would not say this to another," she whispered half-resentfully. "I would not say this even to you had you not shown yourself earlier so kind. But you are as you are, the kindest man I have ever known, the only kind person I have met in all my life, and I cannot deceive you.

"Hosea," she said quickly. "Hosea, I do not love you. Do I like you and admire your goodness? Yes. Respect you? As no one else in all the world. But the desire for you, that desire which they say a woman should feel for the man she weds, that desire is not in me for you. Though I perish for saying this, say it I must. Shall I, who have nothing else to give to a husband but love, defraud you of this also, you who deserve all good things and only good things? I will not do it. You shall know the truth."

A great sadness near to bitterness was in his heart at her words. But through it, he was well aware that he had always known that it was so, that never had he really expected her to love him. His thoughts turning from himself to her, his eyes clearing from the blurredness of pain and disappointment, he looked at her again. This time he saw not the wild dark cloud of her hair, nor the running flight of her brows, nor the surge of her breasts, nor the clean length of her limbs, nor any of those things in which he had always delighted, but instead the bowing of her head, like that of a petitioner before a judge. He was aware that this was for her, as it was for him, an hour of trial. But when his eyes caught a glimpse of her bare feet beneath the hem of her dress—pale, fragile, defenseless, the more pathetic for being dusty—his sadness for her was of an instant greater than for himself, the tenderness toward her almost too great for him to bear.

"It changes nothing," he murmured, then took her by the hand and led her from their glade to the homeward road through the quickly deepening twilight.

• • •

ON HOSEA'S RETURN TO NOAM'S WORKSHOP, he devised a secret game with the exercises in composition, which continued the main discipline of his studies: whatever his master's assignment, Hosea took delight in giving his imagination free play with it.

Had Noam asked that he conjure up a letter such as the steward of an estate might write to its absent master? Then he would seek to imagine what manner of man the steward might be, and strive to make every one of the sentiments ascribed to him conform with his supposed character. This was a sport to which there was no end. For having caused the steward to write as befitted his nature, it was then possible to go further and deeper with him, to suppose him a guileful flatterer who wished to cajole his master without appearing to do so, or a dissembler who, imparting evil tidings of the estate, was seeking to exonerate himself by setting them in a favorable light.

From the elaboration of themes set by Noam, it was but a short step to experiment with themes of his own choosing—a step made not only easier but almost inevitable by the very facility with which he wrote. For what was he to do with himself when the others were still engaged in some task which he had long since completed? He was not one to fold his hands in idleness. Nor to make pranks at the expense of his fellows.

Once, he wrote a eulogy to the memory of Gadiel, describing that sorrowful hour when the mutilated body of his brother had been brought home. On another occasion, he strove to capture in words his sense of Iddo's wondrous beauty and grace. He wrote of many things, but most of all he wrote of Gomer.

Of his own wild, frightening feelings toward her—the vague aching hunger of his spirit, the restless stirring of his flesh—he did not write. Yet everything he composed, and not merely those pieces which dealt with her explicitly, was informed by the awareness of her. In some mysterious manner which he could not fathom, a living bond united his writing and his love. Because he loved, he wrote; because he wrote, his love found both transient release and continuous renewal.

Hosea was very careful to indulge in his writings when no one was likely to look over his shoulder. Always he kept half-written potsherds and sheets near to hand, should someone draw nigh his bench. And he broke into the smallest pieces any potsherd, erased to unblemished smoothness any sheet or tablet onto which he had poured forth his heart. One notion, however, did remain from all his efforts, which he ventured to air with Noam.

"Master," he inquired once, at the end of the day, "is there nothing else for a scribe to write than chronicles, letters, edicts, and accounts?"

"And what else could there be?"

"Might not a scribe write what is in his own heart? His thoughts and feelings about things?"

"That depends," said Noam, smiling benevolently, "what

might be the nature of these thoughts and feelings. Give me a clear example and I shall give you a clear answer."

But Hosea was unable to reply. The illustrations which came to mind were not to be voiced, and in the stress of the moment he could not think of others. His face reddened.

"Here, now," Noam said. "Do not take on so. It is not unusual that a man knows what he intends but cannot express it. If you cannot find an instance to give me, let me see whether I cannot supply one for you. Do you mean to ask whether a scribe may not invent writings of his own? Suppose he has heard reports of events which have befallen others, or has himself undergone experiences, reports and experiences such as afford instruction and reproof to men? Is this the purport of your question—may that scribe properly write down the incidents and thoughts concerning them? If that is what you intended, the answer is clear. Of course the scribe may write these things down, except that he would be foolish to do so. If he must record incidents to study and therefore improve himself, can there be any instances superior to those related of the patriarchs, the prophets, and the judges? And if it is precepts he wishes to impart, can any precepts of his invention equal those of the wise men of days gone by? My son, no scribe need so lack for tasks with which to occupy himself as to invent his own tales and devices which might, as likely as not, turn out empty—if not indeed mischievous. Why should he devote the skill which the Lord has given him to the composing of a book, a single copy of which may be superfluous, when there are so many books of which there cannot possibly be an excess of copies?"

"I was thinking of something else, not of tales of instruction or of precepts, but of a man's deepest feelings."

"Deeper in a man's soul than wisdom?"

"Nay then, not deeper, but other."

"Such as," Noam prodded.

This time, Hosea did not lack for illustrations which he was capable of speaking forth. "Such as what a man feels when a kinsman dies; what I felt when the body of my brother Gadiel, of whom you have heard, was brought home. Or the sadness which comes at times with dusk or the sound of music. Or the excitement of watching a dance. Or the exhilaration of the morning's coolness. Or the lifting of the spirit when one looks up at the skies and sees through the lowest clouds other clouds above, and through these still others so that one sees not only the heaven but the heaven of heavens."

"Or," Noam broke in, "speculating on what goes on in the heart of a guileful steward or putting oneself in the stead of a master so stupid as not to know when he is being led round by the nose. For think not, lad, that I have not observed the sport you have been making with your lessons."

A stab of concern pierced Hosea.

"Do not be perturbed," Noam hastened to reassure him. "I have not been vexed. To the contrary, I have been amused. After all, while you are almost a man, something of the child remains with you, and it is right for children to play. But only for children, not for grown men.

"And here is my answer to your question, which I can give now that I understand you aright. A grown man does nothing that is purposeless, that benefits not himself or others or God.

"Now, of what good can it be to you or anyone else if you write as though you were another person, and that other not real?

"As with your letters, composed as though not by you, so with the writing forth of your inmost feelings. To what purpose can this be? I ask. What those feelings are, you already know. And as for other men, who having feelings of their own, what need have they to know yours?"

Hosea could find nothing to say, though he was not persuaded.

• • •

HOSEA WALKED INTO HIS FATHER'S HOUSE and was startled
to see Talmon sitting idly in the public room. Not that this was
the steward's first visit to his master's house since the household
had last come up from Jezreel. For six months, during the days
just after each New Moon, he had come and gone but without
Hosea so much as laying eyes on him. For there were kinsfolk to
visit in Tirzah, which was a few hours' distance from Samaria, and
where the steward preferred to lodge. *The hour of decision must be
at hand.*

As soon as Talmon caught sight of the youth, he rose from his
place and embraced him in greeting.

"Devise to follow me when I depart. I have news to tell you…
in the outer doorway…," the steward whispered in his ear.

A few minutes later they stood together in the shadows of
the corridor. "It is a strange message I bear," Talmon said. "And
from a strange source. Yesterday came to me a servant of Charun,
one of the two still remaining to him, who requested of me most
urgently that I say to you and you alone: 'The buyer of slaves is
returned.' He said that you would understand, and I see from
your countenance that you do."

Hosea nodded distractedly. "I understand, and I thank you for
your service."

Talmon observed Hosea's face, his manner, the concern and
intentness which had seized him, the intentness which held him in
its grip.

"Young master," he said. Failing to catch Hosea's attention,
he repeated, "Young master."

"Eh?" Hosea came to with a start.

"Master, may a word be spoken to you, and you not take it
amiss? This matter, I know, is no business of mine. You are a young
man, almost a grown man, and settled, too, for your years. But I
am older than you. I have known and cherished you since birth.

Therefore I am resolved to speak, even though you may be vexed with me for it...."

"Please," Hosea said, "what is in your heart, speak."

"Master," Talmon resumed. "I do not know what the interpretation may be of the message I brought you. I hope only that it does not portend an entanglement on your part with Charun, or with anyone in his household. He is a base fellow and, as the peasants say, lambs follow the sheep and goats the ram. And there has been much talk of late in the valley concerning you and his niece."

"*Step*-niece."

"Aye, step-niece, but still too close. And in her own right, people say, willful, quick-tempered, undisciplined. You are not angry, young master, that I speak my heart?"

"How could I be angry," Hosea reassured him, "when you mean what you say only to my good? Only you err concerning Gomer. You know her not, therefore you believe rumor. She is not as people say."

"So," Talmon mused, "then it is not as I feared. Well, I am not your father, nor would I wish to be in this matter." He turned to leave, but on impulse Hosea took hold of his cloak and detained him.

"Tell me," he asked anxiously, "does my father know of this? Did you tell him?"

"Concerning the message I brought you? No. I had pledged myself to secrecy. But concerning the linking of your name and Gomer's, how could he not know when the whole valley buzzes with it? And how could I not tell him? Is he not your father?"

Hosea looked around to assure himself that no one in the household was listening to them. He leaned over to Talmon and in a low voice asked, "And what said he?"

"Only that with the fevers of youth there is naught to be done except to hope that they will burn themselves out."

"Where is my father? Is he in the inner chambers?"

"Nay, when our business was finished, he did go off to sit in the east gate."

Muttering hasty thanks and farewell to Talmon, Hosea set off at once, before his determination could dissolve. He strode vigorously up the steep roadway which led beyond his home, to the crest of the mountain of Samaria where stood the great ivory and marble monuments to the nobles of Israel, and then precipitously down its far slope to the city's massive eastern wall.

There, before the gate and facing the open square, with its ceaseless traffic and its busy merchant booths, sat the elders, the chief householders of Samaria. Each had an imposing chair with an ivory- or gold-tipped long staff between his knees and in his hands. No formal duties engaged them. At one time in Samaria, as in all the villages and towns of Israel, the elders had done service as judges. But now that the city had grown great, courts had been established according to the practice of other lands, with judges appointed by the king and paid from his treasury. The elders were left with nothing to do except to assemble each afternoon and discuss with one another the day's events and other matters of interest to heads of households, men of wealth and power.

Beeri left off his conversation with his companions at the sight of his son coming toward him.

"Blessed be he who cometh. Is all well with the household?"

"Peace, my father. All is well."

"Then why comes my son to seek me out?"

This was indeed the first time in a long while Hosea had visited his father at this place.

"There is a matter I would discuss with you...."

"And it cannot await my return," Beeri said and smiled indulgently. He turned to his companions. "Such is youth," he observed. "It must pluck fruits before buds show." He addressed

Hosea. "Well, son, if the matter burns, the fire must be extinguished. Come, we will discuss it as we walk."

"Let not my father hasten his return homeward," Hosea urged, at once contrite over disturbing Beeri, and afraid he might have prejudiced his petition.

"It is as well," Beeri insisted. "The time for going homeward is at hand."

Rising, he took courteous farewell of his companions, holding his staff with one hand and leaning on Hosea's arm with the other.

Hosea restrained himself as they threaded through the jostling, crowded, public square and passed through the dark, vaulted gate, obscure and damp with shadow, resounding with echoed and re-echoed footfalls and words.

Soon they were in the clear sunlight and the quiet of the avenue which led toward their home.

"Father, I wish to be married."

Beeri threw a quick, sidelong glance at his son's face.

"You are of age for marriage. I am pleased to hear it. To be wed is God's first commandment. Did he not bid Adam: 'Be fruitful and multiply'? And it is time, too, that I held a grandchild born of a son."

"Aye, father," Hosea agreed hastily, "and there is a particular maiden whom I desire."

Beeri slowed their pace. "Is there indeed?" he said.

And Hosea, supposing that his father knew that it was of Gomer that he was speaking, and fearing that he would express his disapproval, went on.

"I did not mean to sound presumptuous, to seem to be telling you whom I would wed rather than to ask you as beseems a dutiful son to his father. And I know that you hold her family in slight esteem, as it deserves, and that she will have no dower, but I love her; I can love no other."

Only from his father's weight on his arm was Hosea aware that his father had slowed for another matter. Beeri was standing limply, his shoulders hunched over, his right hand pressing the staff it held to the middle of his chest.

Alarm surged up in him. "What is it?" Hosea whispered. "Is my father ill?"

"Nay, it is naught. A passing pain in the chest."

Beeri smiled, but Hosea was shocked at the pallor of his face, the perspiration in which it was bathed, and his heaving intake of breath.

"Let my father seat himself a while to rest," he urged.

Beeri shook his head. "It will pass. We need only stand still."

A shocking possibility flashed into Hosea's thoughts.

"I did not mean to distress my father," he said. "I hope that it is not because of my speech that he is ill."

Breathing more easily, color beginning to return to his face, but still speaking in spurts for the shortness of breath, Beeri said, "I am not certain that I approve your words...but this illness...has come before, often...whenever I walk rapidly...climb hills...not young as once..."

"Then let us speak no more now," Hosea urged. "It takes your breath."

Beeri nodded.

In stillness, they waited until Beeri felt able to proceed. When he did, they went on wordlessly, slowly, and with frequent pauses for Beeri to recover his breath. At last, they approached their home. Just before the door, Beeri broke the silence.

"Is it Diblaim's daughter, Charun's niece, of whom you were speaking before?"

"Yes, father."

"That was my fear," he concluded heavily, and said no more.

By the next morning, when Hosea was summoned to his father's chamber, he was in an agony of despair. During the night he had weighed and reweighed his father's words, and concluded that there could be only one result. He went as in a nightmare to Beeri's room. Hosea's hands and feet were cold, his mind a chaos of dread and contentions.

Beeri was standing at an eastern window, reciting his morning prayers in praise of God who was causing the sun to rise. From his appearance, he seemed completely recovered from his illness of the day before. He was no longer pale; his movements as he bowed and gesticulated were vigorous, and his lips formed the familiar words firmly. Motionless in reverence, Hosea waited.

"Praise to the Lord, God of Israel," Beeri concluded his devotions, "who did fashion the luminaries of old and has this day given us light."

"Amen," Hosea responded, "and praise to Him also that he has healed my father from his illness of yesterday."

"Praise him for that also, though it is a little matter, as they tell me who are expert in such things. Some disturbance of the stomach, they say, or the taking in of a foul wind, or else simply advancing years," Beeri recounted. "And now, my son, sit down. I have something to say to you."

Hosea sank onto a stool.

"I was not made happy," Beeri began abruptly, "by what you told me yesterday. Not that it came to me altogether as a surprise. I have heard rumors this past Passover that it was Diblaim's daughter whom my son was escorting. And I have been given to understand that such was the case also on the Passover preceding. I would have spoken to you then concerning her. She is not one such as I would choose for a son of mine." Hosea opened his mouth to protest. "Nay, bide with me," Beeri said, heading off the interruption. "I have naught against the girl, though they do say that she is headstrong. It is Charun's household that I distrust—its indolence, slovenliness, irreverence, and impiety. A rose may grow amidst briars, as the song says, but in my observation, only seldom. More often, the rose which appears in such a setting turns out in the end to be not a rose at all but only a flowering of its parent weed.

"Therefore, as I just said, I was inclined to restrain you. But I did not do so. At first, I hoped that if I said nothing your attachment would disappear of itself. Alas, it did not turn out so. But something else deterred me...."

Beeri broke off, reflecting, savoring something he found better to the taste.

"When I was young, I did imagine that a father decrees and a son obeys. So it had once been between my father and me; so I have observed it still is in many households. But not in mine. On one son I laid commandments; not only did he not heed them, he perversely did their contrary, and so doing he perished. On another son I enjoined precepts, and he fled them...and me.... Twice wounded, terribly wounded, I would not expose myself to wounding once again. Therefore, even to you, seemingly so dutiful, I forbore to say anything—whether of yea or nay. I cast the burden of this matter onto the Lord. And He, in His inscrutable wisdom, has brought it to this pass. To us He has returned the determination of this matter. But it is a hard thing and a grave thing. Therefore it must be closely and carefully considered."

Again, Beeri fell silent.

Hosea's compassion for his father mingled with impatience. Yet such was his piety toward his father that Hosea sat, waiting, disclosing neither by word nor movement the urgency which threatened to explode in him.

When Beeri resumed, however, it was with a series of questions, pointed and brief, and in their purport so hopeful that at first Hosea was stunned and incredulous, then drunk with joy.

"Tell me, my son," Beeri began, "why do you now, after keeping your own counsel so long, speak openly to me? And at just this time? And so pressingly that unable to await my return home you sought me out at the city gate?"

Hosea, in a flood of speech, poured forth the tale of Gomer's peril and of the signal on which they had agreed and of how it had been brought to him.

"I see," said Beeri. "Either you speak up for her now or you shall lose her altogether."

"Yes, father."

"And would it be a great calamity to lose her?"

Beeri searched Hosea's eyes. His answering glance unswerving, Hosea said simply, "Sooner would I forfeit life itself."

Beeri nodded.

"I did ask it only to make sure. And now still another question. Answer me honestly from your heart, and I shall believe it. For though you be not wily and cunning, my son, good you are and therefore able to recognize the good. Tell me, concerning your Gomer, is she, despite the place of her dwelling, and regardless of what others say concerning her, is she a good girl?"

"As the sun is bright, father, and the summer day long. By the Lord I swear it."

"Nay, there is no need for taking His holy name. Your word suffices."

For a long pause both were silent, considering what each had said and heard.

"Then so it is," Beeri said.

"Do you mean...?" Hosea began incredulously.

"Aye, you may take Diblaim's daughter to wife."

"Oh, thank you, thank you," Hosea cried out, clasping his hands before himself in the fierceness of joy and gratitude.

"Nay, thank me not," Beeri went on, unable to restrain himself for explaining his decision, even at the risk of marring Hosea's joy. "I would have preferred otherwise. And under other circumstances I would have insisted that it be otherwise. Were you, for example, your older brother, my heir, on whom and on whose wife our house must be built. But that, whether for good or ill, you are not. Therefore it is not whom you wed but whom Iddo takes to wife—God grant she be a virtuous woman and one of the daughters of our people—on whom the fortunes of our house depend. Since over that I have no power, why should I deny you whom you desire?"

But there remained a peril, the presence of which Hosea could not forget for even a moment, so terrible was it and so insistent. Emboldened by the fear of it, he interrupted Beeri.

"Father, I shall be forever grateful for your kindness to me of this day. But it will avail me naught unless we forestall what Charun intends. Father, we must go to Jezreel at once. If not you, since you were ill yesterday and are still weak, then let me go."

Beeri hesitated.

"You must," Hosea insisted, "or all is lost."

Beeri nodded his head. "But you must not go alone. It is not seemly for a youth to speak for himself in marriage, and it is not safe for a young man in love to arrange his own marriage settlement."

"Then what shall we do?" Hosea cried in distraction.

"Peace, my son. There is a way. Talmon returns tomorrow to Jezreel. Though he is but a steward, he is freeborn, devout, all in all a worthy spokesman for you and our family. And I can instruct him as to the settlement."

"Father," Hosea broke in, "there will be no dowry."

"So you told me yesterday. It does not matter."

"And this marriage price may be high."

"Whatever the trafficker bids, we will equal and more also. So I shall bid Talmon to say. Then, in a few days, when I am strong again, I shall come to Jezreel and make a solemn covenant of all this."

"But I go with Talmon, do I not?"

"You want it very much?"

"I will not be able to endure it otherwise—the waiting, the trusting all my hopes to another, even if that other be Talmon."

Beeri allowed himself a smile.

"Then you shall go. And not for your sake alone but for mine, to whom you will otherwise give no peace, and for Noam's, to whom assuredly in your present state you will be worthless. Only be mindful always, for all your ardor, to comport yourself with dignity."

"Oh, I shall. Believe me," Hosea said. "How can I even begin to thank my father for his countless kindnesses to me, and this his greatest of all."

"Nay, thank me not. It is by this that a father's heart is made glad, that he shall look on the gladness of his children. If that joy was withheld from me with your older brothers, then it is good to know it at least with you."

Once again there was pain in Hosea's gladness.

• • •

"YOU SHALL NOT DO IT," Talmon insisted on the second afternoon of their journey, as they approached home ground. "Do not come disheveled and dusty from the road to the house of the maiden you court. Not for any suitor is that befitting, especially not for you who are a son of your father."

Hosea snorted in disdain.

"Nor," Talmon continued, "shall you arrive until first a servant has gone before to announce your coming. Would you have them unprepared for you? How pleased think you your chosen bride will be to be found unbathed, uncombed, robed in her workaday dress?"

At this and the memory of his Passover morning visit, Hosea yielded. When they reached the fork in the road, he did not go onward toward Charun's homestead but silently turned the ass which bore him toward Beeri's house and his own.

The arranging of an appointment with Charun proved more difficult and time-consuming than either Talmon or Hosea had expected. Charun's servant returned the next day with the report that his master was profuse with his regrets but occupied that day on vital, nondeferrable business. Hosea's disappointment was palpable. When the next day the same report was returned, Talmon came forward with the theory that perhaps Charun had not yet completed his preparations for their visit. Meantime, on that second day, the steward developed an air of anxiety and preoccupation, much like one who has come by disturbing news and knows not what to do with it. When on the third day came another rebuff, Talmon was angry.

"That son of Belial," he stormed, "that seed of evildoers, the Lord protect us from such as he. A fool is hard enough to endure, but a fool who sets himself up as clever, because of him the very earth trembles. And that he should be a liar too, a base deceiver, and in so grave a ma—"

Here he caught himself abruptly, like one on the point of making some unhappy, unintended disclosure. Hosea was too deep in his own fretting to cast judgments.

"Then what are we to do? Wait forever?"

"Nay," Talmon answered firmly, "not forever. That will not be needed. But until that slave ceases to play the master, yes."

"What do you mean?"

"Tonight begins the Sabbath, so that on the morrow we could not visit him in any event, a circumstance on which he is no doubt counting to whet our eagerness, so that we may increase the marriage price we are prepared to pay—which is of course his purpose throughout this crookedness."

Hosea groaned. "Must we, because he is base, bring ourselves low likewise?"

"What would you have?" Talmon all but snapped at him. "Shall we throw the pride of our house behind us? Have you no concern for your father's dignity, if not his silver?"

"But that trafficker in slaves and cattle..."

"Have no fear concerning him," Talmon said firmly. His lips were tight, his face set. "I promise that you need not disquiet yourself on that score."

And Hosea steeled himself as best he might to endure the interminable days that lay between him and those for which he yearned.

But, as it turned out, he was not to wait long after all. That very noon, as Hosea and Talmon sat together over their repast, the servant who watched over the gate came in to them.

"Masters, a young woman stands in the doorway. Gomer, Diblaim's daughter. She asks to see Beeri's son."

"I come at once," Hosea cried, jumping to his feet.

"Nay, we go both of us," Talmon instructed.

So to the two of them Gomer bowed low in greeting and said, with quiet, formal dignity, "You will forgive your maidservant that I come here unbidden and at an unseemly time. I would not have you think that I know not better. But as you shall soon observe, mine is not a situation in which I can choose times or stand on proprieties. I came," she said, a touch of defiance entering her speech and manner, "when best I could."

Then her composure deserted her altogether. Oblivious of the steward, she spoke breathlessly to Hosea.

"I must speak quickly and be returned before my absence is noted. Hosea, it is a fraud which Charun seeks to work upon you. Othniel the trafficker came not to our house this season, nor did he make an offer of marriage. Charun says so to beguile your father to paying a greater price."

Talmon pounced like a cat on a mouse. "Then how came the message to Samaria?"

"Charun sent it," Gomer said to Hosea, unaware seemingly that it was not he who had interrogated her.

"But the secret words...?"

"He extorted them from me. First he plagued me until I admitted that Hosea had made me an offer of marriage and was concerned, lest I be wedded to another. That I admitted in the end because he taunted me for my lack of suitors and because my pride was stirred—and because I thought that with it he would be satisfied. And so he was, until it became apparent that Othniel would not come to Jezreel this season. Then he became as a madman. He gave me no peace with his questions. 'Surely,' he kept suggesting, morning, noon, and night, 'your lover, if he loves you so, has not left you defenseless, to be taken by another without his knowledge. Surely he has instructed you how to appeal for his aid.' This I could have endured. But when he took to tearing my hair and beating me, that humiliation I could not sustain. And I said to myself: 'Then let Hosea come if he can and will. At least I shall have relief. And before he falls into Charun's trap, I shall warn him'—as I do at this moment."

She paused.

"You believe me, Hosea?"

He noted that her gaze was indeed direct. "Yes," he answered. "Of course."

"Then all is well," she said. Suddenly there was great bitterness in her voice. "Not to me is it given that anything go evenly, normally, as for others, not even when out of the heavens a boon is offered."

"But what will be with you now?"

"I have had the relief I bargained for. Now, as I perish, I perish."

The outburst was over, subdued as quickly as it had come.

Talmon broke in. "By the Lord of hosts, not so."

Gomer looked at the steward in surprise, so tardily aware of his presence.

"You shall not be punished," Talmon went on. "You need not be punished for speaking truth. Whatever Charun may inquire, tell him not a word of where you have been or what you have done. And I shall send a servant to come to Charun's house with tidings which shall please him. He shall say…yes, he shall say that since the Sabbath comes, the matter must be held over to next week. And since our master, Beeri, may not arrive for many days later—and in any event no betrothal could be pledged without him—we would be wise to wait for him. Charun will be too confident to molest you. And now go, for each moment increases your peril."

For an unforgettable instant Gomer stood in the doorway, the steadily falling rain a wall behind her, her drenched robe sodden, her hair falling in wet strands about her face. Her eyes and cheeks were near red, like dark fire. Then she was gone into the wet obscurity.

Hosea stared into the misty void until Talmon's voice woke him.

"It is a noble thing the maiden has just done."

"Then you believe her too."

"Of course; she had all to lose and naught to gain by disclosing what she related."

"But my father, when he comes, will he do as you predict, knowing of Charun's deception? Will he himself go to his house?"

"I cannot be certain. But it is likely, more likely than if she had not come to tell us."

"But how?"

"Because, my son, I have known since the second day we arrived that Charun was lying. I had made inquiries and learned that the trafficker had not come to Jezreel this season. The only question in my mind was whether Diblaim's daughter was, as seemed likely, a partner to the fraud. Of the fraud itself, I will of course inform your father. You may well thank the Lord that your maiden has established her truthfulness."

And, discerning the abyss he had just skirted, Hosea did just that.

As the outcome established, Talmon knew his master right well. Beeri's response when he heard the story upon his arrival was to commend Gomer.

"It is better so. Of what sort Charun might be we needed no further evidence. The sole question was concerning the girl. This much, then, has been established—that in respect to the truth at least, and it is no trivial respect, she and her uncle are not of a piece. For the first time since this matter came to be, I feel myself heartened."

Charun, on the other hand, was emboldened to arrogance. Of the fact that he had been detected in his deceit and exposed by

Gomer, he had no notion whatsoever. He knew only that as a result of his stratagem, as he supposed, not Talmon but Beeri himself was to come to him to press Hosea's suit. When the meeting took place at last, he was all bland self-confidence, condescension, and grasping cupidity, demanding five hundred shekels of silver and a great number of sheep and goats, as well as a trousseau, not only for the bride but also for all of his household.

Beeri sat in Charun's private chamber, Talmon at his side.

"Not only insulted, but cheated too," the steward whispered to him.

"We shall not be cheated. Have I so little regard for my son as to agree to such fantastic terms that men should later say in the gates that for less I could not get him a wife?"

"Then what will you do?"

"When he is finished, you shall see."

Beeri answered Charun quietly but with a firmness that left no room for argument. "It is not concerning cattle and sheep that we speak now but our children—my son and your niece. Your step-niece. And concerning one's flesh and blood it is not fitting to haggle. Therefore, I shall tell you the sum I have in mind. It will be not too much, for I would not lessen the dignity of my son. Nor will it be too little, for I would not have a daughter of my house acquired cheaply, to her shame. The sum I say will be proper. I will not depart from it.

"For your niece—your step-niece—I offer one hundred shekels of silver. As to sheep or cattle or house furnishings, since one hundred shekels is a generous price, I offer nothing."

Charun burst forth with a hoot of derisive laughter.

Unperturbed, Beeri went on.

"I did listen until you were done. Now pay me like courtesy. As for garments, I shall present to each member of your household, including your two manservants and one maidservant, one change both outer and inner, as befits the station of each, to be worn at the wedding."

Mollified as he was by the concession concerning clothes, Charun sobered instantly at Beeri's next point. "As for dowry—and I would not take a daughter to my son without it, lest the very maidservants mock her for having come penniless—there must be with Gomer a dowry equal, except for the changes of clothing, to the marriage price."

Charun blanched. The negotiations for some time had proceeded contrary to his expectations. Now they had truly taken an adverse turn, for it was on his most vulnerable point that Beeri had touched. He knew he could rely on Beeri's courtesy not to raise issues certain to be embarrassing, but this would not be the end of it, as his neighbor was a shrewd man, shrewder than most.

It was some time before Beeri spoke again, and then with a balance of delicacy for Charun's pride and bluntness as to the facts.

"It is rumored, Charun, that your fields and flocks have not prospered of late. Perhaps such a sum might prove a burden to you. Therefore, since we are men, brothers, or may soon become such, I offer this compromise. Let the marriage contract say that on the day of the wedding you will pay me the one hundred shekels, so that Gomer's repute will be protected. But to spare you, I shall give you, secretly at the time of the sealing of the contract, a receipt for that sum, bearing my seal and that of Talmon here."

Relief flooded Charun. He shrugged his shoulders, grimaced deprecatingly, and waved his hand as though to brush Beeri's entire utterance aside. But he said nothing, not daring to utter any of the answers or arguments which occurred to him, for fear that they would be either too much or too little, too bold or too appeasing.

Beeri knew his antagonist.

"Charun," he said, "you know that I am a man of my word whose yea is yea and nay is nay. I tell you that I will not depart by a hairsbreadth from the offer I have made. Accept it or reject it you may, but not alter it. Nor will I sit here all day for you to decide.

"Look in the brazier, where we can both see it. There is a large charcoal—there in the center—all but consumed, but not yet fallen apart. I shall bear with you until it disintegrates, whenever that may be. At that moment I arise and return not, and my offer is withdrawn, perhaps permanently. I await your word."

Charun looked at the coal, gray without glowing red within. He remembered Beeri's response to his need so many years before, and remembered how uncannily the man had tried to seize the advantage then. Hot anger flared in him, and subsided. Like the coals, his hopes, too, were diminishing.

"I agree," he said.

"To all terms?" Beeri insisted.

"Yes."

"Then," said Beeri decisively, "let us strike hands in pledge." He rose at once, walked briskly across the room to Charun, who rose slowly from his chair, and extended an open hand. With false courage, Charun touched it with his palm.

"Before the Lord, I am witness to this," Talmon said, taking quick advantage of the favorable moment. He turned at once with a questioning look to Charun's crony, Thedka, who, since there was nothing else to say, could only assent.

"And I, too," said the crony, only vaguely aware of the questions which Beeri proceeded to put to him, the decisions to which he was giving numbed assent.

It was agreed that the marriage contract be drawn and the betrothal be celebrated as soon as possible, but that the marriage be not solemnized until the spring, just before the Passover. It was stipulated that the marriage contract contain, in addition to its specially covenanted terms, all the usual clauses traditional in Israel as to the obligations of the bride and groom to each other and their respective rights: that the groom binds himself not to take a second wife without the explicit consent of the first, and that the family of the bride warrants her virginity, to be attested by the tokens of the bridal bed. If she is not a virgin, the marriage might be annulled by the groom, who then might not only keep the dower but may also assess the bride's family double the marriage price paid by him. The two men decided further that, though Hosea was well qualified for the assignment, the writing of the marriage contract be turned over to some scribe who was not himself personally involved in the transaction. Finally, they determined that at least two days would be required for sending after the scribe and his coming, and that accordingly the betrothal be set for the third day hence. The delay would serve further to afford Charun time to prepare for the occasion, in which, though it was the proper prerogative of the bride's kin, Beeri had asked and was granted permission to participate.

Then, these matters disposed of, Beeri said, "And now, if it please Charun and the maiden is attired to be seen, I should like to look on her, for I have not met her heretofore."

Like the daughter of any house for whom suit is being made, Gomer was ready, having been robed in a dress which Charun had borrowed for her. Pulling aside the hanging over the doorway, stepping from his own room into the courtyard, Charun first called her name in a loud voice, after what was apparently his wont, then, recalling the proprieties, sent the servant who stood there to fetch her.

Through the open doorway they could see her approaching, walking with unhurried, quiet grace. She was dressed in a crimson robe which became her, setting off the darkness of her hair and eyes, and by its loose flow accenting the delicate richness of her form and disclosing the loveliness natural to her movements. Her normally tumbled hair had been combed to a black cascade, descending to her waist and falling in two plaited tresses before her shoulders. Beeri drew his breath in amazement.

"That my daughter-to-be is comely, I had heard. But I had not imagined her to be so beautiful."

"Aye," Talmon mused, "our Hosea, it would seem, has an eye for more than script."

Then they both fell silent as Gomer crossed the threshold.

Her hands crossed over her breasts, one knee bending almost to the ground, she bowed her head before them, so low that the tips of her braids brushed the floor.

"May my lord live forever, and may his maidservant find favor in his eyes."

"Arise, my daughter, and let me see your countenance from near."

She came erect and raised her face for his contemplation. As she stood there, a wave of color suffused her cheeks. Something of timidity appeared in her expression.

"Beautiful you are, my child," Beeri said at last. "May you be as virtuous. And then my house will rejoice in you. For, as you have no doubt surmised, your uncle here and I have just covenanted to wed you to my son Hosea. Are you pleased?"

"The honor paid me, my lord, is greater than I merit."

"And what think you concerning my son?"

"He is wise and just and kind. I esteem him beyond all men."

Beeri studied her reflectively, considering her choice of words.

"And do you love him also?"

Her eyes did not waver.

"I shall love him," she said, and there was no doubting her

earnestness, "as a wife should love her husband."

Beeri was not altogether content. There was a reserve in her manner, a careful choosing of speech which left him vaguely dissatisfied. He thought of how he withheld his own heart from his youngest son, and painfully admitted to himself that it could not be expected from strangers, if it was not forthcoming from flesh and blood. He sighed.

"God hear your words to confirm them." He raised his hands over her head. "The Lord make thee like Sarah, Rebecca, Rachel, and Leah, that in thee our house and all Israel may be built."

After which he bent forward and kissed her on the brow.

CHAPTER VII

NOT IN MANY A YEAR had there been a wedding in Jezreel equal to that wherein Hosea, son of Beeri, took Gomer, Diblaim's daughter, to wife.

Servants went forth day after day bringing invitations to the wedding, to the prophets who were in Dothan, to the priests who dwelled nearby, to kinsfolk such as Hosea's sisters and their husbands and children, to the princes of the tribe of Ephraim, and to all the judges, the rich and the great of the vicinity. As for the poor of the land, they, it was understood, would come by themselves.

The courtyard of the house where the ceremony would take place was whitewashed. A supply of seasoned torches, well steeped in scented oils, was prepared. Calves and lambs were set apart for slaughtering; jugs of wine were sampled and marked. Goatskin tents were procured, to be set up in the fields, for the guests would be too many for the courtyard and the bedrooms. A large airy apartment, a wing to the main house but quite isolated from it, was set apart for the bridal group and plastered afresh, strewn with carpets, and hung with Beeri's finest draperies. The bridal couch itself, made of wood inlaid with ivory, was sent down by Beeri from Samaria.

On the morning of his wedding, Hosea stood with Beeri, Noam, and a great company as the priests brought peace offerings in his name, made supplication to the Lord for his welfare and Gomer's, and asked that children be born to them. Then, he and his father went to the cave in the hills where they prayed for peace for the dead in Sheol. They neither made sacrifice nor left gifts there, since to do so would be a heathen practice and not lawful to an Israelite who might sacrifice to the Lord alone. Then they returned home.

By noon Hosea, in anticipation of the wedding, felt himself already fatigued and slightly giddy. But much remained to be done.

Noam and Talmon were sent to instruct Hosea in how a groom comes near to his bride and takes her. The steward, though honored with the appointment, had little regard for the duties it entailed.

"I have never held with such teachings," he said bluntly as he, Noam, and Hosea were closeted together in the bridal chamber. "I have seen the beasts of the field, the fowl of the air, the very insects. Who instructs them in such things? They know of themselves or the Lord instructs them. Is man less intelligent than they, or less cared-for by the God who made him? Let the boy be, is my mind. He will find his way."

But Noam would not have it so. As always with tradition, humor deserted him.

"And think you," he countered, "that you are wiser than those who have gone before us? As they ordained, so it behooves us to do."

Whereupon Noam, painstakingly, with the same earnestness, orderliness, and concern over detail with which he dealt a manuscript, began his counsel. And Hosea, listening in weariness and embarrassment, grew more confused and frightened by the minute, and so ashamed that he no longer knew where to look, whether at the men who were speaking so openly of such intimate matters or at the room with its seemingly enormous bridal bed, where the deeds which Noam described in such excruciating detail were to be performed.

When Noam's meticulous instruction was finished, they were admitted to the room. They set a ewer behind a curtain in a corner, filled it with warm water scented with myrrh, and bade Hosea to retire behind the screen to bathe. When Hosea had washed and dried himself and put on the loincloth which the menservants had furnished, they summoned him to lie on a bench for the anointing with olive oil and aloes. Then they dressed him in linen undergarments, and an outer robe, and the chaplet of flowers like a crown. Like every groom of good lineage, he would come to the marriage pavilion attired as was Solomon, king of Israel, in the days of his glory.

The guests were assembled in the courtyard, and the men singers had raised their voices in a chant to the accompaniment of musicians. For all Hosea and his attendants knew, all was in readiness—except for themselves.

Once the chaplet had been set on Hosea's head, it seemed suddenly that everything was finished. At the same time, they learned on inquiry that all was not in readiness, either in the courtyard or in the bride's chambers. The frenzied rushing gave way to a period of idle waiting, empty except for a tenseness which Hosea found even harder to bear than the excitement which had preceded it. Burdened by the weight of his robes, constrained by their stiffness, all but intoxicated by the heavy scent of the perfumes and spices, tremulous from the many and confusing activities which had been his lot that day, Hosea stood in the center of the room praying that time would stop so that he might never need to step forward to face the assembled multitude.

But though the passage of time seemed interminable, there came a moment, whether too soon or too late he did not know, when Noam and Talmon, now themselves in stately attire, stood on either side of him, leading him forth through a dark corridor into the out of doors.

In his bewilderment and the blinding light of day, he was aware only in fragments, of a great throng filling the courtyard, of festoons and wreathes of flowers, of a silken bower standing beyond. Vaguely, too, he identified the song which the choir and musicians were rendering as the hymn composed in honor of the marriage of Princess Athaliah of Israel to Jehoram, king of Judah, now commonly sung at all weddings. It was of him, he told himself, incredulously, that they were chanting.

> *Fair art thou among the sons of man;*
> *Therefore God hath blessed thee forever.*

And then, somehow, he was standing in the shade of the bower, and the music had changed. Now they were singing:

> *Hearken, O daughter, and consider, and incline thine ear;*
> *Forget thy people and thy father's house*
> *That the king may desire thy beauty*
> *Since he is thy lord; do thou homage to him.*

Gomer, he was aware, must be coming. From afar, he caught a glimpse of the bride's white robe. Then, lovely beyond words, she was at his side, and all were singing:

Altogether glorious is the princess as she enters the palace.

After which the assemblage fell silent, Hosea's vision cleared, and his heart stilled. Perceiving only her, conscious only of her and how indeed she was altogether glorious, he said in a firm, unfaltering voice the traditional words:

"Be thou, Gomer, daughter of Diblaim, my wife, after the Laws of Moses and Israel."

Then he added a message of his own, as much a promise as a prayer: "I will betroth thee unto me in righteousness and in justice and in loving kindness and in compassion."

Hodiah led the assemblage in a series of blessings for the couple, seven of them in all—for prosperity, for children, for the land, for the priests, for the prophets, for the nation, and finally one over a brimming goblet of wine. Hosea was given to drink and then Gomer.

Hosea lifted the veil. As his bride sipped the wine, he said, "And I will betroth thee to me in faithfulness. And thou shalt know the Lord."

• • •

THE NEXT MORNING, before the servants had come into the courtyard to set forth the bridal feast of the second day, Charun came to the door of the bridal pavilion, bleary for want of sleep and blowsy with wine, with his steadfast companion Thedka, equally drowsy and besotted, but both making a great pretense of dignity.

Beeri, who had expected their arrival, was present to receive them.

The courtesies of the occasion having been exchanged among the three men, and with a permissive nod from Beeri, Charun knocked on the doorpost.

"I stand here," Charun proclaimed, "to assure the honor of my house."

From within, the curtain was drawn. Hosea and Gomer stood together in the doorway, robed in the clothes of night, Hosea with a voluminous linen cloth in his hands.

"In the presence of these men," Charun intoned, "I do ask of you, Beeri's son, who did yesterday take my niece, Diblaim's daughter, to wife: did you find in her the tokens of virginity?"

"Yes," Hosea answered, his voice strained.

"And where be these tokens?"

"Here, on this spread on which we did lay together as man and wife."

Charun took the sheet and unfolded it, exposing it to the view of the others.

"Here," he said to them, "is the spread of the bridal couch, stained with blood, which, as you have heard from the lips of Hosea, Beeri's son, and now husband to Gomer, my niece, is the blood of her virginity. Are you witnesses therefore that there were not missing in her the tokens of virginity?"

"We are witness," Beeri and Thedka said in unison.

"The Lord hearken to your words," said Charun, thus concluding the ritual.

Though he left at once, Charun returned soon after, demanding a private interview with his niece. He was shown into a side chamber, to which she came soon thereafter.

Charun studied her for a long moment, then stepped quickly to look outside the door and behind the window lattices to make certain no one was within hearing. Gomer, who had appeared pale in the earlier morning, turned ever paler.

"What would my uncle have?"

"Ho," he crowed, coming closer, "already she is a great lady filled with reverence for her kin. What would I have? I shall show you."

He grasped her wrist and pulled her to him.

"What would I have, eh? I would have an explanation for something I saw this morning, something more than the pallor and unhappiness of your face. I wish to know how came you to a wound here," he said as his other hand swept up her left sleeve, exposing a bandage ringing her left arm, just below the shoulder. "Here," he repeated, "when yesterday you were without blemish? And now," he went on fiercely, "your uncle would see what manner of thing lies here concealed."

She struggled to resist him, twisting her arms to break his grip, but in the end he had his way. The bandage ripped away under his fingers, uncovering an arm incised with a clean, fresh cut on its inner surface.

"And how," he panted in her ear, holding her close, "how comes a bride in the soft bed of her espousal to a knife cut such as this? Have you played the strumpet in my house? If that old hawk caught a glimpse of that bandage as I did, if he thinks what I thought, I am ruined. Double the marriage price would I owe, when I have already spent half of it!"

In his fury he shook her to and fro, so that her hair came tumbling down.

"I am innocent...before God...."

There was an indignation in her voice which rang genuine. Without releasing her altogether, he stopped shaking her.

"Mean you that you were indeed a virgin after all?"

"By the Lord, I swear it."

He considered her intently. "So," he reflected, "had I ever believed. Always have I been certain that for all your wildness you were one of the virtuous ones. But if so, then what can be the meaning...?"

He grew altogether still. Then a gleam of cunning came into his eyes, and a single hoot of discovery and derision burst from him.

"So," he cackled in glee, "so that is the way the wind lies. Of course, so it must be. If you had to resort to tricks, then it must be for his sake." With relish, he continued. "Tell me, my sweet, my niece, perhaps your husband is not altogether a man? And if so, why if it were so...oh so wonderful...should Beeri be brought down from all his hauteur...and I, I would keep the marriage price and take back the bride...perhaps even compensation beyo—"

"Stop it," she interrupted him, trembling with disgust. "Don't say another word against him...." The fury of a spitting cat was in the staccato of her words, her curving fingers, her blazing eyes. "Not another word against him, you who are not fit to lick the dust under his feet."

"Nay," he taunted, "not a word. Except that he is no man."

She glared at him.

"There is nothing lacking in him."

"Yet his wife remains a virgin on the morrow of her bridal night."

Her eyes darted about the room as though seeking escape from what she had to say. But there was no way out. And so she lifted her head, looked into Charun's eyes, and spoke with cold contempt.

"It pains me that I must degrade and defile my husband by revealing to you what is between him and me. The fact is that he is completely a man. There is nothing lacking in him. Save that..." And here her words faltered. "He is so innocent. So eager and yet so unskilled. He knew not...oh...go away," she cried. "I hate your sight and sound and smell; your foul smell that I have detested all these years and detest now more than I can endure; that you have caused me, compelled me to uncover my husband's shame. But this device," she breathed, a vengeful joy overtaking her, "this shameless device you shall not profit. You shall see, at this season next year I shall be nursing Hosea's child.... You shall see and then you shall know."

As she spoke, so it came to pass. Before the year had gone its round, there was born to Hosea and Gomer a son to whom they gave the name Jezreel, after the place where he was conceived—and in prayer that the name which means "the Lord will sow" might portend still more blessing.

CHAPTER VIII

IN THE EARLY SUMMER, when Hosea first arrived at the Hall of the King's Scribes, the high-ceilinged and many-windowed chamber was filled with light and gentle breezes. It was far more spacious than the cramped house where he had served his apprenticeship under the tutelage of Noam the Naphtalite. But now, during the winter rains, when the windows were latticed and curtained against the season's cold, a heavy, acrid gloom filled the place. The many oil lamps that hung each over a work table and the charcoal braziers standing here and there achieved little to light or warm the room. Meantime, by their smoking, flaring, and sparking, they rendered the air murky and biting. The eyes of the scribes, already overstrained from intentness, smarted, teared, reddened, and often blurred.

Perhaps it was for this reason, because his vision was dim, or perhaps it was because of the man's garb, a great cloak of goat's hair and a broad-brimmed hat after the fashion of dwellers on the islands of the Great Sea, or perhaps it was because he thought never to see him again, that Hosea stared up at the stranger whom the slave boy had brought to his table and did not recognize him.

"You know me not?" the man asked.

Hosea squeezed his eyes closed and opened them again to sharpen his sight. He saw the stranger more clearly now—his stalwart, broad-shouldered frame, the luxuriance of his purple-black chin beard, the high color in his cheeks, and the luminous darkness of his bold eyes.

"So, I am a stranger before you," the man continued, amusement near to open laughter in his words.

But now there was something in his voice, some timbre or inflection, that rang distantly familiar in Hosea's ears.

"I know your speech," Hosea said, slowly, gropingly.

"You know more than that." The mirth in the man's utterance had now broken free, so that he spoke and laughed together. "This is a fine 'peace unto you.' A man returns home after many years, and his own flesh and blood, his own brother..."

"Iddo," Hosea whispered. "Iddo!" he cried, leaping to his feet, rounding his work table in a rush and falling on his brother's neck. "Iddo, Iddo," he repeated, holding him close to himself.

The many years were undone in an instantaneous flight, so that he was again the little boy he once had been, clinging with the little boy's worshipfulness and love-hunger to his older brother. "Iddo, blessed be your coming, the more blessed because I had despaired of it."

"A fat inheritance awaits me," Iddo drawled, holding his brother's embrace, "and you despair of my coming? For the old man's sake, I might not have returned. Nor, I will admit, did I come out of brotherly love. Why, had I long since been a shade in Sheol, as you feared, I would somehow have managed to get here." Iddo patted Hosea on the back. "You have grown older, "but you still do not know the world's ways." As Iddo spoke, Hosea was increasingly aware that the shoulders he embraced were not yielding toward him quite as he pressed toward them. Now, before Iddo's speech, and even more before its impersonal, amused remoteness, his ardor chilled. Suddenly he felt himself awkward and embarrassed for the embrace in which he was implicated. So as not to break it too abruptly, he pulled back half a pace and, still holding Iddo by the arms, turned the conversation.

"But where have you been all this time? I sent for you two years ago, when our father became gravely ill, and again thereafter when he had died. By the hands of merchants and travelers and the king's emissaries I sent after you—anyone who was going the way of the cities of the Philistines. And when none found you, Talmon and I went ourselves, to Ashkelon and Ashdod, to Gaza and Gath, as far even as Ziklag. Everywhere we found men of your acquaintance, but none who knew where you were to be found. And I came to fear that some evil chance had overtaken you, somewhere in secret, away from the eyes of men...."

By now their arms had fallen away from each other's and they were standing apart, neither far nor near. Meantime the other scribes, having witnessed their meeting and knowing of Hosea's search for his brother, had risen from their places and stood in a circle about them, listening to their conversation with undisguised curiosity.

Iddo chuckled and prodded Hosea's chest with a playful forefinger. "Evil chance, did you say? Far from it. A rare good fortune. It happened that my master, the seren of Ashkelon, was asked to send a levy to the assistance of his kinsman, the king of Caphtor, against his enemies in the other islands of the sea. And I was designated second in command, after the prince, one of my master's sons. As for none knowing my whereabouts, this came about because the whole matter was secret, lest the weakness of the king of Caphtor become known and the very attack which he feared be invited. As it turned out, he had naught to fear. There was no war, and we received our wages for feasting, drinking, and wenching, the wages of officers in the field. Alas, it came to an end. The Caphtorite grew weary of spending his money on us to no purpose and sent us away."

"And so," Hosea suggested, "you came back to find my message."

"To be *pursued* by it," Iddo corrected. "It was impossible to escape. Everywhere I went, at my lodgings, at the palace, in the open places in Ashkelon, in the other cities of the sea, everyone had one and the same message for me—that I was required at home. A few said that I might see my father before he died, but most that I should enter into my patrimony. I pieced the reports together—it was not difficult—and came at once."

Then he addressed the scribes and apprentices who stood about, all of whom were fascinated by the drama of the meeting, by Iddo's charm and handsomeness, the vivid foreignness of his garb, and, most of all, the excitement of his adventuresome mode of life. "There is that which I must say publicly, to all the world. Has there ever been such a brother as this one here? One man coming into possession of another's inheritance might have pretended to seek out the rightful heir—if only to close men's mouths—but the messengers he sent would have been instructed secretly never to find the one they sought. A second man, to quiet his own soul, might have looked once or twice more and then told himself there was naught more for him to do. But this one here sent to inquire after me not once or twice but times innumerable, and always genuinely. And he went himself! It would have been different had we been men and brothers close one to another. But we have not seen each other these fifteen years, and even before that we were less than David and Jonathan. Now, I ask you, is this not something to be commended?"

A murmur of approbation swept the assembly. Hosea blushed and averted his eyes, but only in lesser part because of the compliment which had just been paid him. Since the tenor of Iddo's speech had become clear, he had been disquieted by it—and now his disquiet was acute. He did not see it as any extraordinary righteousness that he had not attempted to appropriate a kinsman's inheritance. But most of all, this was a private matter. Why then was it being published to the world?

The conversation had shifted to another theme. Someone had asked after life among the Philistines, and Iddo was replying. His enjoyment was as unmistakable as the relish with which a hungry man wolfs his food. This was bread to Iddo—nay, wine—to stand, the man of bold adventures and rare knowledge, in the center of a rapt, admiring circle.

A mature man again, bedazzled no longer by a little boy's adoration, Hosea observed his brother and in a flash understood him. There had always been in Iddo something of this hunger to be marveled at, it scarcely mattered by whom. Therefore he always pushed himself into people's eyes, whether they were his familiars, such as long ago in the dancing in Jezreel, or strangers, as were the scribes of the king and their attendants.

But this was a childishness, Hosea reflected unhappily, ill-befitting a man.

And then, with vision cleared by disillusionment, he studied his brother's appearance, noting one by one the samenesses and the differences across the years.

Iddo was as handsome as ever, even perhaps more handsome, what with the oblong darkness of his spade-shaped chin beard in startling contrast to the bold color of his lips and clean-shaven cheeks. But his features, while still well modeled, had taken on with time and self-indulgence a heaviness approaching coarseness. His high complexion, set off by a beard, seemed almost gaudy.

And his frame, though it continued strong and graceful, had filled out to near corpulence. All in all, Hosea noted with surprise, Iddo now resembled Gadiel more closely than himself as he had been as a boy. And as with their oldest brother, there was in his beauty a disturbing suggestion of the lush, the overripe, and the excessively rich, of a damp, fecund animality.

Hosea suddenly was conscious of the unkindness and disloyalty of his thoughts. Shame and self-reproach engulfed him so that he dropped his eyes, unable to look openly at the brother he had just wronged in his heart. As much because he did not know what else to do with himself in his guilt as because there was need for it, he occupied himself with sending word to Gomer of Iddo's return.

Slipping through the wall of listeners, quietly so as not to divert their attention, Hosea looked about for his slave boy. He found him at last on the outermost fringe of the circle, bobbing and craning in the effort to see and hear over the shoulders of scribes, apprentices, and adult slaves. Hosea tapped him on the shoulder and beckoned him aside.

"Ukal," he whispered to the lad, "you will run at once and inform the Lady Gomer that our brother Iddo is returned. Bid her, please, to have a chamber prepared and a fitting meal ready. She, the child, and the servants should be bathed and robed in festive clothes, as befit a household whose master has come home after a long absence. And make haste, since her work will be much and the time short."

"I fly, master," the boy answered, going on to add, his eyes dancing, "What good fortune is ours! Our master returns, with such stories to relate. The other boys will perish with envy. Their ears will stand out to hear from me what I shall hear from him."

"Yes," said Hosea, smiling at the boy's enthusiasm. "All very true, but meantime do not tarry."

When Hosea turned back to them, the scribes and apprentices

were as he had left them, still arrayed about Iddo. But he was no longer speaking about the ways of the Philistines. Instead, he was discussing, perhaps in response to a question addressed to him in the meantime, that theme of which the men of Israel never wearied: the danger of Assyria, and whether it was imminent or remote, real or exaggerated.

"If I am right that Assyria is not to be feared, you ask me," Iddo said as Hosea worked his way unobtrusively to the center of the circle, "why then does King Jeroboam go on paying a heavy tribute each year?"

He shrugged his shoulders and went on.

"My father—*our* father," he corrected, with a smile including Hosea in his speech, "was as full of sayings as a pomegranate of seeds. I cannot abide pomegranates, and I could not endure most of his sayings. But one, I remember, which he used to quote in the name of Solomon, is as good an answer to the question as any I can invent. 'The sky has no upper limit,' Solomon said, 'the earth has no lower limit, and the hearts of kings have no boundary at all.' What Jeroboam knows and thinks, I know not. But some things I do know. I have seen Assyrian soldiers—some of them mercenaries or fugitives from their king—serve my lord, the seren of Ashkelon. They are neither better nor worse as fighters than the men of Israel. I know further that five years ago, Assur-dan-il, the Assyrian king, laid siege to Hadruch and took it not, that four years ago he attacked Arpad and took it not, and that he has not come into Syria since. And if you will say that before then they took both cities and Damascus also, then I reply that those victories were fifteen, twenty years ago—and that Jeroboam also not so long ago stood at the gates of Damascus.

"Nay, I fear the Assyrians not. They sweep forward, but they can be beaten back. And if arms defeat them not, then other things may: the pestilence, such as was nine, ten years ago; an invasion from another direction by the Babylonians, Elamites, or Medes; or else rebellion in their provinces, or conspiracy in their palaces. I do not say like some that the king of Assyria is but a noise, but neither does he terrorize me."

He was talking, Hosea recognized, not only vividly and well, but wisely also. And if there was still in his eyes the fevered joy at being attended to and marveled over, there was also earnestness. And as he let himself slip into fascination with the man and absorption in what he was saying, Hosea felt again the pride in his brother that he once knew, a lightening of the heart to be freed of guilty disapproval, and, with all this, a returning of joy and love.

• • •

THE EARLY DUSK OF WINTER had settled on the earth—so long had they tarried in talk—by the time Iddo and Hosea departed the Hall of the King's Scribes. On a tripod near the entranceway, a brazier burned, the wavering glow above it accentuating the depth of the enveloping night. A raw wind blew, a fine cold rain fell, and they paused by the brazier, Iddo to fasten the buckle of his great cloak and Hosea to pull his robe upward through his girdle, so that its skirts would not trail in the mire.

Hosea looked upward. Behind and above the Hall of the King's Scribes, the Citadel of the Palace hulked, darker than the sky it shouldered. Before them was the Great Square and the broad avenue running from it—in one direction toward the open place by the city gate and in the other up the slope of the mountain of Samaria—a river of darkness stained here and there with the diffuse, misty yellow of lamps shining through lattices and open doors, flecked with intense points of fire. The torches, borne by invisible pedestrians, gave the illusion of carrying themselves.

Iddo looked up from the buckle with which he busied himself.

"With all our talk of other things," he said, "I have forgotten to inquire after our private affairs. This house to which you lead me—where is it, and is it yours or mine?"

"It is the selfsame house on the mountain which our father purchased. Of course it is yours, by inheritance."

"But you have continued to live in it?"

"It seemed better so," Hosea explained. "You were not here to declare your pleasure concerning it. Nor did I wish to rent it to a stranger, for then, should you return and require it, you could not redeem it until after a year. Besides which, it was not certain that I had any authority of contract over it. To leave it untenanted, on the other hand, would be wasteful and might be dangerous, since, as you remember, it lies not too far from the Ravine of Achor, and though the city watchmen keep guard—"

"Please, please," Iddo protested, "there is no need for explanations between us. That you have had the use of the house pleases me. And you shall not offer me rental for your years of tenancy."

Hosea stared at his brother. That Iddo on his return might desire his house he was prepared. But that he might so much as raise the question of rental compensation had never occurred to him, even remotely.

"My brother is kind," he managed to say. He picked up a wood stick, stuck its tip into the coals of the brazier, and watched it intently, as though it were absorbing his full attention.

The Great Square of Samaria at night, Hosea recognized full well, was not a fit place for the discussion of business affairs. Nor was this, the first night of the reunion of two long-separated brothers, a proper time. But Iddo's suggestion regarding compensation had irritated him and stirred his pride. As they walked on, he struggled to restrain himself, only to yield in the end.

"I would wish," he said stiffly, choosing his words with utmost care, "that you do concerning the house whatever is most agreeable to you. It is yours. You are under no obligation, you may not find it comfortable, to share it with anyone else. Nor is there any necessity that you should do so. Should the need arise, the wages of my employment are sufficient to maintain a household. I say this forthrightly because you need consider only your comfort in making your decision."

For some moments, they walked on in silence. Then Iddo spoke. "I am pleased," he said, "that you have means of your own." Though his words were deliberate, there was the lightness of unmistakable relief in his tones. "So then we have your question: do you continue, for the present at least, to lodge in my house? Who knows? Perhaps I shall decide after a while to return to Ashkelon. It would be foolish in that case, would it not, for you to purchase a home for yourself, only to have mine left empty soon thereafter. Shall you spend your money so that the thieves of Achor may make free with mine? No, let us leave matters as they are. Meantime, we shall learn whether we can dwell together, you and I, in amity."

This was not, Hosea told himself ruefully, such a meeting as he had imagined. Nor, he thought in a spate of resentment, was his brother such a one as he had hoped for. In all these hours, to have thought never once to inquire after the mode of their father's death—let alone of his brother's life.

After the first night of their reunion, Hosea could not maintain his grievances. This disappointment of his, he wondered, was it truly warranted? Could judgment be pronounced on any man on such hasty, superficial evidences? And as for his unconcealed eagerness toward their possessions, might it not be less insensitivity than candor and straightforwardness? So also with his attitude toward their father. On this score, his brother had never made pretense. Nor was he at all unique among men, very many of whom were less than ardent about their kinsmen. But where most feigned affection, he would not. In which case, Iddo's failing was not without its virtue.

And what if, Hosea concluded, it were all true? What if his brother proved to be as a man what he had been as a youth—selfish, vain, pleasure-seeking, unloving? Still he remained his brother, of one flesh and blood with himself. Were brothers to accord or withhold love according to their approval or disapproval of one another? Rather, should it not be between them as Solomon had said long ago: "A brother is born for times of trouble"?

As the hardness left his heart, his body relaxed. His voice was now warm, his words cordial.

"Shall we not talk of nearer things? I had heard when I was at Ashkelon that you were not wed. Is it so still?"

"Aye, it is true. I never found need for a wife, seeing that in the cities and isles of the coastland women of all sorts, free and slave alike, are readily available as concubines."

Hosea was reminded of Iddo's repute, of which he had heard when he was among the Philistines, as a pursuer of women—and one much loved by them.

"But now that you are again among your own people and the head of your father's house—"

"Say, I thank you," Iddo interrupted, "but I have ever been more akin to the bull, to whom one cow is like another, than to the ox trained to bear a yoke. And as for our father's house, that can be built by others. By you, for example, when you wed, if indeed," he added as the thought occurred to him, "you are not wed already."

"Indeed I am," Hosea laughed, "for three years. Our child is nigh two years old and is now being weaned."

"By Dagon!" Iddo exclaimed, "By the great Dagon!" Then, mindful that he had committed the offense of invoking the name of one god in the domain of another, he paused, raised his eyes and hands toward the heavens, and muttered quickly, perfunctorily, "Forgive me, Lord God of Israel. I purposed no irreverence."

This prudent precaution disposed of, he returned to his surprise. "I never dreamed it!"

"But why," Hosea queried, amused, but also touched by the first evidence of interest in him on Iddo's part. "After all, I am a grown man."

"Yes, a grown man. And I continued to think of you as a child, as indeed you were when I saw you last. But you must...why, you must be all of a score and five years old."

"A score and seven," Hosea amended.

"Do you know," Iddo went on, "I have not so much as seen your face clearly, what with the gloom in the scribes' hall, and the dark now. Here, let me look at you."

Iddo swung Hosea about so that they stood facing each other, seized his brother's torch from his hand, and held it so that its light fell full on him.

He could have seen me earlier, Hosea told himself ruefully, had he desired it.

But of his resentment he said nothing. And since his words had been tempered by pleasure and amusement, he offered his face to Iddo's scrutiny and smiled, somewhat wryly, to be sure, but warmly also.

Hosea was slighter than his brother, being in person slender almost to fragility, but was quite as tall. His face, narrow and thin, its structure defined in a high forehead, prominent cheekbones, and hollow cheeks, was pale even under torchlight—paler for the shock of graying hair and the dark, sparse beard, also touched with white, about his jaws. His lips were thin, but with sensitivity rather than tightness, parted now in a wide smile that revealed firm, large, white teeth. His mouth was no less appealing for the ruefulness that lurked in its corners. The pallor and skeletal quality of his face, the invading grayness of his hair, and the seriousness manifest even under his smile made him appear at once young and, if not old, then ageless.

"How much like our father," Iddo marveled, "taller than he and in many ways different, but in many other respects his very self."

"In any case," Hosea bantered, "a grown man."

"Not such a one," Iddo teased back, "as I would enroll for battle duty in my command—you were a reed as a boy and you are a reed now—but for years and no doubt in wisdom, indisputably a man."

Hosea reached forth, retook possession of the torch, and led off, Iddo following, both striding in step and smiling over the playful exchange.

"But who is your wife?" Iddo asked.

"Do you not know? Did I not tell you?" Hosea was astounded. "Why, it is Gomer."

"Gomer...Gomer..." Iddo echoed.

"Do you not remember her?" Hosea responded, now more amazed than ever.

"I think not. Who is she?"

"You must recall her. She is the daughter of Diblaim. Charun's niece," Hosea continued when Iddo still gave no sign of recognition. "Or do you not remember him either? The owner of the farm down the valley from ours, the one our father wished to purchase, which Hodiah the prophet prevented."

"That I shall never forget, and now the man too comes back to me. But his niece—"

"Why," Hosea protested over the absurdity of Iddo not remembering Gomer, "you danced with her once. It was the time of the Festival of Booths, and none of the maidens dared to step forth to dance with you and she did and you danced wondrously together."

"No!" Iddo exclaimed incredulously. "It cannot be."

"Cannot but is, though I can understand that you find it hard to believe."

"But she was a little leopard, that one."

Hosea said nothing, looking ahead.

"I meant no offense," said Iddo.

"Of course not, and what you said is true. She was a little leopard. But if so, she has changed. She is dutiful and looks well to the ways of the household. She bears herself with dignity." Here a new note came into Hosea's voice, gaining steadily until it was disquiet. "Indeed, I sometimes wonder whether she has not turned too restrained and quiet, too subdued."

He fell silent.

Iddo's interest in the topic was ebbing. But feeling that some comment was required of him, he ventured wit.

"All the world complains of women that they are disobedient, frivolous, excessive in speech. Yet my brother, possessing a wife free of these faults, is not content."

The jest, feeble to begin with, by its completion had died. Hosea, far away in his thoughts, scarcely heard it. Iddo, his duty done, said no more.

They completed what remained of the ascent in silence.

• • •

JUST INSIDE THE DOOR OF THE HOUSE, in the passageway that led to the courtyard, Talmon the steward waited to greet his master.

"Blessed of the Lord be he who comes," he called as Iddo appeared, his rumbling voice unsteady with emotion. Then the decorousness of age and formality of prayer vanished, and he was a tremulous old man again, seeing after many long years one whom he had loved as a child. As by themselves his arms flung wide open, and his feet carried him forward in a rush.

Iddo, who had ever been fondest of Talmon of all the household, stepped forward to meet him.

"My boy, my boy," Talmon cried, his voice breaking. "Praise be to the Lord God of Israel that He has brought you home. And praise to Him, too, that He has given me the joy of seeing you again."

"Aye, it is good, old one," Iddo said, calling Talmon as he used to do in childhood. "It is very good to see your face," he said, with a warmth that had not been there all that day.

Iddo suddenly felt ashamed of his emotions.

"Did I say it is good to see your face? As though it were possible to see faces—or anything else—in this gloom. And all this while a light burns so near to hand."

Their arms about each other's shoulders, Talmon and he moved a few paces further into the passageway to where a hanging lamp burned. There they turned to each other to renew their mutual scrutiny.

"It is not only good to look upon you," Talmon said after a moment, "but you are good to look upon. Alas for your poor father, that he did not live to behold how strong and handsome is his second son as a grown man."

"Alas," Iddo echoed, "but as for you, the years have passed over you but touched you not. You are young as ever."

It was kindly spoken, but not true. Talmon's frame was gaunt, the flesh of his face hung in loose folds, his head was bald, and the hair which spilled down about his face was thin and white.

He smiled knowingly and poked a playful finger at Iddo's ribs. "The truth was ever a small thing in your eyes," he said. "But tell me, you who have been a soldier among the Philistines, did I instruct you well in the use of arms?"

"Well enough, old one," Iddo teased. "If I was not the best of swordsmen when I came to Ashkelon, I was not the worst either. And they did teach me tricks of which even you have never heard. There is with the two-edged sword a twisting that—"

"Think you not," said Hosea, appearing at the door of the house, "that we shall all be warmer indoors?"

The old man clasped his hands in a return of memory.

"The entire household waits within. My Shualith..."

"She lives still?" Iddo marveled.

"Spry and clever as the vixen after which she is named," said the steward, gently drawing Iddo across the courtyard toward the living quarters. At the clattering of their boots, the door to the common room swung open. To a chorus of "blessed be he that comes" from within, they entered.

On either side of the entranceway the servants stood in line bowing, the three slaves to the left, the two freeborn to the right. Between them Shualith, bent low to the ground. Behind her, to the rear of the room, Gomer, her child in her arms, rose from her chair.

Iddo glanced at the servants. Knowing none of them, he nodded, passed them by, and approached Shualith. He extended his hands to raise her to her feet, but she seized one, drew it to herself, and kissed it again and again, weeping.

"That I should have lived to this moment," she cried and then continued, though her words grew unintelligible for her sobbing.

Iddo smiled down on her and then, after a moment, pulled the old woman to her feet.

"Now, now," he chided, "does my coming after these years grieve you so that you can only weep and wail? A smile would be more befitting. Come now," he said, cupping the old woman's chin with a forefinger.

At his touch, she raised her head and smiled timidly. Her face was all wrinkles, her quivering mouth toothless. But her eyes, though swimming in tears, were keen and shrewdly appraising. As they considered him, the forced smile became easy and broadened until she seemed to shine with gratification.

"It is not good for a man to be so comely," she sighed, shaking her head in a pretense of disapproval. "Those Philistine women, no doubt, pursued you as once they pursued Samson. And they fed you too much, no doubt, of their unclean, detestable foods. And you did eat and grow fleshy. Still, better so than with my old man and me, all bones, or that pole, he was ever such, who is your brother." She clasped her hands in dismay. "But I babble on, and you have not yet been greeted by our Lady Gomer."

Hosea stepped forward to present his wife. Iddo, who had been listening to Shualith with obvious pleasure and equally obvious condescension, turned to face Gomer.

She had been standing, waiting quietly, the little boy on her left arm nestled against her, his head drooped on her shoulder and against her cheek. She bowed very low, almost to kneeling, and rose again.

"Your servant is glad to look on the face of her husband's brother, the master of our house."

She spoke softly, dutifully, with neither subservience nor boldness but with poised deliberateness—and, as ever, with a muted timbre of voice and lassitude of manner.

The promise of her girlhood had been fulfilled. She held her head high as ever, and though her wild tumble of hair had been tamed—and even partly concealed by a fine veil—the two tresses that hung down before her shoulders were darkly luxuriant. Her face had rounded somewhat and matured much, and the hollows under her high cheekbones were no longer as deep as they had once been, but the line of her brows still winged upward after a straight flight, her teeth were still white, her lips were still warm. And there was a sad secretiveness to her glance, an expression more alluring in its quietude than in its erstwhile boldness.

As for her body, it had ripened. Her arms were rounded, and her bosom, especially now in the season of nursing and weaning, was full and strained at her robe.

The grace that had been hers endured, save that it was slower and more measured.

"And my heart also is gladdened to see my brother's wife," Iddo answered. "I remember the Lady Gomer from her girlhood and would have known her anywhere."

It was one of those polite little falsehoods which Iddo struck off so effortlessly, habitually, and by which the world had ever been enchanted.

Gomer's tone was no more sprightly than before, nor had her expression changed, when she said, "Our master's charm is surely even sharper than his memory."

Both men looked at her—Iddo with the annoyance of one unaccustomed to having his compliments parried, Hosea with the pleasure of her not having been taken in by his brother. His heart rose pridefully.

Blushing under the scrutiny of the two men, Gomer turned so that the baby was between her and them.

"And shall no heed be paid to our son?" Hosea broke in.

The child slept soundly on his mother's arm, plump in his healthy babyhood, of one coloration with his mother, all rosy now with slumber.

"I should have wished," Hosea offered tentatively, "that he greet his uncle."

"Nay," Gomer interposed firmly, "let us not wake him, or he shall not sleep again this night—nor we either. His uncle will listen to his wisdoms on the morrow. And, if he has children of his own, he will not be offended."

"Alas," said Iddo, "your kinsman is childless, indeed unwed. And the child is most pretty and, I doubt not, clever also. But I shall not be vexed to wait to hear his speech."

"Then let me put him again in his cradle. And do you meantime take off your cloaks." She turned toward a man and a maidservant. "Mibsam, Keturah, let one of you take away your masters' robes, and the other fetch water for the washing. My lords will sit themselves to eat and drink of the dinner which has been prepared for them. They need not wait for me. They are hungry, no doubt, and the food is overcooked already."

She turned and left the large room, departing through a curtained doorway into one of the bedrooms which, lying to the rear of the house and away from the street, were reserved for the master and his kin.

"My brother's wife is fair to look upon," Iddo remarked while Hosea, Talmon, and he washed their hands in a basin which the maidservant had brought them.

"So I have ever supposed," Hosea replied, leading the way toward the table about which Shualith and another bondswoman bustled. "The child," he went on, "is he not fair also?"

"Aye, a sweet child," Iddo agreed, picking up the wine goblet set at his place and tilting it forward so that a few drops spilled on the table before him for libation, murmuring an invocation. He did not notice that Hosea and Talmon were praising the Lord, God of Israel, over bread.

The three men looked at one another and burst into laughter

as they became aware of the discrepancy of their actions. Then Talmon and Iddo sobered.

"Supplicate Him," the steward urged.

"Aye," Iddo said, apologetically, "this is not the first time. Once before this day I invoked the name of an alien god in the Lord's land."

"His anger may be kindled," Talmon continued. "Appease Him."

Iddo rose and repeated the formula he had already pronounced once that day. "Forgive me, Lord God of Israel, I purposed no irreverence."

Hosea, watching him, was more disturbed by the expiation than by the original offense. Iddo's ritual was an everyday matter which he had seen enacted times beyond number. He himself had never performed it. Having traveled outside the confines of Israel or Judah only once, and then briefly to seek his brother, he was not habituated to the names of strange gods. Besides, his father had learned from the Lord's prophets and taught him that it was sin to an Israelite even to pronounce such names. This commandment had so impressed Hosea that to this day his conscience was troubled when he wrote letters to foreign kings and perforce had to salute not only them but their deities. But such compunctions disquieted only the prophets and their followers. For the rest, all the world knew that gods, like men, were jealous of their rights—and none more so than the Lord God of Israel, of whom Moses had said there must be no other god before Him.

And yet there was something in the act of appeasement with which Hosea's heart had never been at one, the troublesome puzzle of the nature of these other gods. If the Lord was indeed so great a God as Israel asserted, if indeed He had made heaven and earth, then certainly He was the greatest God. Yet His people and land were not the most powerful; they did not seem, if the

Assyrians or Egyptians marched against them, even safe. Who then was the Lord their God?

The question was old and stubborn, a vexation of the spirit, and there was no answer to it. Hosea shook his head to throw it off as does a swimmer coming up from deep waters and returned his attention to his table companions.

In the brief interval of Hosea's distraction, his companions had plunged into talk. And under the encouragement of Talmon's questions, Iddo was again, as that afternoon in the Hall of the King's Scribes, telling about the people on the island of Caphtor: how they spoke, dressed, and lived. Then he began to tell of his experiences among them, thence to the adventures, both perilous and amusing, which had befallen him. His color high, his eyes flashing with wine and excitement, he related the perils he had undergone. In the telling of each, the blood of his listeners chilled. He also described ludicrous incidents in which he had figured, over which they all laughed, admiring him the more that he made himself laughable and so near to them.

Shualith and the handmaid who had been waiting on the table all but forgot their duties in their eagerness to listen. The other servants, who had been loitering on benches or on mats along the walls of the large room, rose one by one, their curiosity roused by bursts of laughter or exclamations of amazement, coming near and standing where they could hear, until they were all assembled in a circle about the diners. The Lady Gomer returned, slipped unnoticed through the circle, took her place at the table, and in a moment was lost in rapt attention.

Thus on the first night of his homecoming, Iddo won the hearts of all his household.

Seated opposite his brother, Hosea was at first one with the company that ringed the table, fascinated, admiring, transported, as were they. But there came a moment when he looked about and saw the faces around him—Gomer's as intent and alive as he had seen it in many a month, Talmon's and Shualith's glowing with pride and gratification, the servants' at once awestruck and affectionate. And none held a glance for him, neither now nor at any time since Iddo had crossed the threshold, so totally was the old master forgotten for the new. So it had been in the Hall of the King's Scribes: his associates, by whose side he had worked for years, were in one instant won over by Iddo. And so it had been in their boyhood, in their father's presence. Always brightness and warmth about Iddo, always gray obscurity for himself.

He looked again at Gomer, noting the faint smile curving the corners of her mouth, the slight knitting of her brows, the dark luminosity of her eyes. Jealousy pierced him. It writhed through his being in spasm after spasm until it was one continued anguish. How could it be that another could so quickly, carelessly, arrogantly assert mastery over this household, and with not even a nod of gratitude toward the one who had cared for it in his absence?

Now Hosea understood why, for all his pleasure at his brother's homecoming, he had been so quick to criticize him. The man was vain and selfish and pleasure-loving, endlessly preening and strutting like a barnyard cock. No doubt Cain had found like reproaches against his brother, but not for these did he shed Abel's blood but out of envy, because the Lord had looked with greater favor on his brother than on himself.

Then Hosea saw in himself a great evil, the enormity of which he had never heretofore suspected. A great fear descended upon him. Was his heart different from that of Cain? To be sure, he was no man of violence. He had neither shed blood nor, he was relieved to observe, did he feel any impulse to do so. But in intention, was not his the very sinfulness of Cain?

Sitting immobile in the chair, abstracted in his tormented thoughts, unheeding of the wind of words blowing past him, he willed himself to change.

His inward parts would not obey, however. He bade his heart to be generous, but his eyes continued to bear a grudge. Whereupon it occurred to him that not only was evil deeper and more variegated in him than he supposed, but that he was weaker against it than he liked to believe.

It was all, he decided, too much and too difficult for him; he could neither puzzle it out nor prevail against it. And it was too disquieting to dwell on. With effort he tore his thoughts free and fastened them to the story Iddo was telling at the moment.

But late that night, when all the household had retired at last and he lay beside Gomer, feeling the warmth of her all down his side, hearing her even breathing and that of Jezreel in his crib, it occurred to him that he had no occasion for envy. Those in the room with him were his, and such as these his brother had naught. The scale was not altogether weighted to one side.

But even as he solaced himself with such thoughts, he realized that they too were signs of envy, evidences of an envy deeper than he had heretofore supposed. For only in desperate battle does a man throw his dearest possessions onto the scale.

Confused, guilt-ridden, and aghast at his powerlessness over his passions, he thought then to ease his heart by speech. But to whom could he talk? Gomer slept, and were she awake he could not lower himself in her eyes by confessing his shame. In the end, he prayed. To be sure, matters such as these were not properly presented to the God of Israel. What had the Lord, who sustained Israel and made the land fruitful, to do with the inmost recesses of the heart? But there was none other for Hosea to turn to. Therefore, though he felt himself to be intruding on God and troubling Him with matters not His concern, Hosea besought in the dark stillness of the night forgiveness for his sin.

• • •

DURING HIS FIRST WEEKS AT HOME, Iddo from time to time alluded to the possibility of going off again to Ashkelon. But as the days passed, such references became less frequent and positive, then ceased altogether. He developed the habit of going off each morning to sit, not in the gate with the elders, but in the corners of the marketplace where the younger, less grave heads of households congregated. He struck up friendships with some of the army officers stationed in the Citadel. In the evenings, he almost always had something to do—some banquet to attend or place of amusement to frequent. And when he was at home, he seemed to take pleasure in the ways of the household and its companionship. He played with Jezreel, talked military matters and exhibited swordsmanship with Talmon, bantered with the menservants, and teased the maids. With Gomer he was courtesy and deference, with Hosea all amiability. The initial awestruck admiration of him ripened into universal affection. As for Hosea, the initial jealousy which had so troubled him melted away as both he and the others became accustomed to Iddo's presence. In the end, Hosea became one with the household in taking pleasure in it.

It was with reluctance, then, that Hosea one evening reminded his brother of his readiness to find new quarters for himself and family. And it was with gratification and relief that he heard Iddo's protestations.

"I will not have it," the elder brother said. "Is not this your father's house? Are we not men and brothers? Why then shall we live apart, you there and I here?"

"But doubtless we disturb you. The child cries or makes noise—"

"Only a little," Iddo interrupted, "and that little pleases me. He is my kin, is he not? And were he not, he would still please me."

Gratified, Hosea put forth his last contention.

"But the house is small, too small for the souls who inhabit it. You have but a tiny chamber for yourself, and in the large room you have neither privacy nor peace."

"Aye, the house is small. Our father—may his spirit not be vexed with me for saying so—had his virtues, but an easy way with money was not one of them. But what he did not build, I shall—and more generously than would he. This I have had in mind ever since I first thought not to return to Ashkelon. If you wish, toward this and toward the maintenance of the household you may pay your share. But as for the presence of others and for your fear that it mar my peace, are not these others my own flesh? Have I not been a wanderer long enough? Is it not written that it is not good for man to be alone?" He smiled at Hosea. "And would my brother deprive me of the companionship of my kin, now that I have just tasted of it and seen that it is good?"

Won now by Iddo's smile and warmed by his friendliness, Hosea agreed willingly and with a sense of eagerness that did not abate at any time in the months that followed, so pleasurable and varied was life in the household with Iddo in its midst. Always there were animated talk, interesting visitors, and after a while the exciting business of planning the refashioning of the house and the happy confusion of the building.

To be sure, there were things with which Hosea, had he been paying attention, might justifiably have taken issue. For instance, Iddo made no repairs to the house without first discussing it in family conference. But after having discussed it, he would disregard the preferences, even the strong preferences, of the others and do as he felt inclined.

Thus, on impulse, he ordered the digging of a cistern in the courtyard for the storage of rain water. It was not seemly, he said, that the servants of his house be compelled to fetch water from the public well, though it was in solid rock that the cistern was dug and the well but a few steps from their door.

For the common room, Iddo commissioned the making of two couches inlaid with ivory and covered with embroidered spreads, such as one saw only in the houses of the very rich.

He built upper chambers on the roof for sleeping quarters for himself, with an open portico where the household might refresh itself from the heat of summer days.

He engaged the most skilled of artisans to set ivory inlays into the doorposts, as had become the fashion among great families in recent years.

In Hosea's eyes, much of this was both superfluous and extravagant, being not only too costly for his purse but, as Talmon made clear in their family conferences, for Iddo's as well.

There was but one score and one score alone on which Hosea did resist Iddo. There came a day when Iddo proposed that into the vestibule wall they cause a niche to be cut in which they might place Terafim, so that their household, too, might enjoy the protection and favor of the souls of its ancestors. The "no" which erupted from Hosea was so violent and out of keeping with his normally quiet manner that he was startled no less than his listeners. Somewhat shamefaced, he apologized for his outburst. But in this, at least, he had his way without dispute.

Beyond this, Hosea was, if not altogether approving, at the least content. He justified it by telling himself that it was not only their house that Iddo was beautifying, but Gomer's life and his also.

CHAPTER IX

IN THE EARLY SUMMER HOSEA went up to Beth El at the command of the overseer of the scribes. He was to travel there with Elinadab the priest and serve as secretary to him.

Elinadab the priest was of those who looked often on the king's countenance. The head of the house of Nadab, he was well-versed in priestly traditions and rich with wealth, both inherited and earned by the discharge of his official duties. Elinadab was distinguished for uprightness and for the absence of the avarice so common among his colleagues. Content with the perquisites of his office, he did not engage in money lending to exact usury on loans. Nor did he join house to house and field to field until there was no room left in the land for its people, but he obeyed the ordinance of Moses that the priests were to have no inheritance in the land, the Lord being their portion and the offerings to Him their sustenance. King Jeroboam, then, had done well to bring him near to the throne, that it might take strength from his prestige and counsel from his expertise in sacred things.

And yet the people, though they respected Elinadab, disliked him. They did not cheer as he passed through the streets of Samaria, as they often hailed the less worthy of the priests and nobles. Hosea himself had seen the man only from behind the wall of companions and attendants who invariably surrounded him. Now, looking at him closely, watching his demeanor, Hosea saw that the man rode on a milk-white Egyptian mare, whereas his companions and servants traveled on asses. His head, unyielding to the movement of his horse, was crowned by a jeweled turban. The line of his forehead was vertical; his eyes fixed forward and oblivious to those about him; his beard full, curled in ringlets and oiled; and the flow of rich robes billowed out about the fullness of his strong frame.

There was arrogance in his appearance, but even greater arrogance in his conduct. For he made no effort to slacken the gait of his horse out of consideration for the others who traveled on slower mounts, not even when he called one of his companions to his side. So it came to pass that all the party traveled in discomfort, but most of all the men whom he summoned that he might speak with them. For the rest were free to lag behind or overtake him, but the person with whom he conversed was compelled somehow to remain by his side.

All this moved Hosea to anger.

Samaria left behind, the party now traveled the foothills and the mountains of Ephraim. It was a land of rolling hills, normally carpeted with fields of grain in the valleys, olive groves and vineyards on the slopes, and ancient trees at the crest. But that was not the view now. Winter's drought season had not abated. The late rain, like the early, had failed almost altogether. And now the shadow of approaching dryness was over the land. The heavens had yielded some water, and to the unskilled eye that might have seemed enough. But Hosea knew well the ways of the soil from his boyhood in Jezreel, and to him the signs for the future were evil indeed.

Farmers still harvested the barley, but the piles of it were scant. Having sowed, the farmers tilled out of habit, in the faint hope that the rains might yet descend out of season. The wheat land lay abandoned; weeds and thin, pale blades grew together. As for the trees, though it was the season when the white figs ripened, the fruit was sparse and small on the branches. For the black figs, there was almost no hope whatsoever. Even the leaves of the sturdy olive were paler than usual, its fruit thinner.

This was all a sad, burdensome sight, the more ominous for the fact that the very fowl of the air, usually so multitudinous at this season of the year, seemed also to have abandoned the land. Hosea's ears rang with the the silence.

What will be, Hosea fretted, with the land and its people, especially with its poor? If already some had starved and sold their children or themselves into bondage, what evils would befall them in the winter to come? Hosea sighed heavily. What is the significance of all this? What is the Lord's meaning in sending it to His people? Against what was He vexed, and, being vexed, would He show His intent to the priests and prophets? Or was His anger too fierce?

Someone nudged Hosea, startling him out of his abstraction. It was one of the attendants who rode at his side. Wordless, the man jabbed his thumb in Elinadab's direction.

"The scribe, which is he?" Elinadab was saying. Hosea prodded the flanks of his beast and pushed him through to the center of the troop.

"Did my lord call his servant?"

Elinadab stared down at Hosea. "You are a scribe from the King's Hall?"

"Yes, my lord."

"Why came you not when first I called?"

"I was considering the land in its thirst and in my sadness knew not that I was being summoned."

"Be it known to you," Elinadab pronounced, "that it is the wont of my servants to attend when I speak, that I shall not need to call once and again."

"As my master commands." The man's arrogance stung him so that Hosea lowered his heels and allowed the animal to drop back. It was childish of him, he knew, but he was no slave to be addressed so.

"When I talk to a man," Elinadab roared, turning his head, "let him remain in my presence."

"Then please, my lord, slow your mare. My ass cannot keep up with her."

It was respectfully spoken and altogether innocent on the surface. But there was that beneath it to render Elinadab suspicious. His head turned and he considered Hosea. Then he faced forward and rode on for a distance, his massive shoulders unrelenting. But in the end, he drew in his reins and slowed the mare so that Hosea might overtake him. Even so, he did not wait until the two beasts were abreast. He began to speak when the ass was somewhat behind and continued thus, so giving the appearance of speaking into the void, whereas Hosea answered forward toward a face of which he saw only the fringe of a beard, the curve of a swarthy cheek, and the stoniness of a brow. Little wonder, he told himself, his anger smoldering within him, that the land languished under the Lord's displeasure, if the priests of Israel are such as this one.

"What is your name?" Elinadab asked curtly. When Hosea answered him, he went on to inquire, "How long have you served in the Hall of Scribes?"

"Somewhat beyond two years, my lord."

"And by what master were you instructed?"

"By Noam the Naphtalite."

"Then you should be fleet and accurate in your writing."

"I think so, my lord."

"And so it had better turn out. For it is not for want of scribes in Beth El that I take you thither. Are there not priests at the sanctuary, and may one not expect of priests that many shall be skilled in writing? Was there not a time that priests alone were the scribes in Israel?"

Elinadab fell silent for a while, giving no sign to indicate whether Hosea was still required or dismissed. Then, abruptly, he resumed.

"Thrice have I required priests to record transactions, twice at Beth El and once at the shrine at Gilgal. And each time I was cursed, once with a dolt who wrote too slowly, the second time with a fool who could not read what he had written. If you are such a one as either of these," he said, glaring back at Hosea as though he were already guilty of the offense, "then get you back to Samaria at once. There is sufficient vexation for me whither I go without my bringing more to burden me."

Again he rode on in silence, resuming his speech as suddenly as he had interrupted.

"For another reason, too, have I asked the overseer that one of his scribes accompany me. I would have one with me who is my man, that I may trust him and not need to fear lest the record come out not according to the happening, but as his superiors from the sanctuary might prefer. Once before it befell me that when I returned to Samaria my secretary read to me what had been written down, but my ears did not recognize the events which my own eyes had witnessed. That time I had a scribe who was lent to me by Amaziah, my cousin, who though he be my kinsman and high priest at the highest altar of the Lord, which is in Beth El, is no more to be trusted than a Canaanite."

He broke off then, and drew in his reins. When Hosea was at his side, Elinadab thundered at him in a voice so angry that the beast started and the furthermost slave trailing behind on foot heard clearly.

"Hear me now, scribe. Our business now is with a prophet, a Judean named Amos. He has spoken treason and blasphemy, I am told, before the shrine in Beth El. And you, I can already see, who lack in subordination, are such a one as might be a follower of these troublers of Israel who call themselves prophets. If this be your malady, I wish to know nothing of it. You will write what I bid and speak only what and when I allow. Concerning all else, you will hold your tongue. Do you understand?" His eyes bored into Hosea.

"As my lord commands," Hosea answered quietly, his gaze unwavering and altogether unperturbed.

It was after nightfall that day, for Elinadab was wont to travel at his leisure, that they came tardily into Beth El, riding down the wide main street to the Broad Place in the city's center which was flanked to one side by the Shrine of the Pillar, which Jacob had set up, and on the other by the Temple of the Golden Bullock of the Lord, erected by the first Jeroboam, king of Israel.

To Hosea these thoroughfares and buildings were both familiar and strange, familiar because he had been here before often with his father and by himself, yet strange also for always he had looked upon these scenes at a time of festival when the streets were thronged with pilgrims, the night bright as day from the multitude of torches, and the air bitter with the smoke of sacrifices and sweet with incense. Now even the Broad Place was empty save for themselves, quiet but for the sounds they made, and dark except for the flames which burned on the altars in either shrine.

"Tomorrow we shall worship; now we go to the dwelling of my kinsman," said Elinadab to the company. He led them round the Temple of the Golden Bullock to a great palace almost as large as it which lay beyond.

Like the others, Hosea was escorted to a chamber and, when his traveler's pouch had been brought to him, prepared for the night. But though he was weary and the hour late his sleep was long deferred. Just as he was about to retire an attendant brought word that his services might still be required that night, and that therefore he should not disrobe but should have his scribe's utensils ready to hand. It was half a watch later that the summons came for which he had been forewarned. A servant led him along corridors, up and down flights of stairs to a curtained door through which he directed him.

The room he entered was one of the most magnificent Hosea had ever seen. Its splendor seemed sure to rival the chambers of the royal palace itself. The ceiling and walls were of finely carved cedar wood; its floor was inset with parti-colored marble slabs in an intricate design. The three-wicked bronze lamps that hung from the center of the room and the tripod braziers that burned in two opposing corners were cunningly wrought with eagles' heads, lions' feet, and adornments of flowering wands reminiscent of Aaron's staff. Couches arranged in a triangle at the center of the room glowed with inlays of ivory and silver and flowed with tapestries and pillows so abundant that they spilled onto the floor. On one of the couches sat Elinadab's kinsman, Amaziah the high priest. A man of middle years, he was a dark little creature—swarthy of skin; slight of body, face, and limb; black of beard; with eyes and brows even darker.

"This is the scribe whom I brought with me from Samaria." Elinadab indicated Hosea. Then he waved him to an unoccupied couch.

Hosea bowed low and murmured, "May it be God's will that

my lord the priest lives," seated himself on the couch, and put into readiness the polished wooden packet and sharpened stylus he had brought with him. But he was not to write for some while, for the two priests resumed an altercation in which apparently they had been involved for some time, behaving as though he were not present at all.

"I tell you," Amaziah snapped angrily at his kinsman, "that I do not exaggerate. At any time that man would be dangerous... now especially...the locusts two years ago...this year the drought... the king not well...the country restless...and the Assyrians..."

The man's body rose slightly between spurts of incomplete phrases.

"I know, I know," Elinadab replied testily, "the times are doubtless evil and therefore our hands should be firm. We have been over all that before. But I still do not have a clear statement of what the man said."

"As in the letter, does my cousin not believe me?"

"Nay. But when I come before the king, I would have your very words as my own ears heard, and as my scribe shall write them down." He turned abruptly to Hosea. "Record this with great care. Write first of all, 'Thus saith Amaziah son of Hophni, high priest of the House of God, and of the royal house in Beth El. The name of the Judean concerning whom my complaint has already been made to the king in Samaria, may my lord live forever, is...' What is the name?"

"Amos," Amaziah answered a moment later, and Hosea's stylus resumed its scratching.

"His father's name?"

Amaziah shrugged. "Do such as he have fathers?" he said.

"Leave room for the name of his father," Elinadab instructed Hosea. He turned again to Amaziah. "And his city?"

"Tekoa."

"Tekoa?"

"Yea, the little town overlooking the wilderness to the south of Bethlehem, as one goes to the Salt Sea."

Elinadab nodded. "Write down 'Tekoa in the wilderness,'" he commanded, "and write also that he is a prophet by occupation and a member of the company of prophets which is in...where does his company dwell?"

"He has no company," the high priest replied.

"But you said he was a prophet."

Amaziah leaned over his couch, tilted the urn to refill his goblet, and without raising himself looked up at Elinadab. He smiled wryly.

"This is the worst of the business. The man claims he is neither a prophet nor a member of a prophet's company, but a herdsman and trimmer of sycamore trees. Yet he speaks in the name of the Lord."

"In short," Elinadab added, "he is one of those who has been appearing of late. The wild-ass prophets I call them, for they go their own way."

"One of those," said Amaziah, "and the most troublesome of the lot, say I. They will not abide reproof, nor have they fellows to restrain them. And since they eat not the king's bread, there is no controlling them in that fashion."

"And his prophecy?"

Amaziah's voice grew tense. "It was as I wrote to Samaria. The man declared in the name of the Lord that Jeroboam our king would die by the sword and Israel be led into captivity from this land. Therefore did I inform our lord the king that a conspiracy had arisen against him, and that words were being uttered which could not be endured."

"And these words," Elinadab said. "You heard them yourself?"

"No, not myself, but from faithful persons whom I trust as I would my own ears." He sat back and glared at Elinadab.

"And these persons are here in Beth El that I may speak to them?"

Amaziah hurled the cup to the floor and sprang to his feet, quivering with rage. "How you put me to shame, believing not my words. Were I not high priest of Beth El, I would be warranted in taking offense. Were my word directed against a priest of high rank, or a nobleman, it would need to be believed. But all this now is for whom? By the Sacred Bullock of Beth El, for a Judean herdsman! Is it not enough for you that I say that the man troubles Israel?"

"But I question not my kinsman's word, but that of those who informed him."

"And are not my friends to be believed like me?"

"I doubt not their word either. I do not say that they have spoken erroneously at all, or if so, by intention. But a man's ears may deceive or his memory fail him."

"I stand sure that those who informed me are to be believed."

"Let not my cousin be vexed," Elinadab said, though without softness in his voice or manner, "but it does not suffice that he stands sure for his informants. I shall ask one question and you will see wherefore. Where spoke this Judean these words with which he is charged?"

"At the gates of the Temple in Beth El."

"Before whom?"

"Before whomever was there, of course."

"And how many were there at the time?"

"It was the Passover season; the Broad Place was full end to end."

"Since it was a multitude that did hear this man speak, it is not likely that those who brought word to you are in error. But if they should be, then the error would be grave. Allow me to remind you of another matter of which you have no doubt heard—who has not—the matter of questionable evidence concerning a vineyard, no more than a vineyard. And yet, because of it the House of Omri fell and that of Jehu, from which stems our lord King Jeroboam, ascended to the throne. In that, too, a prophet was involved. That business may be in no wise akin to this which is before us, but the world is wise when it says, 'On the stone on which a fool has slipped, a prudent man steps not.'"

Amaziah hooted his derision. Elinadab flushed with anger, rose to his feet so that he towered over Amaziah and continued, his voice unsteady with indignation.

"My cousin the high priest esteems not his kinsman's counsel. So be it. He may hold it for little worth if so he desires. But perhaps it is not too late for me to give you instruction. Let me then ask this: It is the way of these prophets, even these wild-ass prophets, that they win followers. This Judean, how is it with him?"

For the first time, Amaziah's indignation was tempered by considerations of caution.

"Strangest of all, the man's words were hard, not pleasant as the crowd likes…. Many took offense, but many believed him…. Therefore I waited for the spring pilgrims to depart…but even now, among those who dwell in Beth El, there are some who go after him…. They call upon the people of the land for repentance, from the king to his slave who sits at the millstone."

"And those who go after him, they are men of name and power?"

"None of great name or great power, but some who are not unknown or powerless either. Do you think had it been otherwise I would have troubled the king?"

"Do you not see," said Elinadab, pressing his advantage, "why I believe we should move with caution? This whole matter may be naught. But as you yourself must have suspected, it may be weighty. Else why did you send to Samaria for instruction, when it was within your power to deal with the Judean as you desire?

"Follow my counsel, cousin. Tomorrow, after I and my companions have worshiped and brought sacrifice to the Lord, we shall see this Judean. Then we shall speak to those who brought you the report concerning him. Meantime, I suggest you make inquiries in Beth El as to the opinion of the townspeople concerning him, and who among them put their trust in him. Then we shall see."

Elinadab turned to Hosea. "Return, scribe, to your chambers. Tomorrow you shall go with me and we shall begin again."

It did not occur to Elinadab to express regret that he had kept Hosea from sleep after the hardships of the day's travel. But Hosea's vexation was not hot as it had been on other occasions during the day. It was tempered and cooled by the awareness that if Elinadab was not gracious or considerate as befitted a priest of the Lord, he was not altogether devoid of uprightness either. But even if he could eke out a small virtue in Elinadab, he saw none in Amaziah. It disgusted him that one such as he should stand as intercessor between Israel and God. Could the Lord find favor in offerings which came from such hands, the hands of a scoffer, and one not averse to justifying wickedness and condemning the righteous?

He wondered as he retired to his chamber that night what incontrollable madness had leaped upon him that he, who was neither priest nor prophet, should dare to think at all after what the Lord God of Israel had ordained, let alone think so presumptuously.

• • •

HOW GOOD TO RISE EARLY, Hosea thought, even if still weary from the travail of the road and for lack of sleep, to worship the Lord in the holy places at Beth El. It was now neither Sabbath nor New Moon nor festival and, except for the ministering priests and a handful of pilgrims, the sanctuaries were empty.

Elinadab and his company stood together in a little knot in the large enclosure, open to the sky, about the Sacred Pillar. The air, for all the dryness of the summer, was cooled with morning. Shadows were everywhere, under the rectangular porticoes that bounded the sacred precinct on all its four sides, on its level earthen floor, on the stone dais in its center, and on the pillar which reared from it. It was toward this that they all looked, curiosity and awe mingling in their glance. It was a cylindrical column the height of a man, showing even in the half light the twelve separate stones of which it had been fused. These were the number of the tribes of Jacob, who had rested his head in this place and had dreamed of a ladder reaching from earth to sky with the Lord standing over it, and then had risen to declare this a gate of Heaven and to set up the stone pillow on which he had slept as a thing sacred to himself and all who would spring from his loins.

They all waited with unbroken silence for the rising sun to touch the pillar's tip.

It came at last. The line of light which had been slipping down the western colonnade struck into light the rounded top of the column. When this happened, twelve priests emerged from behind the colonnade, crying out together as they marched solemnly to cross the enclosure:

"The Lord is God and hath given us light."

The leader among them added, "Surely the Lord is in this

place; and I knew it not.... How awesome is this place. This is none other than the House of God. This is the gate of Heaven.

"He who seeks to face the Lord for whatever reason, let him first pour oil on this stone as did our father and send up his prayer to the Lord for, since here are the portals to His presence, He will hear more easily and answer more readily.

"Cruses of oil may be purchased for half of half a shekel which is five gerah. This is a sacred oil, scented with spices, compounded according to the instructions of Moses by apothecaries of the House of Aaron. This is an oil of sweet savor which will be acceptable to the Lord, inclining His heart to hearken to the voice of those who call upon Him."

As the chant of his proclamation died away, attendants came from out of the side colonnade, each bearing a tray in which was set small horns of oil. The pilgrims undid their purses from their girdles, purchased each his portion, and then waited to approach the pillar in order of rank.

First Elinadab came near, poured half his portion of oil onto the top of the column and, holding the horn still in one hand, raised his hands and his face to the heavens and prayed aloud. His speech was fluent and he seemed unembarrassed by the presence of others. His prayer was long, for as the head of a great household it sufficed not for him to pray on behalf of himself and his kin only; he must ask God's favor of long life, health, and victory on the king also, whose face he saw often, and on the people and on the land, especially in these evil days. On the last matter, his words came less readily for this was not a usual utterance; they rang with greater fervor and genuineness, mounting as he continued until he wept as did all those who heard:

"Look down from heaven and see," he cried, "Thou who sittest enthroned in thick darkness, how the land mourns, the pastures are desolate, the vine fails, the fig yields not its fruit, threshing floor,

wine press, and oil are emptied, the stores diminish. Wherefore
would the nations say of Thee, our God, Thy power is too small
to feed Thy people and bless Thy earth. O do Thou feed us and
tend us, as in days gone by, as Thou didst feed and tend Jacob our
father when he passed here, saying that Thou wouldst give unto
him and unto his seed the land on which he lay and that in him
and in us would all the families of the earth be blessed. Look then,
Lord God of Israel, to Thy covenant. Heal Thy land, save Thy
people, lest we perish."

When he was done and had poured what remained of his oil
onto the pillar and had stepped back, none spoke or moved for a
long interval, as though they desired to allow time for the words
of the priest to make their way to the Lord's throne. Then at
last, at his signal, the others stepped forward in turn, one or two
praying and speaking aloud, but most briefly and in their hearts,
moving their lips only and whispering their supplication. It was
so also that Hosea did, for his awe of the place was so mighty that
he could scarcely have brought forth a sound had he attempted
it. He also felt ashamed to uncover his heart before others. For
how could a man ask aloud and in the presence of strangers for
the welfare of a woman whose sweetness of flesh he missed, or
for the health of a child toward whom his tender mercies were
awakened each time he recalled him, or for God's protection for
the household in which they dwelled? In praying for the land, he
didn't even dare to speak aloud. For who was he to presume to
present the needs of the house of Israel to its God? And so he
murmured out his heart quickly but passionately, looking straight
toward the sky, where somewhere directly above him must be
the gate which had opened for Jacob. And feeling from the joy
and lightness which sprang up in his heart that his prayer had
penetrated the blue barrier and had been accepted, he stepped
away, gladsome, confident, exultant.

• • •

AFTER THE LAST PETITIONER, the call of trumpets sounded beyond the walls of the sacred precinct. The silver trumpets, which they all recognized, were sounded each day in the Temple of the Golden Bullock of the Lord beyond the Broad Place, when the burnt offerings and peace offerings brought in the name of all Israel came up upon the altar. In a few moments then, the temple would be free for individual rites. Whereupon the pilgrims hurried away in a body, each one depositing a box in the doorway as his special gift for the repairs of this House, and giving coins to the beggars who loitered in the entranceway of the shrine.

The Broad Place was no longer empty as it had been when they first crossed it earlier that morning. On all sides, merchants stood at their booths in the hope of catching whatever trade the few pilgrims then present in Beth El might have to offer. All sorts of wares were on sale, from amulets, charms, and chips of stone taken from the sacred enclosure, to the rarest of imported textiles and tapestries. But the greatest business was being transacted on the far side of the Broad Place just before the Temple. There were gathered in a swarming, shouting, bellowing crowd the dealers in sacrificial necessities: cattle, sheep, goats, doves, wine, oil, meal, and spice. To these Elinadab and each of his companions repaired to purchase whatever was required by the sacrifice he sought to bring. It was a noisy business. The prices, always high in this place, were even higher now. To the protests of the pilgrims the merchants argued the locust and the drought. Offers and counteroffers were exchanged to the company of expostulations, solemn oaths, curses, and vituperations. A great hubbub arose. Then slowly it quieted as each pilgrim, having completed his purchase, entered the Temple doors as quickly as he might, for, except for persons of high rank, those who brought sacrifices were received by the priests in the order of their coming.

Hosea was the first of their group to finish his transaction. Whenever Beeri had come to Beth El, though he had prayed and poured oil over the pillar, he had steadfastly refused to bring any sacrifice of consequence into the Temple. For the prophets were of divided heart concerning the Temple. It was to them as to all Israel a house dedicated to the Lord, but within it the Lord was represented by a graven image fashioned in the shape of a bullock.

The prophets were not content that the invisible God be incarnated in stone. Deferring to them, Beeri would bring nothing so large as a beast to be put upon the altar. Yet, as he also pointed out, it was not seemly for a man who feared the Lord to come to His House empty-handed. Nor was it likely that the Lord would take such an act without displeasure. Therefore, by way of compromise, he had made it his practice to provide only a meal offering, a cake of fine flour baked in the oven, mixed with oil, with a measure of extra oil to pour on it and to make it all of sweet savor. As for the money he spared himself in this fashion, he computed the price he would have extended had he bought a bullock as a burnt offering of atonement for his sins and those of his household; the difference between the two sums he was wont to divide half as a heave offering for the priests and half for distribution to the beggars at the gate.

After Hosea had made his simple purchases and completed his calculations—counted out from his wallet the money which was to be given away, placed one half in one knot in the hem of his garment, and the other in a second knot—he went through the gate into the great Temple.

Before him a vast, high-ceilinged chamber opened, at the further end of which loomed the gilded Sacred Bullock of the Lord. Dominating the entire sanctuary, this heroic statue was elevated on a platform and towered over the likenesses of four calves on the four corners of the pedestal. At the feet of this figure a brazen altar smoked with the sacrifices which had already been brought on behalf of the king, the priests, and the congregation of Israel. The air billowed with clouds of smoke and was sharp with the biting smell of scorched flesh and the sweet fragrances of spices.

About the altar priests were clustered clearing away the remains of the sacrificial beasts, removing the portions allotted to them and their fellows, clearing the top of the altar of ashes, and washing it free of the blood which had been sprinkled and poured upon it.

Amaziah stood apart from this bustle to one side. He was drying his hands after bathing them in a laver Levites held before him. Meantime others took from him the insignia and robes of his office. As high priest, he officiated only at the great public sacrifice, leaving his lesser fellows to attend to individual offerings. He was an impressive figure when Hosea first saw him in the sanctuary, clothed as he was in the time-honored, majestic accoutrements of his position. But he became again, step-by-step, the ugly, tense little man whom Hosea had seen the night before as, one by one, the badges of his dignity were taken from him.

First the Levites removed the high mitre from his head and the silver plate inscribed 'Holy to the Lord' from his forehead, setting a turban in their place. Next they removed the breastplate of judgment with its twelve precious stones arranged in four rows and bearing each inscribed upon its surface the name of one of the tribes of Israel. After that they undid the cloth ephod that circled his chest, bearing both away held high in reverence. The robe of twisted thread of blue and scarlet in which he was clothed was slipped from him, the little bells dangling from its hem tinkling sweetly in the process. For a moment he stood exposed—a slight, agitated little figure, clothed only in the linen trousers, vest, and girdle which were the assigned undergarments of an officiating priest. Then in his insignificance he seemed to Hosea, who liked him neither for his reputation nor for what he had seen of him, to be not only no high priest in Israel but less than a man. But the time of his exposure was short, for the Levites covered him quickly with his own clothes, a garb exceeding in magnificence that which he had worn as an officiate, a robe of cloth embroidered with gold and silver threads. Rings and bracelets were put upon his arms and a circlet resembling a crown, though not quite one, about his head. He assumed once more the signs of his arrogance.

Robed for the street, Amaziah proceeded solemnly, two priests following in his wake, to the altar, past beyond it to the pedestal of the image. There he kissed in turn the feet of each of the four heifers at its corners and then, in the center before the great bullock, knelt down, bending low until his forehead touched the floor. He remained so for some time, ostensibly in prayer, though in his resentment of the man, Hosea did not believe so. As he started to rise his companions raised him. After which he turned to face the priests and the worshipers, now swelled to a sizable congregation; lifted his hands; and pronounced over them the blessing of Aaron.

Hosea inclined his head to accept the blessing. Though he strove to receive the words of the priest with the reverence and savor which they merited, he felt dissent within himself surge into open rebellion and disdain.

From his father he had inherited misgivings concerning this imaging forth of the God of Israel in the shape of a bullock. It all seemed to Hosea to be too near to the ways of the idolaters and altogether inappropriate to a God who could not be seen. The sights of animal sacrifice, blood, entrails, dung, raw meat, the flies swarming about them, and even more the thick, clinging smell had always sickened him and did so now once more. But most of all he was perturbed that such a one as Amaziah should stand as intercessor between Israel and its God. Could the Lord find favor in offerings which came from such hands, the hands of a usurer and scoffer and one not averse, as he had disclosed himself the night before, to justifying wickedness and condemning the righteous? And yet, on the other hand, whatever he might be as a man, was he not also the scion of Aaron, and therefore through whom else, if not through him, could Israel approach its God?

As befitted his exalted station, Elinadab's sacrifices were accepted first and out of order of his arrival by the priests. They were elaborate and expensive, a bullock brought as a whole offering in atonement for sin, a peace offering, a thanks offering, and abundant amounts of oil and incense. The spurting forth of the fresh blood of the animal, the reddened hands of the priests, the gutting and dissecting of the carcasses were even more repellent to Hosea than ever before. Deliberately he turned his eyes and thoughts from the spectacle being enacted before him. When the revolting smells billowed forth from the altar once more, he breathed as lightly as he might. He concentrated on the chanting of the priests and Levites and on the prayers they uttered. But even these did not reach to his heart, rebellious as it was for his suspicions of the officiants. Had it not been an affront to God he would have already turned and left this place. At last the priests, having disposed at long last of Elinadab's offerings, turned to him. Hosea's rebelliousness was not appeased by the manner the chief priest adopted as soon as he looked upon his offering.

"Is this the whole of your sacrifice?" he asked, and the scorn in his look and words was unmistakable. Hosea made himself unhearing.

"It is my entire sacrifice," he declared unperturbed.

And when the priest asked him next for whom and to what end he brought it he answered only, "For the healing of our land and the welfare of the children of my house."

The burning of the meal and incense on the altar gave forth

an odor pleasant in itself, the more pleasant for the surcease from the smell of scorched flesh. Through the smoke the image of the bullock stood before Hosea, and he was grieved that it was into the nostrils of the graven image that the sweet savor was ascending. When subsequently one portion of his offering having been consumed in fire, the rest was set aside for the priests, he could not avoid wondering whether those who would eat of his gift were like Amaziah. If so, slight as that gift might be, he begrudged it to them. Nor at the end did he kiss the calves or bow to the bullock, but he hurried out eager to get away from this place which had suddenly come to seem to him not merely distasteful or questionable but, for all the ritual scruples, unclean.

Hosea did not understand what was happening to him. This was after all Israel's great shrine. It was by Israel's God that these rites had been established, by Him too that the sons of Aaron had been chosen. Why then did he, who had arisen that day rejoicing that he might worship the Lord in the holy place of Beth El, become so bitter?

• • •

THE HOUSE OF DETENTION belonging to the high priest of Beth El lay at the end of the alleyway separating the shrine from the palace. A one-roomed building of cut stone, its thick and firmly mortared walls allowed for two tiny apertures for light and air. Its massive door was equipped with a slide bar, bolted now, since a prisoner guarded by one of Amaziah's bodyguards sat within.

The guard rose as Elinadab, Hosea, and two of the most stalwart members of the priest's company came single file down the narrow path.

"We would speak to the Judean who is your prisoner," said the priest.

"As my lord commands," the guard answered. "My master has prepared me for your coming." Turning, he took hold of the tongue of the bar, tugged it free from the hole in the doorpost, lifted it from its brackets, and pushed the door open with his shoulder.

Elinadab paused on the threshold. "I have brought attendants with me. Will I need them in there?"

"To protect you?" The guard chuckled. "No, my lord. There will not be room. And as for the Judean, a lamb could not be gentler."

Elinadab nodded, gestured to his attendants to wait outside, instructed to Hosea to accompany him, and entered the room.

The chamber was shadowy, lit only by the two apertures near the roof and by the doorway behind them. As their eyes eased to the dark they discerned, to their surprise, that the chamber was occupied by two persons.

"There is more than one here," Elinadab called back to the guard.

"Yes, my lord, I had forgot to say it; the second comes almost every day. He is a kinsman or a friend and since he does no harm and I have not been ordered contrariwise, I allow them to sit together."

"Then I order contrariwise," the priest snapped. "Is this a house of pleasure or of detention? Not this one here or anyone else henceforth is to be admitted."

"As my lord commands," the guard answered. "It did not seem wrong to me. They are quiet together. One talks, the other writes—"

"Silence at once," Elinadab said, annoyed. "It is not you whom I have come to hear."

Elinadab turned to the two men.

"Which is the Judean who calls himself a prophet? And do you rise when spoken to by one higher in rank than yourselves."

Both men rose to their feet. Now that his vision was adapted to the half light, Hosea could discern, if not their features or expression, then that one was taller and younger than the other.

"I am the Judean," said the older of the two in a deep, strong voice, the syllables clear and deliberate.

Elinadab waited a moment and then asked angrily, "And say you not 'my lord' to one greater than you?"

"I know not my visitor," answered the Judean. "Nor if I knew him could I recognize him now, what with the sunlight streaming in from behind. Let him declare who he may be, and I shall pay him the honors which are his due."

The Judean was so much in the right and his amused tolerance so manifest that Elinadab, having bristled for a moment, had no recourse except to identify himself.

"I am Elinadab the priest, head of my house, kinsman of Amaziah. At the command of our lord, King Jeroboam, have I come hither to inquire whether it be so, as has been reported, that you have spoken treason against the king."

His wrath hot within him, he regained the initiative by turning to the other man.

"And who are you?"

"Your servant is a follower of the Judean prophet."

"So, he has followers, like a genuine seer. And what do you hear in his presence each day?"

"We talk."

"The word of the Lord, no doubt."

"Yes, my lord," the man responded, taking seriously what Elinadab intended as mockery. "He instructs me in the word of the Lord, both that which he has already declared to the people and that which is still unspoken. And when he permits, I write down the chief things he has spoken."

"You are a scribe?"

"No, my lord, your servant is a merchant, but not unskilled in letters."

"So you have a full account of what this Judean has said?"

"Not a full account, alas, but some."

"And where is this writing?"

There was an interval of silence before the man spoke again, and then with much caution in his words. "What would my lord want with this writing?"

"What? You dare question me?" Elinadab seethed. "When I ask, dare you inquire wherefore I ask?"

"Let not my lord be vexed with his servant," the man said with the haste of one who seeks to avert a threatening peril. "But the writing was sent only yesterday to acquaintances of the Judean prophet in Jerusalem. It would be much trouble to fetch it back again."

"Lie not to me," Elinadab interrupted angrily. "Do you think me a fool to be so easily deceived? I shall have that writing."

"Will my lord be angry if I say a word?" It was the Judean speaking now, slowly, calmly.

"Well, speak on."

"Wherefore should our master, the king's messenger, fret himself over the writing when I am not at all loath to declare it to him, to its last word."

"And why shall I trust you not to conceal what it profits you to conceal?"

"Hear me now, my lord. Wherefore should it profit me to conceal aught when it was to disclose all that I was taken by the Lord from tending my cattle?"

There was a persuasiveness to what the Judean said, but Elinadab, far from being appeased, was vexed yet further. Once again the right had somehow come out in favor of the Judean rather than with him. Torn therefore between wrath and reason, the priest turned all the more heatedly on the merchant.

"I will have you know that I am not deceived by you, and should I have the least need for the writings you will fetch them. Or you shall sit in the stocks before the shrine and be lashed each day until the hardness of your heart is departed from you. What is more, for your brazenness toward me, from this moment forth you will see this Judean no more. Do you attend?"

"Yes, my lord."

"And so that my bidding may be done, declare your name that I may give command in the household of my kinsman the high priest."

"My name is Amishadda the merchant."

"And your father and tribe?"

"My father is Reuel, also a merchant. We are of Manasseh from across the Jordan."

"Mean you Reuel the Gileadite?"

"Yea, so men call him."

Then Elinadab was perplexed and chagrined at the same time. For Reuel was of the great merchants of the land and, as was most rare among merchants, who were almost all newly-made men, the head of an ancient and distinguished house. Here, the priest told himself, there was need to walk carefully and yet not to shame himself by changing too abruptly. Wherefore he barked to the guard, "Is this man who he says?"

"Aye, my lord."

"Then we shall know how and where to find him. Meantime, as I said, he is to come here no more."

"So be it, my lord."

"Now go," he ordered.

The merchant bowed first to the priest and then to the

Judean, but the second lifted him up as he bent and the two men embraced, bidding each other peace, commending each other to the Lord's care.

"Peace be with thee in thy coming and going," said the older man. "May the God of Israel continue with thee."

"And with thee, master," said the younger, and, disentangling himself from the other's embrace, was gone.

After a moment's pause, Elinadab spoke. "It has been charged against you," he said, "by Amaziah the high priest and others also, that you have plotted rebellion against the king. What say you?"

There was still gruffness in Elinadab's manner, but less than was his wont. Hosea wondered whether it was because the Judean had been revealed as having powerful friends or because, having twice been set in the wrong by the Judean, he was on guard not to be shamed again. Then, remembering the priest's basic uprightness, he decided it was more of the latter than the former.

"It is not so, my lord. I have in no way conspired against the king." The answer was quiet but firm and assured, suggesting no contradiction.

The man was standing midway in the prison room, between its threshold and its further wall, so that no light reached his face to illumine it. But the outline of his frame could be discerned: neither tall nor short, broad of shoulder and deep of chest, powerful and yet in no way fleshy. Hosea's impression was of immovability and permanence. The impression was heightened by the imperishable skirts of his leather cloak, his columnlike legs, and his splayed, earth-clinging feet. He could also now discern a slender thong that was twined about the fingers of the man's right hand. It hung down almost to the ground and was tipped by some object of dull metal, shaped like an arrowhead but blunter, which swung gently to and fro. Looking at it, Hosea conjectured it to be some kind of amulet.

"Then said you not," Elinadab pursued, "that the people of this land would be led captive?"

"Aye, that I did say—and so it will come to pass."

"And of Jeroboam our king, that he would die by the sword?"

"Nay, that not, for the Lord disclosed it not to me."

"I do not understand," Elinadab cried in exasperation. "Part of what is charged against you, you admit. The rest you deny. Scribe, read to him the complaint of Amaziah and let this Judean say what in it he claims to be true and what false."

Hosea picked up the tablet he had inscribed the night before and read:

"So says Amaziah, high priest of Beth El, unto Jeroboam the king: 'Amos, a Judean from Tekoa, has conspired against thee and spoken words which the Lord cannot endure. He has said that Jeroboam shall die by the sword and the people of this land be led away captive.'"

"This is the indictment," Elinadab said. "Now what is your answer?"

"One part true, one part false, and one part half true and half false," said the Judean, with more than a suspicion of humor in his answer.

"By the altars of the sacred place, read me no riddles and stand not in the shade where your face is hidden. Step forward into the light so that I may discern your countenance and not your voice alone."

The man stepped forward. As the light poured onto his head and face, Hosea could see a great shaggy broom of dark hair and beard, a swarthy complexion, a strong aquiline nose, broad thin lips, and strong white teeth under his moustache—altogether the countenance of one of the desert folk, a Kenite or a son of

Kedar. Except for his eyes. These were large and startlingly blue, in their largeness and brightness almost ingenuous, like those of a child. And yet they were no child's eyes, for there was in them a knowledge of good and evil, an experience of pain and hope which made them older than the sum of his years.

"I meant not," he said, "to baffle my lord with riddles. But I must be clear. The part which is false, totally false, is that I have conspired against the throne. The part which is half false is that I prophesied that Jeroboam would die by the sword. I said only that the Lord would rise against his house with the sword." The man's humor ebbed away as he spoke. His eyes and voice chilled, the color fading from the former and the warmth from the latter. "As for the people of this land, it will be—woe unto them and me also—as I have foretold. The maiden Israel will fall; it cannot be otherwise. And if once she falls, she shall rise no more."

There was that in the intentness of his look and the tragic purport of his utterance that froze Hosea and even Elinadab. The priest shook his head slightly to throw off the spell. Coming to himself, he said harshly, "But still you have threatened the king's house with the sword."

"But master," Hosea broke in eagerly, "if this Judean spoke as he says, the offense is less. For to say that the Lord shall raise the sword against the House of Jeroboam is not to say that He will overthrow it. And observe, this Judean said that it was to be against the House of Jeroboam that the sword will be raised, the house mind you, not the king himself. But that may be at any time, perhaps in the days of his son or grandson, or even later. And though thanks to our king this land has long been free from war, can one expect peace forever?"

"Did you not read me aright yesterday on the road? And was it not this I feared, a scribe who mingles himself with this which is my business?" Elinadab bellowed. "Who has asked you to appoint yourself this man's advocate? And now, hear me, scribe, speak no more, save at my bidding. Or as the Lord dwells in this place you shall be whipped from this city and I shall let it be known to the king what manner of bold-faced dogs minister to him.

"And even if it be so as you say," Elinadab said, now quieter, "that the offense is less, it is the word of this Judean against the high priest of Beth El. Who then is to be believed?"

"Nay, my lord," Amos corrected, some of his earlier calm returning to him, "it is the word of the servants of the high priest, for he himself was not present when I spoke, and it is their word not against mine but against the multitude who heard me, of whom many remain in Beth El."

"But why should the servants lie concerning your utterance?"

"Not lie, my lord," the Judean answered, his playfulness now flowing back. "Far be it from me to suggest that the servants of the high priest might lie. But exaggeration, yes, they being mortal men, of that they are capable. All the more since the graver their report, the more important they make themselves out to their master. And as for the high priest—well, my lord, he loves not prophets in general and in particular prophets who walk alone like myself."

"As the Lord lives, you are a plucky one," said Elinadab. "Overbold to be sure, presumptuous and arrogant, but by no means deficient in courage."

"Scribe," he ordered Hosea, "sit down and write on your tablet—after the place where you have recorded the complaint of the high priest—as follows: 'The Judean, however, answers that his words were otherwise, being as follows.' And now," he instructed Amos, "say it for yourself."

The Judean closed his eyes to recall the words he had used, then brought them forth in a chant like a lamentation, infinitely burdened, and so potent that the priest and scribe alike—one standing unbending in his arrogance and the other seated cross-legged on the floor, his face raised, his stylus poised expectantly—remained motionless until it was finished.

> *And my Lord declared:*
> *"I am going to apply a plumb line to My people Israel;*
> *I will pardon them no more.*
> *The shrines of Isaac shall be laid waste,*
> *And the sanctuaries of Israel laid to ruins;*
> *And I will turn upon the House of Jeroboam*
> *with the sword."*

The chant died away, leaving a preternatural stillness. Hosea busied himself to write what he had just heard, which persisted in his mind so vividly that his stylus flowed without hesitancy to the end. Elinadab stirred. The Judean opened his eyes like one awakening from slumber.

"These were the words, my lord, not one altered, which I spoke in the Broad Place."

"So you swear?"

"In the name of Israel's God."

Elinadab studied the Judean for a while.

"Sit down," he commanded. "I have more to inquire and it will be wearisome to stand so long."

"But how shall I sit when my master stands?"

Elinadab looked about the chamber. Except for a water pitcher and a straw mat, it was empty of furnishings.

"Will my master sit, perhaps, on one of these mats? The floor is no novelty to me."

The Judean stooped toward the mat to draw it near.

"Nay, I will not," said Elinadab.

"Then if it troubles my lord not, let me stand also. It would not be fitting—"

"Sit down, as I command," Elinadab said gruffly, unwilling to reveal his cognizance of the herdsman's courtesy. "And enough of this 'do you sit,' 'nay do you.' It was not for such talk that I have come hither."

The herdsman nodded and lowered himself to the floor, but crouching on his heels as shepherds are wont to do about their fires, so that he might be lower than Elinadab, but not too far. The leather thong he had wound up about his wrist as he sank down, so that the metal tip continued to swing gently, clearing the floor. He looked up expectantly.

"Hear now, Judean," the priest began. "I have more to ask you, questions which may or may not touch on the complaint of the high priest. If it turns out that they do, the answers will have worth should you come to trial. But even if not, I would have you respond to them. You are a strange fellow, perhaps a mad one, but you have awakened my curiosity. I would know what manner of thoughts are within you."

"Whatever the reason," Amos said, "let my lord ask, and I shall answer as best I can."

"Then first tell me this. Is it the burden of your prophecy that the Lord, who is Israel's God, means to destroy His own people?"

"Yes, master."

"But His own people?"

"All peoples are His."

"And Ashur and Baal and Chemosh, whom the Assyrians and the Canaanites and the Moabites worship?"

"These are things of naught, the imaginings of men."

"So it was a thing of naught which made Assyria great."

"Not he but our God."

"All the world says one thing and you say otherwise. Who is to be believed, all the world or one man?"

"The one man, my lord, if the truth be with him."

"The truth!" Elinadab laughed scornfully. "Has greater foolishness been spoken? Foolishness? Nay, madness, to suggest that the God of Israel would make great not his own people but some other. Think you the Lord so witless that He should do so? Who is it that brings Him sacrifices? Israel or Assyria?"

"What are sacrifices to Him who made the Pleiades and Orion, who turns deep darkness into dawn, and darkens day into night?"

"What are sacrifices? They are the gifts that incline Him to look with favor on those who seek His face."

"Is the Lord, then, some covetous village elder who, save for a bribe, will not judge a cause? And was there any time when the Lord's favor toward Israel was more manifest than when He led her and fed her and made miracles for her on the way out of Egypt?"

"What then?" Elinadab asked.

"What then? Were sacrifices brought to the Lord those forty years in the wilderness?"

Addled by the argument, Elinadab was tempted to anger, the more so as the Judean smiled up at him—the smile with which a grown man regards a child's fancies. But the priest restrained himself, for to show vexation would be to confess defeat. Whereupon he bridled his spirit and changed the subject.

"This prophecy of yours, concerning the house of the king, why should the Lord raise the sword against it? Declare that, since you know His heart so intimately."

"I know only what He has seen fit to reveal to me."

"And has He seen fit to reveal this?"

"Aye," Amos replied quietly. "For two sins of the house of our king will the Lord raise up the sword against it, and both sins of blood. For the blood of Joram, king of Israel, who was slain by Jehu so that he might set himself and his descendants on the throne of Israel where they sit to this day. And for the blood of the poor of the land, who are oppressed and despoiled that the rich may lie at their ease on their ivory couches, and though the word of this comes to the king he hinders it not, but elects rather to have the favor of the rich, the great nobles and merchants and—let my lord forgive me—the chief of the priests. For they are the strong and of profit to the king, whereas the poor—"

But this was too much for Elinadab, who trembled with rage.

"Silence," he thundered, stepping closer to the Judean, his fists raised to smite him. "Silence, I say, or as the Lord resides here in Beth El, I will beat you into a proper awe for the great of the land. I have heard enough, whether from you or anyone else, of that moldy scandal of how the house of our king, may he live forever, came to the throne. A hundred years it is by now. And as for that other babbling about rich and poor, what would you do instead, you Judean worm? Would you overturn the pillars of the world? Would you undo the decrees of the Lord Himself? For who makes one poor and one rich, one weak and one strong, if not the very God in whose name you speak? And by what warrant? Answer me, and hold not back, or I shall beat you yet."

"I shall not hold back."

There was no fear in the Judean's voice, no averting of his face, no throwing up of an arm to protect himself against the impending blow, not even a stiffening of his square shoulders.

"Then speak."

"It is the Lord who has commanded me to say these things."

"The Lord, say you? Which would make you a prophet. And yet there is not in you one token of prophecy."

"Does my lord mean that I wear not a goatskin cloak? If that be the proof of a prophet, then I am none."

"And possession, has the Lord ever possessed you?"

"So that I fell in a stupor or was beside myself with ecstasy, uttering strange words and making wild movements? Nay, by that sign too I am no prophet."

"And as for being a member of a company of prophets, that also you are not. Then, will you tell me, wherein and by virtue of what are you rendered a prophet?"

"Because the word of the Lord has come to me."

"Where, how, in whose presence that he may serve as witness to confirm what you say?"

"In my own heart. And there is no witness, save my heart."

"Ho," Elinadab hooted, "a prophet of the Lord he calls himself, and when he is asked for evidence he answers that he must be a prophet only because he says so."

"That I am not worthy to bear the Lord's burden I know. But He chooses for his messengers whom He desires, sometimes a king of Israel like Saul, but sometimes also a farmer in Gilead, as was Elijah."

"And now, having chosen the herdsmen of the land, he may elect the potters next and after them the beggars and after them the scavengers until there be no churl anywhere from Dan to Beersheva on whom His hand has not rested."

"And why not, my lord? What was the word Moses said when they brought him the report that Eldad and Medad were prophesying in the midst of the camp and asked that he restrain them? Said not Moses then, 'Would that all the people of the Lord were prophets'?"

All through their contention, Elinadab's face had been red for passion and shouting. Now his cheeks flared even more, until they were like those of one smitten with the burning plague. He bit his lips and glared at Amos.

"Well then, Judean," Elinadab said. "You speak in the name of the God of Israel. Let Him afford you a sign and wonder that you can show us, and I shall believe that you are indeed His prophet. Nor need it be some great sign. I do not ask that you turn my staff to a serpent as did Moses or cause it to flower as for Aaron. Let it be a little wonder, the tiniest. Let the sun brighten at your prayer or tell me what have I at home in my black chest which is in my bedchamber or where may I find the seal ring of onyx and gold which I once had. Do any of these or one akin to them, and I shall not only believe you myself, but I shall proclaim to all the world that it is indeed the Lord who has sent you. A tiny sign," Elinadab taunted, "the merest dust of a wonder."

Amos studied him, the blue of his eyes icing again as once before.

"I shall give you a sign," he said rising, "a sign but not a wonder."

The Judean undid the leather thong from his wrist. "See you this, my lord? Know you what it is?" He caught the metal object at its end, and held it out first to Elinadab and then to Hosea.

The priest and Hosea considered it in turn.

"A charm?" Elinadab asked. Hosea shrugged his shoulders.

"Nay, my lord, nothing so marvelous. Merely a plumb line, a cord with a lead weight attached to it such as masons use to test a wall of hewn stone or brick whether it be true. And now here..."

He turned away to a corner of the room, stooped quickly and came back carrying in his hands four hollow cubes of clay, each a span as to length and breadth.

"These," he explained, "are builder's tiles. And now see what I show you."

He bent over and piled the tiles one onto another so that they formed a pillar, as high as almost to a man's hip.

"What say you, my lord, and you, scribe. Are these straight or crooked?"

"Straight," said Elinadab.

"So they seem to me," Hosea agreed.

"Then let us see."

Unfurling the cord, he let it fall along one surface of the pillar. The lead weight swung back and forth at first before it stilled. As it did so, the weight fell before them by as much as two fingers breadths.

"You see, my lord the priest and you the scribe, the tiles by the eye seem straight but by the plumb line are proved crooked, leaning forward toward you. Now I shall show you something more."

He raised his bare foot and brought it down onto the ground near the tiles. They shook, shifted the least bit one on the other but did not fall. He stamped again, and a third time, and the fourth, and still the tiles stood. But they had been unsettled more than could be perceived and with the fifth tread they swayed and toppled.

"They were crooked one with another," Amos interpreted, "therefore they could not stand. One blow they resisted and another and yet another, but in the end they fell; it could not be otherwise but that they must fall, seeing that they were not straight."

He looked at them but detected no comprehension on their faces.

"This is my sign, do you not understand it?"

"This a sign?" Elinadab asked bewilderedly.

"Aye, my lord. Do you not see that as was the column of tiles, so is the House of Jehu? It stands on an uneven place, having been established in murder; it is built awry since it troubles not itself with the injustices of the land. Therefore I say it cannot continue to stand. But so too is all the House of Israel, crooked with the Lord its God, crooked one man with his fellow, the merchants with their dishonest weights to those who buy from them, the masters by oppression and overreaching to their servants, the priests by their greed and corruption with the worshipers, the wives with their adulteries and extravagances to their husbands, and husbands with their whorings and resorting to the groves, and all by their idolatries to the gods. Therefore, even before the word of the Lord came to me, did I know that this people would fall, that sooner or later but inevitably it must fall.

"Only I knew not how. Then came the locust of two years ago and I said: this is a trampling from on high, and I prayed, 'O Lord God, forgive I pray Thee. How shall Jacob continue to stand? For he is little.' And the Lord repented of the evil, but Israel repented not.

"And now, this year, the Lord stomps again: the drought is upon us, even now devouring the great deep and the tilled land. Therefore each day I pray to Him, 'Lord God, forbear. How shall Jacob continue to stand? For he is little.' But the people heed not, neither king nor priest nor prince, but continue in their evil, crooked ways. Perhaps this time too He will be merciful.

"But not forever. Unless Israel learns to do good that it may live, there will be a third treading more terrible than these. Whence may it come? I have looked to see and I have found it. There to the north a fierce people has arisen, swift as the hawk, savage as the leopard, mighty as the lion. And when I saw it, I understood wherefore the locust and drought had come upon us. These were warnings from the Lord wherewith He desired to turn us from our evil ways before it is too late.

"For if once he brings the Assyrians upon us, then as little will remain of this people as a shepherd may save of his lamb from the lion, a pair of shinbones mayhap or the flap of an ear."

"But the sign," Elinadab broke in impatiently. "Where is the sign."

"This is the sign," Amos answered and held up his plumb line again, indicating with his toe the pile of tiles lying helter-skelter or one upon the other. "And as for what they signify, it is that the crooked shall not endure but only the straight shall stand."

"This," Elinadab jeered, "this piece of lead and a pile of bricks!"

"What thinks my lord," the Judean hurled back, "that the Lord deals in one law for things and another for man? Nay, so surely as one sun shines over all, as God has ordained, so sure is there but one law, also of his ordaining, for all, whether for kings or kingdoms, Israel or the nations, men or tiles, and that law is, as I have said, that the crooked shall not stand but only the straight endure."

Elinadab clapped his palms to his temples, tilted back his head to look toward heaven, shook it from side to side so that his beard waved to and fro like a flapping banner.

"And this, O God of Israel," he cried, "this he calls a sign."

Then he chuckled. "As is the sign, so is the prophet. Aye, prophet and sign are equal." After which he laughed, then laughed again and then laughed more, so violently, with ever mightier gusts and spasms until he shook all over and, ceasing to clasp his head, drew his hands down from his temples to his belly to hold it in. Meantime, with wisps of breath he wheezed now and again, looking toward Hosea in unspoken invitations to him to join in his mirth.

"This he calls a sign.... Like prophet, like sign.... He throws down tiles...and says it is from the Lord...a sign...a wonder."

With each utterance the priest burst into fresh paroxysms, renewing his glances at Hosea.

But Hosea did not laugh.

• • •

WHEN HOSEA RETURNED from the house of detention to the palace of the high priest, he could not think clearly at all. For what he had heard quietly spoken from the lips of the Judean had broken over him like a mighty storm, its thunderclaps shaking the earth to the foundation. Then, later, as his mind cleared, he realized that those truths uttered by the prophet—making small the merit of sacrifices, elevating the worth of good deeds—were familiar to the point of evoking his father Beeri. Yet Amos's wisdom was new and unimaginable.

How long, Hosea reflected, had he puzzled over the gods of the nations? Yet was it not clear as the dawn, once it had been said so, that only the Lord is God, whereas the others are—he did not know what—but in any case no gods at all. And was it not manifest, as the Judean had asserted, that the laws of things are not to one side and those of men to another, but both alike are the ordinances of God who made one sun to shine over all the earth and commanded one righteousness over all its families?

A hunger arose in Hosea, a hunger and a thirst to see and hear the prophet again. Whether he was truly a prophet Hosea had no doubt. He longed to ask of him countless questions, some vague as mists, but others keen, hard, and as unbearable as flints in the flesh.

Therefore, having ascertained that Elinadab had no present need of him, Hosea came again at the hour of noon to the house of detention. But this time the guard would not admit him. Instead he sat on the ground midway down the alleyway, not troubling to rise for a mere scribe and not speaking, for he was taking his repast and his mouth was full. He only shook his head in refusal.

"And why not?" Hosea protested.

The soldier worked an olive pit free in his mouth and spat it forth. "You heard with your own ears what your master said."

"But I am his servant, his scribe."

"Is it at his command you come?"

"No."

"Have you a writ from him authorizing your entrance?"

"No."

"Then bring one such and I shall admit you, and let it be sealed with his seal, for I cannot read letters."

So saying, the guard reached into an open pouch before him on the ground, wrenched a piece of bread from a loaf, picked up another olive, and continued eating.

"Then do not open the door but permit me to speak with him from outside. That my master did not forbid."

"Who knows of these exalted persons what they mean to permit or forbid? Say you stand outside and speak. You are seen. Your master says that this, too, he wished to prevent. What befalls you I care not. But this I know, that if I should be lashed, you will not take the blows on my behalf. If I am dismissed from the employment of my lord, the high priest, you will not sustain the children of my house. As I said before, a sealed writ."

"Very well," Hosea capitulated, "I shall seek one from my master. But what," he added anxiously, "if he grants it not?"

"Then," the soldier mumbled through his food, "you do not see the Judean." He swallowed and his speech cleared. "I sit here all day and have no desire to look on his face or hear his voice. Why should you?"

Without hope of making the fellow understand, Hosea said only, "It is important to me."

Something of Hosea's urgency came through to the guard. The man studied his face, chewing slowly. "Important, you say," he said at last.

"Aye."

"Mean you, truly important?"

"Truly."

"But if so, you will pay a little something, not too large a sum, half a shekel, for instance?"

"To whom?" Hosea inquired, unsuspecting.

"To whom?" the guard countered in amazement. "Why, to me, of course."

"But that would be a—"

"A bribe. If so, what then? Is there anyone in Samaria who does not take rewards? What are the sacrifices and the portions the priests take, and the heave offerings and the tithes and the royal levies, but bribes? Save that they go to the priests and Levites, so the king and nobles are therefore called by names of good repute. Nor do any of them risk a beating as do I."

"Nonetheless, I like it not," Hosea insisted.

"You like it not? Then bring me a writ and a seal."

But Hosea was not at all certain that a writ could be procured.

"If it is necessary—the gift, I mean—how shall it be done?"

The soldier thought for a moment.

"It must be by night, in the dark," he said slowly, thinking his way along. "Otherwise, it will not be safe. I stand sentry here from the end of the first watch of the day to the end of the first watch of the evening. Then another comes to relieve me. But it is now the summer season. The sun is slow to set and its afterglow lingers long. The time then is short between the onset of darkness and the end of my round. But it will have to suffice you. The one who replaces me is not a bad fellow and not averse to silver. Nevertheless, as men say, the fewer in the secret, the safer. Besides, the captain of the guard comes at times at that hour to supervise the change of guards. I don't want him to find you here."

"But how long," Hosea asked anxiously, "might it be between dusk and the end of your watch?"

"At this time of the year," the man estimated, "about one quarter of a watch."

"Little enough," Hosea mused. "Well, we shall have to see. I shall speak to my master. If he is gracious, I shall return this day with a writ—yes, and a seal on it. If not, you will see me...there is no other way...as soon as it grows dark."

"And a half shekel in hand," the guard reminded.

•   •   •

THE QUESTION OF HOW HOSEA might find occasion to lay his request before Elinadab agitated him all his way back to the palace. However, the solution presented itself during his noon repast while he sat in the common room of the free men.

The body servant of Elinadab came over to Hosea and summoned him to their master's presence.

His arms laden with shards, tablets, a papyrus scroll, a leather sheet, reed pens, and a stylus, and an ink horn dangling from his girdle, Hosea appeared before the priest in his chamber.

Elinadab was manifestly in a fouler than usual mood.

"Sit down, man," was his greeting to Hosea. "Can you write standing up? Or must I instruct you in everything, even when to cover your feet and how to clean yourself afterward?"

At the crudity of the last remark, Hosea bridled. But he remembered that he wished a favor of the priest. He bit his lip, seated himself cross-legged on the floor before a low table, arranged his writing supplies, and waited to be told what to write.

Elinadab was apparently too full of indignation to be concerned with whom he was speaking. He began to stalk the room.

"I would have you know," he said, "that the high priest and I spoke today concerning the self-styled prophet and what needs to be done with him. We proved not of one mind. The man must be executed, he insists. The fool! To bring to trial one who has powerful followers, on charges which are in all likelihood false—for I believe the Judean on that score rather than Amaziah, though he be my cousin and the high priest of Beth El—when it is safer merely to expel him from the country. He called the Judean dangerous. 'Dangerous!'" Elinadab here mimicked Amaziah's high-pitched voice. "I admit there is some danger in the unruly things the Judean has said, and in his followers. But not half so much as my precious cousin and his counsels fear.

"Therefore, hear now, scribe. I know the heart of my kinsman. He must have his way, though it may be folly and injustice, lest he burst himself and destroy the world in getting it. When I rendered my decision, he refused to release the Judean, denying that my authority supersedes his. And this very moment—I am as sure of it as if I had seen it with my own eyes—he is devising letters to be sent to Samaria contending that since he is high priest it is conducive to the public order that the final word rests with him. But I will forestall him. He shall not shame me so or do the injustice he devises.

"Therefore, scribe, write first of all to the king himself. Do it on shards first that we may correct it before inscribing it on leather or papyrus. Write as follows:

"To our master, Jeroboam, the anointed of the Lord to be king of Israel, may he live forever, vanquishing his enemies and conferring his great mercies on his friends, from Elinadab the priest, the least of his servants.

"My lord, I did come to Beth El, in accordance with my lord's command, in the matter of the Judean who claims to be a prophet, against whom Amaziah, son of Hophni, the high priest of Beth El, has made complaint, saying that the Judean has conspired against our lord the king.

"Having inquired diligently, it has become clear to me that the report concerning the utterance of the Judean which was brought to the high priest, for he heard it not with his own ears, departs somewhat from the truth, that the Judean conspired not against our lord the king, nor did he say that our lord the king—the Lord protect him from all evil—would fall by the sword.

"Nevertheless, Amaziah, out of his devotion to our master's house, did not investigate the report but believed it, and, out of his zeal for the welfare of our lord the king, wishes to execute the Judean, in which counsel he persists to the present.

"From which counsel I, your servant Elinadab, depart, saying that it would not be in the king's interest to do as the high priest urges. For the Judean has many who can testify that he spoke not as is charged against him, and among them men of wealth and station in Beth El and other cities of the land. And to what advantage will it be to the king that a tumult shall arise unnecessarily? As for the words of the Judean, of them some are wise and others foolish, some obedient, others preposterous. There is danger in them, but the man is but a herdsman and not a true prophet. And would it be seemly for a great king to contend with such a one?

"Let it be good then in the sight of our lord the king that this Judean be expelled from the land, for so we shall be rid of him and his words alike, and yet we shall have stirred up no strife and shed no innocent blood.

"And may it be good further in thy sight, my lord the king, that instruction be sent to Amaziah bidding him in this matter to bow to the word of your servant who is the king's messenger, for though your letter to this effect was set before the high priest he heeds it not, out of his devotion, no doubt, to the welfare of our lord the king."

"Now, read it over to me," Elinadab ordered Hosea.

In the fierceness of his anger he had spoken the letter in a rush, not stopping to think what next should be written, indeed scarcely pausing for breath. But Hosea, who had kept up with him not only easily but willingly, once the purport of the letter had become clear, read it back accurately and fluently. Elinadab listened, ordering now one small correction, now another, smiling from the first line onward ever more broadly with satisfaction.

"This will do," he pronounced. "I shall not mar it by writing to others in the palace. Wherefore should the king think that it does not suffice me to address him alone? That mistake we shall leave to my cousin. As for you, scribe, you will copy this over onto the finest leather in your most careful script. Put onto the ending the usual greetings to the king and benedictions for his welfare and bring it to me, that I may seal it and send it off by fleet messenger. And delay not, for if it is dispatched by sundown it will be in the king's hands in the morning. We go forth tomorrow to Gilgal."

This was not welcome news. Even the matter of the sending of a letter to Samaria and awaiting its answer, for all that it pleased him for the prophet's sake, had an unpleasant aspect of which he only now took notice. Inevitably, it would postpone their return to Samaria. But no more than that, if the king was prompt to reply by not more than two days. This was to be an affair of perhaps as much as a week, he reflected, a long time for a man to be apart from his wife and child and household, not only for him but for them also who expected not so long an absence. He must remember, he instructed himself, to ask the courier to inform his household of the turn of events. But Elinadab was speaking again, and Hosea turned his attention to what the priest was saying:

"I had not thought to go to Gilgal, but now I shall. The king did say that if it was convenient to me I should visit the shrine both to see that all is well with it and to bring sacrifices there in his name. Since wait we must in any case—two, three days—I shall meantime go off to Gilgal and return thence and so be able to say, when I look again on the face of the king, that I have fulfilled his word. Nay, hold now. Why shall I wait till then? Do you, scribe, write also on the letter that though he commanded not but merely suggested it, I, his servant, depart at once to Gilgal, knowing that when I come hither again the verdict of his wisdom will greet me. Scratch something at once to this effect that I may see it before it is copied onto leather."

To frame the letter Elinadab had requested was nothing for Hosea, and his stylus was soon quiet. Meantime, he reflected, since on the morrow they would depart from Beth El, he must speak his request either now or later that day, when he brought back the finished letter.

"I have finished, my lord," he said.

"Read it, read it."

Hosea read the lines he had composed.

"Good," Elinadab said. "Now get you to your chamber. And remember, let not a breath of this be breathed."

This is as favorable an occasion as would arise, Hosea judged, now that Elinadab was so exhilarated by the coup he had devised against Amaziah.

"If it please my lord," he began.

"Yes? Yes?"

"I would ask a kindness of my master."

"Just at this time when there is that which needs urgently to be attended to?"

"Aye, my lord, for if not now, I know not when it may be."

"Well, what is it? Speak, loiter not."

"I would have my lord's permission to see the Judean in the house of detention."

"And wherefore?"

"I would speak with him."

"Concerning what? What business can you have with him?"

"Concerning his prophecies."

"Prophecies? Is it so you call his babbling?"

There was no other course except to face up to Elinadab.

"So they appear to me."

"I wonder not. Did I not detect in you the first time I laid eyes on you that fire of insubordination, which burns no less in the adherents of these self-sent prophets?"

"But," Hosea protested, "you yourself defend him to the king—"

"Against the charge of treason," Elinadab yelled, "against that of which he is innocent. Think you therefore that he is not guilty of other offenses: of reviling those better than himself, seeking to overturn the world by dragging down the exalted of the land and raising up the lowly beyond their station, and speaking lightly of the house of our lord the king and the temples of the Lord, God of Israel? Nay, you shall not see him."

• • •

WHEN THE SENTRIES WHO STOOD at the threshold of the palace of the high priest crossed their spears before him, denying him exit, Hosea's heart sank. It had not occurred to him that permission might be required for going forth at twilight.

"Whither bound?" asked one of the guards. "Is it that there are no women in the shrine, that you must be going forth both by day and by night?

"The sacred prostitutes in the grove of the shrine beckon," the scribe responded, "and, having done his duties to God, is not a man entitled to take his pleasure?"

His ploy had worked, but it filled him with disgust when he realized that it was for jest the sentries had stopped him. He contrived to smile, brushed the crossed spears upward to clear a way for himself, and strode through. Yet since it was better that they continue to think as they did, he walked first toward the sacred grove.

After a short distance, he turned into a side street from which he might backtrack to his actual destination.

But in that short distance, the music of drunken revelry and shouts of debauchery came loud to his ears, first from the groves to either side of the road and then, as he progressed, from the pleasure houses.

With what heart, he wondered bitterly, come the men who favored these places over their homes? How ventured they to come near their wives, when their limbs still smelled of the perfumes of other women? And all this with no expiation or atonement. For an accident in the night, some dream in which his seed came forth he must purify himself, else he may not touch anything holy, let alone enter a shrine? Yet is not the person of one's wife, was not Gomer, to him a sacred thing, and was not coming into her like entering into a sanctuary? It was a twofold desecration therefore which was here perpetrated: the name of God was profaned and the person of the wife of one's bosom defiled. This too was a crookedness—surely the Judean would say so—for which a people might fall. This much he knew.

"So, you came after all," the guard whispered at the entrance to the alleyway, "and took your time about it too. It is some while since nightfall, which means that your time is so much the shorter."

"Then let us hasten."

"The half shekel first. Good. And now, a word of instruction. It will not be long before I am relieved. You will therefore be prepared to come out of the prison house as soon as I ask it and take yourself off. But if the other guard or the captain is at hand before you can leave the alleyway, then pretend to be at ease. I shall say that you are a friend who has come to converse with me. And now come, I shall bring you to the door and slide the bolt for you. In this dark, you will never find your own way. Now do you go first, ahead of me. I shall guide you from behind. And my hand is on my dagger against treachery, should such be your purpose."

Guided from behind by the guard's touch, his own hands out to the walls on either side, cautiously setting one foot before the other, Hosea made his way down the alleyway.

"The door is before you," the guard whispered. Put forth your hand and feel for it. Then find the bolt. It pulls to the right."

"I have it."

"Then go in. I shall leave it open that you may come forth quickly if the necessity arise."

Hosea pulled at the bar, pushed on the door, and stood peering into the solid, soundless darkness. Now that the moment was at hand, he did not know what to say, nor even by how to address the Judean, whether by name or as a prophet. Indeed, he was not even sure that the man was awake. But the moments were precious, and he must speak. Therefore he uttered the first word that occurred to him, recognizing only later that of all possible salutations, this one was supremely appropriate.

"Master," he whispered, "master, do you sleep?"

"Nay," a voice sounded from below and before him. "Who is it that calls me master?"

"It is I, the scribe who came here yesterday with Elinadab the priest."

"And what would your master have with me?"

"I have not come on his behalf, but on my own."

"And what would you?"

"If it please my master, I would hear, if it please him to grant my request, more of the Lord's word which is in him. And let him not fear to speak to me, for though I serve Elinadab my heart is not with him in this matter."

"Do not seek to reassure me," the Judean said softly. "I do not fear men. Nor is it a labor but a refreshment to me to tell to another what the Lord has set in my soul. Do not the herdsmen say, 'More than the calf desires to suckle, the cow desires to feed.' Besides, I did mark your face and manner when you were here yesterday, and I did know that you are one of ours, not theirs. Who are you, my son? What is your name and your house? And who readied you for my word, for few are they whose ears are open to it."

"My name is Hosea, the son of Beeri, of an Ephraimite house in Jezreel. I am one of the king's scribes in Samaria. As for my nurture, my father and his fathers have all been of those who revere the Lord and His messengers, as do I after them. But never did I hear from him, nor from any of the prophets, such sayings as came from your lips, sayings like light and flame. Therefore my soul has had no rest within me, for having heard this little I must hear more. But master, I came here unauthorized and in defiance of Elinadab's order, having bribed the guard who stands outside. Therefore may I not be found here when the guard is changed. The time is short, what I wish to hear long. Let it be good therefore in my master's sight to speak to me not about myself or other unimportant matters, but concerning the truth he has to impart."

"Then let me rise, Hosea, as is proper for the utterance of the

Lord's word. So also shall we stand together, as befits men who are brothers. Now," he continued, his voice on a level with Hosea, "concerning what would you have me speak?"

"I scarcely know. I have so many questions to ask."

"Ask, my son, whatever your heart prompts, and I shall answer briefly that you may ask again."

"Then tell me this first, master. You have spoken a burden of doom on our people. Is there then no hope for it?"

"None, unless the people cease to do evil and learn to seek good."

"But is there no hope for this, for their repentance?"

"Once I did think so. Is not the Lord's word true and mighty? And has He not raised out of the children of this people prophets to declare it and Nazarites to show how it may be obeyed? But the Nazarites they make drunk with wine and the prophets they command to 'prophesy not,' for they love their evil way and will not be turned from it. So sin piles on sin until the weight is too great to bear."

He paused for a moment and then continued.

"Hear now, Hosea. I am a man of the fields. There in the open, one has much to learn. Have you been ever in the country in the harvest season?"

"Yes, master. Often."

"Then you too have seen this. It happens sometimes that the crop is large and the farmer brings his oxen and wagon into the field to carry the sheaves to the threshing floor. And he piles the grain onto the wagon, more and more and more. And men say to him, 'Cease, for the wagon will break.' But he heeds them not. He heaps more onto it, until it creaks under the burden. Now they caution him again. But—how often have my own eyes not seen this—he will not be counseled. And so, in the end, the wheels spread or the axle cracks or the wagon is burst altogether and the sheaves are spilled, and all is lost. Hosea, my son, the whole House of Israel is a wagon, a wagon which creaks to heaven, and still they pile on their sins in sheaves. What shall be the end?"

Hard and bitter were these words in Hosea's heart, too hard and bitter to be swallowed. Therefore he resisted them. "But is there with God no other way? Is there in Him no power to mitigate the judgment, though the judgment be just?"

"What, would you have God do injustice?"

"But are we not His people whom He brought out of Egypt?"

"All peoples are His. Did He not bring up the Philistines from Caphtor and Aram from Kir?"

"Then is our sin greater than theirs?"

"No. The evils we do they commit, and more also. Did not the Assyrians thresh Gilead as with sleds with iron runners? Has not Edom attacked as from behind? Did not the Moabites render an abomination in the dealings of nations when they desecrated the sepulcher of the king of Edom by burning his bones to lime? Over all these, too, His judgment impends."

"But if we are not set apart by our God for special blessing, which would not be equitable, shall we be set aside for a special curse?"

"It is just. For it is to us that He has revealed His word. Our offenses are knowing; theirs are blind. Them therefore He may rightfully spare, but not us."

"But master," Hosea said apologetically, "the judgment is so harsh. Though it may be merited I am loath to acknowledge it, for I love this land and this people."

"And think you," Amos asked softly, "that I do not?"

There was then, Hosea reflected, no escaping it. This land would fall; since the Lord was just, it could not be otherwise. But why would they not hear or heed, this people destined to exile and death?

As though he had heard Hosea's thoughts, Amos addressed the question.

"This people, though it talks much of the Lord, knows Him little. They think Him small, whereas He is most great, beyond all conceiving or expressing.

"It is because they deem Him small that they make images of Him, setting up the idol of a golden bullock and saying of it, 'This is thy God, O Israel, who made heaven and earth and brought thee out of the land of Egypt.' This to a thing of gold.

"Deeming Him small and knowing the world to be great, they cannot imagine that He alone shall rule over it. And so they set up other gods, each over some land, to divide the kingship with Him, as though He who is mighty enough to bring one sun over the earth cannot rule over its peoples.

"Deeming Him small, they know not what it is He desires of them."

"And what might that be, Master?"

"What but justice! Even as His word came to me and as I declared before the multitude at the Festival of the Ingathering:

"I hate," says the Lord, "I despise your festivals;
I take no delight in your sacred assemblies;
Though you bring me burnt offerings
*   and your meal offerings*
I will not be pleased,
And to your peace offerings of fatted calves I will not look.
Remove from me the noise of your songs
To the playing of your lutes I will not listen.
But let justice roll on like waters,
And righteousness like an unfailing stream."

The Judean, quoting his prophecy, had slipped into the soft, sad chant in which he had spoken once before in Hosea's presence.

Then as now, there was in it a spell that filled Hosea with joy, so that he felt as might a strong man summoned forth to run a course, but also with awe, born of the knowledge that He who summoned him was more than man. Such, he thought, and chilled to think it, is the power of the word of the Lord.

"Master," he whispered, speaking impulsively or he would never have presumed to say it, "how comes the Lord to his servant? How is it with you when His hand is upon you, His spirit within?"

The response came not from the Judean but from the guard outside.

"Scribe, you have talked enough. Your time is ended."

"But I have not yet begun," Hosea started to protest.

"You did promise," the guard reminded him, "that you would depart as soon as I required it. What would you? To be found here?"

"You must go," Amos interceded, "for your sake and his—for the sake of all of us. As for the questions left unanswered: had I the years of the hills of old, I could not cause you to feel what I have felt when the Lord descends on me."

"But there are other matters also," Hosea said humbly, "which, being not clear, burn within me."

Amos laughed softly, but without mirth.

"Think you, my son, that the answers to all riddles have been spread before me?"

"But the word of the Lord—"

"Aye, the word of the Lord is light. Yet every light, though it illumines, also casts shadows. So with every revelation one darkness is illumined, but another, hitherto unsuspected, revealed."

"Even so, even if there be some questions you cannot answer, there are others in your power. What of these? Having gone hence, who knows whether I shall see you again to speak—"

The guard outside muttered angrily. "Was not this my word, that when the time came—"

"Fret not, brother," Amos interposed calmly. "He will be gone in a moment."

He turned to Hosea. "If God wills it, we shall meet. If not, all my word is available to you. Go you to the home of Amishadda, the son of Reuel the Gileadite, the merchant who was here when first you came with the priest. Bid him show you the scroll of my prophecies."

"Then it was not sent to Jerusalem?"

"One copy, another remaining here. Amishadda spoke neither the truth nor altogether a falsehood."

"But will he believe me? And you too, master, that you trust me so, and I unknown."

This time there was a ring of gaiety to Amos's laughter. "It was not great venture, and your face like a polished mirror. But as for Amishadda it may be another matter. Therefore I will give you a token. Come, take it."

In the thick darkness the men groped each for the other. Their hands met, and the Judean placed an object in Hosea's palm.

"What may this be, master?"

"It is the plummet. Amishadda will know its meaning, as do you."

Hosea's fingers closed about it.

"Go now, and the Lord be with you."

"And with you, now and forever."

That night, when Hosea sat in the house of Amishadda, copying the utterances of Amos's, the words he recorded were no sooner written in ink than they were blurred with his tears.

• • •

NO ONE WILLINGLY DESCENDS TO GILGAL during the summer. The place to be sure is among the holiest in the land, seeing that here Joshua circumcised Israel, removing from them the reproach of Egypt. But it lies in the Jordan Valley, eastward of Jericho, a region proverbial for the fierceness of its heart but never, according to the testimony of its inhabitants, so fiercely hot and parched as in this season when Elinadab and his attendants came down to sacrifice.

Now the drought had fastened itself on the land in all its fury. The very dews failed under it. Nor did any hope for rain, even the faintest, remain, especially after the wind from the east set in. Descending hot and clear from the plateaus of the desert, devoid of the last traces of moistness or least hope of rain, blowing not in gusts but relentlessly, it was such a wind as neither fanned nor cleansed but only scorched: the mighty wind of the Lord in His fierce anger.

It polished the sky into intolerable radiance. It rendered the earth gritty with dust on the surface, hard underneath, and everywhere hot to the touch, like some pan left unoiled on the hearth. The river ran so low that it ceased to be a fluid brown ribbon, having been turned instead, as it appeared from afar and above, into a string of brazen beads, linked together by threads of mud, steaming and cracking under the sun's glare. The strip of vegetation running along its banks, usually unbroken in its luxuriant greenness, was seared at the outer edges and interrupted here and there where the yellowness of the land and of the river bed flowed together. From this universal wasteland there was no escape, not even in Jericho, for all its orchards, gardens, and springs.

Through this wasteland Elinadab and his companions made their way, panting, wretched, dazed, visiting one after another the twelve stones which Joshua had brought up from the riverbed when the Ark and tribes had crossed it. Before each stone in turn they stood, barely able to see the sacred things for the sun's blinding light. They prayed, laboring to bring forth speech through their cracked lips and dry mouths.

In the evenings, they found no respite. The slaves and underlings retired to inns where they tossed through the nights, Elinadab and his exalted companions either to the home of the high priest of Gilgal or to some house in Jericho. None enjoyed sleep's refreshment, for if no breeze stirred they stewed in their own perspiration, whereas whatever wind stirred was like the draft that comes from a refiner's furnace.

Meantime, from the smallest to the greatest, they murmured among themselves against Elinadab that he had brought them hither, all so that he might make a show of his devotion to the king. They invoked evil on his head for building himself up at their pain. They yearned and dreamed of Samaria. Though the heat prevailed there also, it was not what it was here and, furthermore, in his own house a man can, in some measure, make himself at ease. So, weary, spent, seething with resentment but sustained by their impending return home, they stumbled back to Beth El.

Scarcely had they occupied their quarters again in the house of the high priest when a fantastic rumor swept Elinadab's entourage. The king, troubled by the drought and the evils it had occasioned— and fearing the greater evils to come—desired to appease the anger of the Lord. Therefore, he himself would depart his summer palace on a pilgrimage to the shrines to the north, at Carmel and Dan. Elinadab was commanded, since he was already on the way, and since only a priest of his rank might fittingly stand in the king's stead, to take himself and all his company southward. They were to visit, in turn, all the sanctuaries in the land of Judah—as far as

Beersheva at the remotest border and returning thence through Gilead beyond the river—so that in every place He had showed Himself, sacrifice might be brought and supplications poured forth. Thus the anger of God would, perchance, be turned aside.

This pilgrimage through the mountains and wilderness of Judah could not be completed in less than four weeks, and could last as long as two months. Hosea was not alone in opposing the journey. He was sick in his heart for Gomer and for Jezreel, his yearning after them becoming greater every day he was away. But even more so, he fretted over the message of the courier, who, having assured him that all was well with his household, went on to add, "They regret that you will be delayed, but from what I could see they grieve not as do you."

"It is ever so," Hosea had defended his family and his status in it, "that those abroad are naturally more lonesome than those who remain at home."

Still, the comment rankled in his heart. Especially since, if it were true, he could understand wherefore. For why should he be missed when a man remained in the household—one stronger, bolder, more colorful than he, one who had ever been preferred over him? It was a vexing thought.

A visit to the prison, as soon as he was in Beth El again, availed him not at all. Another guard was on duty, a stern, sullen giant whom Hosea feared to approach unless there was no other way. Amishadda the merchant was missing from his place and none in his bazaar or at his home knew his whereabouts. Many anxieties burdened Hosea then as he returned to his room in Amaziah's palace.

But he was soon summoned by Elinadab to the priest's apartment. There, he learned much of what he sought to learn.

He found the priest elated and annoyed at the same time.

"It is no little trust with which the king has invested me," he said, confirming the report of the pilgrimage down Judah and up Gilead, "to set me up as his spokesman, and that of the whole people before the Lord. But it would be a hard road at any time, and especially in this summer of drought. But then, shall I remonstrate when the king himself goes forth from the comfort of his summer house?"

All very well for you, Hosea reflected. He did not believe the Lord would be appeased by sacrifices and prayers, instead of a return to righteousness.

A wild hope surged up in Hosea, a glimpse of a possibility, and one too promising to be passed over.

"Master," Hosea broke out, "let a word, I pray, be spoken in your ears and on your heart. Would you see it fit that your pilgrimage be of use to all this people and the land?"

Elinadab stared at him, his brows arched in inquiry, a light of curiosity and annoyance in his eyes as he waited for Hosea to continue.

"Master, it is for the sins of the people that this drought has come on us, and that even greater evil impends, whether from Assyria or Egypt. Master, when you come to the sacred places, do not sacrifice only or pray on the king's behalf, but summon the people, both small and great, to return from their evil ways."

"Such as?" Elinadab taunted him.

Hosea barely noticed the threat present in the priest's tone of voice.

"Such as the oppressions of the poor which go on every morning, noon, and night, the buying of fields from under their feet, the exacting of interest on loans, the denial of justice."

"And what else?"

"The offenses being done even now in the groves nearby, all

abominable before the Lord but never so abominable as when perpetrated in His name."

"And is there no more?"

By now Hosea, even in his passion, could not fail to mark the priest's meaning and the rumble of his erupting anger. But there rose up in him a boldness, a reckless impulse to speak that left no room for prudence.

"Yes, my lord," he answered defiantly, "there is more. There is the worship of idols, bullocks and calves, as though a stock or stone can be the living Lord, the God of Israel—"

Elinadab exploded. "Silence! Not one more word or by the altars you revile I shall stop it with my fist."

Hosea couldn't help but feel intimidated, frightened, and ashamed of his weakness. He was no prophet, he told himself. And even when God's word had come to him from another he was too afraid to speak it.

"Was not this ever my judgment concerning you? On the road when we came hither, I smelled it in you, disobedience toward authority, wantonness with the ways of the world established by our fathers. It was in you before you arrived hither; it has been worsened by what you heard from the Judean."

At the reference to Amos, Hosea emerged from his absorption and was all attention, listening to hear whether Elinadab would reveal anything concerning what the king had written.

"He at least," the priest raged on, "will no longer abide here to encourage the folly and wickedness of those who, like you, are already foolish and wicked, or to implant such sins in others, hithertofore sound. This very day he is to be expelled from this place and from the land altogether. So the king has commanded, confirming my authority and approving my judgment. Though when I consider the Judean's influence on you and no doubt on others, I regret that the rogue is to get off at all, let alone so easy."

Returning to Hosea, he still spoke harshly but no longer with spontaneous anger. "Now, get you to your tasks. You will write a letter to the king telling him that his will shall be done in the matter of the Judean. Inform him also that as for the pilgrimage, I set forth with all my entourage on the morrow. Use your own words but return it to me fully written, that I may fix my seal upon it and dispatch it at once."

Hosea did so and also sent another to Gomer, Iddo, and Talmon, informing them of the prolongation of the mission, bidding them not expect his return before six weeks, nor to fret if he tarried on the road as long as eight. He commended his household to the Lord's protection and sent to each of its members his greetings of love and peace.

• • •

THE BROAD PLACE OF BETH EL was almost as crowded as was typical during the pilgrimage festivals. The cause of the Judean had stirred much excitement; added to that, the high priest himself was to preside. On both scores virtually all the townspeople had assembled, as well as a number of strangers who chanced to be in the city.

They stood, a field of turbaned heads, reaching from an open area before the steps of the Temple, which had been kept clear by armed men, all the way across the Broad Place to the doorway of the Shrine of the Pillar. Above them, on the lower steps, stood a crowd of priests and dignitaries. On a row of chairs under the portico of the Temple, with soldiers to either side and behind them, sat the priests of topmost rank, the elders of Beth El and, in the center, Elinadab, the king's emissary.

Raised even above these, on a throne erected on a dais, was Amaziah. The little man seemed even littler for the great chair he occupied, his elevation above and remoteness from the others, and the voluminous robes by which he seemed half engulfed. Since he would go hence to sacrifice, the garb of his office was on him. It was heavy and oppressive in the fierce heat, the more so for that he was exposed to the full glare of the westering sun. Even to those who stood at the rim of the crowd, as did Hosea, it was apparent that the high priest was uncomfortable and ill-tempered waiting for the Judean. He perspired much, fidgeted constantly, and muttered intermittently to the attendants and lesser priests who stood below and before him.

Abruptly his patience snapped.

"By the horns of the altar," he cried out. "Shall we be kept here forever? Go…quickly…. Tell the overseer of the house of detention…"

But just at the moment, the crowd stirred to one side; the whisper swept through it: "He comes." "The Judean." Amaziah sank back into his chair and waited while the eddy among the heads of the spectators flowed toward him, issuing in the figures of the Judean and two guards with him.

The Broad Place fell very silent. Prophet and priest looked at each other. The one in his leather robe stood so calm that his eyes never wavered from the figure before him; nor did the chains clatter which manacled his wrists and ankles; nor did his bare, dusty feet shift from the spot on which first they planted themselves. The other, in embroidered crimson and purple, perched tensely on the edge of his throne, never ceasing from the darting of his limbs, the sudden writhings of his body.

"Hear now," Amaziah began. His voice cracked for excitement and the crowd tittered so that he was compelled to wait until quiet was restored to begin again.

"Hear now, my kinsman Elinadab the priest, sent of Jeroboam our king, may he live forever, and you the priests and judges of Beth El, its householders and those who have come hither to appear in the Lord's presence. Before us is one, a Judean herdsman who has come hither, unasked by any of the men of Israel, and who has spoken here, in the ears of many, harsh and base words concerning Jeroboam the king, and the Lord and His sacred places and His people and land, words which I shall not repeat lest you be affrighted by them, words which merit death."

He paused after the last word, letting it sink in, his roving eyes scanning the crowd, his tongue flicking forth to lick his lips.

"Nevertheless, since our lord the king, may he live forever, is slow to anger and quick to be appeased, it befits his ministers to seek to be so also. Therefore, though he deserves it not, the life of this Judean shall be spared."

The crowd stirred, a murmur as of applause rose from it, to be cut off as Amaziah continued.

"Nevertheless, it is not meet that he be allowed to abide in this land. Therefore is it decreed of our lord the king with the consent of Elinadab the priest, who is his emissary among us, and by me also that this Judean is exiled from this land. On pain of death shall he return to it. Furthermore, as soon as our sitting here is ended, he will be brought by armed guard to the border and be driven over into the realm whence he came, that this land be no more defiled by him."

He paused so long that men would have assumed that he was done, save that his posture denied it. For he continued perched forward on his throne and bent over.

"Yet listen now," he went on at last, a heightened excitement in his voice. "Though his life be spared, shall this son of Belial go unpunished for the words he has spoken? The judgment of the king has been pronounced, not death but exile. Hear then my judgment, I who preside over this city and shrine where his mouth has sinned. He shall not go unpunished. This, then, is my decree. I order that this Judean shall be stripped to his breechcloth that all may look on his shame, that as he came reviling and despising he shall be cast out being reviled and despised."

"No, my lord," a voice broke in.

Stricken speechless by the bold suddenness of the interruption, Amaziah for a moment could do no more than glare at the crowd from which it rose.

"Who is it," he finally brought forth, "who dares speak when I speak, saying no to my aye?"

"My lord," the voice came again. "You have given your word."

"Who speaks?" Amaziah shrieked, flinging himself from his throne toward the descending steps, to stand leaning over them so that he seemed like to fall. "Remove him," he commanded, "from those who are about him that I may look on his face."

In the center of the throng a withdrawing began, as though a leper had been discovered in its midst. But in the open space, when it had been made, stood not a single individual but a band of half a score and before them—the merchant.

"Ho, it is you," Amaziah called, as he recognized Reuel the Gileadite amidst his company.

Amaziah, so soon as he had identified the merchant, ceased to be beside himself with rage, nor did he threaten aught. But if he could not work his desire on a great merchant as he might on some lesser personage, he was not one to be gainsaid by anyone. Indeed, by the smile that squirmed over his lips, the kindling in his eyes, the near dance of his limbs, he would seem to be feeling the challenge by which he was being confronted the more pleasurable as his antagonist was the less unequal to him in strength.

"And what," he drawled, "is the desire of the chief of the traffickers of this city?"

Reuel the Gileadite flushed crimson but answered with restraint.

"The fulfillment of the oath of the high priest."

"Aye, I swore to you. And what did I swear? That I would spare the life of this Judean troublemaker. What I undertake, I do. His life is being spared."

Reuel the Gileadite stepped forward several paces, his face working with outrage, an outstretched arm tipped with an accusing forefinger trembling before him.

"Did our lord the high priest," he cried, his words tumbling forth, "call his servant a trafficker? Did he charge me with taking money for one merchandise and delivering another—he who has in his pocket divers weights and measures, one set for buying and a second for selling? Surely now, if ever I wished to commit such transgressions, who would be better capable to instruct me in such guile than our lord the high priest."

Amaziah began to tremble with rage. One of the merchant's companions tugged at his robe to draw him back, and clapped his own hands over the merchant's mouth, stifling further indiscretion.

The event hung in balance while Amaziah determined in his heart what to do with the accusation and the accuser.

"Hear now, men of Beth El," he said at last, "shall the Lord's high priest stand here to bandy words with base fellows? And yet, shall they affront him and not be chastised? What then shall be their punishment? What better than that the one they are so stupid to revere shall be shamed yet further than they feared? Therefore, this is my decree: not only shall this Judean depart naked from this place but he shall be pelted with stones and unclean things as he goes as well. I ask you, men of Beth El. Is this not just judgment?"

From those on the steps and under the portico phrases of assent sounded here and there, but even from among them only sparsely.

The crowd below, despite its usual eagerness for spectacles, was silent and seemed sullen.

Through the sallowness of Amaziah's skin a flush crept.

"So, it pleases not the heart of the men of Beth El, the decision I have rendered. And wherefore not?"

A cry came from the furthermost fringe of the assemblage. "Has this too been bought?"

As regards Reuel the Gileadite's gift to him, Amaziah was ready, having by now thought out an answer.

"What think you, men of Israel," he called, "that it is for myself that I accepted their money? It was for the sanctuary."

A heavy stillness reigned over the Broad Place. And with it, palpable hostility.

Amaziah was too overwrought to turn back.

"Who will be the first to lay hand on this Judean traitor, to strip off his garment?"

A young priest came forth from among the steps unto the open space between Amaziah and the Judean.

"Permit me, my lord," he petitioned eagerly.

"You shall not go unrewarded," Amaziah assured him. "First his turban, then his girdle, then his robe."

All eagerness to do the will of his master, the youth sped down the steps, approaching the Judean, who waited unmoved now as all the time before. Nor did the priest pause at any time except once. As he reached toward the herdsman's head to take off its covering, he looked into the man's eyes. It was then that he withdrew his hands hurriedly as does one who has almost touched something hot. But an instant later he recovered. The turban was hurled to the ground, the plaited girdle next; the tunic, a single leather shift fastened in a knot at one shoulder, slid down. The prophet stood exposed, only a breechcloth left.

In the presence of shameful things men are wont to snicker. But not now. Perhaps it was because of the quiet, uncringing dignity with which the Judean carried himself. Perhaps it was because there was nothing of the ludicrous in this body, not flabby arms or pendulous breasts or bulging belly, but only massive tightness and strength. Whatever the reason, men glanced and turned their eyes away, refusing to look at the nakedness of this, their fellow.

But Amaziah, though he sensed the hostility of the assemblage, had no choice, if he would save face, except to go on. Indeed, by very virtue of his uncertainty he became the more resolute and passionate.

"The pelting," he called, "let it begin. And to him who first sets his hand to it I give a reward."

The words rang out over the Broad Place, but neither voice nor move responded. Amaziah bit his lip.

"Two silver shekels," he offered.

It was no mean sum, more money than many a man within hearing saw in a number of months. But the suspicion of injustice was on the proceedings and the fear of the Lord's anger, if perchance the Judean be sent of Him.

"Five," Amaziah bargained, and a hum of amazement swept over the crowd, for this was as much as a quarter of the price of a man when he sells himself for a slave. But great as was the wage, the work was more perilous still, and none hired himself.

By now the high priest, vexed and raged to madness, trembled from the crown of the head to the sole of the foot and all but danced in paroxysms over the open space before his throne under the portico, so that men looked in a mixture of amusement over the strangeness of the spectacle and shame that a high priest should so demean himself.

"What," Amaziah bellowed. "In all Beth El is there none to do my will, not even," and here he turned to the lesser priests, "among my kin and intimates, those who are ready enough to eat my bread and drink my wine? You there Nemuel, and you Perez, and you Itamar, aye, and the rest of you. Your choice is before you. Either this moment you pick from the ground what you may hurl at this Judean son of Belial or, as the Lord lives in this place, you shall not look on my face again. Hear you? And this very moment."

There was nothing for it, but they must do his bidding, for his glance swept from side to side, giving them no escape. They bent, all who stood on the steps, to pick up whatever they could find which might serve as missiles. Yet the ground on which they stood was not some alleyway or common staircase to be covered with litter and excrement of beasts but the approach to the House of the Lord God of Israel and, if not itself sacred, then being near to sanctity, was kept as clean as might be. Indeed, this very afternoon the stairs had been swept and, for all the scantness of water, sprinkled also, and—unless one were to tear up the very flagstones or scrape the dust—bore nothing which a man might take in hand.

"And what is it now?"

"Master," one ventured the answer, "there is naught to throw."

The high priest clenched his fists and looked up to the heavens in the extremity of his exasperation.

"Lord God of Israel," he supplicated, "with all the filth which there is in this land these dolts can find none. But hold…"

He went rigid; his eyes gleamed.

"Aye," he crowed, "I know where there is an unclean thing and one most befitting him who will receive it. Did this Judean not speak unbearable words concerning this sacred place? Then from it shall come that which is to punish him."

He paused that he might relish the more thoroughly what he had conceived and, by holding it secret a moment longer, all the more pique the crowd's curiosity.

"Stands there not within, men of Israel," he inquired exultantly, tossing his head to indicate the Temple behind him, "the lamb of the evening sacrifice? And has it not stood there since noon when it was examined for blemish? With what that beast has provided, with that shall the Judean be condemned. Bring forth its dung," he shouted, and pointing to attendants commanded, "you, and you, and you...."

A gasp rose from all. The attendants whom Amaziah had designated hesitated before setting off to do his bidding.

In that interval, a firm yet calm voice sounded. It was Elinadab.

"If it please the high priest," he said strongly so that all could hear, rising meantime from his chair and mounting toward Amaziah, "let a word be spoken in my kinsman's ear."

He drew near to his cousin and in hushed tones continued a colloquy with him. Of their conversation naught reached the multitude who watched, yet all could see the calming gestures of the taller man and the passionate shakings of the head, the waving of the arms of the shorter.

Amaziah raised his voice. "No," he declared, "once already you have presumed to interfere in this matter and, since you come in the king's name, I could not other than defer. But this time you speak for yourself and I shall not so much as listen...."

Elinadab spoke again, still so low that none but Amaziah could hear, and again Amaziah answered aloud.

"Is it for this that you have come here, to teach me, the high priest in this place, how and in what manner I must rule its people? Of your instruction I have no need. As for the populace, let one among it, from the greatest to the least, venture in the matter to whisper nay to my aye and I will do to him worse than I shall in a moment have done with this Judean yonder."

Elinadab set his hand on Amaziah's forearm and spoke to him with great earnestness. But the high priest refused to be counseled. For a moment he listened and then, infuriated at what Elinadab was saying, tore his arm free and cried out in a very frenzy.

"So, it is not conformable to the dignity of the high priest to be angry before the multitude or to prescribe vile punishments, that such devices befit peasant children, but me they demean. Demean, say you? Then stand and look on and you shall see how the high priest will demean himself in the eyes of all. For not only have I pronounced my judgment, I shall execute it. My hand will be the first…"

"No, by the Lord," Elinadab cried out. "That you shall not do."

"By the Lord, I shall. I swear it; it is a vow. The dung, bring me the dung."

Elinadab turned away. In his face there was such rage that men cringed away, parting before him as he strode not to his chair but diagonally down the stairs and across the Broad Place in the direction of his quarters. Meantime, Amaziah bellowed again and again. "The dung…bring me the dung."

Squeamish over the foulness of all this, embarrassed for the indignity of the high priest, shamed before the Judean even though he was naked and not they, the populace at the first was only quiet. Then it became aware of the grotesque nature of the spectacle being enacted. There, dancing in his passion, was a man, and he of the greatest in Israel, shrieking to a multitude that he must have brought to him instantly…he could not abide to wait for it…the droppings of a sheep. The ludicrousness of this seemed to strike the entire assemblage all at once. Laughter erupted. Mouths gaped. Beards wagged. Heads bobbed. Hands pointed and then held strained bellies. And there was a roaring as of the sea in tempest or a host at war.

A moment later the attendants Amaziah had dispatched bore

to him on a large brazen salver the dung of the sheep, some freshly dropped and still moist.

His nostrils wrinkled and his mouth twisted.

"Our lord the high priest," one called from the crowd, "relishes not the dish he demanded."

At which the laughter mounted even higher. But when the high priest put forth his hand and let it hover over the pellets while he sought the one that seemed driest, for all the world like a glutton selecting from among dainties on a platter, all bounds were burst. Men shrieked and pounded their fellows on the back; they doubled over; they clung one to another.

With the quickness of his disgust, the high priest hurled from him the foul thing he had picked up. But for his haste it fell far short of its target, spattering itself on the bottommost step. Then he would have turned to flee, but the crowd desired not to have its sport so soon ended, and one cried, "Your vow, you have not fulfilled it so."

The call was not heard far, but those whose ears it reached saw here an occasion for prolonging its game.

"It is true," another agreed.

"You have not struck him as you swore," chimed in a third.

And soon the entire throng chanted together.

"Let the high priest keep his word."

"Hit the Judean."

Amaziah yielded reluctantly to their insistence, turning back to hurl a first and then a second bit of ordure, both of which, however, fell short.

But the next pellet reached its goal, striking Amos on the neck and spattering down over his shoulder and chest.

Then of a moment the laughter faded sharply until nothing remained of it. Nor, now that he was free of his revolting task, did the high priest depart, nor did he ask any other to do as he had.

He stood in the place from which he had hurled the dung, staring blankly at the Judean, in the meantime absently wiping his soiled right hand on the skirts of his robe. His madness departed from him; his restlessness stilled. The Broad Place was altogether quiet.

Then Amos said in a loud voice, "Hear now, Amaziah of the sons of Aaron, you who did despise the word of the Lord and have sought to silence His messenger, laying on me the commandment:

Prophesy not against Israel;
Preach not against Isaac's house.

"That which you have required will be granted. Prophecy shall be withheld from you and vision from the children of this people.

Lo, days come saith the Lord God,
That I send a famine on the land,
Not a famine of bread, nor a drought of water,
But of hearing the words of the Lord.
And men shall run from sea to sea,
And from north to east;
They shall run to and fro to seek the word of the Lord,
And they shall not find it.
Then, in that day, shall fair maids faint
And youths from the thirst—
All those who swear by Samaria's guilt—

In the course of his utterance, the Judean all imperceptibly had passed from speech to song, that eerie brooding keening with which he had given forth his burden in the house of detention. Now, as its last cadences throbbed away, men held their breath and strained after what he would next pronounce.

His eyes on the high priest, Amos took up his burden once more.

"Hear further, Amaziah, high priest to that which I have just called Samaria's guilt, for such is the thing in the Temple behind you.

"Since first the Lord took me from behind my herd and brought me hither, I have prophesied concerning Israel and its king, but concerning this place I have not prophesied, for of this vision was withheld. But last night, while I sat in the house of detention, the hand of the Lord rested upon me and now, 'ere I go hence, I shall declare what will be here in time to come."

The eyes of the Judean closed; the crooning intonations returned as he whispered awesomely:

> *I saw the Lord standing over the altar; and He said:*
> *Smite the capitals of the pillars till the columns shake*
> *Break them to pieces on the heads of all these men*
> *For the last of them will I slay with the sword;*
> *There shall not one fugitive flee,*
> *Not one survivor escape,*
> *If they dig through to Hell,*
> *Thence shall My hand take them;*
> *If they climb up to Heaven,*
> *Thence will I bring them down.*
> *If they hide themselves on Carmel's peak*
> *Thence will I search them out and bring them down.*
> *And if they do conceal themselves from my eyes, on*
>   *the floor of the sea,*
> *There will I command the serpent and it shall bite them.*
> *And if they go into captivity before their enemies,*
> *There will I charge the sword that it slay them.*

For I have set Mine eyes upon them,
For evil and not for good.

He paused yet again, the hush now that his voice was momentarily no more heard was a silence beyond all the silences which had been before. For men were frozen with the terror of his prediction concerning them and could neither speak nor move. Then he went on to compound dread with dread. His eyes still unopened but his face and speech directed at Amaziah, he said:

"Nor have I heretofore prophesied concerning you, Amaziah. What think you, high priest of Beth El? May it be that judgment shall be visited on a wayward people but not on those who have misled it? Shall harlots be punished, but not the wives of the great of the land who have played the harlot with the sacred Sodomites? Shall all the arrogant not be visited for their pride, save only the most arrogant of all, the children of princes and priests? Or the covetous but not the greediest of all? Therefore hear now, Amaziah, what the Lord will do to you and your sin-laden house:

Your wife shall be a harlot in this city—among its conquerors.
Your sons and daughters shall fall by the sword,
Your estate shall be divided by lot,
And you yourself shall die in an unclean land.

But now the measure of horror and fear was overfull. Voices, some of protest, some of discussion, some of lament, flowed together into a tumult. Through the midst of it a single cry rang out, sharp and mighty as the thrust of a sword. It was the prophet. He had leaped from the pavement onto one of the lower steps, facing about, so that though visible over the heads of the multitude he was not far elevated above them. Therefore they felt him close to them, among them. Nor, except for those in the foremost ranks, were they shamed or diverted by his nakedness. Only from his shoulders upward could he be seen. His head uncovered, his long disheveled hair sprang free. His swarthy, bearded, intent face was that of a man of war—all strength, resolve, fierce passion. His eyes flared as with sheet lightning. He stood so for a moment, waiting to be attended to. But when the hubbub, though it ebbed, did not cease altogether, he raised his arms for silence. They were like the shaft of Goliath's spear for solidity and strength and, though held unmoving on high, they seemed to strain in battle as did those of Moses when he contended with Amalek.

Regarding him, men expected that when he spoke it would be as he had spoken before, as his posture now foretold, after the fashion of a lion's roaring or a ram's horn's blaring or a captain calling over the shouts of attack. But it was not so. As quiet returned, his arms dropped and his voice when he gave it forth pleaded:

"O Israel," he sang softly but penetratingly, so that those furthest distant heard clearly and their hearts melted, "think you it is a light thing for me to utter evil things against you? And if it be hard for me to prophesy, must it not be harder for the Lord to charge me so, let alone fulfill? Or think you that it is for no cause that all this comes upon you? Consider the transgressions of this people, those which I recounted to you when first I came hither, and judge between the Lord and yourselves.

"Do not the princes and judges sell the righteous for silver, and the needy for the price of a pair of shoes? Do not the rich in their lust for possessions begrudge the poor the very grime on his face and pervert the cause of the humble? Is it not so that in this very city, in its sacred groves, a man lieth with a woman and then his son enters and comes unto her after him? And as for the priests, are not the garments they wear, the spreads of the couches on which they sprawl by every altar, are these not pilfered from the treasuries of their temples? And the wine they drink in the houses of their gods, is it not paid for out of the common till? Is it not so, O House of Israel?

"Is then the Lord not vindicated when he sent to you through me that harsh thing which I uttered when first I came hither, namely that flight shall fail the swift and he that thinketh himself strong shall flee away naked on the day of the Lord?

"O, men of Israel, brethren to Judah, my brothers, will you not do what the Lord has counseled through me saying..." Here the accent of supplication was stressed, the pleading grew stronger as the Judean wept his last words to the people of Israel.

> *Seek ye the good and not the evil*
> *That ye may live*
> *And that so the Lord may be with you*
> *As ye boast*
> *Hate the evil, love the good.*
> *Establish justice in the gate!*
> *Perhaps so the Lord, God of Hosts,*
> *Will have compassion on the remnant of Joseph.*

Then, the man fell silent. He swept up his leathern robe, threw it around his waist and, through the multitude dividing before him, departed the place.

CHAPTER X

THE WATCHMEN ON THE RAMPARTS were crying out the end of the first watch when Hosea, having raised his hand to knock on the door of his house, observed from the light which lined one jamb that it was ajar.

Startled, he pushed it open. In the light of the overhead lamp, now burning low, the eunuch Ephai lay sprawled across the corridor. He was deep in sleep, a wine jug at his side, an empty cup tilted loosely in his limp fingers.

Hosea's lips tightened. He was not one to begrudge a servant meat or drink, but neither had he forgotten his father's frequent admonitions about the folly of masters who tolerated drunkenness in their households. He was about to stoop to wake and reprove the sleeper, when he spied through the corridor another recumbent form. His anger mounted.

Hosea took a lamp from those on the shelf, kindled it with the flame overhead, and, holding it high, strode into the common room. Every servant in the house, male and female alike, was as stuporous with strong drink as the lad in the entranceway. Mibsam, the caretaker of the house, lay on the floor, prone, his face cradled in his crooked arm. Shualith was propped in a sitting position against a couch on which another handmaid lay supine. Talmon alone occupied a chair, but the upward pitch of his head, which jutted his beard into the air, as well as the depth of his breathing and the resonance of his snoring, attested that he was no more wakeful than any other.

For a moment, as he took all this in, Hosea struggled to think what occasion it might be which could account for the drunkenness of an entire household. He had lost track somewhat during the last harried days of the calendar, but that this was neither Sabbath nor New Moon nor festival he was certain. Nor had he heard, whether at the city's gate or at Elinadab's house, of any event worthy of national thanksgiving, nor had he seen elsewhere any signs of any such.

This, then, could not be other than something peculiar to his household, some happy occasion, though what celebration would warrant the dispensing of wine to the servants he could not imagine. It was a singularly happy occasion indeed, he judged, from the number of jugs that stood about.

No longer angry now but only curious, he tiptoed across the common room to his own bedchamber, eager to awaken Gomer and learn from her wherefore this might be. But though the baby Jezreel slept in his crib, Gomer was not in their bed. The spreads he could see were rumpled, but no longer warm to the touch. Nor was there any answer when he tugged at the curtain that veiled the privy corner.

Mystified, he returned to the common room and considered of whom he might make inquiry. He spoke to one, then another, then shook a third by the shoulder. None answered with any more than a wordless mumble. Amused now in his perplexity he mounted the steps to the upper chambers, hopeful that Iddo, better accustomed to strong drink than they, would be capable of speech.

He was well past the entrance curtain and into the room when his heart stopped its beating and his breath its flow. It seemed as if all of him then began to tremble, so that his teeth chattered and his clothes rustled and the lamp held high in his left hand danced, sending tides now of brightness and now of shadow flowing over the couch where Iddo and Gomer slept side by side.

He lay prone but with his face turned toward her, his arms and legs spread abroad, his massive shoulders and back moist with perspiration. She was lying on her back, her head averted from him, one arm clutching to her bosom the crumpled coverlet that shielded their nakedness.

As he stared at them, he was suddenly aware of how her arm curved over her head, and how often in the privacy of their chamber he had considered her lying so and found her beautiful. He had treasured the sight as a secret, precious for being his alone. And as though this were the substance of his calamity, a sadness over it welled up in him, too great to bear. Still staring, still trembling, still holding the lamp aloft, he wept, tears flooding his eyes, grief shuddering through him like some deep tide beneath the sea.

As he wept, a moan sufficient to wake her escaped him. Her eyes regarded him, blank at first. Then, with the dawn of comprehension, she glanced to the side where Iddo lay, and looked back to Hosea with eyes like deep, dark pools of terror. And so they continued long, she staring at him, he trembling and weeping, and both wordless.

And so it seemed they might have remained forever, had not Iddo stirred in his sleep and, half unawares, half remembering, stretched his hand after her. Gropingly it reached toward her, found her arm, and spiderlike crawled up it to find and cup her breast. A loose smile worked across his lips. Gomer, her eyes still fixed on her husband, stiffened and shrank.

Hosea snapped.

"No," he breathed, speaking for the first time. "No," he protested more loudly. "No, no, no!" he shouted hoarsely.

Iddo did not hear or heed, and so he turned on Gomer.

"Depart from him," he rasped.

Unanswering, she turned her head and frantically scanned the room.

"And do you tarry?" he taunted. "Is the bed of whoredom so dear to you that you are loath to leave it?"

"I seek my robe to cover myself."

"Before your husband you are too modest to stand naked," he hooted savagely, "but to lie uncovered with his brother, for that you are not ashamed. Up, or as the Lord lives I drag you forth this instant."

She arose without further protest and searched the room, looking for the discarded robe.

And he who had never looked on her full nakedness stared at her with contempt. But as he regarded her, marking the whiteness of her person shimmering in the lamplight, the litheness of her limbs, the fullness of her bosom, and remembering the sweetness of her flesh, the hatred faded from him, and his anger dissolved again into heartbreak. The sadness was so great that by the time she had found her robe and, arms erect, was slipping it over her head, he could not see at all for tears.

Meantime Iddo stirred. His eyes opened languidly and were about to close again when he became aware of the light of the lamp that burned above him. His eyelids flew open. Except for a tensing of the body, a slow turning of the eyes to Hosea, and a quick turning away, he lay immobile, continuing so for a long instant. But it sufficed for him to force a smile to his lips and to fashion words for his tongue. He rolled over and sat up, facing Hosea boldly, his hands busy meantime in spreading the coverlet over his groin and so far as it might reach over his upper legs.

Hosea had been watching him since he had first stirred. Now, at the sight of his brother's overripe redness and his massive chest gleaming with sweat and suggestive of the animality that had once marked Gadiel, a sense of disgust invaded him, turning to nausea when at last Iddo opened his mouth.

"The seeming of this—"

"Seeming?" Hosea interrupted scornfully. "Is it semblance or fact that this night you have lain with the wife of your brother?"

"Yet," Iddo urged, "it is not as bad as it appears."

Hosea groaned. The fingers of his free right hand dug themselves into his breast in the fierceness of his grief. "Lord God! 'Not so bad,' says he. The wife of my bosom, the light of my eyes, my woman, my only one whom I love, plays the harlot with my own brother, uncovering her nakedness, permitting him to know her flesh, and he makes it all seem a little thing."

"But it has not been often," Iddo offered.

When Hosea grasped the words, the understanding was like a knife in his entrails. "Then it has not been only this once. You have lain together other times when you were not drunken but in all awareness."

Fury flared in him.

"Whore," he hurled at Gomer, "that could wait each night in cold sobriety a whole evening through and then, when the household slept at last, muster the shamelessness to climb here into a strange bed. All these many moments, all those steps, at each of which a turning back was possible, but not for you."

"Nor for you," he turned on Iddo, "waiting here to the

shame of your father's house and the defilement of your brother's bed. You who have taken women without number, Israelite and Philistine, young and old, ugly and fair, and did need to take my woman also, my only one.

"Son of Belial!" he screamed. "Rutting beast!"

He went on, but not for long, ashamed of the ugly epithets he was speaking and very soon at a loss for them. Besides, Iddo was trying to tell him something, repeating it again and again.

"Quiet, man," he was saying, "I beg you, do not shout. For if the household is awakened, then all Samaria will know of this."

"If a thing be right to do," Hosea taunted, "can it be wrong to make it known?"

"But the disgrace to our house."

"And since when has Iddo, son of Beeri, exercised himself with his family's fair name?"

Anger was still in Hosea, but it was cold now.

"Son of lies," he scorned, "think you my eyes are pierced out that I cannot see? It is not disgrace that concerns you but fear. Yes, even you, the mighty man of valor, tremble in your skin, quaking lest this night's sin become noised about, lest there be witnesses to it. For then you will be stoned. You and your paramour who was my wife, stoned to death in the city's gates, having been caught in adultery."

He paused and went on, savagery in his voice.

"Said I you would be stoned? Nay, this is the penalty for normal adulterers, men and women who have done no more than transgress a major law of God and man. But yours is no such simple crime. You have lain with your brother's wife, uncovering his nakedness through her. This, says the Law of Moses, is an abominable thing—incest—for which the penalty is death by fire. Rightly are you anxious lest the household and

Samaria learn of this, for if they do, you will burn."

His anger was again hot as his words, but not so hot that he failed to see Iddo tensing. "It will not avail you to attack me," he warned. "You are stronger than I, but even when we were children, not Gadiel, not you, could down me readily."

One of Iddo's hands clutched the coverlet, his legs curled aside. His eyes fixed on Hosea, he spoke sidewise to Gomer.

"As soon as I spring, you will run, quickly, to your own room, before the servants wake. Get into bed at once. Then, even if he shouts before I can choke him off, if he lives, what can he prove? If he dies, I shall say I took him for a thief in the night."

"You shall not escape so," Hosea said as his right hand went forth unerringly to seize Iddo's spear propped against the wall near the door. With a quick twist, he pointed it forward. At the same time, he lowered the lamp, carefully, to a bench nearby, becoming aware, only now from the aching protest of his arm and shoulder, of how long and stiffly he had held it aloft.

"Do not spring," he warned, "or I shall run you through. When we were children, you were wont to mock me that even in pretense I was loath to thrust with spear or sword. Of that reluctance I am now cured. Nor shall I be punished for it. Your lying together with her in death will be proof enough of your lying so in life. Nor," he went on, detecting the glow of calculation in Iddo's eyes, "shall you wrest it from me. Am I not your pupil and Talmon's in the use of arms?"

But Iddo was not yet resourceless.

"Approach him from the side," he commanded Gomer.

"Fear not," Iddo reassured her when she failed to move. "You will not need to come within his reach. Only turn his glance, cause the spear point to shift—it will suffice me."

Still she did not respond.

"Do you not hear me?" Iddo snarled.

"I will not do it," she whispered.

"Fool," he cried, "is your life so little worth in your eyes? Are you so eager for the flames?"

"You will kill him if you can," she said dully.

"Of course."

"I will not have his blood shed."

"Then I will spare him."

"I do not believe you."

"I swear it."

"I will not do it."

And there was a finality in her tone which convinced him.

"What do you purpose to do?" he asked Hosea, his devices not at an end.

"I do not know," Hosea answered.

Even while his wife and his brother had been dealing one with another, feeling had been ebbing from him—the rage and indignation, the wistfulness and regret, the love and hate that had ravaged him since he had entered the chamber. Now, even the need to be alert against peril had passed. He was emptiness within, a great void untenanted but by weariness.

And by confusion also. It was true what he had said to Iddo; he did not know what he purposed to do. To rouse the household, to call the guard to turn them over to public justice, to disgrace his household, to see the fire kindled on their flesh—this was unthinkable. But the alternative was no better. That his brother should go unscathed, to mock him, as he no doubt would, for a cuckold, that she who had betrayed his love should suffer nothing.

A fog of fatigue, confusion, indecision clouded his thinking. He must have time to reflect, but time—he perceived this much clearly even in the haze—not purchased at the price of freedom of choice.

He stepped backward toward the door, the spear and his gaze undeviating. The curtain pushed aside, he shouted over his shoulder.

"Talmon, Talmon the steward, awake!"

At the third outcry, the sound of stirrings was heard from below. Lights shone forth.

"I want Talmon," he called then. "It is I, Hosea. I want Talmon only. Let none else come near."

The hubbub below resumed. Then out of it steps emerged.

"Master Hosea," the old steward called up from the foot of the staircase, "blessed be you who comes. Why knew we not of your arrival? And wherefore do you call from Master Iddo's room? Is aught amiss?"

"Naught. But first bid each servant to go to his own room and draw its curtain. Let none look out to see or be seen. And then do you come hither."

Again, a subdued tumult below, then silence. Finally, the sound of feet on the staircase and the light of a lamp coming brighter as they mounted.

The curtain behind Hosea rustled, and a panting sounded in his ears.

"I call you to witness—you, Talmon, the steward of this house—what you see in this room."

For a moment there was silence, then a quick intake of breath, then a great oath, then silence once more.

"See you my calamity," Hosea said bitterly.

"Aye, master. I see too wherefore he dispensed wine to us of evenings for no seeming cause. I see too what an uncleanness it is which I reared and raised."

"Then you will be witness against him?"

"Aye, as once I loved him so now I shall be the first to raise my hand against him."

"Before the Lord," Hosea bound him, "you are a witness."

"Before the Lord," the steward swore. Heavily, he asked, "Master Hosea, shall I go to call the guard?"

"Not yet."

"Not yet? Is it not commanded: 'Thou shalt burn out the evil from thy midst'?"

"Not yet," Hosea repeated.

"Master, please, shall I call the guard?"

Hosea's lips opened to utter the word of assent, to speak that which must be spoken, which could not go unspoken. But his eyes were open also, and he saw—he could not help seeing—the expressions on the faces of those on whom he was about to pronounce doom. Iddo's stunned consternation, Gomer's abject submissiveness, the terror-stricken expectancy of both. And suddenly they seemed only pitiable, too pitiable to be looked on. He turned his glance aside and his lips closed slowly.

"Master," Talmon repeated, "shall I call the guard?"

This time, Hosea told himself, he would not look at them. But when his eyes were averted, he saw them not only as they were in this moment but also as he had known them these many years. He could not bring himself to say what must be said. Later, perhaps, but now it was impossible.

"Not yet," he said, shaking his head.

"Master," the steward urged, "you cannot purpose to hold them guiltless. It is forbidden."

"I know, I know. They will be punished; they must be punished. The law requires it. But later, not now."

Talmon groaned. "Master, I too desire to wait. Oh, how I

desire it! And not for a while only but forever. But am I not a witness against them? Will not my hand be required as the first to be raised against them? But with an evil case such as this, it is like charging in battle. One must not delay, or the heart will melt."

"Not yet," Hosea repeated dully.

"As my master will. And meantime?"

"Meantime, you will stand guard over him in my stead. I shall go down to bring Mibsam to this chamber that I may have two witnesses, aside from myself, as the law requires. Aye, I shall wake Shualith too. Let her sit watch over Gomer and over the child."

Hosea put the spear in Talmon's hand.

He crossed the room and went down the stairs, his steps heavy with his burden.

CHAPTER XI

A MISTY MORNING GRAYNESS seeped into the window, filling the crisscross of the lattice but flowing no further and touching nothing else in the room. Seeing it, Hosea conceded his defeat. He knew then that, strive as he might, he could not give them over to death.

All night long, since he had descended the staircase, he had lain here, on a couch in a bedchamber not his own, and struggled to bring himself to do that which needed and ought to be done, to give the word for which Talmon waited. But each time he had brought his will almost to the point of decision, his imagination had leaped before him. He had heard with his own ears the cries summoning the street guards and the hubbub mounting to a neighborhood tumult as more and more people were wakened from sleep. He saw the lamps flaring in darkened windows and other lights—shock, revulsion, derision, lustful pleasure—kindling in the eyes of those who came to understand wherefore was this commotion. He watched a woman and a man being led forth by the guards, passing through two lines of spectators, silent until someone, bolder and less clean of tongue than the others, called out an indecent jibe, upon which the chorus of those who joined with him conflicted with the chorus of those who would silence them. He experienced the lash of that staring, the blow of those words, the sting of their shame as they would feel them.

But the most hideous of his imaginings, the most disgraceful and terrifying, was the execution itself. It was too indecent, too impossible even to conceive, let alone to bring to pass. He could not do it.

He tried to rally his hatred and outrage to force himself into an awareness of what the law required. With all his strength he strove to whip himself to a pitch at which nothing would matter to him except their punishment. He lived again deliberately, vindictively, the sight of the two of them lying, their limbs intertwined, asleep from gratified desire. He forced himself to imagine the whisperings and caressings and writhings and tensings that had gone on before and told himself that this had been not once, in some single half-drunken spell, but several times, perhaps many.

But instead of burning with anger, he felt sad, lost, and despoiled. Gomer had been precious to him. How could he give her over to hideous death? He could not abide that those soft lips he had kissed so often and hungrily—though they were now foul—should be closed forever. The very whiteness of her person should not, would not be exposed to alien eyes more than, alas, it had already been.

He could not rouse himself to action, and so became less in his own eyes. Twofold is the penalty for faintness of heart, he told himself. A man would suffer neither were he not a weakling who deserves to endure both.

But what now? How indeed, he asked sardonically, does a man in his situation comport himself if, like him, he is incapable of what the law ordains? With what mien and utterance does one address a brother who is his wife's paramour? How about the wife?

Does one show displeasure, and, if so, is it to be angry or stony? Or does one pretend indifference and perhaps even affability? Does one say:

"How lovely is the appearance of my adulterous wife this day"?

Or: "Will my brother who has lain incestuously with my wife be so kind as to pass the salt?"

After he had left off lacerating himself, he became aware that much needed to be done. He must find a new home for himself and his child, it being manifestly unthinkable to remain under one roof with Iddo. He must arrange a divorce from Gomer, but it must be so devised that the cause be not known. Else, would the name of their house be disgraced and his son bear shame forever.

Aye, much needed to be thought through and done, and none of it pleasant. Therefore let it wait; he had enough pain for the present. But one thing he must do at once: send Talmon off to bed. The man was too old to be kept standing guard even one moment after there had ceased to be any point to it.

He grimaced with distaste, anticipating Iddo's reaction. He would say nothing, that brother of his; to speak would be dangerous. But his eyes would kindle, first with relief that his life would be spared, then with amusement and mockery at the weakness which allowed it to be so. It was a little thing against the burden of his misfortune, and yet somehow the harder of the two to abide. Well, if he could swallow one, he knew he could get the other down also.

Wearily he crossed the common room on his way to the stairs. As he passed before the room which belonged to Gomer and him, Shualith came out of Jezreel's room to meet him. She had sat these many hours where he had stationed her, just inside the threshold of the child's chamber, so that she might keep the baby always in view but also, with the curtain raised, keep watch over the next doorway.

"All is still, master," she volunteered.

Hosea nodded. "I shall return soon, and then you will be free to go to bed."

"Fret not concerning me; I am not overly tired. Think rather how to care for yourself and your poor, poor baby."

She began to weep quietly. He bent forward, kissed her cheek in a token of his gratefulness, and turned away. Wearily, reluctantly, he trudged up the staircase to the landing before Iddo's chamber. There Talmon sat. He faced the door, humped about the spear held erect between his knees.

The steward neither looked up nor spoke as Hosea approached. To the contrary, he seemed to slump even lower and closer about the shaft.

"He is gone," he said. "I took my place and sat here," he explained, "most of the night. Then, at earliest dawn, I heard the sounds of stirring within. I knew what it signified. I shall not lie to you, master. As surely as if my eyes looked on, he was knotting coverlets together to lower himself from the window. I never forget my duty to you, but, master, it was as though a weight were on my shoulders holding me down and a hand over my mouth keeping it silent. Perhaps, had I seen into the room where his offense was committed, I would have hated him as he merits. Or had I been able to watch him, the hero trembling for his skin like a cowering dog, I would have despised him and so been made capable of bestirring myself. But the curtain was before me and upon it images without end of what had once been, and against these I was without strength." Not stirring or raising his head, he continued. "The day had broken…and, in his chamber, it had been still a long time, more than sufficient time for him to reach the city gates. Master, I have betrayed you. And not you alone, but the law and the right. I, the old soldier, sworn to loyalty, to dutifulness. Hate me, slay me. It is the recompense I have earned."

The steward's great, gaunt shoulders hunched over further. His old head bowed so low that the gray locks, tumbling forward, all but touched the knees. There was silence except for two breathings—one laboring sighs, the other quick pantings.

Hosea wavered between anger and relief. Anger because injustice had escaped its due, relief that now Iddo would have no occasion for victory over him and his weakness. There would be no need to look on an unholy joy kindling in the eyes of one delivered from the doom he had earned.

And through the anger and relief was a gladness of malice. Iddo had fled away empty-handed and all but naked. Almost certainly he had had no money with him in the upper chamber, nor clothes except for what he wore, all his possessions being stored in strongboxes below. It was a thought hotly sweet to think on, and, for a moment, Hosea dismissed all else that he might think only of it and so fully savor its delight.

"Master," Talmon broke in, "whatever your judgment on me, no matter how harsh, utter it. Do not seek to spare me."

"I have naught against you," Hosea answered. "You have done what I would have, had I been in this place. Besides, it is better so. The riddle I could not unravel for myself has been solved for me. Go below, Talmon, and sleep. You have been up almost the entire night."

Hosea dropped a reassuring hand on the stooped shoulder and turned away.

One problem, he thought, the easier one, is solved. But the other...

Ephai, bearing a ewer of water, mounted the staircase. "Do not trouble to go aloft," Hosea instructed the lad. "Master Iddo is not there. He has gone away on a journey," he improvised in response to unspoken inquiries, "to the cities of the Philistines."

Which is almost certainly the case, he told himself. Not

knowing that he has nothing to fear, he will not rest until he is in another land.

"But master," Ephai protested, his brows arched in incredulity, "in the deep of night, and without warning or farewell, and none coming to summon—"

"Enough," Hosea cut him off. "So it was."

A slave boy he could brush aside with a straw, but what would he tell others—Iddo's acquaintances especially, and perhaps also the city elders inquiring as to the sudden and strange disappearance of a householder? Could the truth be forever concealed in such a matter as this? Already three knew who were not of the family: Talmon, Shualith, and Mibsam. Trustworthy as they were, he must caution them again as to secrecy. For if ever their knowledge escaped, even if only to the other servants, it would be all the world's.

It did not seem hopeful. Nevertheless it must be ventured, for Jezreel's sake if not for his own. If people wondered and guessed and gossiped, better suspicion and whispers than certain knowledge shouted aloud.

Thinking this, he followed Ephai down the stairs into the common room. He looked at the curtain that hung over the door to what had once been his and Gomer's bedchamber, now the place of her confinement. No longer could he postpone the most difficult and painful decision of all.

His heart was a tangle, like the growth along the lower Jordan, steaming, venomous. He plunged into it. Thoughts and memories like stinging insects swarmed over him, piercing and poisoning his entire being. He pushed ahead, striding meantime to and fro across the common room, his body struggling with his spirit. He could see no way—no wisdom, no counsel, no device—against the ordeal which awaited him. A weariness flooded him then, a weariness of despair, overflowing the many wearinesses that already held him. He could find no way to avoid it because none existed.

Then, his strength spent, his ingenuity exhausted, he needed mightily the comfort which earlier he had refused, the only presence in which the possibility of comfort resided.

Shualith rose as Hosea came into Jezreel's room and accompanied him to the crib. "The child has slept the night through, the poor mite, who knows not his misfortune."

"And she?"

"She has made no effort to approach him. Indeed so quiet has she been that from time to time I became alarmed and looked into the other room to make certain that she had not somehow, stealthily, done harm to herself. Though," Shualith interposed hatefully, "she could do us no greater kindness than quietly to cut her throat. It would be some restitution for the evil she has done us. I never trusted her, master. I always knew deep in myself that there was wickedness in her. Ever so proud she carried herself, she who except for you would now be a second wife somewhere—if not something lower even than that—who came to us naked of dower except for what your father supplied for appearance's sake. That such a one, who should have kissed the dust from your feet every morning, noon, and night, should—"

"Hush, now," Hosea said. "You will be heard."

"Let her hear. She will hear more also from me, I promise it."

"But Ephai and Keturah—"

"Wherefore should we be concerned lest two servants overhear me when all the world will soon stand agape at the report?"

"The world must not know."

For a moment, her little eyes bored pinlike into him.

"Soft you always were," she whispered unbelieving, "worse than a woman. But so soft I did not dream." He did not answer. "To spare that brother of yours—"

"He has spared himself. Iddo has fled."

"Fled? What mean you? That husband of mine let him go? Aye, they say women are foolish and men wise. But that brother of yours never fooled me for a moment. Through all his sweet cajoling, I smelled the rottenness inside him. Well, wherever he is, let evil fortune pursue him. May leprosy pale his cheeks and ague burn his insides. That, alas, we must leave to the Lord. But the one in that room, she remains in our power. Ha," she crowed, "it turns out all the better that Iddo has escaped. He is, after all, your flesh and blood. But she is a stranger."

A stranger, he mused, whose body had known his in the inmost of all intimates. How is it written in the Book of Moses—"and they shall be one flesh"?

Again the sense of loss waxed strong in him, the feeling that the greater part of himself had been torn away from him.

Meanwhile, Shualith, her tiny frame quivering with hate, buzzed in his ears. And though unsure as to his course and unable to discern the way ahead, he was sure that hers was not a good counsel.

"And what, if I do as you say," he asked quietly, "will be with the child?"

The momentum of her passion carried her well past what he had said. Then it came through to her, and she fell silent at once.

"Yes," she said. Shualith winced, and then her resolution returned.

"No matter what," she insisted, "she must die. Think you an abomination like this can be concealed from the eyes of men, let alone God? They will discover it and hold you guilty for covering over an offense that merits death. And He above knows it now. Master, for lesser sins He has stricken down houses and brought plague and famine on all Israel. And think not," she went on, her fury mounting, "that I am deceived by your contention concerning Jezreel, true as it may be. It is but your own softness that constrains you."

She was speaking the truth. He was beginning to waver under her assault.

"Silence!" he said. "I will not hear one word further. Have you been ever thus, and I knew it not, brazen of brow and unbridled of tongue?"

Then he caught himself.

"Nay, the anger I bear myself, I am diverting to you. You are in the right. I cannot give her over to the flames. Call it softness, weakness, unmanliness, what you will. It is so that the Lord made me."

He smiled in apology.

"My child," she crooned, "my wronged child."

But once again, he could not accept sympathy. Already his throat was choking and tears springing in his eyes. In yet a moment, he knew, he would be weeping out of sorrow for himself.

He turned from her that she should not detect this further evidence of his weakness. Then he approached Jezreel's crib.

"I would be alone with you, my son," he managed to pronounce. "I have seen you only once, for an instant, since I came home from my journey. Shualith, do you go to your room and sleep. You will require it after this night."

Once her footsteps had muted themselves in her own chamber, Hosea gently put his hand on his son's head. An insufferable compassion welled up in him.

"Little orphan," he whispered, "bereaved this night, but knowing it not."

Because of the heat, the child slept, except for a breechcloth, uncovered. His skin, faintly moist with perspiration, in its olive hue was like Gomer's, as was the mass of ringlets framing his head. But the cast of his features and the high coloration of his cheeks, heightened now by sleep and the summer, were, Hosea noted, as after the likeness of the kin of Ophra rather than of Beeri, but fortunately, he reflected further, without the coarseness of Gadiel, resembling in slenderness and grace the appearance in boyhood of—

An icy apprehension froze him, so that he was incapable of either breath or thought. Recovering both, he calculated fiercely, then relaxed slowly as the absurdity of his suspicion became apparent. Nevertheless, an ugly association had been established in his mind, not readily to be dissolved, if ever. This would not be the sole time, he recognized with prescient clarity, when he would see Iddo in his child.

Would he be able at such times to love his son, or would Iddo's likeness stand between them? Would he impute uncleanness to the child, holding him impure by the defilement, after his birth, of the womb which gave him life, and shrink from him in consequence? That she had compelled him to such thoughts—and perhaps to such an estrangement toward his son—caused him to hate her, as he had not at any time since his return home.

And now that the gates of mistrust were opened, other suspicions came flocking through. If Iddo, then who else, and how many others, and when? Even her virginity on their bridal night—he winced as always with a distressful recollection but went on the more angrily for it—even that assured only that no man had known her altogether. But there were other fashions for the making of love between a man and woman, as he knew full well since his marriage, as the Book of Moses informed all the world when it said: "And behold, Isaac was sporting with Rebecca his wife." Who then, if not her husband, had sported with his wife before she became a wife? Perhaps, it occurred to him, it was Iddo himself, as long ago she had danced opposite him, her eyes only for him. Had this game on which he had stumbled been played before, if not to its end, then with more successful secrecy?

And now, with hate that needed to be vented and suspicions that required to be voiced, not so much that they might be allayed as they might wound, and in wounding appease hatred, he swept aside the curtain between the rooms and strode over the threshold.

She was sitting on a stool in the far corner, her head bowed. Her face, as far as he could see it, was paler than the light which fell on it from the window above and behind her. Her body, though erect, yet sagged also. Her hands were clasped loosely, powerlessly, in her lap. She was at once so lost, so wretched, so hopeless and pitiable that in one mighty gust hatred and jealousy were swept from him. He felt only pity and an overpowering desire to put his arms about her and hold her fast and speak to her words of solace and reassurance against the calamity which had befallen them both, saying *Beloved, bride of my youth, be comforted.*

But in that very instant of remembering, hatred, jealousy, and rage were rekindled, burning yet more fiercely than before because now he was angry with himself, that his softness had so nearly traduced him.

"How often," he rasped, asking jealousy's questions first of all, since they were hottest in him. "Tell me how often it has been." And when she did not answer but only sagged lower, he repeated the question, deliberately adding to its explicitness and cruelty.

"How often have you climbed those stairs to my brother's chamber that he might take his pleasure with you, and how often have you received him in this room and on my bed?"

"Here, never."

"Then how often above?"

Her clasped hands tightened in her lap.

"Hosea," she faltered, "please…to what purpose—"

"Answer my question," he ordered.

"Five, perhaps six times."

"She does not know the exact number," he said. "What is one adultery more or less to an adulteress?"

Then she wept, but soundlessly, only the shaking of her shoulders disclosing it. And because pity engulfed him again, he cried out:

"How could you? Did I not love you?"

She did not answer.

"Did he make you drunken, perhaps, as he did with the servants?"

"He gave me strong drink," she said with difficulty. "But I was not drunken. Would that I could say it, but it was not so."

His ebbing pity vanished altogether with this last question, leaving him all coldness. "Did you love him, then?"

"I know not," she murmured.

"Seek not to brush me off so. To this much I am entitled in restitution for my wrong."

Halting, tormented, despairing, she replied, "I know not what to say…. He drew me…. It was a madness. Even when I went to him, I could not puzzle out wherefore. As a child, I did think I loved him, and always afterward did I regard him as the comeliest of men. Then, when he came and I saw him again, he was no longer so handsome as I had remembered him, and I was glad. For some reason, I was glad. But still he drew me. And always, from the very first night, he looked at me with desire, bold, open, as outspoken as if with words, and though it shamed me it stirred me also. And whenever the opportunity offered, he spoke words of love to me, such words as you would not permit to pass your lips, and they were like fire. And then, after you had departed with Elinadab, he began to entreat me to come to him. He gave me no surcease, and a desire was kindled in me, not a desire for him so much as to know what would befall a woman with a man like him. I fought against it but it was too strong for me, and so I went."

By now Hosea was on fire, wanting only to wound her in return for the torment she was inflicting on him.

"Was the event," he snarled, "equal to the expectation?"

When she fell silent, he shouted at her.

"And who else?"

"Who else?" she echoed.

"Aye, who else has known you besides Iddo? And in the years before we were married, who else and how many more have made sport with you that kindled you so?"

She failed at first to take in the question. When she did, she stiffened, but only to say in a low voice, "No one."

"Not even Iddo in the days when you were wont to think him so comely?"

"He did not so much as speak to me, except once at a dance."

"And what," he cried, "what of other young men, those days you were in Charun's house, and that buyer of slaves, Othniel, aye, and Charun himself?"

"None," she repeated, "not one. Was I not a virgin when I came to you?"

"That you were. But a woman's breasts give no sign of having been fondled or her lips of having been kissed. Of that how much did you submit to, and with whom?"

"Nothing and with no one."

"Mean you that none attempted to lay hands on you, or that you would not submit?"

"Aye, they attempted, many. Was there anyone to protect me?"

"And, I suppose," he scorned, "none succeeded."

"Not by my consent, and then no longer than I might struggle free."

"But touched you were," he persisted.

"Aye, sometimes when I could not escape."

"And no doubt you burst into fire, you who are so flammable."

"No, not that. It was never for more than a moment until I could struggle free and never, never even once, with my desire or submission. I despised them and their groping hands. My disgust would rise. Until you, there was none whose touch I could abide."

"And me," he said, "you have loved. Lord, God of Hosts, how you have loved me."

Then she wept, with such wild shuddering and sobs that it seemed her frame must burst. Several times she quieted and made an effort to speak, only to choke over the words and plunge into another paroxysm of abandoned grief.

Finally she recaptured her composure, a composure such as one achieves who has made peace with death.

"Hear me now, Hosea," she said, her voice husky from her weeping but otherwise flat and devoid of all feeling. "I do not expect you to believe me. I have lost the right to be believed. But I have loved you and love you now."

Only, Hosea thought, at once with sadness and bitterness, without flame, without even so much as a spark.

But of this he said nothing, for the pain of her sorrow was still lively in him.

"And I know," she continued, "that my doom is decreed. As I perish, I perish. Only until the guards come, do not torment me with questioning. To this too I will submit, if that is your will. Whatever you wish you may have of me. This much at the least you have merited at my hands. But, if you can, as an act of mercy, do not make me speak of my offense. The weight of it is too heavy upon me that I should be able to bear speech concerning it also."

He said nothing. Though she could not know it, he was incapable of speech. She continued.

"You have been good to me, Hosea, beyond my desserts. This much I must tell you, now that I may, though I will say it again at the end, if I can. Many things I regret, Iddo beyond all others. Concerning you I have no regrets, only gratitude. And if gratitude and reverence, too, be love, then I have loved you always and you alone among men. And now, I beg you, summon the guards so I am not left to wait and wonder any longer."

Through a long pause he wrestled with himself, clinging still to the wish to hurt her. But he could not withhold from her his mercy.

"The guards will not come," he managed to say, "not now, not ever. You are not forgiven, but your life is spared."

CHAPTER XII

IT WAS FULL LIGHT BY NOW. In the hope that there might be surcease in it from his pain and confusion, Hosea turned to the routines of a normal day.

The sweat and dust of the last stage of the journey homeward were still on him. He also felt a ravenous hunger within, for he had had no food since the night before when, while they waited before the gates of Samaria, the members of Elinadab's party had eaten parched corn and dried dates and figs from the pouches they carried.

In the room he had occupied the night before, he bathed from head to foot, then summoned Ephai to the room to anoint him with fragrant oil, trim and order the hair of his head, and comb but not cut his beard, the latter being forbidden by the Law. He put on him a fresh linen tunic and laid out, in readiness of the time he should desire to go out, an outer garment, a girdle, and a head kerchief, together with its bands and fillets.

Swift and competent from habit, the eunuch performed his duty as though there was nothing unusual in it except that his master had just returned from a long absence. But Hosea could see him brimming with curiosity as to why his master had slept that night in a chamber not his own, and why Iddo had departed the household with such suddenness and mystery. Repeatedly he referred with elaborate obliqueness to one circumstance or the other, groping cautiously for an explanation. But Hosea either pointedly ignored the invitations or alluded to the servants' drunkenness and neglect of duty the night before. Ephai, rebuked, would slip again into offended silence. But when, his dressing completed, Hosea gave instructions to bring into the room furniture and all his changes of clothes and other personal possessions from his own chamber, the servant could not but risk another venture.

"Then it is to be so permanently?"

Hosea was fully aware that the eunuch meant the estrangement, of which signs were multiplying. He deliberately misunderstood Ephai and at the same time made an announcement through him to the entire household.

"Not permanently. We shall not long continue in the house of—" Trying to pronounce his brother's name and failing, he ended instead, "in this house."

Reminded that this was, in fact, Iddo's house he found the thought insufferable. He must seek out other lodgings, and at once. Before dusk, if possible. He would suffocate must he remain here another night.

"But whither shall we go?" The eunuch followed the scent eagerly.

"I know not," he answered. There was near frenzy in his voice. "The Lord must provide a place."

"Goes the entire household, all its members, to the new dwelling place?"

This was the question for which he had yet no answer. It had been easy the night before to resolve to thrust a bill of divorcement on Gomer. But that had been before he looked on her misery and wretchedness. Now he was not so certain. He needed to consider how Jezreel would be better served, whether motherless or not, and how shame on his house would more likely be averted. All along, as he considered these things, he sensed, though he would not admit it, that he was daubing over the weakness of pity in himself. But when he found himself reflecting along other lines also—that when he divorced her she might return to Charun's house, that coming with her dower money she would be even less safe there than in the past—it was no longer possible for him to deny the solicitude he continued to feel toward her.

Then he was aghast at himself that he should not only be so devoid of strength as to fail to punish a faithless wife as she deserved, but even to put concern for her from his heart.

At this point, a resolution crystallized in him. He would delay not one day in divorcing her, and, having done so, would never think of her again. Let her go where she will. It was no longer of consequence to him. To this he swore. If firmness did not spring spontaneously within him, he could nevertheless muster it forcibly.

The slave boy before him was suddenly a symbol of the powerlessness of his own spirit and he turned on the lad, pouring against the boy his anger against himself.

"By my life, by the life of my son," he vowed, "you have asked your last question concerning the affairs that touch you not—Lady Gomer's, Master Iddo's, mine. Show but one more presumption of curiosity, and, the Lord be witness, I shall sell you out of hand to the traders."

Shaken by the unexpected fury of the assault, Ephai replied with a show of innocence, his ingenuity standing him in good stead:

"As I live, Master Hosea, I was not inquiring after Master Iddo, or our Lady Gomer or you, but over the servants and slaves of the household, myself first among them. I meant to ask how it will be with us, whether we would go with you to the new residence or return to Jezreel or, the Lord prevent it, be severed from Beeri's household, the free ones to find other employment and the slaves Keturah and I to be sold—"

It was a lie, Hosea was certain, but he was ashamed of his outburst and so he did not challenge it.

"Let it be," he ordered, cutting into Ephai's continuing protestations. "Concerning whatever goes on among us, no matter how strange its guise, no one is to say anything, neither Keturah nor you nor any of the freemen. Or, as the Lord lives, it will be the last word he will speak as one of this household. Now go, that I may pay to the Lord my morning obeisance."

But the intention was more easily declared than carried out. For when he had taken his stand before an open window and lifted up his eyes and hands to the heavens, his heart was unable to follow.

How could he come before the Lord or bow himself before God on high, he who had thus wantonly transgressed not only the ordinances which Moses at His bidding had set before Israel, but, more gravely still, that commandment summoning to righteousness which from Amos he had learned to be the greatest of all?

That Iddo and Gomer should be punished, and according to the statute, if not both of them then at least the one on whom the judges and elders could lay hands, was the clear requirement of God's Law. But this was the course on which he had turned his back. Shall a man, his hand still busy with wrong, presume to approach God?

Nor was it himself alone on whom he was inciting wrath. He remembered that there in Moses's Third Book, just after the judgment concerning him who lies with his brother's wife, there is found the warning lest through transgression the land vomit out its inhabitants as it had earlier vomited out the nations who dwelt on it before Israel.

He saw again the line of tiles which were not straight with the plumb line, heard once more the thudding of a bare foot on the ground, and witnessed as before the shifting of the heap toward collapse. Such was he in the midst of his people, a crookedness, not the largest but not the least either, that set its edifice awry, and at the same time an incitement to the foot of doom that it descend the sooner and the more strongly.

Had he never met Amos he would no doubt be thinking now that his offense was his own only and by nature no more than a breach, serious enough to be sure, of some two or three of the ordinances of the Lord. But now he saw it in its true gravity and import. Not he alone would bear his guilt but this whole land and all its inhabitants. It was not an affront merely against the Law—but against God.

The very sky, as he studied it, white rather than blue, glaring and metallic with the heat of the drought, seemed to confirm his awareness of divine displeasure. He must bring a sacrifice, he told himself, nay, two sacrifices, one a sin offering for his flouting of the Law, the other a peace offering to placate his God.

And then he recalled lines, which he had copied down from the prophesies of Amos. They read that not in sacrifices did the Lord take delight but in justice rolling down as waters, that He was appeasable not by the voice of prayer or the song of psalms but only by righteousness like a mighty stream.

But Hosea was incapable of exacting the justice the moment required. He stood there. His uplifted hands dropped slowly, he desisted from the attempt to pray, and he turned away from the window and the baleful sky visible through it, guilty now not only before himself and against the Law and the people of Israel, but before and against his God.

• • •

HOSEA APPEARED IN HIS OWN EYES like a madman he had once observed. The poor wretch, stricken by the Lord, had stood in the Broad Place before the king's palace, quiet in demeanor, his hair and beard combed, his face composed, and had proceeded, without shame or regard for the bitter winter weather, to divest himself of his clothes—his headgear with its cords and fillets, his heavy woolen cloak, his linen girdle and inner garment, even his undertunic. All this time, a throng of spectators had stood about, too horrified to interfere. Not until the madman had laid hands on his breechcloth and was about to uncover his nakedness was the spell broken. Some men rushed to prevent him while others called for the city guard, and a great tumult ensued.

Soon, Hosea's own stripping would be in process. A stripping not of clothes, but of wife, home, and servants, of all things except for one child, his small hope and joy. Now as then it would be carried out calmly and deliberately, a nightmare that would be incontrovertibly actual.

The stages and details of the "stripping"—so he referred to it always in his own mind—painful as they were to plan, would be, he foresaw, even more painful to execute. The least of them would have in it something of the torment a man experiences when he tears off a loose flap of his skin, a hangnail perhaps. It must be done quickly or the heart will melt and it will not suffer itself to be done at all.

Swiftly, therefore, Hosea set about doing what he had to do.

First he hurried down to the Hall of the King's Scribes in

the lower city to ask leave of the chief scribe to be free that day. Perhaps it was superfluous for him to do this. Perhaps, this being the morning after his return from so long a term of service, it would not have been held against him had he simply absented himself. But his employment was not dispensable to him; and it was wise for him to be careful of it.

His stride lengthened as he made his way from the Hall of Scribes toward a neighborhood where families resided not each in its own house but several under the same roof, sharing the courtyard, the oven, and mill, but each occupying its private bedchambers. As he went from house to house, inquiring after vacancies, the prospect of it became increasingly distasteful. The courtyards were littered and noisy, the apartments malodorous and dark. And everywhere people swarmed in hordes: women baking bread in the central oven or tending pots over open fires, children at play, idlers gossiping, artisans at work before their doorways. It would not be pleasant living among such sights, sounds, and smells. But there was no avoiding it, now that he must sustain himself on his own wages. It was in quarters such as these that most of his fellow scribes dwelt, and seemingly without discomfort. What they could endure, he could also.

He went from house to house and street to street, holding to the faith that if only he searched long enough he would discover some place cleaner, less crowded, and more quiet than the others. However, in the end he gave up hope and settled on an apartment which was like all the others, and struck hands with the caretaker in token of their agreement.

As he hurried off, he gave thought to the next matter that needed to be determined, the disposition of the other servants. Shualith and Talmon, even were he less attached to them, he would need to retain with him to care for the child and tend the home while he was at work. Ephai and Keturah, he resolved quickly, must be sent from Samaria. They had seen too much. Nor could they be counted on to keep silence concerning what they knew or conjectured. He would dispatch them to the house in Jezreel at once. For Mibsam, he no longer had need or room. Yet it was not possible to send him away also to Jezreel. Being a freeman, he might refuse to go. Besides, he was one of the two witnesses to Iddo's offense. If Hosea had not wielded the weapon he held against his brother he was neither so willing nor so foolish as to throw it away. Better to keep the man near at hand and in view. But how, since Hosea could no longer afford his wages?

A notion occurred to him that caused him to stop abruptly. He considered it for a while, smiled wanly, and went on his way smiling so broadly that passersby on the broad thoroughfare which climbed the shoulder of the mountain of Samaria looked at him with curiosity. He had found a solution to the problem of Mibsam. He would set him to be the caretaker of Iddo's house—it required it—and, since he was serving Iddo, Hosea would pay him from Iddo's monies. This pleased him, that it should be his brother who, all unawares, would defray the cost of maintaining a witness against himself.

He turned to the next of the matters he must settle—how he would find the money required by Gomer's marriage contract. A hundred shekels was a sizable sum and Hosea did not need to calculate long to conclude that what he possessed in the strongbox—the remnants of the money Beeri had willed him and what he had succeeded in saving—fell considerably short of it. There was no choice except to have recourse to the usurers, bringing as pledge…bringing what? Furniture and other household effects? Except for Jezreel's crib and bedding, he had none of his own; they all belonged to Iddo. His scribe's tools? Then on what would he live? His books? What moneylender would accept such security? Adornments of gold and silver? Of these he had but one, an ancient armlet which his mother had brought to her marriage as part of her dowry and bequeathed to him. Such a possession no man pawns. There remained only his clothes, outer garments and inner garments, of which he possessed a fair supply of good linens and woolens. If only these would suffice to span the gap between what he had in hand and what was needed.

Arriving home, he proceeded forthwith with the plans he had devised: Ephai and Keturah he bundled off without delay to Jezreel; Talmon and Shualith he dispatched to the marketplace to purchase beds and bedding, a table, stools, lamps, pots, and dishes for the apartment he had rented. He opened the strongbox and extracted from among the fine linen and jewelry the swollen purse belonging to Iddo, and his own slim money sack and armful of garments, and counted out his money. He entrusted the pledging of the clothes to Mibsam in the sure knowledge that he, accustomed to bargaining, would realize a larger sum than his master. When the servant returned with the report which Hosea had hoped not to hear, he sent him back again, this time with the armlet also.

It was by now late afternoon; the third watch of the day was more than half over. Carried along by the impetus which had brought him so far, he busied himself with preparations for the final task, the gravest and most difficult of all.

From a cabinet he took his scribe's supplies and implements, an inkhorn and quill, a penknife, and a leather sheet. He carried these into the chamber he had occupied the night before, set them on a table and seated himself before it, thinking to write out the bill of divorcement while awaiting Mibsam's return.

But, being weary from the day's exertions and sore of soul from its stingings and lacerations, Hosea was deserted by the determination which had heretofore sustained him. Compared to the ordeal that lay ahead, those which had gone before were as

flesh wounds to a head-to-foot flaying. So though the pen was
sharpened, the sheet unfurled, the inkhorn unstoppered, and the
formula for a bill of divorcement rehearsed too often in his career
to be doubted now, he did not write but sat, neither thinking nor
feeling, numb and depleted. When Mibsam returned, he was still
sitting.

The servant counted out the coins that completed the hundred
shekels of dowry—and the surplus, which was slight—into Hosea's
purse. Looking wordlessly to his master for further instruction
and receiving none, Mibsam departed. He was still sitting when
Shualith set before him a ewer of water for bathing his hands, then
curds, honey, shallots, bread, and salt for supper.

Meantime, the day turned and declined. The light dimmed
in the latticework in which it had dawned for him that morning.
Through his numbness he recalled that documents must be written
and legal proceedings transacted in daylight to be valid. Should he
delay until sunset, it would be too late to divorce Gomer that day.
And by the morrow…he came to with a start. It must be now,
he saw, his mind clearing. Weakling as he was, he could not be
trusted from hour to hour, let alone from day to day.

"Mibsam," he called, rising. "Mibsam."

"Yes, master," called the servant from the common room.

"Summon into the common room the Lady Gomer and
Talmon. I shall join you as soon as I have written out a bill of
divorcement."

Now that his resolution had been revived, it took but the
fewest moments to write out the formula:

*On the fifth day in the month Av, in the thirty-third year of
the reign of Jeroboam, son of Jehu, king of Israel, in the presence
of Talmon son of Keturi, a Gadite, and Mibsam son of Nachon,
an Ephraimite, Hosea son of Beeri, an Ephraimite, did pay*

*out unto his wife, Gomer daughter of Diblaim, an Ephraimite,
one hundred shekels, silver, in discharge of her dower rights and
declare unto her:*

*"Thou art not my wife; I am not thy husband. Henceforth art
thou free to marry any man."*

This bill in one hand and the shekels wrapped in a kerchief in
the other, Hosea entered the common room.

Gomer was standing at the far side of the large table. Hosea
tried to avoid looking at her again, fearing the sight of her,
recognizing in it a threat to his determination and the dispatch
with which he meant to carry it out.

"Here," he said briskly, taking a position opposite Gomer but
directing his glance and words to Talmon and Mibsam who stood
together at the table's head. "Here is money. Do you declare its
sum."

They accepted the kerchief, opened it, and gravely, as if
performing a morbid act, counted out the coins.

"One hundred shekels," Talmon pronounced.

"Yes, one hundred," Mibsam agreed.

"Then," Hosea instructed, "do you observe that this silver
I set before Gomer my wife, offering it to her in discharge of
my obligations under the marriage covenant and as a preliminary
to my divorcing her? Take it," he bade her. He turned in her
direction, but not so far as to see her face. "Take it and deliver to
me the marriage contract in its stead."

Her voice when she answered was soft, yet firm.

"No, I will not."

"Take it," he reiterated.

"I cannot. It is not due me."

"Take it," he repeated monotonously, determined not to be
trapped into feeling.

"It is not mine," she insisted. "My uncle gave me no dower; that stipulation was but a pretense. And if he had," she said, her voice now barely audible, "it would now be rightfully forfeit."

"Take it," he said still again.

"But you cannot spare so much money," she protested, her speech coming alive for the first time.

Now the temptation to wound her and look on her hurt was stronger than he could resist. He raised his eyes and said deliberately, "How solicitous is my Lady Gomer of her husband's welfare and happiness!"

Her pale face went dead white, her suffering eyes suffering yet more. But for a flash there was in her speech her old boldness, but tempered by gratitude.

"And how shall I not be when my Lord Hosea is so solicitous of mine?"

It was true, but it was a truth he could not concede, especially since by denying it he could wound her again.

"Nay, not for your sake," he said coldly, "but because I would insure the validity of this divorce beyond all challenge."

Her head came up, her eyes caught fire, her cheeks flushed, and she breathed deeply. He was certain that when she spoke, it would be with the hauteur that had marked her, that had always drawn him. But she was so for an instant only.

"Then let the Lady Gomer accept the money and give me her marriage writ."

Perceptibly, her defiance deserted her. She grew limp like some puppet from which the support has been withdrawn. But though she faltered, she did not fail. She drew from the bosom of her dress the furled marriage writ which had been given her in Jezreel under the bridal bower. She laid the writ before Hosea and, turning toward the head of the table where Talmon and Mibsam stood, took up the money.

But the shekels were many and her fingers were unsteady. The neat piles collapsed into disorder. Coins rolled away, several toward the edge of the table. Her hands full, she tried to forestall their falling. But she was too slow and awkward to preempt a mishap. Shekels rang down on the stone floor. What she held in her hands she deposited on the table while stooping to pick up what had fallen. In her haste she had not set them down securely and some of these too rolled from the table, dropping about her head and onto her shoulders.

With this humiliation she could no longer contain herself. Scrabbling on the floor at their feet—for none moved to help her—she began to weep. But even now, pride kept her silent. Her lips quivered, she was blinded with tears, her throat was constricted so that she could not breathe, but no sound escaped her. She was slow to find the coins and, shaking in humiliation and despair, they seemed to elude her fingers. Hosea could go no further with his pretense of indifference. The flash of malicious joy he had experienced when she had had to stoop to pick up the money had been short-lived. He clung to it and sought to keep it alive, but the impulse to spare her this humiliation became stronger and more urgent until he ached with it, until he felt he must yield to it or its tightness in him would stop his heart. Groaning, he sank to the floor. Pushing her groping hands aside, he proceeded to pick up the coins.

At the nearness of him, at his touch and help, she was altogether undone. Propped up by one hand, the other pressed against her mouth in an unavailing last effort to keep back the sounds of her grief, she wept openly. It seemed that all of her guilt, terror, fear, shame, and despair shook and twisted her.

Seeing, hearing, sensing her sorrow, Hosea ceased to collect the scattered coins, wanting only to extend his arms to her that her grief might break itself against him. Then he recalled that this was a solace she might no more take in him or he in her. A great sadness welled up in him, and he would have wept with her. But Hosea thought of the ludicrousness of it—two grown people weeping in unison under a table—and then of the cause of all this. He picked up the last coins.

"Come," he said, not kindly but not brusquely either. "Get up."

She quieted somewhat, rose slowly to her feet, placed the coins she had picked up onto the table, and wiped her eyes in the hem of her head veil. Still weeping, though no longer violently, Gomer awaited numbly and unresistingly what would be.

At Hosea's bidding, the coins, having been recounted, were wrapped in a kerchief before being presented to Gomer.

"You will pick them up and walk three paces in token of acceptance," he instructed her. She did so. He asked of Talmon and Mibsam, "You are witnesses?"

"We are witnesses," they declared.

"Before the Lord?"

"Before the Lord."

Hosea unfurled the writ of marriage and exhibited it to the two spectators.

"This," he declared to them, for neither could read, "is the writ of marriage which I gave to the Lady Gomer at our wedding, wherein it stipulated the dower obligation of a hundred shekels which I have just now discharged."

"You, Talmon, did seal it with your seal. Do you identify it?"

"Aye."

"And you, Mibsam, though you cannot decipher it and have not set seal on it, have seen the Lady Gomer produce this document, asserting of it that it is her writ of marriage. You have also heard Talmon identify his seal on it. Is it so?"

"Yea."

"Then observe what I do with this."

With his penknife, he pried away and broke into pieces the seals set years before by Talmon and Thedka, Charun's friend and witness. Then he cut the leather sheet into shreds.

"You are witnesses," he asked, "that I have now destroyed my wife's writ of marriage?"

"We are witnesses."

"Then do you attend most carefully what I now proclaim to all."

He turned to Gomer.

"I, Hosea, son of Beeri, herewith declare to Gomer, daughter of Diblaim, to whom I have heretofore been wed: 'Thou are no more my wife; I am no more thy husband.'"

Calmly, deliberately, he said it a second time, and then a third.

They were face-to-face, and Hosea, noting her pallor—the passivity and hopelessness with which she heard him out—forgot to complete the proceedings.

"We are witnesses," Talmon volunteered and Mibsam echoed, when Hosea failed to inquire.

"Before the Lord?" Hosea asked, suddenly roused.

"Before the Lord," he answered.

"Then it is done," he declared and started to turn away.

"Hosea," she said after him. Hosea paused and looked partway backward in her direction. "Hosea, will it be granted to me to see the child?"

The desperation in her request uncovered a vulnerability in her he had not thought of, but he had now no heart for vengeance of any dimensions, let alone of such cruelty.

"Yes," he replied. "If it be not too often nor when I am at home."

"Hosea," she continued, "this I must say and perhaps now

that there can be no purpose in it except the truth, you will believe it. Hosea, in spite of everything, I have loved you."

Such was the hostility that blazed in his eyes that she faltered and fell silent.

He lay awake late that night in the room he had rented, unable, for all his weariness, to sleep. He marked the long, even breathing of Jezreel from his crib across the room, remembering how the child had cried himself asleep asking for his mother. Hearing the noises of this restless house, smelling its smells, disturbed by its novelty and wretched with its wretchedness, he relived achingly the distant past and in a chaos of passion the more recent also. How best to shape his child's future? While he tossed and turned, he tried in vain to suppress the anxiety he felt. He wondered whether Gomer had found lodgings for the night and how it went with her in her aloneness.

CHAPTER XIII

WHAT IS A MAN TO DO WITH HIMSELF who, having suffered mortal wrong at the hands of those dearest to him, cannot erase their names or blot out their images from the ever-open scroll of his awareness? Hosea's present seemed formless and void. He knew not what to do with himself, nor how to proceed from here so the future offered a degree of hope.

He felt as if he had lost not only the world but his God also. Surely Hosea had been alienated from Him for having been derelict in executing the judgment clearly written in the Law, and the greater, unwritten judgment that the crooked must always be made straight. And so he, who had heretofore prayed each day when he rose up and lay down and sacrificed at the ordained times, now knew himself exiled from His shrines and altars, from His presence everywhere.

Hosea worked with fierce intensity as though the materials of his trade—the sheets of leather and papyrus—were the loved-hated ones and its tools the instruments whereby judgment is visited upon them.

In the evenings he sat in the ugly common room of his home, cramped not only with three adults and a child, but with the sounds and smells of the multitudes swarming in the houses and in the courtyard. He played with Jezreel, rejoicing in the games they played together. Hosea ached each time the child spoke of his mother, and, when he ceased to make mention of her, that this child in his motherlessness be forced to bear sins of which he was innocent.

At night, after the child had been put to bed, he lay awake, brooding. Sometimes he tormented himself by recreating the sights of Gomer and Iddo in the embraces and tossings of love. Then he would burn with hate and vindictiveness and invariably slip into imaginings of what might have been had he given them over to the judges and elders, their disgrace and pleadings for mercy, their hideous deaths. But the pleasure of this, while fierce, spent itself too soon, and he would be left weary, ashamed at the same time of his vengefulness and his incapacity to have satisfied it. Sometimes he relived moments of happiness which had gone on between Gomer and him, but never for long; the poison of the end always seeped back to make bitter the memory.

Sometimes he yearned for her in loneliness and the hunger of desire. Sometimes he wondered, when he forgot to guard himself against it, how things went with her, what she was thinking and feeling. But most often he tossed in bed, his heart awake, with only the hope of sleep, so that he might briefly rest from the weariness, emptiness, and confusion which were his constant companions.

Hardest of all to endure were the Sabbaths and festivals. To remain at home through a long holy day, staring at blank, soot-grimed walls when all the world was rejoicing was impossible.

Yet, for his offense against the Lord, he debarred himself from the prayers and sacrifices which occupied the graver among the populace of Samaria—and, by temperament, from the carousing of the frivolous. He took then, when holy days forced long hours of idleness on him, to wandering the streets of the city. Because he seemed to himself the lone griever amidst throngs, times of happiness for others were to him occasions for resentment. What was his offense that he should be exiled from friendship and joy? Where was the equity in it? Especially—and this was the invariable climax of his aggrievement—where was the justice of God?

It was because he was angry with the Lord that he made his way to the houses of harlotry up on the mountain of Samaria.

Two months had dragged by since he had banished Gomer and himself from the house of Iddo. Both the holy day of the Sounding of the Shofar and the Day of Judgment had come and gone. Now the Festival of Booths was at hand. In recognition of the harvest, Hosea and Talmon erected a hut in the courtyard, and Shualith adorned it with palm, willow, and myrtle. She had proven adept at finding for them a few citrons, which were scarce, and costly, far too costly for any except the farmers who raised them or the rich to bring them as offerings to the Lord.

Then arrived the solemn eighth day, with its prayers for the well-being of Israel. Hosea could not remember in his life the prayers for rain ever having been more fervent than they were that day. Yet once all entreaties to the Lord had been made, the people turned quickly to feasting and drinking. The streets of Samaria were filled with baskets wreathed with garlands and heaped high with autumnal fruits, borne aloft to the shrilling of pipes and the chanting of songs. Last year's wine was in good supply—and cheap. As for what would be next year, when the full effects of the drought would make themselves felt, the apprehension provided all the more reason for eating, drinking, and making merry.

Out of the ferment of Hosea's heart came a mood of rebellious abandon. He recalled the same festival years before where he had discovered Gomer among the maidens, and had marveled at how graceful and beautiful and alive she was. He could still see the tangle of curls that had flowed to her waist, and the excitement on her face. Unfortunately, the vision of her was replaced by the image of two dancing, whirling figures moving together as one. Hosea felt a familiar stab of pain. Need he remind himself that the two had been drawn to each other even then?

Seeking some kind of salve, he left his home.

The wine shops, alone of places of trade, were open for business. Street vendors carrying drink in goatskin sacks accosted passersby, urging them to purchase their wares. What with the universal example and ever-present temptation before his eyes, as well as his own bitterness aching to be slaked, Hosea drank heavily—more heavily than ever before in his life. Soon he was all but intoxicated, but with no trace of the lightness of heart which heretofore wine had induced in him. Instead, the rebellion inside him had turned sullen and vindictive. When passersby jostled him, his impulse, restrained only by lifelong habit, was to strike out at them and snarl. Whenever the voice in himself warned against looking on strong drink, in defiance he turned to the nearest wine shop or vendor to down another cup.

To the twofold heat which was in him, of wine and of anger, a third was added as the afternoon wore on. Desire. The demands of his flesh had become of late all but intolerable. Yet being Beeri's son he had refused to acknowledge his desire and, when it would not be dismissed, had suppressed it sternly. Now, in his rebelliousness, he would not fight it. Unresisted, it burned the more fiercely, not only for the wine he had drunk but also for the sights he saw. Perhaps it had always been so in Samaria on festive days that groups of young girls strolled the streets, flaunting themselves in the eyes of men; or that drunken couples staggered along, arms twined about each other, giggling as they went; or that men and women stood together in doorways and shadowy corners; or that harlots came up from the cleft and solicited trade. If it had been so before, Hosea had never taken much notice. But now he was a man whose eyes had been opened. He looked on Samaria and saw that it seethed end to end with fire. At which he was like a lamp burning before a furnace whose little flame was sucked into the greater. Nothing in him resisting, all things within and without moving him toward the conflagration, he set out, misty of sight and thought, but determined.

Befuddled as he was, he still was not free from old scruples. He did not turn in the direction of the cleft. Nor did he consider resorting to the groves of sacred prostitutes and Sodomites. He made his way instead up the mountain of Samaria by the left roadway, to the special quarter where houses of harlotry were permitted. He had passed this way before, on some errand or other, and had been solicited, hearing the invitations against which Beeri had cautioned him. "Though at their beginning they drop honey and are smoother than oil, their end is more bitter than wormwood and sharp as a two-edged sword," his father used to say.

Before each house of harlotry, in the narrow entranceways which he could see by standing on tiptoe, men stood in throngs, conversing, jesting, looking frankly into one another's eyes, unabashed as though none knew the shameful purpose of the other. But when he thought of that purpose, how each man waited but to mingle his seed with that of his fellows in the orifice of a woman's body, he had for some time been nauseous with excess of wine. Now his gorge rose so that he could only with difficulty keep back his vomit. Had anger and desire not burned in him still, he would have fled the place. Instead, he remained where he was. He even purposed to go further up the hill where the more expensive houses were situated and matters might be more acceptably resolved. But then, as it chanced, a man came forth from one of the houses and forced his way through the crowd, colliding forcibly with Hosea on the fringe. Teetering under the impact, the man threw his arms toward Hosea and clung to him to avoid falling.

The man's face was gross and flushed. His arms and torso were fat and heavy, his breath sour with wine. All of him exuded the acrid smell of stale sweat and, Hosea imagined, an after-scent of perfume. But what revolted Hosea beyond all else was the touch of the man's hands on his own arms. They were moist and sticky.

Now Hosea's gorge would not stay down. Leaning against a blank wall on the roadside he vomited forth the wine he had drunk, and the meal he had eaten before going out, and he continued to retch long after there was no food or drink in himself.

After a while he quieted and was able, though weak and trembling in every limb, to depart the place. At a water trough partway down the hill, he stopped to scrub his arms. But even as he washed them in the cleansing waters, he knew that it was only the physical reminder he was removing. The desires he had been feeling, Iddo and Gomer's desire for one another, the harlots in those houses on the mount and in the cleft, the men who resorted to them, and all Israel, from the king on his throne and the high priests at the altars to the hewer of wood and drawer of water—on all was the sin of corruption. The whole land was a harlot against its God, unclean before Him. Beyond the sins of oppression of which Amos had spoken, or the special sin of Iddo and Gomer, was a universal sin of all the children of Israel: the sin of uncleanness.

Hosea returned home wondering why He, who for much less cause had brought a flood on the world, should now be so patient.

• • •

AFTER THAT DAY, Hosea ceased to roam the streets on those days on which he was free from work. Instead he got into the habit of taking himself to the community of prophets in Tirzah, an ancient village near Samaria. Beyond all things, Hosea desired to go about undefiled. The road between Samaria and Tirzah, even the droppings of animals that littered it, felt clean compared to the filth in the city. The rolling hills terraced in vineyards, the olive groves and almond orchards, the fields of grain and vegetables seemed cleaner yet. And the heavens above, blue and bright with autumn, were purity itself. Walking this road was like being washed in cleansing waters.

The community of the prophets had a sense of purity about it. Hodiah, who had been revered by Hosea's father, was long gone. But his followers, clad in skins, still wore their hair and beards long, went about bare of foot, and lived in tents, refusing, as did the Rechabites, to dwell in houses. Israel herself once did dwell on the ground, in tents. In fact, she did so when the Lord was nearest to her. Others, however, were no different in garb from any of the people one might see on the streets of Samaria. They were all earnest men who tolerated no impiety or wickedness in their midst.

Afternoons of Sabbaths and the New Moon, they read aloud from the Law of Moses, discussed the commandments, sang songs of David to the Lord, or related the deeds of the prophets of old—Samuel, Elijah the Tishbite of Gilead, and Elisha. At those times, they allowed whomsoever desired to be in their company.

They spoke much of Amos, the Judean prophet of whose preaching they had heard but of which they had no written text. Discovering this, Hosea prepared not one but two copies of the sayings of Amos, which he brought to them as a goodwill offering. Whereupon the members of the order took special notice of Hosea and treated him as though he were one of their fellows.

So he came to attend discussions to which none were admitted except the prophets. There, he discovered that, though they lived together in brotherly harmony, they were not all of one mind concerning many grave matters.

Some among them, the greater part it seemed, held to the notions of the fathers concerning the fashion in which the word of the Lord might be induced, asserting that music and dance availed, as Elisha himself had established. These also contended that there is no prophecy unless the prophet be possessed, falling into a trance. The other party would have none of the playing of instruments or dancing, and, while not denying that the word of the Lord might be disclosed in a spell of possession, said nevertheless that it need not be so, contending not only that a man might keep his senses when the hand of the Lord was upon him, but see and hear with a clarity such as he never experienced. At such times, they claimed, the voice sounded not from without but from within the prophet. Which was the meaning, according to their notion, of what befell Elijah in the cave: not in the storm nor wind nor earthquake was the Lord's word to be discerned, but only in a still, small voice.

Had Hosea held convictions in these controversies, shyness in all likelihood would have prevented him from voicing them. But having himself never been favored with a descent of the spirit, whether in possession or quietly, and knowing that his sinfulness would prevent both, he was unable to take sides with either.

This much only he knew. Here life was not loathsome with corruption and injustice. Here he was refreshed.

This helped Hosea the day Shualith brought him tidings about Gomer, several weeks after the Festival of Booths.

With his permission, Gomer had been visiting Jezreel regularly when Hosea was away from home. The arrangements had been made and were carried out through Shualith.

Hosea had sternly instructed Shualith not to talk to him about her, but Shualith believed it was her duty to keep her master informed. She hated Gomer and never alluded to her without bitterness, and only spoke about her as long as necessary to impart the information required. So it came to pass that with no effort on his part, Hosea did not lack for knowledge concerning his former wife, including her decision to remain in Samaria so that she might continue to see their son and her difficulty in finding a suitable place to live, for none took in a kinless woman unless with the intention of despoiling her.

But this, Hosea told himself, touched him not at all. He listened, as he always did, and made no comment.

It was different with the news which Shualith had to impart this day; he could sense it as soon as he returned home from the Hall of Scribes. He expected some comment from her, for it was on first and sixth days that Gomer paid her visits, and usually Shualith did not delay in spitting out whatever she wished him to know. But on this occasion, she at first said nothing whatsoever. Then she seemed on the point of speaking but kept silence after all. Something—it was obvious—had unnerved her. And since this was a day of Gomer's visits, it was something, he suspected, of a most extraordinary nature.

Not until early evening did Shualith disclose what perturbed her. They were sitting together at the table, the three of them—Hosea, Talmon, and Shualith—at the Sabbath meal which even now in their straitened circumstances was distinguished above others by brighter illumination and the serving of meat, bread of fine flour, and unmixed wine. The air was heavy with dread. Each of them had toyed with food and drink rather than partake of it, and now they were at an end even of that.

"I have evil tidings," Shualith began abruptly.

Hosea sighed. "And what new evil can there be?"

"A terrible evil, master, sufficient to put one's hair on end. Alas, that I should be its harbinger."

Still confident that nothing worse could come to him from Gomer than he had already received, he asked calmly, "And what may that be?"

"Gomer is pregnant."

Through the reeling of his brain, he seized on the sole hope that it was not so. "It cannot be," he said simply.

"Alas, it is true. She told me so herself."

"Mean you," he challenged, "she came here and told you of her own initiative? Not she. She would keep her own counsel."

"Yea, but I asked."

"Out of a clear sky?"

She flapped a hand at him in angry impatience. "Is a woman near fourscore years not to be able to spot the signs, the rounding of the face, the filling out of the figure? A fortnight ago I spoke of it to Talmon here, and he mocked me. Today it would be evident to anyone except a man. I scarcely needed to ask, or she to answer."

Dislodged from the refuge of disbelief, he asked the fateful question.

"Whose?"

Shualith shrugged her shoulders and put out her hands helplessly.

"But you must have asked her. What did she say?"

"Of course I asked, and she answered what I expected—and perhaps it is true. She says it is yours."

"But on what ground?"

"That after you had departed to attend Elinadab and before she had dealings with Iddo, she missed a period but thought little of it at the time. Now she recalls that such an event was quite unusual with her. Is it so?"

"And shall I know? She told me from time to time that it was with her after the manner of women, and I did not approach her, but whether it was regularly or not—"

He broke off for a moment, considering possibilities. Then, if it such a thing be possible, he cried aloud in a whisper, "A monster. It will be a monster."

For if what was in Gomer's womb was from his seed, then it had been rendered unclean for having been polluted by his brother. If it was his brother's, though, then it had been from its very inception an abomination of adultery and incest. A nausea was in him like that on the Festival of Booths when the drunkard had laid slimy hands on him. Then, flight had been possible. He had torn himself loose and escaped and washed himself in water. But how was one to flee from the hideous thing which was inside Gomer, and where and what were the waters that could erase the thought of it?

"What is to be done?" he asked, more of himself than the others.

Talmon, who had heretofore said nothing, answered.

"As I said to Shualith I say to you, Master. It is none of your concern. She is no more your wife. What is it then to you if a strange woman bears a child?"

"Fool," Shualith snapped contemptuously, "I say to you again as I said before, that you speak nonsense. If the child be our master's, is it no concern of his? And if not his, then is it of no consequence that he and Jezreel after him and all their house now have as kin this…this…nay, there is only one way, that which I bade her do. The child must not be born. She must rid herself of it. Let her do as the base women when they conceive. Let her bear burdens to strain herself. Let her bathe in hot waters. Let her drink effusions of wormwood. Let her do the other things also whereby women cast unborn children."

"And she consented?" Hosea asked.

"What she knows of such things, she is attempting even now. As for the rest, which she knows not, nor I except by hearsay, I sent her to a midwife whom all declare is skilled in these matters. God grant that the child be cast, then our master and his son and house and all Israel will be rid of an evil thing."

"And if not?" Hosea ventured. "If the midwife should fail?"

"Then I say yet again," Talmon broke in, "what I said before: it does not come near or touch our matter."

But as he sat at the Sabbath table, darkening and invaded by shadows as the lamps above burned lower, Hosea knew that the truth was not as Talmon had said. The child, be it his or a bastard, was kin to him, coming near to and touching him intimately. For can a man turn away or close his eyes to his own flesh?

• • •

BEFORE LONG, THE REALITY OF THESE FEELINGS came far closer to Hosea than even he had foreseen.

Abruptly, without warning or explanation, Gomer ceased to visit Jezreel.

"I shall not go to inquire," Shualith all but vowed, directing her protest to herself rather than Hosea or Talmon, neither of whom had suggested such a course. "If she is ill, good. Dying, better yet. When she has rotted ten years in the grave, I shall give her the pleasure of a visit."

But a fortnight later, she was arguing with herself to another effect. "If she has cast the child," she thought, "it is something which I should much desire to know."

In the end, then, it was the hopefulness of her curiosity which took her to Gomer's lodgings.

Her words concerning her former mistress were as harsh as ever when she returned home, but the venom was out of them.

"Gomer is ill," she reported to Hosea. "Not so ill as she deserves, but ill enough, from the philters and medicaments no doubt, but most of all from the willow wand which the midwife used on her. The fetus, alas, seems well. She wastes, and her belly swells."

Hosea saw that Shualith, though she would not confess it, was deeply shaken by what she had seen.

"Now that she lies among strangers, with none to bring her so much as a cup of water, she is learning to value better the care and comfort her wantonness cast aside."

"But surely," Hosea asked urgently, too concerned to fret over the propriety of his concern, "surely she has a maidservant to tend her."

"*Had,*" Shualith answered. "There was a wench, but she ran off not only with the wages due her but with all the money in the strongbox—and it was no small sum. Now there will be no silver to hire another maid until Gomer can get it from the moneychanger to whom she has entrusted the larger part of the dower you paid her."

He should exult over the punishment which had overtaken her. Let her, as Shualith said, learn in bitterness the good she had lost in losing him. But there was no gladness in him, only the pain of pity and a desire to help her, a desire that for the moment at least obscured all hateful memories. Only his pride before Shualith and fear of her contempt restrained him.

"Master," Shualith continued, "you know that I hate her for the wrong she has done you and your house, a wrong the greater for your loving-kindness to her, and that you raised her from a dung heap to sit beside you. Were she dead now, I could look on her corpse and rejoice, aye, praise God for it. But she is not dead; she suffers."

She looked up at Hosea's face and, misreading the strain of containing himself for obduracy, forgot her own hardness and began to plead.

"Master, you who cannot endure to look on anything in pain, even a beast or a bird, the merest insect, surely you will not prevent that her plight be eased."

"Then what do you purpose? Shall I hire another maidservant to tend her?"

"Can you afford it, master?"

He grimaced. "Not easily."

"So I thought. But she has money remaining—"

"No," he exploded. "If I do aught for her, and mind you, I say *if*, I shall do it of my own means."

"Indeed, master," she hastened, hoping to placate him. "Besides, there is no advantage in a strange maidservant. She will pocket of the money with which she is sent to market, lie concerning the prices, and then of the food she has brought back will steal for her own family."

"Then what is your counsel?" he asked.

"I shall tend her."

"But the child," Hosea protested, "and this household, who will look after them?"

"I also."

"And how will you be in two places at once?"

Shualith's face took on the look of long-suffering tolerance of a woman explaining something so obvious that only a man can fail to comprehend it.

"Obviously, if she remains where she is it would be impossible. But when did Moses ordain that she must live there and there alone? In this courtyard, in the corner house across the way, is an empty chamber. Let her be brought there. Then to what I cook, I shall add enough for her, and when I clean here I shall clean there also, if need be taking the child with me."

He was drawn and disquieted by the prospect which had opened up so unexpectedly, drawn and disquieted with such power that he had to deny it instantly.

"You must not expect me to see or speak to her."

"And who says, foolish one," she appeased, "that you must?"

It was easy then for him to assent as a concession to what he desired mightily in any case.

"So be it then."

Now that she had achieved her purpose, her vindictiveness returned, perhaps genuine, perhaps feigned to conceal compassion.

"Fear not—I have not forgotten," she concluded. "And neither shall she."

•   •   •

NOT UNTIL THE VERY HOUR of the birth did Hosea decide what would be.

All through the autumn and early winter, during the time of its gestation, Hosea was convinced the child was a monster. That it would be born with two heads, perhaps, or no eyes, or a hairy skin like a goat's cloak—might its father be the goat of a man who was Iddo—or a brand on its forehead like that of Cain, he was certain.

And yet, contrariwise, the thought of the child awakened in him a gentle curiosity, and, sometimes, a quickening of the pulse. After all, the baby might be of his creation and fashioning. There was, then, a sense of its possible innocence. Thoughts such as these were never more prevalent than on those rare occasions on which he caught glimpses of Gomer.

These glimpses were not frequent and occurred only during the winter, after she had recovered from her malady, and before the flowering of the almond trees. In the early mornings and later afternoons of this season, when the heat was not too strong, she sat on a stool before the doorway that led to her chamber, taking in the fresh air, and Hosea, passing by, spied her now and again. The short course along the opposite side of the courtyard between his apartment and the open street prevented long gazes, while children at play and housewives at the mills, ovens, or open fires intercepted his line of vision.

But these glimpses sufficed to reveal the pallor underneath the duskiness of her skin, the listlessness of her posture and of the folding of her hands in her lap, the ravaged thinness of her face and bare arms—all of her except where she swelled with new life. She was so pathetic, so pitiable, so seemingly innocent that his morbidity concerning the child she carried seemed altogether ludicrous. But always memory returned, and the knowledge of right and wrong, sin and expiation.

At the New Moon of Adar, on a black night of heavy rains and booming west winds, her time overtook Gomer.

The neighbor she had sent to summon Shualith cried her news to all the world as she ran across the courtyard, and, shaking the latch violently, shouted it through the door to Hosea's apartment. Startled into wakefulness, Hosea sprang from his bed. But Talmon had already raised the wick of the night lamp and unbolted the door, while Shualith, as he could hear through the partition, was dressing hastily. There was nothing for him to do. He quieted little Jezreel who, having been disturbed but not wakened by the tumult, stirred uneasily in his crib. Then he crept back into his bed, wrapped the covers about him, and, telling himself that he had no part in what befell her and the child she was bearing, resolutely closed his eyes.

But sleep was impossible. He relived the birth of Jezreel, the torment of anxiety and hope, the upsurge of elation, the giddiness of joy when the child had been born. The contrast between what had been then and was now stunned him with sadness.

And he could not let off calculating, counting back the months. People said that a child born in the eighth month could not live. By this then, by whether the child lived or died, he might learn whose it was. Second thoughts chilled him. How could he be sure of the rule? There were those who scoffed at it. And if it were true and the child lived, thus disclosing its nine-month birth and that it was his, was its conception any less polluted?

The night dragged on. The town guards called the beginning of the third watch and then, interminably later, its end. All the while, Hosea held the bedclothes against himself, firmly, waiting for word.

In the graying dawn, as cocks crowed in the many chicken runs of the vicinity and the stirring of daytime activity began in the courtyard, Hosea, his fingers and limbs stiff with strain, gave in to himself. Shivering, and with forced deliberateness, he put aside the covers, rose, dressed, opened the door, and, through the dim light and chill, walked across the courtyard to Gomer's doorway.

He was glad it was the neighbor woman who came to the door rather than Shualith, for then he did not need to ask the questions for which he desired answers.

"Alas," she began.

His heart plummeted.

She observed Hosea's face and said in a joyful tone, "Alas, a wondrous thing."

His pulse raced with relief.

"It lives?" he asked.

"It?" the woman asked. "You mean the mother? She not only lives, I have never seen her like for strength. Lips tight and not an outcry from her, not even at the end—"

"I meant the child," he corrected curtly.

She smiled.

"Let me see," he commanded.

The woman nodded and went inside. The bundle when she returned seemed all swaddling clothes.

He stared down at it, looking for the opening in the wrappings.

The woman chuckled. "Eh, men, all alike, all helpless. Here, if you would take her, I shall uncover her face."

"No," he said, drawing back. There was such passion in his voice that she looked at him first in bewilderment, then with shrewd comprehension.

"I intended it not as a token of fatherhood," she began to explain, "but only because it would be easier—"

"Show me the child's face, as I commanded," he said, "and spare me your speech and snooping alike."

"At once, my lord, at once."

She cradled the bundle in one arm and with her free hand put one flap of cloth aside in one direction and one flap in another.

He was all of him rigid and unbreathing as he waited, his eyes fixed and straining toward the place where her hand busied itself.

"There," she said and tilted the bundle so that he might see better.

Before him was a tiny face, a girl with dark eyes, wide open and staring back at him. She was an infant like all others, only fairer than most, and though he scanned her over and over looking for some ugliness or stigma such as he had felt, yet he could see only the sweetness of a newborn baby. Hosea found himself yearning toward her. And when he thought of the fatherlessness of this mite, and of the great black guilt that even now overshadowed her white innocence, he all but reached out to take her in his arms to comfort her.

Poor, poor little creature, he thought. Then, in a flash, he despised himself. No, not that. Let there be an end of weakness.

"I have been sorry enough for those who have sinned against me. This one will not be pitied," he said. "Let her be called Lo-Ruchama."

CHAPTER XIV

FOR WEEKS, Hosea saw not so much as a glimpse of either the child or her mother. It was full into winter, and none sat in the courtyard these chilly days, let alone a woman just risen from her confinement. Nor did Hosea come near her apartment. What he knew of either mother or child he learned from Shualith. The baby, he was given to understand, was, by some perversity of the Lord, beautiful and flourishing. Gomer was, though well, lethargic and withdrawn. And Hosea gathered that, for every kindness she conferred on Gomer, Shualith exacted full compensation in suffering, determined so far as she could effect it that her former mistress should experience neither pleasure nor peace. Knowing the servant's capacity for malice and her ingenuity and perseverance, Hosea disliked to think of the subtle torments she was inflicting in speech and silence, in gesture and in glance. But Gomer was no more his wife, and were she, she was being accorded no more than her desserts. And so he listened, and said nothing, never once chiding Shualith or remonstrating with her.

So it went until the approach of spring, when two events

occurred simultaneously: Talmon fell gravely ill, and Gomer, through Shualith, asked to see Hosea.

Talmon always claimed to have been born in the nineteenth year of Jehu, king of Israel, so his age was the by-no-means inconsiderable sum of three score ten and five. And yet to this very season he had been robust. To be sure, he complained now and again of sleeplessness and loss of appetite, of aches here and pains there. He grumbled too that he had naught to do and that time hung heavy on his hands. Watching Shualith at her many duties, he often quoted the saying of the people of the land: "An old man in a house is a curse; an old woman a blessing."

Actually he was not as busy as he might desire, but he was not altogether idle either. There were few household chores which he was incapable of performing or from which he abstained out of shame on the ground that only women might with propriety do them. An old soldier like himself was proof against the taunt of unmanliness. He cooked, baked, washed, and even sewed. All in all, though he spoke of himself as rusting away like an unused weapon, there was little truth in his saying. And as for health, he was for all the world as frail as an ancient cedar which is twisted, gnarled, and largely leafless, but tough enough to outstand the wildest storms.

Shualith was convinced, and Hosea disposed to agree with her, that the cause of her husband's sickness was neither old age nor idleness, but grief over the misfortune which had befallen his master's family. That he should be required to despise any of Beeri's sons, and most especially the one who was the apple of his eye, and that he should see the household he had served these many years, not the greatest in Israel yet not the least either, brought down to the dust, consumed him like a worm at the heart of a tree and, like it, in the end brought him low.

It was at this juncture, when having taken to bed he scarcely ever rose from it and then only to totter feebly about the room and return to bed once more, that Shualith, having run across the courtyard for a moment to see what was with Gomer and Lo-Ruchama, came back saying to Hosea, "She desires to speak to you."

Hosea frowned. "I have no business with her."

"So I said, and so she acknowledges. Nevertheless, she desires to speak to you and will come here for that purpose if you so desire."

"Tell her no," he said firmly.

But within a day or so, Shualith brought it to him again. "She insists on speaking to you," she reported.

"Insists?" Hosea snorted. "And on what ground is she so bold?"

"She says that were it concerning herself she would never trouble you, but it is on the score of the little girl."

"Who is even less to me. Bid her keep herself and her child at a distance."

The third time, however, Shualith had no request to make but an offer to impart.

"She says she is about to offer the child for sale and desires to know your mind before she gives it out, whether you would wish to purchase her yourself."

Now he was shaken in earnest. It was pointless for him to insist that this concerned him not. Bastard or legitimate, his brother's or his, the baby was kin to him. She was taking too much on herself. Reluctant as he was to see her, let alone speak with her, she needed to have a lesson read her.

He muttered a word of explanation to Shualith and, without putting on a top cloak against the spring shower which was falling, strode across the courtyard to her door. He knocked on it. As soon as he heard the sound of voice, he entered.

She was standing on the far side of a waist-high, tripoded charcoal brazier. Her face was raised to the door, and she held a steaming pot, just removed from the fire. The room in its further corners was shadowy with dusk, steam, and smoke, but in its center where the coals glowed all was clear, and he could see her plainly.

Her face was paler than he remembered it and very thin, so that there were hollows under her cheekbones, and her eyes seemed larger, too large indeed. She was startled now to see him so that her expression was animated, but about and through it was a quietude of resignation and sadness. And he was taken aback to observe that all these changes which should have diminished her beauty had somehow made her more beautiful, hauntingly, wistfully so.

"You are kind to come," she said. "Pray be seated." She indicated a stool near the door.

But he would have none of the amenities.

"What means this which I have been told, that the girl child is to be sold?"

She was about to answer but the pot was in her hand. She looked at it helplessly for a moment and then back to him.

"I desire not to delay my lord, but if he will wait for a moment, no more, until I have completed what I am doing, I shall be able to speak to him with composure."

She took his silence for consent and proceeded to put a lid on the pot and carried it to a box in a corner where she covered it with sand almost to its rim to hold in its warmth.

He noted the meager furnishings of the room—a crude table, a lamp, two stools, a narrow bed, and near it the crib for the infant, all bare of tapestry or ornament, except that a bowl in the center of the table glowed with several hyacinths, procured somehow from the countryside where they were now in blossom.

Hosea's eyes followed Gomer. Her arms too had thinned, and her body also, but her breasts were full from motherhood so that she appeared at once painfully frail and yet disturbingly lush. Disquieted, he averted his eyes determinedly, but not without a spasm of regret over his loss. Then she was returning to the doorway where he stood and he thrust away all feeling except scorn.

"Yes?" he said, renewing his question laconically.

She pointed inquiringly to a stool but when he took no notice dropped her hand and said listlessly, "I must give up the baby and I did not know but that you would desire to take it."

"And why must you give her up?"

"Because I cannot remain here."

He raised a shoulder and arched a brow in inquiry.

"I cannot," she replied to his unspoken question. "You have been good to me, once sparing my life when it was forfeit and a second time saving it when it hovered on the brink of Sheol. I have troubled you enough. Now I would go hence before you send me."

"I have said nothing to this purpose," he said curtly.

"Nay, but soon you will. Why then should I tarry to trouble you?"

"Besides," she looked him directly in the eyes, "I do not forget my guilt against you, not for a moment, be it morning, noon, or night. Sin makes all things bitter, but there is nothing bitterer than kindness from the hands of the one sinned against. I cannot eat your bread, Hosea, nor sleep under the roof you have provided. Your generosity does not ease, it makes intolerable my unworthiness."

She paused, waiting for him to speak.

He remained silent, as was she for a moment.

Her speech when she resumed it continued gentle and controlled. "It is hard to accept charity at any time or circumstance, harder to accept it undeserved, harder still when it is rendered instead of judgment, but it is an impossibility beyond all conceiving when, in addition to all else, it springs from and is further fueled by hate. You have all been kind to me, Talmon, Shualith, and most incredibly you, Hosea. But yours has been...there being no word for it, I have framed one for myself...yours has been a *hating* kindness."

For the first time Hosea was aware what she meant. This must have contributed to the hollowing of her cheeks and draining of their color, the sinking of her eyes and casting over her countenance the shadow of suffering and wistfulness. But of all this he would disclose nothing.

"So be it," he said. "You will not remain here. Being free, you may go when and where you please, and as for reasons, you owe me no explanation and I desire none. My interest is only this: what you purpose with the child and wherefore."

She flushed. Once she would have reared in high-spirited indignation, but now when her eyes flared, it was with hurt, and her lips opened not to speak protest but submission.

"I understand. But it is because I depart from here that I must dispose of the child."

"And why can she not accompany you?"

"If only..." Gomer breathed, then recovering her control, went on. "No, not whither I go."

"And whither may that be?"

"Whither think you?" she asked, a flash of her spirit breaking through. "What is a woman to do who has no family to whom she can turn, Charun being far worse than no kin at all, who, having been divorced, is undesirable for a wife, of whose dower money some is already spent and some stolen so that between one and the other a substantial part is gone? Shall she wait until it is all gone and then sell herself to slave? Or shall she, while she still has silver, establish herself?"

"And where may that be?"

Now she was bitter. "You will compel me to say it aloud. Then hear me, I go to the Left Shoulder."

Still he did not understand, whereupon she went on in a fury of flagellation of herself and perhaps of him also.

"Do you hear me, Hosea? I, Gomer, your former wife, become a harlot. With the money you have furnished, I establish myself, and in one of the best houses. With your writ of divorcement, I am exempt from the prosecution to which respectable women are liable for lying with men wed to others."

He wanted to cry out in denial and prohibition. But dazed as he was by what she was saying, he remembered that he had no authority over or claim to her, that if she wished to sell herself for gain, to give the lips and breasts, the limbs and body he had loved to others, he could not gainsay it. Harrowed at the thought but powerless before it, he struck out at her.

"You purpose wisely," he said with icy indifference. "To be a harlot comes naturally to you."

It was as though someone else than himself were uttering this incredible cruelty. Hearing it, he was horrified by its callousness. Ashamed of himself also that he should be capable of taking advantage of her defenselessness, he realized that he was like one who puts a stumbling block before the blind or curses the deaf.

When his mind cleared sufficiently for him to observe her, his heart all but died for remorse. She was relapsing from the indignation into which she must have stiffened. There had been fight in her but it was there no more.

She said quietly, "Therefore, I must give the child away...." Her eyes began to glisten with tears. "To adoption, I pray the Lord, and not into bondage. Only, where in Israel is the household that desires a girl baby? So I am brought to ask you for still another act of mercy."

Hosea did not answer.

"If I sell her as a bondmaid," she pleaded, "even into a God-fearing household, who knows what will be with her? Who will make sure that she does not hunger and thirst, that she is bathed and combed? Who will tend her when she sickens? Her master, to whom she is a thing purchased for five shekels? The overseer, to whom she is one more responsibility? The older maids, bitter with their own lot?"

She was frightened now and speaking more urgently.

"And how is one to be sure that she will not be maltreated, kicked and pinched and beaten? Who will there be, wherever she may be, who will stand to protect her?

"And when she begins to grow up, who will guard her from abuse at her master's hands, or if not his, his sons', or if not theirs, other servants'. And suppose she is sold out of the land, so that I never see her again."

Her fright had become sheer panic.

"Tell me I merit all this. I shall cry amen and amen. Tell me her birth has been unclean; I shall not gainsay it. Yet she herself has done no wrong. Whatever the sin, it is not hers. One need only look at her to be assured of that. Would the Lord have fashioned her as she is were she condemned by Him, white and pink and well favored and sweet, so very sweet? Look at her, Hosea, I beg you, look at her, and your eyes will tell you whether my sin is on her."

The torrent of her supplication swept over him, but he was no longer aware of it. He was thinking bitterly how always and forever he was trapped, betrayed by pity and, if not by that, then by conscience.

At this moment he was not much moved by Gomer's distress. Why or how he could not tell, but for the present at least he looked on it unstirred.

But his freedom from one master was swallowed up in bondage to another. The child, his own or bastard, was his kin and a man does not, except of direct necessity, sell his own flesh into bondage.

"Bring the child hither. I shall take her."

In an excess of relief and gratitude she threw herself to the ground at his feet. This seemed intolerable to Hosea. He winced and drew back, and she, bowed over to the floor, sensed his recoil. Instantly she was silent. Then she rose, keeping her face, even after she had come erect, averted out of shame. She went to the crib, looked down into it, lifted up the baby, and brought her to him.

He extended his arms to receive the bundle but so reluctantly that it all but slid out of them. Both started and grasped it in time to prevent its falling. He said nothing, but she understood. Her face was still averted from him, her eyes fixed on the child she was surrendering.

She whispered. "Have pity on her, Hosea."

And as he strode angrily across the courtyard, the unwanted burden in his arms, he raged inside himself.

The duty one owes his flesh, that she shall have. But of anything more, he couldn't say.

• • •

THAT NIGHT TALMON WAS GATHERED to his fathers, dying with a quietude which was more like falling into an unusually deep sleep. The next noon, Shualith, Hosea, and Mibsam buried him alongside those who lacked the wealth or dignity of family sepulchres. Thence they returned home, wife and master, to mourn the loss together.

Hosea took comfort in the familiar rites. The meal prepared by their neighbors, wherewith they should refresh their souls against grief, awaited them when they returned from the cemetery. In the daytime of all the seven days, Shualith and Hosea sat only on the low, overturned benches, sackcloth about their loins and ashes on their heads, Hosea joining in the rites as though Talmon were to him kin by blood. Their neighbors visited them, family by family, to comfort them. All of which was none other than could be discerned in any stricken household in Israel.

On the second day of mourning came the information that Gomer had departed her chamber, bag and baggage.

On the fourth day of mourning, it was reported that Iddo had returned to Samaria, and had occupied the house of Beeri. Sitting on their overturned benches, Shualith and Hosea shared looks of comprehension with each other. What had happened was self-evident. Through someone or other Iddo must have kept close surveillance on Hosea's household, waiting for some development to liberate him from exile. Talmon's death was such an event. For now only one witness, Mibsam, remained of his offense, whereas it is by the testimony of no fewer than two that an accusation is validated. It all came out even: one day for Iddo's spy to learn of Talmon's death, two for a forced journey to Ashkelon, and two more for Iddo's return.

Then on the sixth day, the rumor came to Hosea's household that Iddo had established his brother's former wife in his own household as concubine.

"Can he do it?" Shualith burst out as soon as the comforters were gone, her own sorrow forgotten in indignation. "Will the elders permit such a scandal? It is his brother's nakedness that he is uncovering, for though she is not now your wife, she was once—alas the day. Is not that forbidden by the Law of Moses… yea, and punishable by death?"

Through his dismay Hosea had been pondering the same question.

"I do not know," he said. "Had she gone to him directly from me, then wedded or divorced, they would have been under the displeasure and penalty of the law. But he took her from a house on the Left Shoulder and, no matter how little time she tarried there, she had become on very entrance as one of the base women, and concerning them some say the law touches them as all others and others say not."

"They must not be held guiltless," she hissed. "Is it not enough for them to have defrauded you and broken your heart, that they must make a mockery of you in all Israel? This you cannot swallow. You must go to the elders, the judges, the king himself if need be, to see that justice be done and you avenged."

Hosea burned with a powerful wrath of his own. But he retained his reason.

"Do you suppose my brother is heedlessly risking of his precious neck? Rest content that, in the day since he returned, he has consulted and been reassured by appropriate authorities."

"And on that conjecture you will let yourself be humiliated and not go to law?"

Hosea shook his head.

"Not on that conjecture alone—though knowing my brother I know it to be more than a conjecture—but for another reason also. He is rich, very rich, and I am poor. Is there any court in Samaria where a poor man will be accorded his justice against one who is rich?"

"And still," she persisted, "you must defend yourself. If it cannot be in law, then let it be by arms. Kill them, Hosea, both of them, and you will not only not be punished, but all Israel from Dan to Beersheva will applaud you. Or if you fear to do this, then hire those who will venture it. In the cleft there are assassins who for a silver piece will slit a throat or two throats. Let their blood flow and in it be vindicated."

She was beside herself, as Hosea might readily have been had he permitted it. He knew himself too well by now for self-delusion.

He shook his head. "It is not out of fear, at least I think not, but out of another weakness that I do not seek their souls. Once I held their lives in the palm of my hand, needing only to close my fingers and they would be crushed, yet I could not because I pitied them. If I behaved so cravenly then, in the freshness of my first wrath over their treachery, can I deceive myself as to how I will comport myself now?

"Do you not understand, Shualith? If I had the two of them bound and helpless before me and held a knife in my hand and Jeroboam, king of Israel, stood by and said, 'Cut their throats and I will proclaim you pardoned and attest it with my royal seal,' then my heart would leap with joy at the prospect—but my hand be limp and powerless to act. Have you in all your days heard of such a weakness in a man?"

Shualith studied him—his thinness, his gray drawn face, his stooped gray form. Half inclined to spit in contempt and half to give him comfort, she did neither, and turned her frustrated anger in another direction.

"And that hypocrite and dissembler," she stormed, "pretending grief that she must take herself to a house of harlotry, and all the time playing on your sympathies, all for the purpose of foisting her little bastard on you and coming disencumbered to her paramour."

This possibility had been suggesting itself to Hosea from the very beginning, with the news of Gomer's going to Iddo. Now that it had been put into words, he had to face up to it. It seemed plausible, and yet he refused to believe it, in part because he was reluctant to be shown up for so great a dupe, but even more because, for all the evidence to the contrary, he could not believe it of her. That she had been lover, half seduced, half willing, to Iddo, yes; that she had preferred becoming Iddo's concubine to being in a house of harlotry, and did so when the opportunity had arisen, yes; but that she had deliberately overreached Hosea, no. A harlot and whore she might be, a trickster never.

But before he could say anything to Shualith, she spoke again, this time of something else.

"But what will you do before men?"

This too he had already considered. Heretofore his ordeal had been secret, a wound to be nursed, an ache and rage to be assuaged in privacy. His divorce of Gomer had been taken as no more than a divorce, sudden and abrupt perhaps, but no more so than a hundred others. In any case, no one, so far as he was aware, had associated it with Iddo's flight, which Hosea had given out and which had been taken for a return to military service in Ashkelon. Now he would have to endure the scorn of the world.

"What will you do?" Shualith repeated.

"I do not know," he replied. "Yet do not fear. Having endured what I have already endured, I shall no doubt contrive to endure this also."

Whereupon Shualith demonstrated that she had not lived with a soldier to no profit these many years. For from her mouth sputtered curses such as are heard only in barracks and about campfires. Hosea stared, and for a few moments amusement mollified the hard edge of his grief and shame.

• • •

THERE WAS, HOWEVER, NOTHING at all amusing about the world's manner toward Hosea, once it became aware of the true state of his affairs. People whispered and pointed after him in the courtyard of the house in which he lived. Once, someone drunken stood before his door in the deep of night chanting:

> *The partridge hatches and broods over*
> *Eggs it has not laid.*

In the Hall of Scribes, too, it was different for him because of Gomer's going to Iddo. Heretofore, if he had not had many friends among his fellows, he had enjoyed, he was certain, their respect. But now he could detect in their glances and speech, nor was it his imagining, condescension, ribald mirth, contempt.

This was an inequity not to be endured: that those who had sinned should go unscathed, while he who had been sinned against should be the butt of the world's despising. If heretofore he had felt himself guilty before God for not having done what was ordained, the Lord, he now felt, owed him an accounting for that in which He was now derelict.

Of Kiryoth Arba, the city which aforetime was called Lux, it was told that in days of yore the angel of death was forbidden to enter its gates to take his prey. The legend says that the people of Lux, when they had lived enough, though they might have gone on living forever, would go abroad into the fields beyond the walls to seek him out. Wherein it is demonstrated that there is nothing, not even death itself, to which men will not in the end accommodate themselves.

As for Hosea, he came to accept the outrage which had been done him. He made peace with his own loveless and womanless existence. He hardened himself against the importunities of matchmakers who, upon hearing that he had put aside his wife, besieged him with offers of marriage. Yet, as soon as they discovered that he had retained none of the wealth of his house, they withdrew their entreaties. He learned to reconcile himself to his children's motherlessness. He gave Lo-Ruchama asylum and became father to her. Once she had been weaned of the wetnurse who nurtured her after Gomer had departed, he would, on returning home in the evening from the Hall of Scribes, feed her and put her to bed. When she began to raise herself to her feet he would give her his forefingers to cling to, exactly as he had done with Jezreel, and when she fell and cried from fright and hurt he would, though he had sworn otherwise, have compassion on her and speak softly to her and dry her tears. He came to terms even with his weakness of pity and with the contempt and self-revulsion in which he held himself because of it.

With these things he made a peace of sorts.

• • •

DURING THE YEAR THAT FOLLOWED, only once did he see Gomer. She was coming down the Avenue of the Left Shoulder as Hosea was coming up it, but on the other side. Even at a considerable distance he knew her by her carriage and gait, and this though she wore, after the fashion of the hour, anklets bound together by a silver chain, so that her steps were shortened and she minced as she walked. He had long half awaited, half dreaded his first encounter with her, uncertain how he would respond. Now he slowed, his heart pounded, and the impulse arose to slip into a doorway so that he might pass unseen. But he was no thief found housebreaking that he should conceal himself. He went on, controlling the evenness of his stride, watching her meanwhile.

Her robe was saffron, the color of the crocus; her veil was green like its leaves and flowed down her sides and back like the haze of spring. A maidservant walked by her side bearing a silver mirror in one hand and a jeweled perfume box in the other. Talking to her, Gomer's face was turned in her direction but somewhat downward, so that without being seen himself Hosea could see her quite well, the ordered array into which her wild curls had been tamed, the silver crescent that danced on her forehead, the kohl about her eyes that set off their dark flashing, the rouge on her cheeks and lips. She seemed brilliant as he had never seen her before and more beautiful even than he remembered her. Then as she was passing him, he caught the faint tinkling of the bells on her anklets, trailing behind her like a perfume, but in sound not in scent. Then she was gone and an instant later the sound that attended her, and he was aware, after the pounding of his heart had subsided, first of a great empty sadness, and then, when he reflected that her face had showed no trace of remorse or sorrow, of anger.

Over the next months, Hosea saw his brother frequently, in the courtyard of the royal palace or in the Broad Place before it, sometimes alone but more often in the company of the city's carousers, who, had they not been rich and of noble birth, would have been numbered among the sons of Belial. On occasion Hosea heard talk in the Hall of Scribes of banquets and drinking bouts in which his brother and his fellows engaged, or of pranks he had played. With each reference to Iddo, with each sight of him, Hosea experienced a knotting of the bowels and a quickening of the heartbeat, like one surprised in a guilty secret, and then indignation against himself that he should be unable to desist from responding as though the offense were his own rather than Iddo's. He felt outrage at the brightness and lightness of his brother's days, the prosperity with which his wickedness was rewarded. The contrast with his own lot was something on which a man might not reflect too long lest he go mad.

But though he saw Iddo from afar not infrequently, Hosea heard his voice and looked on him near at hand only once more. This came to pass on the day of the uprising against Jeroboam in the name of Omri, great-great-grandson to him so named who one hundred years earlier had been king over Israel.

When Jehu, father of Jeroboam, seized the throne, he slew seventy members of the royal family. The young Omri, however, fled to the cities of the coastland. There he found refuge among the Philistines, who gave him asylum and provided him with a house, food, and raiment according to his station, in the hope that someday he might be of use to them against Israel. But Jehu sat firmly on the throne he had seized, and Jeroboam more firmly still. Years before, Omri's followers had rallied a rebellion, and, attended by a mixed multitude of Philistines and Israelite outlaws, crossed the borders into Israel. But few had joined the insurrection, and Omri's followers had fled back to Gaza, shamefaced and without having come even into sight of the mighty host which Jeroboam, then a young man, was mustering against them.

But now it was otherwise. Jeroboam was weary with years and weak with sickness of the belly, and Zechariah, his firstborn, was well known to be feeble of wit, so that if ever he came to the throne, it was said, he would not tarry on it long.

And now, with the army of Israel at Hamath near Damascus, far from Samaria, the occasion was too auspicious to wait longer. Omri conspired with his followers to fall upon Jeroboam and Zechariah on a certain day, slaying them and all their kin. Whatever forces they could raise were now crossing the frontier into Israel. Once Jeroboam was dead and Samaria in his own hands, Omri planned, the army would come to terms.

Those who labored in the Hall of Scribes heard an outcry from the palace across the courtyard. Then shouts and screams, the tumult of doors being forced and furniture and pottery broken, then, unmistakably, the clash of arms. Frozen to their desks at the first sound, the scribes looked at one other, aghast, and then rushed to the doors and windows in time to see a eunuch of the queen's retinue run forth into the courtyard. The eunuch cried to those who stood frozen in the courtyard and to those who crowded the windows and doorways.

"Help! Help! Conspiracy! The House of Omri has risen against our lord the king. Help! The battle is at the doors of the king's chamber!"

Every face among the scribes paled. Men clasped hands in horror as they thought of what this might portend: bloodshed, the plunder of gods, the rape of the women, the devastation of the city and the land. Each man too calculated frantically what this news meant for him, the cold of fear turning yet colder in those whose kin had been close to the House of Jehu.

The eunuch stood in the center of the courtyard, screaming his news again and again. Then his shrill voice was overtaken by the blowing of rams' horns and also trumpets, sounding alarm calls and summoning the king's guard to arms and ordering the closing of the palace gates.

Almost at once there burst into the courtyard an officer of the king's guard followed by a little company of four men, rushing at breakneck speed past the eunuch toward the far gate of the courtyard, which opened onto still another gate, the outermost of the palace.

"Faster, faster," the officer shouted ahead to the sentry who had begun to tug at the great brass-bound doors. "Help him," he ordered his men, himself stopping in the middle of the courtyard to allow them to outrun him. He watched as the leaves of the gate were shut and the bar lowered into the brackets.

He was a giant of a man, with a great beard and hairy arms, formidable though his helmet was awry on his head and only one leg was sheathed with a greave. Hosea recognized him, though from where or what his name might be he could not recall.

"Now," he commanded, "two of you into the postern to defend against attack from without and two of you to guard it from within. If any approach through the exterior court, send word to the royal apartments. As for the rest of you," he shouted above the continuing tumult to those who crowded the windows, story above story, and to those who, having fled the open enclosure of the courtyard, now huddled against the walls under the colonnades, "we know not who is friend and who foe. You will remain, each man in his place."

He looked about the courtyard, sweeping it with a warning scrutiny, then dashed toward the door from which he had come, only to collide on its threshold with another officer. The two men pulled apart, their hands darting to the hilts of their swords but falling away as they recognized each other. The one who was coming out spoke urgently, gesticulating wildly and brandishing an arm toward the courtyard. The other nodded, turned on his heel, and returned to the courtyard.

"Hear me now," he called, pronouncing each word carefully. "If there is any here who is skilled in arms and who loves the lord our king and is faithful to the House of Jehu, let him come forth. There is need of him."

He looked about. From the crowd under the colonnade, several men stepped forward.

"Now," whispered Binyamin, who had worked alongside Hosea since the days of Noam the Naphtalite, "I praise my father that he trained me to wield a pen and not a sword."

"Whoever volunteers himself," the officer now called, "will win the king's gratitude."

When no more than two or three more joined the little knot that had assembled in the center of the courtyard, the officer added: "There will be a reward of fifty shekels."

"Enough for a grave," Binyamin muttered.

"Honors," the officer urged.

"A decent burial, if one's kin recover the body."

"The loving kindness of the king, forever."

"And the torturer's rack, if he is overcome."

"Are there so few, then," the officer cried bitterly, "to stand forth on behalf of a king who has ruled thus justly these forty years? Is there not even one more?"

"One more here," one called from among the scribes. The voice, issuing from his throat to his own amazement, was Hosea's. While his heart pounded, it was also lighter.

"Madman, what is this to you?" Binyamin spat into his ear, and when Hosea started to elbow his way out of the crowd at the window, clung to an arm to detain him.

Hosea tore himself loose. "Has Israel had a better king than this Jeroboam? Is not each son of Israel bound by oath to defend him?"

Only when Hosea had reached the band of volunteers in the center of the courtyard and taken his place among them was he aware that Binyamin had not only ceased to detain him but had himself followed along, together with several of the younger scribes.

"The king is in your debt," Binyamin said. "You have rounded up no small flock of sheep for sacrifice." He grinned shamefacedly.

The officer who had continued his appeal now gave up. He looked at the volunteers, shrugged, and waved them to follow at a run across the courtyard into the palace and down a corridor to an armory room. There he again appraised the band he had recruited.

"Fifty thousand men-at-arms," he groaned, "in the host of Israel, and with gleanings from the dung heap the life of the king must be defended." Then, with raised voice, "Mayhap there will be no need of you. The rebels seem no more than two hundred. On our side we have the same, perhaps a larger number than they. But we must guard this side of the palace, for we do not yet know the mind of the populace nor who else may be with the conspirators. Therefore we fight at a disadvantage in numbers and are hard-pressed. Time, however, is on our side. We need only hold fast til the army comes."

"From Hamath?" someone cried, aghast.

"From Tirzah, where there is a company in rest camp," snapped the officer, attended by so savage a glare at the questioner that no one dared to ask other questions foremost in everyone's mind: how large the company stationed in Tirzah might be, whether it was to be depended on for loyalty, how word of the situation in the palace was to reach it.

"And now to work. Let every man skilled in arms take that weapon in which he is skilled, be it bow, sword, spear, or battle-axe, those unskilled what they desire, but each a dagger, for if the rebels breach the doors of the king's chambers the fighting will be hand-to-hand. Now, be quick."

The racks and stands were full of weapons of all sorts and of high grade, stacked in careful array. It required but a moment for most of the men to find weapons of their choice. Not so the six, Hosea and Binyamin among them, who elected to serve as archers, for they needed to select among bows for weight and strength, to bend and string them, to pick arrows and to pack quivers.

The officer did not tarry for them.

"Be ready against my return," he instructed the archers and led the others off to their stations.

He was back almost at once. "Come," he ordered, "there is need for you."

They followed him along corridors and up staircases, endless corridors and staircases that led always upward, until, when it seemed their hearts would burst and their lungs explode if they went further, they broke into the light of day.

They were brought to a roof garden atop the citadel which was the inmost edifice of the palace, which housed the king's chambers. Below them and beyond a balustraded stone parapet was a courtyard, and beyond it the Hall of Justice and the Treasury, the two buildings forming the eastern and the western limits of the palace compound. To the north and south ran walls as thick and tall as the buildings they linked. Intended to complete the outer shell of the palace, they had been built of great blocks of hewn stone, capable of resisting the stoutest instruments of siege. But their fortifications—the crenellations on top, the loopholes in the walls—all faced toward the city against attack from without. Against treachery from within they afforded no defense. Indeed, their broad flat tops, as wide as city streets, constituted bridges across which the conspirators might complete their invasion of the king's chambers, where the walls abutted on the roof garden. Hosea watched as swordsmen of the king's guard piled furniture into barricades—couches of ivory inlay, tables of acacia wood, statues of kings, images of gods.

"That is where they are, the bulk of them." The officer pointed toward the king's court and Treasury. "They hold also a doorway and a corridor beneath us, on the first story of the Citadel. But there we have contained them. The next attack may likely come here. Your orders are to watch for it and to shoot to kill anyone who starts out along the walls."

"Remember, the fewer that get across alive, the fewer we

below shall have to fend off. They too have archers. Do not expose yourselves needlessly. Now I will post you."

Two of the little company he stationed at one corner of the parapet, two at the other. Hosea and Binyamin he placed at its center, where they could command views to either side.

As he turned to leave them, he saw their faces for the first time. Catching sight of Hosea's, he stopped.

"Are you not," he asked, detaining him, "kin to Iddo?"

Hosea looked at him in amazement.

"Aye, a brother."

His shaggy brows knitted, the officer seemed to be thinking out some problem. But a voice arose from the stairwell.

"Ithamar the captain," it called.

"Eh, to Azazel with it," the officer decided, dismissing whatever thought he had had concerning Hosea and dashing off.

At that instant, hearing the name and in association with his brother, Hosea remembered where he had seen this officer. It was at his own home, the house of Beeri, on the mountain of Samaria, Ithamar the captain having been among those officers who came from time to time to dine and drink with Iddo. The man's perplexity over him, Hosea thought, might under ordinary circumstances have been explained by a groping toward recollection, but certainly not in this setting. Yet Hosea too had other matters with which to occupy himself. He slipped into position beside Binyamin, crouching behind one of the crenellations of the battlement.

The courtyard spread itself before him, empty, except for several figures lying very still on its pavement. About the middle of one of these an oily pool fanned; from the neck of another who lay supine, his bearded chin thrust immobile and upward to the sky, flowed a dark, serpentine rivulet. Hosea tore his eyes away and studied the edifice which rose before him. It was as high as the

Citadel and like it surmounted by a crenellated parapet.

Lying next to Binyamin behind the rampart, Hosea peered through the loophole and strained for sounds. The light of the westering sun fell full on the building across the way, setting the carvings on its facade in sharp relief and penetrating into windows, picking out here the crisscross of a lattice, there the design of some boldly dyed curtain.

But no one stirred where Hosea could see; the entire palace during the lull was so quiet that one would readily have supposed it untenanted. A sense of the unreality of this scene and their role in it beset the two men.

Binyamin said in a hushed undertone, "Can you tell me what you and I are doing here? I swear I cannot believe it even now." He chuckled nervously. "Let me tell you, Hosea, that if I die in this place, my shade will haunt you."

"If it has no more serious business with which to occupy itself."

"What could be more serious than taking vengeance against him who seduced me to drop the pen from my fingers and take up a bow in its place? A bow, of all things. Why, I have not held one in so long a time, I am not sure I know what to do with it."

The feel of the weapon was strange to Hosea, too, but familiar, the pull of it—unconsciously he had been holding it half-drawn—reached into his shoulders and back. But the sight of it, bow in left hand, strung arrow in right, seemed right. A sense of unreality pervaded him. He relaxed his draw, worked his trained arms and shoulders, and said tentatively, "They say of archery that it is like swimming, once learned, never to be forgotten."

"I hope so. Nevertheless, I wish I had an opportunity for a few practice flights."

"To what avail such wishing? When they shoot, it would be not to test their skill but in deadliest earnest." His face to the east, the afternoon sun beating down on him in full force, he shivered with apprehension and started to pray to the shade of Talmon to stand at his side to direct him. Then he remembered that to one who feared the Lord it was forbidden to pray to another. He compromised by petitioning the Lord to the same effect and braced himself for what would come.

But nothing came for a long, dragging time except the circular succession within himself of a strained tautness, imaginings of the enemy's appearance at the far ends of the walls, waves of anxiety lest at that moment he discover that his fingers had forgotten how to wield the bow, pictures of the enemy pouring over the parapet and the flash of daggers.

A figure walked up to the parapet across the court. Hosea's heart stopped and then raced; his breath caught and then came quickly. Tall, strong, casual, almost indolent, Iddo bent over the balustrade inspecting the courtyard below. Hosea watched him with fascination. His resolve began to stir.

An arrow flashed through the air, followed by a flight. The undercurrent of fear and disquiet that had been plaguing him transformed into outrage. With unsteady fingers Hosea drew his bow and aimed. The arrow point danced at the end of the shaft; his vision blurred. He blinked, and shook his head to clear it. He stilled his hands and shot. Intently he followed the arrow's course, meantime instinctively drawing and readying another. It flew straight but a little low, striking the base of the parapet, recoiling and dropping to the courtyard floor. For the trial flight it was not too far beside the mark. Nor had he done worse than the others, none of whom came closer to the target. Automatically he tilted his bow for an arching flight.

His brother vanished as abruptly as he had appeared. Hosea relaxed the string and let the arrow zag. A strength rose within him.

"I have not forgotten," he said.

"Nor I," answered Iddo, his voice clear and resolute though his visage was hidden among the turrets.

"Hosea!" Binyamin's cry was sharp. "Take cover, take cover."

Almost at that instant, something shattered itself against the upper rail of the parapet, less than a span from Hosea's head. Hot sparks stung his forehead and cheek. He hugged the pavement.

"I must have exposed myself," he said tremulously, remarking on the obvious.

Binyamin let out a long breath.

"You may thank the Lord God of Israel that He gave me sharp eyes, sharp enough to see the angel of death on his way."

READER'S GUIDE
for The Prophet's Wife

CONFLICT OF HEART AND MIND
by Rabbi Harold S. Kushner

WHEN I WAS STUDYING FOR THE RABBINATE in the 1950s, Milton Steinberg was one of my heroes, as he was for most of my classmates. The epitome of the modern rabbi, he had been erudite, articulate, and compassionate; fluent in Jewish and classical sources; everything we aspired to be and realized we probably never would be. I read all of his books, including his novel *As a Driven Leaf*, and heard rumors of a second novel left incomplete at the time of his death.

As a result, when Behrman House invited me to respond to the unfinished manuscript of that novel, titled *The Prophet's Wife*, I jumped at the chance. I felt like an archaeologist who had just been told that undersea explorers had found the lost continent of Atlantis and were inviting him to take a look at it.

How does one get inside the mind of a man one has never met, a man who has been dead for more than half a century, a mind more subtle and more creative than one's own? With unlimited respect for the memory and legacy of Milton Steinberg, one does one's best. Perhaps that is how we read the writings of all great people of the past, including prophets.

As a Driven Leaf takes place in Judea in the early second century CE, a time when the Jews had to contend with the culture and cruelty of the Roman Empire. His protagonist is Rabbi Elisha ben Abuyah, a gifted scholar who abandons the path of rabbinic Judaism for the rationalism of the Greeks. *The Prophet's Wife* takes place in the biblical period, the eighth century BCE, in northern Israel. Now the alternative to Israelite faith is not Greek logic but the sexually charged paganism of Israel's neighbors, and Steinberg's hero is the prophet Hosea.

Hosea was one of the earliest biblical prophets whose words have been recorded in Scripture. Though the word "prophet" has come to mean one who predicts what will be, the biblical prophets were defined differently. They were men who told the truth, who brought God's word and God's perspective to the Jewish people when they had strayed from the covenant, substituting other values for those they were bound by faith to uphold. In the words of Abraham Joshua Heschel, "The prophet is a person who sees the world with the eyes of God."

Hosea is the most personally revealing of all the prophets. We know almost nothing of the others' private lives, having been given only passing references to spouses, children, or occupations. Hosea tells us almost too much about his personal life. The first three chapters of the book of Hosea (the last eleven are notoriously difficult to interpret) tell of how he was betrayed by an unfaithful wife. The experience leads him to imagine God's feelings of betrayal when Israel strays from God's ways and prefers the crude sexuality of the cult of Baal.

I can imagine Steinberg being drawn to the story of Hosea as he saw the American Jewish community, and America in general, tempted not so much by philosophical doubts about religion as by the seductiveness of a consumer-oriented way of life. Rabbi Steinberg saw parallels between the two societies of modern America and ancient Israel. The narrative of *The Prophet's Wife* tells of the young Hosea and his pious father trying to hold onto the old ways of serving God even as people around them are drawn to idol worship and the corruptions of wealth. Even Hosea's brothers are exceedingly opportunistic, rebellious against their parents' traditions. But not our hero. He does not stray from his adherence to Jewish law, not even after his beloved wife Gomer betrays him with his handsome, charming older brother Iddo.

The novel as we have it ends with Hosea risking his life defending King Jeroboam's palace against an insurrection, in the course of which he recognizes Iddo among the rebels. The historical books of the Bible do not mention this particular incident, but it actually could have happened this way. There was much civil unrest and turmoil in the ancient Near East. It was a time when many an ambitious soldier could imagine himself king of Israel, and Iddo might well have been such a person.

What might Steinberg have had in mind for the remaining chapters he never got to write? I can imagine a narrative in which Hosea kills Iddo in battle, either inadvertently or, more likely, deliberately. Why else would Steinberg have invented the rebellion, unattested in Scripture, and put Iddo in it?

The killing of his brother in battle would lance the boil of shame and impotence that infected Hosea throughout his life. For Iddo as a youth never offered more than casual regard to his sensitive and righteous younger sibling, and as an adult corrupted Hosea's household and seduced his wife. And so Hosea would slay Iddo not out of jealous rage or personal grievance, but in defense of Israel's lawful king. For the first time Hosea is an actor in his own life rather than the one who is acted on. For the first time he is a dispenser of justice rather than an impotent witness to the absence of justice.

The rebellion, as I imagine it, will be put down. Iddo's death will leave Hosea master of the family estate and all that goes with it. But I cannot see Hosea in his newfound sense of empowerment going back to the house and his former life as a scribe. Perhaps he will deed the property to his loyal servants. Perhaps he simply will abandon it. Most likely, he will sell it to finance the life he is now free to choose for himself. What do I see him doing? What probably every reader of the book would guess. He goes off to the desert to join a band of prophets. There he is able to find his prophetic voice and channel all of his pain and anger into the utterances that will ultimately become the biblical book we know today.

In the company of people whose mission it is to see and describe the world as God sees it, Hosea comes to discern the parallel between Gomer's betrayal of him and Israel's betrayal of God. His prophecies are no cold-blooded analysis of Israel's violations of the covenant. Reading the prophecies, one feels the searing pain that gave rise to lines like these:

I will disown her children,
For they are a harlot's brood,
In that she had played the harlot.
She that conceived them has acted shamelessly
Because she thought,
I will go after my lovers
Who supply my bread and my water,
My wool and my linen, my oil and my drink....
She did not consider this:
It was I who bestowed on her
The new grain and wine and oil,

I who lavished silver on her
And gold which they used for Baal.
Therefore...I will snatch away My wool and My linen
That cover her nakedness.
I will uncover her shame
In the sight of her lovers.... (Hosea 2:6–7, 10–12)

No other prophet speaks or writes that way. No other prophet sees God as vulnerable, hurt by betrayal, the way Hosea does. Moses, Amos, and Isaiah know an angry God, a God Who demands justice. Many of the prophets articulate God's anger at Israel's lack of faith. But no one else pictures God as wounded by Israel's disloyalty with the passion and pathos that Hosea does.

Meanwhile, what happens to Gomer? If this were a Hollywood movie, a newly emboldened Hosea and a truly repentant Gomer, having come to understand how much they love and need each other, would be reunited under a banner that reads, "Love Conquers All." If this were a book written by a Christian theologian rather than by a rabbi, Hosea might take Gomer back in an act of exemplary forgiveness, echoing God's recognition that we are all imperfect people who crave forgiveness for our sins even as we forgive those who sin against us.

But, writing as a rabbi, Steinberg's commitment to personal responsibility is stronger than his attraction to the virtue of forgiveness. Actions have consequences, for good and ill, and I cannot escape the conclusion that Gomer's repeated betrayals prove to be too much for Hosea to overcome. There is no longer love; at most, there is pity. Ultimately, his vision of Israel's future will evolve, in the company of his prophetic companions, to include a belief in a God capable of restoring God's relationship with a chastened Israel, but what is possible for God is beyond the reach of Hosea. The prophetic promises of restoration are set in the future and put in the mouth of God. One day God will be able to forgive a chastened and repentant Israel, but Hosea, who has been hurt and betrayed too often by Gomer, is not capable of bestowing such forgiveness. Steinberg is not writing a parable of forgiveness dispensed by a merciful, loving God. Writing for a modern audience, he is faithful to the spirit of the biblical prophets who tried to warn Israel that God takes us seriously enough as moral beings to hold us accountable for our actions.

We are left with the most important question of all: Why did Steinberg want to write this book? Milton Steinberg already had a prominent pulpit, and a reputation as a formidable commentator and theologian. As a rabbi, he saw words and stories as a means of conveying God's message to God's people. What was it about the story of Hosea and Gomer that led him to invest the time and effort to craft a novel about them?

I suspect that Steinberg saw this book as a complement and companion piece to *As a Driven Leaf*. And I see Gomer, not Hosea, as the parallel figure to apostate rabbi Elisha ben Abuyah. (The book *is* called *The Prophet's Wife*.)

The tragedy of Elisha in the earlier book is that he was driven to be a creature of pure reason, a man for whom a foundation of faith without proof made little sense. Alas, that sort of proof does not exist, and Elisha could not remain loyal to Judaism without it. The only world we have is a messy one in which people do not always get what they deserve.

Gomer is the anti-Elisha, a woman ruled by passion rather than reason, a longing that devours her soul to the point where she does things that she knows are wrong, justifying them by saying, "I couldn't help myself." Where Elisha was driven by cold logic to hurt people he loved, Gomer is driven to hurt them by hot passion. They are both tragic figures because they lack the mediating influence of morality that speaks in terms of good and bad, permitted and forbidden, a sensibility with the power to cool desire to the point where it is no longer a consuming fire and to warm the intellect until it softens enough to accommodate human imperfection.

Taken together, then, the two novels give us Steinberg's view of human nature in a more fully rounded form than he could have done in a sermon or essay. We human beings are extraordinarily complicated creatures, cruel and kind, generous and selfish, introspective and impulsive, a mixture of mind, heart, and soul. We require the wisdom of the Jewish tradition to keep all of these elements in balance. We need it not only to remind us that "there is a time for embracing and a time for shunning embraces…a time for war and a time for peace" (Ecclesiastes 3:5, 8), but also to remind us what those proper times are. Should the elements ever be thrown out of balance, as happened to both Elisha and Gomer; should the mind close itself off to the need for faith in the presence of uncertainty, the need to sometimes give God the benefit of the doubt; should the urgings of the heart and blood ever overrule the restraint of the mind and soul, the result would be the sort of tragedy that blights the lives of Steinberg's central characters.

I imagine that if Steinberg had completed this novel, he would have shown Hosea living out his days in the company of his fellow prophets during the last days of the ill-fated Northern Kingdom, frustrated by his inability to warn the people of the consequences of their uncontrolled behavior, cherishing his faith in a God more capable of forgiving a faithless people than he himself is, and looking forward to a day when God's gift to a repentant people will be the blessing God withheld from Gomer the prophet's wife, the capacity for faithfulness. Then the Jewish people and their God will know the happiness that eluded Hosea and Gomer.

UNFINISHED LIVES
by Norma Rosen

DEPRIVED AS WE ARE OF WHATEVER ENDING Milton Steinberg might have put to his great imagining of the Gomer-Hosea relationship, its unfinished state gives us a way into a number of profound questions. Those questions—they are theological and feminist—concern us today as urgently as when the writing of the novel was interrupted sixty years ago. There are also other, equally interesting questions about the art of novel writing and the nature of midrash.

We know that Steinberg's life was tragically cut short, and that during his last years multiple projects occupied his mind. He had to let *The Prophet's Wife* languish for a while, and then it was too late. One can't help wondering whether there was a schism developing for him between the novel in progress and the unyielding biblical text. From the novel fragment we have, it appears that Steinberg was undertaking nothing less than adapting God's ancient biblical ways to modernity and expressing a feminist viewpoint daringly ahead of its time.

Steinberg's philosophic mind had a strong dramatic side. The novel does not lean on summarized action: events are presented as scenes, in a "you are there" technique. Because of the Vermeer-like detail, the novel seems to move at a stately pace, as if all moments are holy and require equal attention. Yet the swiftness of events yields the excitement of an action novel.

Consider that the biblical text is one of the cruelest in the Bible. In it, God commands Hosea, "Go and marry a harlot." The implication is: let her symbolize the harlotry of Israel and the punishment I will visit upon her; you, Hosea, be as swift to punish Gomer.

This text Steinberg turns on its head. His Gomer is no harlot. His astonishing midrashic innovation is to make her a woman who is as independent-minded as she is beautiful. She is embittered by the injustice of her woman's lot, sold in marriage to someone not of her choice, and in rebellion against her uncle's efforts to wring money from her marriage to Hosea. The Gomer of *The Prophet's Wife* is born into mean circumstances and the iron-hard social subjugation of women of her time.

Steinberg's Gomer has the misfortune, before meeting Hosea, to fall in love with Iddo, Hosea's hell-raising older brother (he is the novelist's invention). The pious Hosea's marriage to Gomer is arranged to his delight but not to hers. It is after her marriage to Hosea and her seduction by the returned brother that Gomer becomes an adulterer and earns the biblical epithet "harlot."

Steinberg exerts a mighty novelistic force against the text. He gives a sensibility and a compassion to Hosea that in the novel he laments is too soft, "too like a woman's." Hosea could have the adulterous lovers killed, but he cannot bear to do it. If biblical Gomer equals the Hebrew people, then, against the Bible text that sometimes insists on unpitying punishment for the people's sins,

Steinberg's novel poses understanding and protective love.

With the outbreak of a rebellion into which Hosea throws himself, the novel fragment ends. Hosea has not yet become a prophet, and Gomer's third child (which brother's will it be?) is not yet conceived, adding still more questions: Why does Steinberg suddenly present us with this unlikely warrior side to Hosea? Was he looking for some novelistic way to launch Hosea into action as a wandering prophet? Was he preparing Hosea to emerge from war with pacifist words?

Steinberg the novelist went even further in humanizing both Hosea and Gomer. Biblical Gomer the harlot is transformed into Steinberg's Gomer the valorous woman, expressing her full sensual nature and her own sense of justice. (After all, who, except for biblical Tamar, who had her own marriage agenda, would choose to be a harlot, anyway? Runaway teenagers from abusive homes or poverty-driven girls from third-world countries fill today's brothels. Destitution leads to prostitution, now as then.)

As Steinberg makes plain in *The Prophet's Wife*, it is the absence of marital support that leads to harlotry. Nothing is lost on Steinberg's novelistic vigilance: the only employment Gomer can find after she is cast out is as prostitute in a place called the "Left Shoulder" where, Steinberg's novel tells us with exquisite irony, married men seek sexual diversion.

With the remarkable sensitivity of his writing, his painting of detail to infuse life into his scenes, his sympathy for the sufferings of his characters, and his daring darts into their souls when they are most in crisis, Milton Steinberg creates a Gomer who is torn between her admiration for the reflective, pious scribe, Hosea, and passionate attraction to his unbridled brother, Iddo.

The Bible text itself reels between opposites. God, like an enraged Othello, ricochets from poles of terrifying threat to tender promises of comfort. In Hosea 13:8: "I will devour them like a lion, the wild beasts shall tear them." In 14:6: "I will be as the dew unto Israel; he shall blossom as the lily." Midrashic commentary adds a layer of parable. What God is really saying is this: you, betrayed by your faithless wife, won't cast her off; how, then, should I separate myself from my people?

The beautiful parable doesn't erase the fact that biblical Gomer is used as a means to an end, a symbol without dignity of personhood, a character who utters no word.

What in fact is the difference between an *eishet ḥayil*, a woman of valor whose price is above rubies, and a harlot whose price is whatever the market will bear? The answer is that there is less difference than likeness, since both are abstractions, the perfect and the tainted alike—dehumanized, denatured, dead. Steinberg's Gomer, in her agonized entrapment, summons such questions.

Milton Steinberg, a modern rabbi and theologian, turned to fiction as the ancient rabbis turned to midrash. *The Prophet's Wife* was created immediately post-Holocaust, at a time when the word "theology" lost its meaning. Out there was a vast expanse of dark matter—God's inscrutable inaction in the face of radical evil and suffering—against which a handful of phrases have been flung: "the turning away of God's face," "God sits at the gates of Auschwitz and weeps," "flickering moments of belief." Theology works best when the other side of it is poetry. Milton Steinberg turned to the poetry of midrash, of fiction, to question this blaming, punishing Hosea Bible text and alter our perception of it and of God.

How far from the original Bible text may a midrash depart? That question, too, is raised by Steinberg's text. It vexes the writing of every midrash, which may be as detailed and inventive as it likes about what is not known, what is left open or left out of the original text, but should not traduce the boundaries of the known. Writing midrash is a bit like writing historical fiction. If you know from history that King Henry VIII had Anne Boleyn's head cut off so he could marry Jane Seymour, you can't very well write that Boleyn escaped the palace at midnight, evading the headsman's hatchet (much as you'd love to save her), in order to return in triumph to take her place as queen. Because then you would have played dice upon the dais of the actual, the real, the historical. And where, then, would you find places for the Queens Elizabeth I and II? Where do you put Churchill and the victory of the Second World War? We have endless space to dilate upon what is, but we cannot move the stars in their courses.

Gomer respects and loves her husband, Hosea, though without the passion she feels for Iddo, the pagan brother. Did Steinberg, steeped in literature, model Gomer in part on the unhappy heroine of Brontë's *Wuthering Heights,* caught between passionate love for the wildness of Heathcliff and her yearning for a safe marriage household? Brontë wrote about the lure of unfettered freedom and the bitterness of life's limitations, by extension a kind of theology. Steinberg is writing a direct theological response to God's voice as it appears in the biblical Hosea text.

Maybe Isaac Bashevis Singer was also thinking of Hosea in his renowned story, "Gimpel the Fool," in which a virtuous simpleton is tricked into marrying the town whore. The deceptions of Gimpel's wife multiply along with his children, until at last his wife dies and confesses everything to him in a dream. Filled with awe at life's mysteries, Gimpel sets off on his humble travels, a fool whose gift for forgiveness has made him holy.

Is this the way Steinberg intended his Hosea to go?

In *The Prophet's Wife,* Hosea is more merciful than God. And this, perhaps, is the point of Steinberg's midrash-novel.

In endowing Gomer and Hosea with warm hearts and deep feelings, Steinberg has run full tilt against the hardness of the Bible text. In place of abstraction he has substituted affecting portraits of personal response; for the puppets of a morality play he has created flesh-and-blood fiction.

A look at Steinberg's earlier novel, *As a Driven Leaf,* may yield a few clues about his intended direction in this unfinished one. For his hero he chose one of religion's most indefensible characters, an apostate. The brilliant Elisha ben Abuyah drives himself deep into isolation, holding to a proud independence of mind, rebelling against the reigning religious leaders, unwilling to renounce the doubts of a seeker. At novel's end, ben Abuyah's life is that of a pilgrim, pursuing the quest that leads to more questions and greater alienation.

How could Steinberg have completed *The Prophet's Wife,* this novel about a woman whose sin earns her the contempt of her society—how could anyone? How can a sexually transgressing woman be vaulted beyond the censure of the ancient world? Milton Steinberg has already, with astonishing prescience, brought the consciousness of his Gomer centuries forward, toward the idea of physical and spiritual freeing of women.

Hasn't Steinberg's Gomer felt the scourgings of the multitude, the lashings of God? Does she not have a tongue of fire, a despair and hope equal to the world's? Something in Steinberg's story seems to be saying, "Let Gomer prophecy!"

We are asked to engage with this amazing fragment, however inadequately, because to engage with it is to keep it alive. Here's a try:

As Steinberg gives Hosea a brother, Iddo, let us give Gomer a sister, Maluti. (Bible characters often come in pairs, opposite in nature: Isaac and Ishmael, Jacob and Esau; Rachel and Leah, Sarah and Hagar.) Gomer is proud, headstrong, impetuous; Maluti, the youngest of the children left in a grasping uncle's care, is thoughtful and prudent. She faithfully carries out her assigned female tasks but longs to study as men do, as Beruriah, the learned wife of Elisha ben Abuyah's friend Meir, had done. Whenever she can, she contrives to take her weaving to the neighborhood of the study house, where she listens to the chanting (and gossip). Learning of Gomer's disgrace and divorce by Hosea, Maluti seeks him out and pleads for her sister.

"If you leave Gomer with Iddo," Maluti says, "she will fall lower and lower. Before your brother returned, was she not a faithful wife to you?"

"But then she was not."

"Take her away with you. Why does God require the destruction of Baal's shrines? If they are left, they tempt. So with Iddo, if left in sight of Gomer. Take her away."

"I am a scribe. My livelihood is here. And for now I am a soldier in the rebellion."

"People will not allow you to starve. You will feed them wisdom; they will give you food."

"But with a wife? Children? Do you know what that would be for them?"

"Gomer longs to prove her worth to you. Isn't this what God intended—that you and Gomer and your children would be a living example to the people? When did a prophet stay shut up in his workroom and talk to the flies?"

"And if my children starve?"

"As you take pity on Gomer, God will pity the children. God will call them 'My People,' and 'Love.'"

Hosea now looked at Maluti more carefully than he had ever done before. He felt sympathy stir between them. They were so alike, and he had never noticed!

"If I travel about the land, it would be far better for me to have a woman like you at my side," he said, "not Gomer."

But Maluti answered, "You and I are fashioned too much alike, Hosea. How would we make one another grow? Even the Holy One must bring the opposites of God's nature together to elevate God's being to One."

Hosea was able to recognize wisdom when he heard it. That day he plucked Gomer from the house of Iddo. She willingly departed, after hearing what Hosea said to his brother: "Through you my father's name has fallen to the dust. But Gomer and I will set out to labor for the Lord."

To which Gomer, in her strong woman's voice, and lifting her children's faces to heaven, added "amen!"

But what, after all, have we accomplished here? The heaviness of the text is so great that if we try to lift it in one place, it sinks in another, and then more questions sprout. What has happened to the idea of Gomer's (Israel's) sin? To the idea of the redemption of Gomer and the Jewish people through the forgiveness and mercy of God? When Gomer (in the guise of Israel) becomes the agent of her own rescue, she loses the drama of a sinner's redemption, and she and we lose the text's explanation of the miseries of Jewish history as punishment for sin.

Is it really for us, in our own lives, to complete Steinberg's story of love and pain, both human and transcendent, and, however broken our world, to look for God's justice and mercy in it?

Who is the driven leaf here? Is it Hosea, or is it Gomer, who is never really given a chance to choose her fate, neither in Bible text nor in Steinberg's version. Elisha ben Abuyah's is a quest story and can embrace the open-endedness of lifelong wandering. But Gomer and Hosea are (divorce or no divorce) a married couple with children—what is more rooted than that? Can they, too, go about the land arguing with God and forging new God-concepts?

In portraying the tormented marriage of Hosea and Gomer, Steinberg reveals the darkness at the heart of the God–human relationship, as well as its lovers' tenderness. God cannot live without the love of the people, however betrayed by them, nor can the people ever love God as much as God requires them to (however many interpretations of that there may be).

If we keep our eyes on Gomer and Hosea, and disregard for now the talk about harlots, then we see that they are a pair who cannot live with one another and cannot live without one another, a recipe for both torment and connectedness without end. Gomer will never love the pious Hosea as much as she loves the pagan Iddo; Hosea cannot live without her all the same. (Read: The Jewish people can never live up to God's standards; God cannot live without forgiving them and then raging anew at each disappointment.) Can such a marriage endure? Apparently not without this painful and improbable pursuit of one another. With it, Gomer and Hosea—and we and God, it seems—can go on.

One thinks of another pair of anguished lovers in another book of the Bible—the beautiful Song of Songs—who are forever pursuing, forever losing, forever finding one another. Theologically speaking, the pursuit is understood to be all about seeking God.

Steinberg's lovers are like that, and so are we. Like them, we sometimes sing love lyrics, as in the Song of Songs, and sometimes we are tormented, as in the book of Hosea. But Steinberg's Gomer and Hosea bring the passion and the struggle closer to our modern sensibilities and enliven our imaginations about the quest for human love and the search for an elusive God.

QUESTIONS FOR DISCUSSION

1. Betrayal, wrestling with conscience, a woman's struggle for a voice — how do the concerns and struggles of the characters in this biblical tale resonate for us in modern times? How does the author succeed in bringing the world of ancient Israel to life?

2. The prophet Hosea, who lived in the Northern Kingdom of Israel prior to its conquest by Assyria in the eighth century BCE, was an important critic of his time. He rebuked the kings of Israel, as well as the people, for their religious and moral transgressions, their idolatry and corruption. Does the Hosea in *The Prophet's Wife* seem a likely candidate to be called for this work? Why or why not?

3. Hosea and Gomer's marriage is presented in the Bible as a metaphor for Israel's Covenant with God. What kind of marriage do the characters have in this novel? Why did their

marriage fail? Under what circumstances could you see Hosea and Gomer reconciling in the unwritten conclusion to this novel? In what ways does the metaphor inform us about Israel's covenant with God?

4. The relationships within the House of Beeri have an important influence on Hosea's childhood—Beeri and Ophra's marriage, Gadiel and Iddo's attitudes toward both parents, the older brothers' treatment of Hosea, the ever-present servants in their lives. What effect do these family dynamics have on Hosea's outlook on God, community, and family?

5. Why do you think the author imagined the young Hosea with artistic talents? How might an artistic disposition inform his view of the world?

6. In her commentary on this unfinished novel, Norma Rosen writes that the author turned the harlot story on its head. In what ways might Gomer be seen as a valorous woman? Do you agree that she is valorous, on the whole? Why or why not?

7. The biblical prophets are often seen as harsh and unforgiving in their words and deeds, even though they were charged by God to deliver them. In his essay, Rabbi Harold Kushner remarks that Hosea is the only Hebrew prophet who "sees God as vulnerable, hurt by betrayal." How does Milton Steinberg's depiction of a gentler Hosea get this point across? Do we see God today as vulnerable, hurt by betrayal?

8. Many Israelites during the time of this novel are less than mindful of God's commandments. They are callous to the

suffering of those among them, they celebrate Canaanite fertility rituals, and they tolerate corruption in their leaders. What was the role of biblical prophets in attempting to warn their people away from self-destruction? Who or what are some modern parallels to these prophets?

9. As Ari Goldman points out in his essay, Steinberg wrote *The Prophet's Wife* at a critical juncture in the history of the Jewish people. The full horrors of the Holocaust were just becoming known. In the Middle East, the modern State of Israel was emerging. In what ways could this novel be seen as a response to world events at this time?

10. How do you think Steinberg intended to finish the novel? How might you have finished it? In what ways do the commentaries by Ari Goldman, Rabbi Harold Kushner, and Norma Rosen contribute to the experience of reading an unfinished work?

Visit www.prophetswife.com to share your thoughts about the novel and its ending.

GLOSSARY

Amos: a biblical prophet who lived during the eighth century BCE

Aram: the biblical region that is modern-day Syria

Asherah: a tree meant to symbolize the sacred deity at Canaanite holy sites

Ashur: the biblical region that is also called Assyria; a city in Assyria; god of the Assyrians

Assyria: a Mesopotamian world power, located in what is now Iraq and southeastern Turkey

Baal: the major god of the Canaanites; a general term referring to Canaanite gods or idols (plural: Baalim)

Beth El: a major city and worship center of Israel

Canaan: the ancient name for the Land of Israel

Chemosh: the god of the Moabites

Citadel: a stronghold or fortress

City of David: a narrow promontory on the southern edge of the Old City of Jerusalem

Cruse: a jar or pot for holding oil or water

Dagon: a major god of the Philistines

Deborah: a biblical judge and prophet who lived ca. the twelfth century BCE

El: a major god of the Canaanites

Elijah the Tishbite: a biblical prophet who lived in northern Israel in the ninth century BCE

Ephod: a priestly garment, similar to a tunic, on which the breastplate rested

Ephraim: a tribe named for the son of Joseph; another name for the Northern Kingdom of Israel

Ewer: a vase-shaped pitcher with an oval body and flaring spout

Festival of Booths: Sukkot, the autumn harvest festival

Festival of First Fruits: Shavuot, a spring harvest festival

Gerah: an ancient Hebrew unit of weight and currency, equal to one-twentieth of a shekel, or less than half a gram

Girdle: an article of dress encircling the body, usually at the waist

Gomer: the wife of the prophet Hosea, mentioned in the Book of Hosea: "…The Lord said unto Hosea: 'Go, take unto thee a wife of harlotry and the children of harlotry; for the land doth commit great harlotry, departing from the Lord.' So he went and took Gomer the daughter of Diblaim…." (Hosea 1:2-3)

Hosea: a biblical prophet who lived during the eighth century BCE, toward the end of the First Temple period, who warned the Israelites against idolatry and sin, and called for them to repent

Israel, Kingdom of: the ancient kingdom in what is now northern Israel

Jeroboam, King: usually called Jeroboam II, the ruler of Israel from 786-746 BCE

Jezebel, Queen: the ruler of Israel, with King Ahab, from 869-850 BCE

Jezreel: a town in northern Israel; also the son of Hosea and Gomer

Judah, Kingdom of: the ancient kingdom in what is now southern Israel

Laver: a large basin used for ceremonial washing

Lo-Ruchama: Hebrew for "not pitied;" the daughter of Hosea and Gomer

Mitra: a Hindu god

Mitre: the official headdress of the ancient high priest

Moab: the territory southeast of the Dead Sea

Nazarite: an Israelite of biblical times consecrated to God by a vow to avoid drinking wine, cutting one's hair, and touching a corpse

New Moon: (also known as Rosh Hodesh) the beginning of the Hebrew month

Nineveh: a capital of ancient Assyria, and its most populous city

Omri, King: the ruler of Israel from 876-869 BCE

Papyrus: a material to write on, made of the pith of the papyrus plant

Passover: the festival commemorating the Exodus from Egypt

Philistines: a people living in the coastal region of Canaan

Potsherds: pottery fragments

Raiment: garments, clothing

Samaria: the capital city of the Northern Kingdom

Shade: a ghost

Shekel: a unit of weight and currency

Sheol: the abode of the dead

Terafim: idols, household gods

Tiglath-pileser III: the ruler of Assyria from 745-727 BCE

Tripod: a stool, table, or vessel resting on three legs

Uzziah, King: ruler of the Kingdom of Judah from 783-742 BCE

Varuna: a Hindu god

Writ: a written order or formal written document